A
PATH too
LONG

The Second of the Sun Sharer Trilogy

JACK GEORGE
EDMUNSON

First published in Great Britain in 2010 by
The Sun Sharer Publications

First edition

Copyright © 2010 Jack George Edmunson

Names, characters and related indicia are copyright and trademark
Copyright © 2010 Jack George Edmunson

Jack George Edmunson has asserted his moral rights
to be identified as the author

A CIP Catalogue of this book is available from
the British Library

ISBN: 978-0-9564709-5-9

Distributed by:
Central Books Ltd, 99 Wallis Road, London E9 5LN
www.centralbooks.com

Printed in Great Britain by the
MPG Books Group, Bodmin and King's Lynn

The Previous Book
The Sun Sharer

Jack George Edmunson is a man in search of spiritual rebirth and 'Real Life' in what appears to be a mid-life crisis but, in truth, is about overcoming weakness found in man when destiny demands courage to find a true path.

This is a tragic story questioning the meaning of love within marriage, affairs, friendship and ultimately with Sun Sharers.

Jack is in a bad marriage pursuing a life of materiality with superficial friends. He can't understand why he has a clairvoyant and an astrologer telling him to pursue a simple life in Catalonia, so he denies their messages and the reality of his spirit guide Nim, who acts as his conscience.

The pain caused by his wife, the manipulative Melanie, and the deep love he has for his son Joseph are exacerbated by the complex lives of his six friends and their secret intrigues. The convenience of their marriages is challenged when Jack has an affair with Bridget, his best friend's wife. An irreverent Jack highlights the complexities underlying the rut of modern living and asks if there is a better way.

Jack is determined to comprehend if he truly has a different path to follow as the family start living in Catalonia, Spain. The pull from his past is accentuated as he meets Karina and falls in love believing that she is his Sun Sharer. This enhances his devotion to Catalonia and its culture which clashes with his hate of 'the Cheshire set' lifestyle. His wife and friends mock his vision for a simple *'Real Life'* and, realising how hard it is to achieve his dream, he becomes more frustrated and outrageous.

The fantastic sex of his dalliances contrasts the poor sex within his failing marriage and his wife's use of her sexual favours to control him.

The love for his son Jojo conflicts with his own for his Alzheimer's-suffering mother, who is gradually deserting him like his wife and friends.

As Jack starts to accept the truth of his future he is drawn further into his past but his best friend and lover Bridget dies tragically, which makes him disillusioned. This reinforces the love he feels for Karina but her responsibilities for a terminally ill husband prevent them being together. Ironically, Jack saves him from dying and thwarts the conjunction of the Sun Sharers.

Depressed and alone in beautiful Yapanc, Jack contemplates suicide.

Failing to create a new simple life he swims out to sea in the dark of night.

Jack George Edmunson fights his way into a world in which we all believe, but where nobody dares venture.

Foreword

L ife has always proved itself stronger than death when there is
a will to live.

There are many known obstacles along the way but many
more are still to be discovered. Exploration of this emptiness takes
spiritual courage and hope in times of distress.

In the world of 2008 there was a dearth of both as crisis
followed crisis.

Jack

Jack George Edmunson, age 55 years.
July, 2009

Acknowledgements

To my Mother, Marjorie who passed away in the early hours of
Tuesday July 27th 2010.

She inspired my trilogy but could never read a word.
She said the cover of 'The Sun Sharer' was beautiful.
Those words will be treasured forever.

1

There is more than death

The Llevant wind died away as the sun absorbed its breath into the dawn spreading above the resorts of the Northern Costa Brava, leaving the Catalan fisherman sighing sympathetically as he trawled his way past its still dark coves.

He still hoped to fill his empty net with any sprat from the barren Mediterranean Sea but was equally content with the motion of his creaking boat as he watched the phosphorescence move from the bow back to his position by the tiller. Happily intoxicated by the ozone-laden air he was dreaming of his breakfast *cerveza* as he slouched in the waning light of the moon and constellations.

His *menorquina* suddenly heeled to starboard, the white gunwale covered by the cold dark sea. The ratchet on the trawl gear noisily disturbed the last hour of his peaceful night as he hauled his stiff body upright and crossed the rolling deck to start the smelly diesel winch. He had great expectations; a possible catch to be examined in the daylight that was creeping its way across the Baix Emporda, and dimming his dreaming stars.

He slapped Jack across the face flinging drops of seawater into the air from the wayward man's beard.

'*Señor!*'

Jack gurgled an incoherent reply as he vomited onto the deck before feeling himself lifted upright again.

'That's no way for my spirit guide to behave.'

'*Señor!*' The two slaps were much harder this time and registered properly.

'Nim!' Jack exclaimed angrily. 'An ethereal being can't hit me.'

It's not me Jack, look around you.

'God it's cold. Why do you stink of fish, Nim?' The English words were mumbled out of thin blue lips whilst his eyes remained tightly closed, fastened together by encrustations of salt. He ground the crystals painfully off the lids with a cold stiff finger and raised himself onto his elbow, whilst slowly opening his eyes to squint at the world he had so nearly left.

'*Asi, vive, señor. Muy bien.*' So you live, sir. Very good.

The fisherman left Jack naked and still entangled in the cutting harshness of the plastic net and moved away towards the small cabin of the vessel. A faded Great Bear looked down at the only fish of the night who painfully returned its gaze whilst shivering uncontrollably and drawing in deep breaths to clear his sodden lungs. Jack coughed and spat again as the fisherman pulled the net to one side.

'*Acqui!*' Here! The accidental saviour wrapped his unusual catch in a red woollen blanket, followed by a layer of silver foil, before pulling a dirty black bobble hat onto Jack's bald head and pushing him forcibly below. As Jack ducked to enter the hatchway he glimpsed Nim's bright white coat merging into the single navigation light of an adjacent trawler accompanied by his doubts that his spirit guide really existed.

His rescuer positioned him roughly next to a rusty electric heater and appraised the miracle man, wondering whether there would be a reward to offset his lack of income. The fisherman thrust a bottle of water into his hand indicating he should drink. After a few gulps, the alabaster-faced Englishman broke the silence.

'*Que llama?*' What is your name?

'Pedro, señor.'

'Gracias, Pedro.' Jack took a few more deep breaths before continuing shakily in English. 'How biblical to be saved by Jesus's right-hand man. How bizarre.' Pedro didn't understand him but needed to check their rolling progress and so he disappeared on deck leaving the survivor to his thoughts.

'Why did I want to abandon my little boy? How crazy have I become? Why Nim?'

You didn't want to, Jack, but you had to follow your
true path.

Tonight was an obstacle that you have now overcome and that means you can start afresh.

You still have three things left to achieve in this
reincarnation: you need to write your Guide to
Life and give people the knowledge about the Fifth
World that only you possess; you have to pursue and
win your Sun Sharer for a final attempt in sixteen
centuries, or let her go into oblivion; and you must
embrace 'Real Life', Jack, and follow my principles,
as you must simplify to survive or you will follow her
and share the darkness.
All of these make you as one.
This is your choice and there can be no more excuses;
no blaming of other people this time.

Pedro returned smiling.
'Piensado un gran bonito, señor.'

He says he was laughing a lot thinking about how he
had caught a huge tuna, not someone who buys the cans.
He has now radioed his best friend to inform him he is
diverting to Yapanc on his way to Palomost harbour.

'He didn't say that, Nim. Spirit guides should be exact when translating. He said he thought I was a big tuna. So leave the Spanish to me and go away. You've done enough damage for one night. I can't believe you let me swim so far out to sea.' Jack was recovering his spirit.

It was of your own free will, Jack. Always remember
that I can never tell you what to do. I can never
arrange or change anything in your life but will
always advise you on how to follow your true path.

Pedro pulled a silver flask of *chupito*, a clear apricot brandy, from the pocket of his dirty blue dungarees and took a large celebratory pull before his rough brown fingers shoved it under Jack's nose.

'*Quiere?*' You want? The big tuna drank, welcoming the burning inside before choking as he gave it back with a cold shaking hand. Hoarsely he replied, whilst looking into the mahogany face of his kind host, 'But, Pedro, there are so few *bonito* in the Mediterranean. You had false hopes … yes?'

They were both laughing which relieved the stress of the rescue. Pedro understood no English but punched Jack's arm in comradeship and confided in Catalan, reciprocating the friendly understanding.

'Maybe you are a little better than a *bonito, amigo!*' His brown eyes marvelled at the crazy Englishman as he prayed inwardly in thanks to Mary, the patron saint of Catalonia, before rapidly crossing himself. Jack remembered to use his limited Castellano-Spanish this time and responded to the words he recognised.

'I hope so, Pedro, but why is that the name for tuna? Are they truly *bonit*o; pretty when not in a tin?' The fisher of men threw his hands in the air as he replied.

'No they are ugly, *señor;* Ugly like my wife and just as savage, but they taste divine, unlike my bitch of a wife!' Pedro guffawed at his joke, slapping Jack's legs. He appreciated the warmth of the humour, followed by the sting of the slap, before the rough fisherman returned on deck.

A cold-blooded tuna would never have the same feelings that were suddenly intense and overwhelming as Jack started to sob. He wanted to be with Karina, his Sun Sharer, his true love who lived so close to the boat, but in reality she could have been a million miles away. He cried for Bridget, his dead best friend and lover, who had supported him as he wrestled to extract himself from his bad marriage. He missed his family; his dead father, his Alzheimer's-ridden mother; but most of all he missed Joseph, his much loved eight-year-old son. The emotional loss and burden of unhappy memories overwhelmed him. He even guiltily cried for his ex-wife Melanie and the pain he had caused her, whilst forgetting the anger and hatred of the separation over the previous two years.

The salty tears dribbled down the silver foil as if he wept the sea itself. The drops seeped into the bilges to be pumped away and lost in the immensity of the Mediterranean, eradicating the sadness and doubts from his old life on the first day of the new.

The first rays of the sun slanted into the hatchway and enticed Jack onto a now stable deck where he stood and drank in the stupendous view of his home, the village of Yapanc. From a mile out he could see it was encapsulated by four ancient hills where natural cork and oak trees stood, like soldiers repelling the encroaching houses and their inhabitants since Roman times. For many millennia the violence of the Mediterranean Sea had eroded the soft tertiary rocks to form the beautiful sandy bay, now bordered by brightly coloured second homes and a promenade with cultivated tamarisk and pine trees. As he looked eastwards towards the towering cliffs, El Far, the lighthouse, blinked its last and welcomed the new day.

'Pedro, that is the most awesome sight I have ever seen.' His stomach turned for almost failing in his quest for a new life in such a special place. Pedro remained silent as he didn't understand the mad Englishman, who had forgotten to speak in *Castellano* again. Jack kept repeating 'sorry' to himself, shivering the words out of his body as he pledged to follow his true path. Pedro's soothing voice broke above the diminishing waves.

'*No problemas, señor. Calmate.*' No problems, relax.' He looked into Jack's green eyes staring so intently at the shore and wondered if the depressed man was regretting his suicide attempt or would try again. As the sun rose higher it warmed both Jack's body and his soul, as Nim, the Sun Bearer, spoke with him again.

> *The Fifth World is arriving, Jack, and a cycle of nature will affect everyone throughout the whole of the earth. Climate change is nothing compared with what will come soon.*
> *The earth will bear an egg and you must prepare for it. A child of the waters was one of our Navajo saviours and he now demands recompense for saving your life.*

'I was lost, Nim, and for years I dreamed my reality away but now I understand. I shall write my novel and explain the Fifth World but I need some time. You must show me what this could be and I will extract myself from my old ways and enter into the new.' Jack hung tightly onto the cabin rail as Pedro swung the boat to starboard to enter the tiny harbour of Yapanc, then throttled back to look for an empty berth and land his special catch.

As Jack shook Pedro's hand and thanked him wholeheartedly, he saw a familiar figure walking down the pontoon on the way to his own *menorquina*. The newcomer jauntily waved his hand.

'*Amigo!*'

'*Hombre!*' Jack gushed with relief as they closed. Manolo was the estate agent who had sold Jack and his family their holiday apartment, and was wrapped in his usual dark blue windcheater and approaching with his typical rolling gait. He was much shorter than Jack with a full head of dark hair and brown eyes. He looked upwards with concern as he grasped both of his friend's silvered shoulders.

'*Hombre.*' He was immediately worried about the shiny tent standing in front of him with a white salty face and encrusted hair.

'Manolo, *amigo*. I had a little accident.' It didn't matter which term was used when they greeted each other as it was a random way of reasserting their friendship since they had met five years previously. Manolo shook his head negatively before replying.

'What is happening here, you crazy English?' Pedro barked out a few phrases in guttural Catalan which made Manolo laugh and then look seriously at the human tuna. 'So my friend how do you feel now?' Jack breathed in deeply and then sighed loudly before replying.

'"None". I am relieved to be here. I'm not excited, I'm not depressed, just "none."'

'Well, "none" is good because you are here and alive, *amigo*.' Manolo smiled widely. He was always bubbly and happy and lived his life to the limit each and every day. 'So, Jack, where do you want to go? I have my car near the square so we can go to the hospital first if you want.'

'No, there's no need for that, but I can't go home to my apartment. I can't ever go back there again. Do you understand that, *hombre?*' Manolo could see his mental discomfort and decided to take control.

'Don't worry. You can stay in my house next to the Hotel Yapanc. Can you walk the 300 metres or shall I fetch my car?'

'Yes, I can walk it if you give me your arm. Let's go now before any people are about.' Jack leaned on his friend's shoulder as they walked slowly from the harbour to the square. He told him about his eventful night.

'I was swimming and I saw Nim, my spirit guide, for the very first time. He told me about "iinaa ji", the life, or beauty way, and told me to follow my true path, but I never believed him until last night.' As Jack incoherently poured out his new beliefs, Manolo wondered about his mental health and resolved to look after him until he was stable again.

'Jack, you have always been a bit crazy, but I think you drank too much seawater and maybe you were hallucinating, yes?' Manolo was a young spirit and didn't care or understand about the deeper, more subjective parts of life, as he only loved life itself.

'Is this *'Real Life,'* Manolo?' asked Jack as he saw every part of their walk in the tiniest and clearest detail. He marvelled at the intricate blue tiles on the wall of a holiday villa dated 1926 and smelt the sweet pine resin, as they weaved across the cracked red flagstones of the promenade.

'Jack, my friend; this is real life. Just put one foot in front of another. Every day you get up and make it happen. You eat, you shit and you walk. That is *'Real Life'.'* They had walked past the Harbourmaster's office and the Wisteria Bar leaving a handful of small fishing boats pulled up on the beach to their left before they reached the village square. They halted to the right of Karina's *croisanteria*, which was next door to Manolo's summer home. Jack shuffled nervously, hoping he wouldn't meet her.

'Wait here, Jack. I must go to my car and fetch the house keys. *Vale*. Okay?'

'*Vale*,' Jack replied and leaned gratefully against the pink wall of the *casa*, watching the back of his chunky friend intently, as he went in search of his ancient Volkswagen Golf.

'Thank god it was him who found me.' He placed both hands on his knees and leant forwards crouching against the lime plaster wall in total exhaustion.

> *He is on your path, Jack, and you need to listen and*
> *to learn from him. There is no scale to friendship and*
> *no balance, but help him and he will repay you.*

Jack shook his head slowly asserting his belief in his guide, then he immediately pushed Nim away. His fixed stare at the pavement was disturbed by a flour-coated hand waving in front of him followed by a familiar voice.

'Jesus what have you been doing, Jack.' Karina's Irish lilt warmed his heart as she pulled the foil sheet closer around his neck. He looked up at the petite auburn lady with the slim waist and sexy legs, topped off with large breasts. It was only her lovely smile that was missing as he replied hesitantly.

'It was just a little accident, lovely. No worries. I got a bit wet fishing with Manolo.' She knew his emotions and glanced at her watch to confirm that his friend would normally be departing from the harbour.

'You know, Jack, although you are alive, despite your obvious suicide attempt, you really are a selfish bastard in trying to take your own life when others like my husband Josep Maria may have none in future. Are you so willing to leave your son Joseph to develop without a father?' The harsh words from his Sun Sharer jarred him but they were justified. Her own husband had less than two years to live before the cancer would return and she suffered with that reality every day but didn't accept the fixed timeline. No one else could have admonished him so truthfully, so he kept his head bowed taking the loud criticism. 'Friends, Jack. We are best friends and you could have come to me if you were that troubled.'

He was more assertive now, remembering how his love had been rejected a few months earlier.

'Based on our last conversation, I can never come to you again and therefore I don't know what best friends I really have.' His words hurt her in turn. He continued. 'At least you have got constant acquaintances at work and with your extended Catalan family, but maybe you have no real friends either. They are all so superficial, aren't they? I would even hazard a guess that Josep Maria would be jealous of any real friendships and so constrains your life.' His words were true but twisted by his thwarted love.

'Jack Edmunson, how dare you say that!' She pushed him a few yards further from the bakery so her husband couldn't possibly overhear.

'You know all about my life because I let you in, and you know very well that he wants to possess and control me. I told you my secrets and you shouldn't use them against me.' She was nearly crying because of the truth in his words and she pushed him harder and even further away to end up close to the sea wall.

She wanted to distance him from her life and her heart but failed again. Turning abruptly and with a final tinny slap on his foil chest she went back to work as she had spied Manolo returning with the house keys.

⋆ ⋆ ⋆

His friend's arrival stopped Jack from dwelling on Karina as he needed food, coffee and a hot shower as quickly as possible. Inside the old family house it was dark and musty with a smell of wax polish mixed with damp. As they climbed the stairs, Jack marvelled at the intricate wrought-iron banisters in the shape of fish and shells and the gaudy plastic lampshades from the sixties. Manolo opened the shutters and the light flooded in from the south-facing windows to reveal a holiday home warped in time since General Franco's death.

'Jack, you can stay here as long as you want. I will return later and bring my things so that I can stay with you and then you can help me tidy the house ready for the new season. *Vale?'* Manolo wanted a positive response before he was willing to leave his suicidal lodger.

'Thank you, You are a true friend.' Manolo was content and bustled off to find Jack some temporary clothes and prepare food whilst Jack went to shower and wash the sadness of the night away. As they sat on the balcony eating a breakfast of bread, cheese and chorizo, Jack tried to explain his state of mind.

'I didn't mean to commit suicide; it was just a reaction to the loneliness I've experienced over the last two months. I hated being alone after all the commotion at home last year. You see I had work then, arguments with Melanie and drunken fun with my acquaintances and suddenly I had no one and no structure. Does that sound strange?'

'*Hombre,* nothing on earth is more important than people; whether they are good or bad in your life, they keep you thinking about its practicalities. As soon as you left the mess behind, that meant you would only make assumptions about what was happening there and none of them were ever going to be right as you were too distant from the truth. You need to be with people and not fantasise about imaginary situations that never happen. Stay here with me and get stronger mentally and physically. I'll make sure there's some company around but you must promise me you'll never do anything as stupid again.'

'I promise, Manolo. Thank you, I do appreciate it.' Manolo smiled through the sunshine that was now warm and penetrating as they sat on the balcony and admired the expanse of the Yapanc bay embraced by the White and El Far headlands and perfectly blue sky. They ate, watching the sea wash gently onto the sands with a delicate and rhythmic sigh. So they shared the sun with Jack content to be alive as Nim sat next to him, happy with the new direction taken by his Centurion who would soon realise his destiny.

Early the next morning Jack slipped out of the house, deliberately avoiding Manolo who was sleeping soundly. Furtively, he turned left towards the beach so that he didn't have to walk in front of the *croisanteria* and risk a chance meeting with Karina. He felt mentally refreshed after his friend had mothered him for the whole of the previous day, having totally annihilated any residual and suicidal thoughts with the three bottles of Rioja they had consumed before an early night. Life seemed infinitely better as he skipped past Hotel Yevant and up the 151 steps to the White Headland and his family's apartment. He didn't dwell and avoided thinking as he collected a couple of bags of clothes and his personal effects. Deliberately he stayed out of his son's bedroom, avoiding the painful sight of childhood possessions like the shells and rocks collected lovingly with his dad. Gently closing the door he placed his old life in a box and firmly put the lid on it, knowing he would have to return briefly when the apartment was sold. Retracing his path he took the right turn that plummeted off the steps and landed on the rocks where he used to sit with Joseph and thought about his junior Sun Sharer.

The weather had changed and it was a cold grey January day. The steely sea was still warm enough for the hardy to swim but looked distinctly unwelcoming as it eased itself in and out of the bay without any urgency. He leaned down and dipped his fingers into a rock pool and decided to sit and take some time for his new *'Real Life'*. His close encounter with death had made him feel incredibly alive and full of energy and every minute felt wonderful and precious in its clarity. He had experienced this feeling once before, when Joseph had been born. Under his breath he started to say his seven daily pleas for other people in the world who weren't so lucky.

'Oh Lord, hear my prayer.' He stared across the bay, letting his mind go blank as he joined the Collective. At each plea he asked for something for others in need but never anything for himself. He pleaded for comfort for his mother, good health for JoJo and then concentrated on the bigger more important issues, from ending the violence in Iraq to providing food in Darfur. The mix was random and he never knew what triggered the thoughts, but there always had to be seven pleas. As usual, at the end of the liturgy, he solemnly crossed himself in unison with the words. 'The Father, the Son and the Holy Spirit. Amen.'

Always seven subjects as seven were mythical and seven were lucky. He cleared his mind of the day so far and prepared it for the day to come, looking eastward for the sun.

Jack cried again for his loved ones and then for himself. He knew he needed time to recover and just be. Being 'none' was good; 'none' would work for him. Looking at the view he had no Joseph sitting next to him holding his hand, always willing to tell his dad, 'I love you, wider than the sky and bigger than the sea.' It is words of unconditional love that make life bearable. Nim stared at the grey view and then at a grey Jack before consoling him.

> *Remember Joseph is safe, happy and well whilst living*
> *with his mother. A child doesn't go around thinking*
> *about you all of the time.*
> *He only needs you to accept his unqualified love and*
> *you will receive his in return.*
> *Joseph is a very old soul and shares your history, but*
> *his time is still to come.*

So Jack left the cold rocks to avoid dwelling on his old life and walked quickly back to Manolo's house where he dumped his bags before taking a fast stroll along the beautiful coastal path to Kaletta. He admired the pink rocks cascading into the drab sea and followed his thoughts to the horizon and beyond. As he walked he pushed his troubles to one side and rigorously focussed on the future. Nearing Cap Roig the track became more natural and solitary as he started to consider returning to England and seeing his great friend Harriet. He smiled as he remembered that, between bouts of extreme caring, she was always happy. He would never forget their visits to the spiritualist meetings at her instigation, and the strange predictions that he now believed. She had always helped him to stay calm whenever he had returned to Cheshire to see his son and had placated him so that he could manage Melanie, the psyche-disturbing ex-wife. He smiled, thinking of the deepest imaginable care from Harriet and also from Matt, her equally supportive surgeon husband, who had never wavered in his friendship.

'Yesterday, Nim, I felt completely washed up, both mentally and physically, but now I feel and truly believe that it's not over until the fat lady sings. And Nim, Melanie isn't here singing.' His smile widened at the insult and the mental picture of the pig he had left behind; her snout always in the trough and just as ugly. Less than an hour later he was back at the holiday villa in Yapanc.

'*Hombre!*' called Manolo, hearing Jack clatter up the tiled staircase. 'How are you today, my fishy friend?' His light-hearted concern made Jack smile again as he grasped his amigo's arm in appreciation before replying.

'I'm much better, thank you, and my first priority is some breakfast as I have already walked and then maybe I should have a good shite.' Manolo was pleased as Jack relayed his base psychology and seemed to be taking his advice seriously. 'Practicalities, Manolo, and then I have to decide where I can permanently live.' Manolo was stroking his chin thoughtfully.

'I have an idea, Jack. My mother's house sits two miles inland from here and next door to it she owns a *barraca,* a small holiday place where we used to go as children. It is a very simple house but it is empty at the moment; just one bedroom, a bathroom and a living area that includes the kitchen, but it is a very healing house and always *tranquilo*. I know this because my father went there to spend his last months before the cancer killed him. What do you think? Shall we go and see it?'

'That sounds just right. Simple and cheap.'

'Hey *hombre*, did I say cheap? Is your credit not good?' They giggled like teenage schoolgirls as Manolo put the coffee pot on the ancient butane stove in the kitchen. He was enjoying having a guest as he, too, was lonely despite the numerous girlfriends and his once-busy Estate Agency. After coffee and fresh chocolate croissants they jumped into the Golf and took the dirt track leading inland from central Yapanc, which wended its way up the steep sides of the pine-clad hill before levelling out past the ancient burial dolmen, eventually crossing to a narrow and very potholed lane, deeply channelled down to the base rock by the torrential rains the week before.

'You drive like Carlos Sainz!' Jack grasped the internal door handle to brace himself as Manolo swerved around the trenches.

'No, *amigo*. I am much better than the World Rally Champion,' and Manolo accelerated out of a bend, sliding the rear of the car by using his handbrake to emulate his Spanish hero. Suddenly he slowed and immediately in front of them stood a small yellow *barraca*, smiling at them with a huge single window all the way across its façade. To the left of the house was a copse of pine trees and on the right, towards the rear, were ancient and neglected lines of olives. Further to the right, was a huge stone house where Manolo's mother lived. Surrounding this imposing structure were orange and lemon orchards filling the hillside with colour and the smell of citrus. The picture of heaven was completed with almond trees and a large field of bare vines.

'Good god!' exclaimed Jack, his heart in his mouth. 'That is so beautiful.' As they pulled up outside he could see yellow osteospermums carefully planted with sets of lavender in between, to give a pretty and fragrant display on entering the rear door. The smell of the flowers mingled with pine smoke drifting across the field from Manolo's mother's house wafted on the light Llevant breeze. Jack noticed the *barraca's* fan-shaped roof and embedded solar panels and remembered what Mabel, the clairvoyant, had said when he was with Harriet the year before.

'Why is the roof that peculiar shape, Manolo?'

'We catch the rainwater so you can wash without the harshness of the calcium from the town mains, and we also use the well between the two properties to save money. The rest of the design helps to charge the batteries that run the lights.' Inside was as simple as he had described, but the magic was in the view. Two miles away in the distance lay the sea, parted by the hill containing the dolmen. To the left were the El Far cliffs and to the right another small hill, before the White and Cap Roig headlands. The view was unobstructed all the way to the midday sun that spread across the fields and energised the little yellow house.

'What do you think, Jack?' They both stood looking in awe and listened to the pheasants and peacocks caged in his mother's garden. After a few moments a stunned Jack replied with a single word.

'Perfecto!' Manolo touched his arm.

'I am happy for you, my friend. This is where I will always remember my brave father and I hold it dear to my heart. I would be pleased if you can be happy here, Jack. So the deal is simple. I will sell your apartment, you give me 500 a month black, no tax, no tell. What do you think?'

'It would be my privilege to stay here. Job done, to use your expression. Job done, Manolo.' Jack wandered into the olive grove and saw the fruit had been left to rot on the earth as he talked to Nim. 'You told me once that spiritual love is the only true love. Giving oneself time to consider it is the only true path. So, Nim, what is my guide to living?'

> *Jack you have a place here that is part of you*
> *already and that will become clearer. You said you*
> *would never give up and you said fifty years down*
> *with fifty to go. Well now you have forty-seven years*

*left, so you need to make the most of this particular
one to show people the simplicity of living. The
simplicity of 'Real Life' and to learn to be yourself
in preparation for your destiny.*

Jack breathed in deeply and took in the unique fragrance of
Catalonia whilst turning 360 degrees.

'Well, that truly is a deal then. I accept my path and will follow
it to the end.'

A week later, he moved into his *barraca* and, within a few days,
had regained sufficient mental strength to speak to his son using
the Bakelite telephone dating from the Civil War.

'Where are you, Dad?' Joseph was very confused as his dad had
gone missing for a month. Jack put on a positive voice that belied
the fragility of his state of mind.

'I have a new house, JoJo, a very small and simple place that
looks down the fields towards the bay but it has a spare bed so you
can come and stay with me anytime, my lovely.'

'No, Dad, I mean which country are you in now?' He had lost
track of his dad somewhere between England, France and Spain.

'Oh sorry, JoJo. I'm phoning you from my new home in Yapanc
where you had such great holidays, mate. Are you okay, son?'

'Of course, Dad, I have this brilliant new game on my Nintendo
Lite.' Jack let him talk about the day-to-day things that interested
his boy and enjoyed listening. After a few minutes he told him
he loved him and, as always, to work hard but play hard, then he
rang off rather abruptly. The first conversation after nearly dying
made Jack sob as he felt so humble and grateful to hear his boy. He
realised that Joseph didn't miss him and was happy, but that hurt
and comforted him at the same time. That left one other person
he had to telephone to square the circle.

'Hi, Mum. How are you?'

'Who's that?' she said in a nasty enquiring tone. The Alzheimer's
disease was now causing more aggressive mood swings.

'It's Jack, Mum.'

'Jack who?'

'Your son, lovey.'

'Where are you, son?'

'In Spain, Mum.'

'Oh, that's funny. Why are you in Spain, Jack? You're usually on the motorway when you speak to me.'

'I live here now, remember? I used to speak to you when I was travelling for my job.'

'Are there no motorways in Spain?' She coughed and then continued without listening. 'Are you on holiday?' Then immediately after. 'I've been to Spain, skiing you know.'

'I came to live here after I left my wife, Melanie, because I love Catalonia and now I'm writing my book. I think you went skiing once but it was in France, Mum.' He ignored the random comment about motorways to try and keep her on track.

'Ay, that's right, it was with Tugdual.' Tugdual had been Jack's best friend in France for over forty years.

'No, Mum. You went skiing with your friends but you came to Spain with Dad on a coach once.'

'Did I? Was it Shearings? I don't remember anymore.' She giggled pointlessly. 'Your dad is dead, Jack. Did you know?' The line went quiet for a minute.

'Yes, Mum.' Jack felt as if someone was sitting on his chest but he continued. 'How are you feeling today?'

'Your brother's holding me prisoner. Can I come and live with you and Melanie in Spain?'

'She still lives in Tettenhill, Mum.'

'Does she? I never liked her; too stuck up with those friends of hers. They are all farts without shitting.' She rambled onto the next subject without stopping, but at least some of it was logical. 'Your brother told me you had committed suicide. Why did you do that?' Jack was still smiling at her accurate expression of Melanie and her Cheshire set friends.

'I only attempted it but really it was an accident otherwise I wouldn't be speaking to you would I? I was very stupid, Mum, and it won't happen again, lovey.'

'Well, my son, I hope you are not so selfish to deprive the world of your smile. You were always a lovely boy but far too imaginative and sensitive. You were always seeing ghosts that didn't exist. Don't leave your son alone. He needs you.'

'No, Mum. I promise I won't.' His mother lost her moment of lucidity.

'How is Melanie? She is such a good wife to you, my boy.' She murmured on about trying to find her glasses that she was sure were in her slippers before she continued. 'By the way, Tugdual, I have a bad hip you know. Jack's brother is terrible to me.'

'Okay, Mum, got to go. Love you lots.'

'Love you ...' She strung it out in a high pitch tone.

Jack replaced the receiver slowly and wiped away his tears, but at least he had made the two telephone calls and that was emotional progress in his new life.

Occasionally, Jack saw a head of beautiful auburn hair as he visited either Yapanc or the little market town of Palafrio a few miles inland, but he never got close enough to see Karina's eyes that he missed so much. After a couple of weeks, Manolo had insisted on a short jaunt on his *menorquina* to help stabilise Jack's equilibrium. The morning was bright and warm as they set out from Yapanc's harbour and as they slowly negotiated the entrance Karina's flying locks caught his eye as Josep Maria raced to be on time to open the bakery. As the boats passed starboard to starboard, Josep gave a friendly wave but she looked at them with a blank expression and Jack felt the utmost rejection. He saw Josep staring at him intently as if they were drawn together but he wouldn't remember the walk they had taken through the Collective whilst he lay in his coma in the hospital in Girona.

Jack had noticed her twice the day before, once in the Palafrio fish market and then again between the vegetable stalls on the main street, but she subtly avoided him by crossing the road and, of course, he avoided the *croisanteria*. When he did see her talking to a common friend like Manolo he saw that she had lost her wide smile and happy eyes but he always felt he couldn't interrupt. He missed her 'hiya, my dear', but Jack knew it was wrong to try and get close to her again, even if he yearned for her warm hugs. But most of all he missed her friendship.

One morning Jack was driving from Kaletta to Palafrio and, as he crested the rise in the dual carriageway, he saw the splendour of the snow-covered foothills of the Pyrenees fifty miles away to the north. They dwarfed the town with their splendid whiteness, an optical *delusion*, he thought, playing on words, but in their essence a vision of heaven. Parking near Carrefour, he quickly strolled towards Manolo's estate agency adjacent to the main square, to be greeted by Nuria the senior administrator. She was a bright and pretty thirty-five year old with mousey grey hair cut into a bob. She had no children but cared for an elderly mother with whom she lived above an electronics shop in the centre of town.

'Hola, Jack, Que tal?' How are you?

'Fantastic, my lovely.'

'You are always fantastic, Jack, always so positive about life.'

'Thank you, Nuria, and you are always so very focussed and serious, especially when looking after your boss.' She smiled at the barbed compliment as he walked through the old fashioned office to the darkest corner at the rear, where Manolo hid from unwanted clients. This was where the real deals were undertaken and was next to the large safe which was full of 'black' illegal cash behind an easy-to-move bookcase.

'Hombre!'

'Amigo! What brings you here? Is it to chat up my wonderful girls?'

'No, Manolo, particularly as you seem to be missing two at present, but you should look after Nuria as I am sure that she would die for you.'

'Hoy, Jack. She is just a woman.'

'Manolo, you remind me of an old English friend, Peter.

You are carefree but can be very selfish. He was my best mate in Cheshire and was always complaining about his business, and optimistic that the next season would be better.'

'*Mañana,* Jack. That's life.' A head poked around the corner.

'Well, you two, as you have no work, are you coming for a beer?'

'Dutch Walter!' They exclaimed in unison and stood to shake the big man's hand. Walter was from Holland and had known them both for about five years and had been suitably nicknamed 'Dutch'. He was built like a windmill, six foot three with a bald head 'apart from a few wisps of brown hair' and exuded bonhomie, but his positive demeanour always diminished in the presence of Freda his stunning wife. Jack asked him if he was there on holiday again.

'No, Freda… sorry, the Duchess and I have moved here permanently now. We have a modern place hung off a cliff near Aguablara. It's inspirational. The east and west walls are made of glass so that you can see the sunrise and then the sunset.' Jack was impressed.

'I'm really glad you're back as it will be great to have some good company. This man here is constantly working!' He nudged Manolo, who had returned to his rental bookings on the computer.

'Well, Manolo,' said Dutch 'I have your expat friends in the bar next door, so are you coming for a drink?'

'Sorry. Walter. Eleven thirty in the morning is too early for my aperitif and I must work to build up my thirst. Thank you, but please take Jack out of my way as soon as possible.' Dutch and Jack were dismissed and walked across to the Centre Fraternal Bar where five other expats were already drinking cold red wine.

The Duchess stood and beamed at Jack. She still looked beautiful like Catherine Zeta Jones even at fifty-five and after three children. Grabbing him into her, she gave him three kisses to the cheeks.

'My god, Mister Edmunson, don't you look well. I heard that you were living out here away from your ex.'

'Thank you, my lovely, you look fantastic too.' Jack turned and looked behind her giant of a husband whose bald head was covered in sweat as usual. Two attentive women sat admiring him as if he was in a cattle market. The Duchess introduced her expat girlfriends.

'This is Pippa, another spiritual believer like you, Jack, and this is Lucy, who comes horse riding with me on Pals beach.' Their handshakes were sensuous which was surprising even to the normally forward Jack, but they were both pretty and looked like typical middle-class, middle-aged women with money to spend. The big designer sunglasses and brand name clothes gave him information about their species of expat, which is often found in their natural habitat of the expensive Aguablara and the cheaper Bagurr holiday villages a few miles further north.

'Nice to meet you both.' He used his 'come to bed' eyes on them and got two delightful smiles in return.

Pippa was demure, short and slightly plump with brown shoulder-length hair and rimless glasses that obscured bright blue penetrating eyes. She wasn't pretty with her thin lips and large nose but something about her immediately attracted Jack. Whether it was her soft voice or the perfect teeth of her beautiful smile, or maybe she exuded hidden pheromones that initiated something far more primal within him. Lucy was the opposite of Pippa, a loud 'full-on' personality, blonde, big and beefy, with large boobs pushing out of her tweedy multi-coloured jumper. Jack spoke to her first.

'I like your top' he said, secretly leching at her breasts and jogging a painful memory about his current lack of sex.

'You like it?' She thrust her breasts out to show him the stripy pink, brown, yellow and green jumper. 'Bought this one at home in Broadway. You know Broadway, Jack? It's got the Lygon Arms, place in the Cotswolds, ya?' She had a public school accent, as a 'ya-ya' horsey type of person. The women continued appraising the newcomer who felt flattered by their attention as their husbands returned to the table with a second round.

'Hello, my name is Nigel, married to the mare over there.' Lucy acknowledged Nigel's comment without taking offence by snorting.

'Ya, Niiige,' as everyone seemed to call him. Niiige homed in on the innocent Jack.

'Do you need to buy, Jack? I have my own property business, ya? Bit of development. Help you out anytime.' Jack filled in the gap.

'Okay ya, Niiige.' He quickly appraised Nigel for what he was rather than his physical appearance which was small, almost frail, with forties style round glasses and slightly balding grey hair. Jack could immediately see why he talked 'big' to maintain his confidence. Which left Roland.

'Hi, I'm Rolly.' A slow drawn-out upper-class accent. 'I'm an artist, Jack. What's your line, old chap?' He had olive-coloured skin and was short and wiry with an amazing dark brush instead of hair.

'IT, Rolly. Not very interesting, unlike your line.' Jack had decided not to engage, so he kept it simple. 'Where are you from, Rolly?'

'Londoners, you know. Country place near Broadway, but originally a bit of Greek in me, like Prince Philip, ya!' Jack laughed inwardly whilst thinking 'Twat' and quickly sat between the two new girls.

'Do you help Niiige in the business, Lucy?' Jack had to lean back slightly as she came so close.

'Oh god, no way; all those builders' arses. No, darling, I run my own holiday consultancy.' He turned to the less aggressive Pippa.

'And you, my lovely?'

'Oh me? Well *J*, I support my Rolly in his art; you know, organising exhibitions and sales.'

'Well, you both do well to live and work here. That's very admirable. Do you speak Catalan or Castellano at all?'

'Oh god, no,' said Lucy. 'There's no need really. We just mix with people who speak our lingo. Isn't that right, Pip?' Pippa backed her up.

'Yes, and we have *Sky TV* and the *Daily Mail,* of course, so it's very civilised here.' The Duchess rescued Jack by enquiring about Joseph and then Melanie.

'Is she still spending your money?'

'No, not since the divorce went through. I'm just sorting myself out now.' She looked into his eyes.

'So did you find your personal legend, Jack?' He squirmed uncomfortably.

'I remember you telling me that I knew what it was, Duchess. I think that was just after reading Coelho's book *The Alchemist*, on the beach with you guys but I don't know yet what is the true answer. I just don't know.' He thought about Nim and wondered if Nim was Coelho's voice on the wind. He remembered one inspiring passage; 'Before a dream is realised, the Soul of the world tests everything that was learned along the way.' Possibly, thought Jack, possibly. She interrupted his thoughts as if she knew what they were.

'Pippa is into spiritual things like you, Jack. She does auras but it's all a load of baloney to me. She's just a crazy witch really.' Demure Pippa had been listening closely.

'Dearest Freda, what a terrible sleight on my character. I could read and interpret your aura anytime *J*. It would be my pleasure.' *J* thought he heard a sexual *come on* before he dismissed it as an unfair reaction because he was so deprived of sex. After a quick drink he felt out of his depth with the expats who were now on their third round before midday, and so he made his excuses and left with Pippa's words ringing in his ears.

'Bye, darling. See you soon, I hope.'

Manolo summed up the expats to Jack that evening as they sat drinking beer on the terrace of the *barraca*. They had lit the barbecue and then piled some wood on top to stay warm in the chill of the night.

'They are unique, *amigo*, what do you say?'

'Yes they are and very different from their equivalents in England. They seem more ...' he paused, '... *worldly.*'

'Hoy, *hombre*, the girls are very *worldly*, my friend. I know them well and they have seen many countries. I love them all, Jack.'

'Are you trying to tell me something, Manolo, as you seem to be very *worldly* yourself?'

'Well, you will find out no doubt as I saw the girls after you left and they were very taken by your company. A new handsome man, independent and sensitive; a writer about *life* indeed. They did like that. Yes, Jack, they like this combination, I think.' Jack looked quizzically at his friend.

'I do believe that I said I was in IT, so I wonder where they got that from, *hombre?*' He gently tapped his friend's leg with the bottom of his beer can before continuing. 'And maybe you were avoiding them for some reason, as you never refuse to socialise. I quote "eleven thirty is too early for an aperitif." I ask you, Manolo; that's like asking, "Is the Pope Catholic?" You, and most of Catalonia, are happy boozing at any time after eleven!'

Manolo maintained his dignified papal silence and so Jack queried further. 'The Centre Fraternal seemed an odd place for a drink though. I know it's next to your office but for the moneyed middle classes it seemed strange to drink in the cheapest place in town, with all the old men.' Manolo ignored this enquiry too but did ask for Jack's first impressions.

'Well, I have met Dutch and the Duchess on and off for about five years now and so I know them the best, but still only as holidaymakers, which is quite shallow of course. They are just nice and normal. Pippa seems quiet and supportive of her husband but, for some reason, I could give her one. In fact, I would be delighted to give her two.'

'Give her what, Jack? *No entendiendo.*' I don't understand.

'Sorry, *amigo*, it's an English expression for fucking.'

'Hoy, *hombre*, I think more than two would probably be required.' Jack looked askance at his friend and wondered what he knew. The frustrated Englishman carried on.

'Lucy I have nicknamed "Juicy Lucy" because she made me hot and bothered. She seems overtly sexy, like a hot mare asking for a stallion to mount her. In fact, I thought frail little Niiige could easily be killed having sex with his wife, or maybe he has to use a saddle on her every time.' They grinned at the thought and could never imagine her being on top as it would certainly crush him. 'As for Niiige, well … I don't know, but that Rolly came across as a complete twat. However, I'll wait and judge him after I've seen his art.' Manolo stared at the twinkling lights in the distance, tapping his fingers together as if in prayer before turning to his friend to confuse him further.

'Well, Jack, I am glad you have met my expats. But beware … they hunt in packs.' He categorically refused to say any more about them and changed the subject to football and his beloved Barcelona as they drank their fourth beer.

At about eleven, Manolo stood to walk across to his mother's house where she would have his evening meal waiting. He shook Jack's hand and asked,

'Do you like your simple home still? Is it everything you expected, *amigo?*'

'Manolo, did you know that Buddhist monks renounce their homes just like I have? My new simple house is Shangri La, 'paradise on earth' as in the book *Lost Horizons* by James Milton. Have you ever read it?'

'No, Jack I only read books about fishing.' Jack tutted disapprovingly and wagged a finger at him.

'Well, maybe you should read it. It's about four people who survive an aeroplane crash in Tibet and are taken into safety at a monastery. Then they go to Shangri La where the air is clean and the living is natural and spiritual.' Jack dreamed on as Manolo edged away, desperate for his *butiffara y garbanzos,* sausage and chick peas. 'A place of peace and constant love that is all at one with nature, and would suit me down to the ground, *hombre.'*

'How much love, *amigo?*' Manolo was more interested in his friend's story now.

'Not enough for you, *hombre!'* They laughed before Jack continued. 'But I have actually been there; to the real Shangri La which is a new Chinese city set in a vast expanse of natural beauty and with very few people.'

'Is it a better place than here, Jack; this mythical paradise?'

'No, just different, *hombre;* a different way of life but life itself is no different. You eat, you walk, you shit and the order is immaterial. The Buddhists there try to find their true path sitting in a beautiful monastery above the city, but really the ones I met were not spiritual in anyway. No different at all from you or me sitting in our Heavenly Temple of the Baix Emporda.'

'Hoy, Jack, you and your path! You can postulate as much as you want, *amigo*, but your truth and my truth are very different. So just remember, Barcelona Football Club has the best team in the world and not your Liverpool rubbish. Secondly, some alternate god like their Buddha seems acceptable to you but for me, *hombre*, well I have my narrow Catholic view, and I am happy. God is God. Catalonia is beautiful and certainly not Spanish and Saint Maria protects us every day. Buddha! You crazy English!'

'Well, Manolo, I don't know if you were drinking before you arrived, but that is the longest speech you have made in the five years I have known you. Mister Practical, the great lover of all things day-to-day, who attends church once a month … but only if he has sinned.'

'I am sensitive too, Jack, but I don't need to scratch it like you every day.' Jack ushered him off his patio and into the dark.

'In that case, as tomorrow is Monday when the agency is closed, I suggest we go walking in the Pyrenees at the Vall de Nuria. Are you up for it?'

'Of course, *hombre*, my body was made for climbing.' Jack eyed him up and down and decided to test the statement on a visit to one of his favourite places in Catalonia.

After an early start Catalan style, at a frustratingly late 10 am, they drove for three hours towards the snow-capped mountains. The friends argued constantly about Manolo's vague directions, just like an old married couple. He insisted they went around the volcanic lake at Banyoles, admiring the bluey-green mineral waters. Half an hour later they passed through pretty Besalu, but remained in the car parked on the new bridge, whilst they sat and admired the twelfth-century model dramatically spanning the River Fluvia. Their appreciation lasted about five minutes until the *Mossos d'Esquadra*, traffic police, moved them on, with Manolo remaining quiet and using the stupid 'English tourist' as a shield from any potential punishment. They also stopped in the patisserie by the square in Ripoll to eat cake with their coffee because the owner had won *world championship* prizes for his pastry although the *world* appeared very small to Jack, as it was just forty odd bakers from around Europe.

Finally, after passing the famous mineral water plant in Ribes de Freser, they turned right onto the steep mountain road leading into the Vall de Nuria. Half-way up they parked and took the *Cremallaria*, literally the zip or funicular train, which wound its way along a track hanging from the mountainside, next to the valley's cascading stream. This ensured spectacular views of the waterfalls as they watched hikers exerting themselves far below. Eventually, and nearly four hours after they had started from home, they pulled into the train station 2,000 metres above sea level and stared at the mountains high above, awed by the simple beauty of the place.

Walking slowly by the calm lake, Manolo was quiet until he reached the dam and turned to stare at the massive hotel set in the corrie.

'Isn't it lovely, Jack?'

'Yes, it's very beautiful.' Manolo continued.

'How did they build such a big and magnificent place up here?' Jack realised that whilst he was looking at the subjective reflections of the mountains on the water, his friend was admiring the practicalities of the property. This would be a permanent void between them as Jack saw the spiritual side of everything and Manolo the day-to-day sensible aspects. Jack pondered quietly to himself.

'Maybe we never see anything properly, only a reflection of reality and a mirror of our individual dreams?' He called to his friend who was tasting the lake's water a few yards away. 'Pure comes to mind, it all looks so pure. Hey, Manolo, isn't *pure* a great word?'

'Pfur. This tastes like shit.' This was a classic and non-subjective reply but Jack tried again.

'That is what bothers me about the environment. We make it impure. Pure versus impure, a constant battle like good versus evil; two broken parts that don't always fit back together.' Manolo grabbed his arm with a dripping hand.

'Come on, my spiritual friend, let me show you the tiny church over there. Purity is always a problem, *amigo*. All the nice girls are married and that is why there are so many divorces. I know these married girls and they are not pure.' Smiling but impure Manolo and pure Jack walked a mile to the far side of the lake to enter the ancient stone building. Inside, the Catalan delighted in showing Jack hundreds of plaques inscribed with birth dates, surnames, all with the same Christian name of Nuria. Jack was confounded and walked around looking for the oldest date.

'So how does that work then, *amigo*? Manolo completed the puzzle for him.

'Saint Gil came here to the place called Nuria in AD 700 and saw the Virgin Mary. He lived here for a few years before fleeing from the Roman invasion, but before he left he buried an image he had made of Her. So the place is sacred to we Catholics and, in fact, as the first statute of Catalan autonomy was written here, it has doubled the appeal.'

'Remember, Manolo. You must light a candle and say a prayer before you leave.'

'Why would I want to do that?'

'For your personal Saint Nuria at the office, who protects you if you are still half-drunk and need to be with a client. She mothers you every day, just like the Virgin Mary, to make it all happen in your life.'

'I don't think so, Jack. You might tell her and she would take it as a sign of love and then she would say to me, *no juegas*.'

'What do you mean?'

'She would tell me not to play games as she is so serious. The marrying kind, hoy!'

As they walked higher using the nearest hiking track behind the small church, Manolo asked a question, suitably inspired by the place.

'So why are you here in my Catalonia, Jack? How is it that you have become so down and depressed?' Jack looked at the tall white peaks.

'Why here? Because I came to my holiday home to forget; to my apartment where I had good times and where I was happy. In fact, it feels like I have known the place forever. I know you don't believe in the same things as me, but I wanted to be in an environment with good *qi* or energy, good feng shui. To escape from my ex-wife. To live a simple life and to be real again.' Manolo stood back and put his hands on his hips.

'My god, *hombre,* that was more than I expected' he clapped his hand on Jack's shoulder 'I thought you were going to say for the cheap beer, sun and girls.' Laughter echoed off the granite cliffs in front of them, resonating all the way back to the coast. They turned back towards the hotel, to alleviate Manolo's physical discomfort from too much exercise with some soothing and medicinal beer. Suitably treated they headed back to the funicular railway station totally satisfied with their day at altitude. As they sat on the train enjoying the lazy return journey into the dusk, Manolo gradually recovered from his breathless spell as the train unzipped itself down the mountain. Jack joked about needing an oxygen bar instead of the alcohol one in the hotel, or even an aerosol can full of oxygen as he had seen in the cities of Tibet.

'My body was meant for climbing', became Jack's taunt to his friend for many weeks, as their comradeship grew to more than the best of friends. Even the journey home was easier as it only took an hour and a half, based on Jack's sole navigation whilst Manolo took a desperately needed but late siesta all the way back to Yapanc.

A considerate Manolo dropped in to see Jack in Shangri La on most of the remaining days of January. He used his mother as a feeble excuse, but in reality he enjoyed his friend's company and genuinely wanted to check to see if he was still stable. Simple life became the norm for Jack, whether it was the minimal two cups and two spoons or a single-ring butane burner for cooking. He even cancelled his English and Spanish mobile contracts, relying on the Internet and a new landline into the house for communications. He made a real log fire every night whilst reading his newly purchased books on the fish, flowers and birds of Northern Catalonia. Then every morning he would admire his natural garden made up of rocks, trees and plants with a vista out to the horizon. He would sit and watch the sky as it changed colour, tinting the variety of cloud forms that drifted past and mesmerising the relaxed admirer. Soon the conversations with Manolo became less intense as his old Cheshire set life was forgotten.

'Everything takes longer now, Manolo. It took me two hours to get up this morning, for goodness sake. When I was in the consultancy rat race, I would be up and out in a quarter of an hour, at a maximum half an hour, including breakfast.'

'Well, Jack, this is good, yes? You are now learning about the real life that you desire.'

'I can never thank you enough, Manolo, for my simple house. It is a wonderful healing place. Have you heard of the sacred science of feng shui from early Chinese civilisation?'

'Yes, but I cannot believe it is important or true.'

'It is real and true, believe me, Manolo. Consider this place as a fine example. Good is where it is open and airy, elevated and hilly with green vegetation and near water. I have all that in my new simple home. I can see the sun all day, the sea in the distance and I have pine and olive trees, and am surrounded by carpets of beautiful wild flowers.' He pointed eastwards enthusiastically. 'Those hills house the green dragon over there,' he swivelled through half a circle, 'and, in the west, you have the white Tiger, with both giving me my energy. But a balance is vital, my friend: yin is female, dark, cold, quiet, shadowy and lunar. Yang must balance with yin, and is male, light, warm, noisy, solar and bright… just like me when I am living here. Can you guess that Chinese society was male dominated? Maybe they were right hey?'

Manolo listened politely to his learned friend without comment. 'But when talking about feng shui you must also ensure you blend the five elements and their colours. Earth is yellow, the colour of my house. Wood is green, which is from my pine trees. Fire is red, the colour of my soil. Metal is gold, which is why I keep my old wedding ring on a chain around my neck as it was made from my grandfather's and, lastly, the water turns black every evening as I sit on my patio. That is the darkness where I died on my personal horizon so I can stare and remember, as it incites me to new life each time I look at it. It was so black that terrible night, but all I see now is the bright blue of the day and that must be the colour of my book cover when I publish it.'

He barely drew breath as he continued on his emotional high and Manolo just sat smiling at the new found enthusiasm for life.

'Did you know that life and death are imparted by your surroundings? I react with my environment through *qi*, that is energy. So I have to make sure I am not at odds with the physical aspects of my new '*Real Life*'. I literally follow the *way* to harmonise with where I am living or working, and that's good as I can do both here. Time is of the essence, it's important to ensure that eighty per cent of your time is harmonised each day, my friend. So I don't harmonise with the bar I drink in, but I do with this house, where I live and where I work. I definitely don't harmonise at all with Cheshire and my old house in Tettenhill.' Manolo interrupted.

'Everything you said was good, but that is where I must totally disagree. I harmonise with any bar, anywhere, and work is just work, to earn money from any property far and wide.' Jack shook his head disapproving of his friend's lifestyle before carrying on harmonising.

'Feng shui means where you die doesn't matter, but where you are buried does.'

'That is good, Jack, as my father is buried about three yards away from you *amigo*.' This assertion did put Jack off his stride as he stared at the ground around him, but he still continued albeit more slowly.

'Where you live and its physical position is vital, and not where you die.' He paused and looked around. 'Is he really buried here?'

'Of course. Where else? Graveyards cost money, *hombre*!' Jack grimaced

'I can perform feng shui, you know. I am a natural geomancer and can identify places with *ling*, or spirit. It is only since my suicide attempt that I have realised my potential.'

'Hoy, Jack. Stop please! My crazy English friend. *Amigo* you do talk rubbish sometimes. I like what you say, but maybe you joke and I never know if you are serious.'

'I am serious, Manolo. For example, bad spirits only travel in straight lines, *hombre,* and this is engrained in many cultures. So it's absolutely brilliant of you to put a curve in the dirt track to this house. That bend is a great feng shui device to deflect evil spirits.' Manolo smiled.

'There you see. Jack, my practical ways always work. The feng shui bend in the track was, in fact, to avoid the ancient well!' They laughed about that, but they laughed about everything now and got drunk whilst having fun together.

And so it was that Jack started to heal.

On 18th January, Jack had called into Manolo's *finques.*

'Mister Jack, we have information for you,' said Nuria.

'You want to take me to dinner, my lovely, is that correct?' She looked shocked as she was a nice Catalan girl trying her best to deal with an irreverent Englishman.

'No, *Señor* Edmunson.' She distanced herself.

'Okay, you want to walk up and down my bad back wearing high heels?'

'What are high heels?' She asked innocently and was shocked again as Jack explained. The other two girls in the office were 'Rent' and 'Sales' as nicknamed by Jack and they were tittering at her discomfort.

'No! *Señor*, please. No jokes.' But she was more interested in him now. 'It is Telefonica. They will prepare your broadband on Wednesday.' 'Rent' and 'Sales' always laughed at Nuria's seriousness and enjoyed his crazy visits, insisting he looked too young to have a bad back. Jack promised them both that one day he would explain how he got it. The sexual innuendo heightened at each visit and the volume of the office radio was turned up to match as they all listened and relaxed to the radio station, Girona, Quarenta Principales.

Leaving the girls he had walked through the Sunday market enjoying the bustle and dodging the huge Rolser shopping trolleys that young or old, man or woman all seemed to tow behind them. The market was a huge social event, where you met your friends, took a coffee or beer and wandered. His wandering brought him close to the door of the eleventh-century church of Saint Marti, built over the old Palafrio castle. Hearing a loud commotion he had gone inside to investigate and found the dark interior was packed with families and their animals to celebrate Saint Anthony's festival.

There were cages full of bright budgies, dogs garlanded and bowed and children in their Sunday best who, were all singing enthusiastically led by the priest on his karaoke-style microphone. Dogs howled, budgies chirped and mothers sang and scolded alternately, as a wayward child poked or kicked someone else's pet. Jack had sat at the rear and watched in amazement as people arrived twenty minutes after the service had started, following the great Spanish tradition of all appointments being *mas ou menos*; more or less. The volume of barking and twittering increased to combat the hymns and slowly the BO seeped out of his fat, poor neighbours on the settle beside him, to merge with the overwhelming smell of booze.

'Only in Spain,' he thought as he left, but at least the church was in use as a happy contrast to many stuffy sanctuaries in England.

Jack saw the expats again briefly as they left the Centre Fraternal and waved to him sat on his favourite stool outside Bar Fun Fun in the Plaza Nuevo; the new square which ironically is in a very old part of Palafrio. He was enjoying the view from his usual spot, with his back to the wall whilst Lluis, the owner, overcharged the *guiri*; taking the piss as often as possible both with regard to money and especially concerning Jack's lack of girlfriends. A 'grockle' or holidaymaker in Catalonia is known as a *guiri*. The cruel side of the locals was sometimes on show when they cynically dressed up their children in the summer to mimic the *guiris*. One evening Jack had bought a box of Lluis's speciality Newtree chocolates from Belgium. It was called a love box with three flavours. Pleasure was a dark chocolate, bitter with an aftertaste. Young was cherry-flavoured, sweet and innocent, and Sexy was ginger, hot and different. So Jack left his stool in the Fun Fun offering chocolates to the girls looking after the shops to the left and the right of the bar, and exclaimed his surprise when they both picked the Sexy variety, even though he had carefully placed them all at the top of the box. He enjoyed chatting to the shop girls and smiling at any passing woman, seeing who looked back and who smiled. Who was a nice girl and who looked away as you would expect if they were faithful?

It was fun and it was therapy, and that was all that mattered.

The end of January was busy for Manolo as clients renewed their rentals and Nuria, 'Rent' and 'Sales' were always there to welcome them and take their money, according to different unwritten and unspoken rules, which depended on how long they had known Manolo's family. Jack dropped by after a brief coffee in the Fun Fun, clutching his eco-friendly shopping basket, which was crammed with *calçots*; long, thin onions best cooked on a griddle or a barbecue, and slurped down in their entirety with an aioli sauce whilst wearing a bib just like a baby. It was a celebrated food at that time of year as *calçot* dinners were organised in the local sports halls so that the wrinklies could eat and drink as much as they wanted for a few euros whilst listening to some traditional *Habaneras* music.

'*Amigo*, how is it going?' Jack stood by his friend's desk.

'*Hombre*.' Manolo grabbed his hand and shook it firmly and happily. 'Job done.' He said quietly and pointed at the queue of people waiting to see his girls. 'This is good, yes?' He stood up and came closer to Jack to whisper the truth. 'Black, no tax, no tell. My Catalan customers love black money for everything, from their property rentals to buying cars, whereas you crazy English never ask and never want, hoy!' He gesticulated at a beautiful tall blonde woman of about thirty years old.

'That woman is the most beautiful in Yapanc, but she is the

only one who will not take me as her lover. I love her, Jack.'

'*Hombre,* you say that about every woman you meet!'

'Ah yes, *amigo,* but I am Latino. I love all women and one day I will find my future wife.'

'*Vale,* Manolo, so what about your lovely Nuria over there? She is pretty, intelligent and dotes on you.'

'What do you mean dotes?'

'She would do anything for you and loves you to distraction.'

'*Amigo,* she is my best employee. Why would I want to spoil such a good commercial relationship?' The practical Catalan businessman would truck no interference in making money.

'Pfur!' Jack humped and looked disappointedly at his constantly romantic, but always practical, friend. 'You should take her into your accounts too, *hombre,* as one day you will look around and realise how much you miss her!'

'Hoy! Jack never!'

'Yes, you will regret it. Just remember how nice she is. I want to find someone who would love me as much as she loves you; loves me for what I am and not what I seem to be. Someone to listen and to accept; not question and change. Someone who loves me for my smile, my conversation and not my achievements. For trying and failing but supporting my trying. To share my hurt and pain and joy and laughter in equal measure without question or complaint. But above all to be happy with me and make me happy.'

'*Hombre* that is magnificent, you should put it in your book!'

'I will, *amigo,* but I thought I would try it out on you to see if the awesome Latino lover approves.'

'Job done, *amigo,* job done, and now I must help the girls. *Adios.*'

Nuria watched the two men closely and leaned close to 'Rent's' ear.

'Look at them. Two little boys needing a mother hoy!'

'But, Nuria, which one do you want to mother and which one do you want as a lover?'

'That can only be decided when I have also made love to the English, yes?' The girls giggled and carried on serving the moneyed customers.

*   *   *

When he arrived home Jack placed a note on the front window of his *barraca* using clear Sellotape and in such a position that he would always see it whenever he was walking past.

Joseph, Joseph, Joseph — if you have money it is easy to stay in touch.

Stop saying I have no money.

Stop talking about your bad health.

Be a man, tough and strong. Harden up.

Not old life. Never old life, no matter what.

Write novel.

No complaints.

No personal chats with Melanie, including money.

Keep it super simple. KISS and simplify.

Assert my life.

Stop being sensitive and responsible.

Don't justify.

Don't engage.

They all seemed good ideas at the time but some days just looking at a list didn't help Jack to change his path.

He had re-joined the land of the living and found his personal Shangri La and now he had to face some old obstacles in Cheshire.

The 'begin' of a beginning but not the end of an ending

Jack sat in front of his hotmail screen and typed cryptically.

> Dear H, my fantastic Soul Shiner friend. Apologies for not emailing last couple of mths but have been dealing with personal crisis. Explain more face to face. Back Cheshire Fri eve Feb 13th staying ten days so can see Joseph two weekends. Any chance of putting me up please? Only if Matt 'OK' and no conflict with old life i.e. upsetting situation ref. ex-wife.'

A day later, Soul Shiner replied in 'proper' English.

> Dear Poppet, fancy flying on Friday the thirteenth; just take care of yourself. I emailed Matt, who replied that he would be very happy to see you for some sound advice and support. I also saw Melanie at school this morning and she said it was 'fine', but she admitted that she didn't like the idea of you being too close to spy on her. A strange comment I thought as surely it is better for Joseph who would be able to come to our house and see you, i.e. just like in the good (bad?) old days.

Why would you need to spy on her, my friend? Is she still paranoid about you after two years, or have you got some secrets to tell me, you dreadful man? However, she and I don't usually socialise together anymore, so it's up to me and I will not take sides. So, my dearest Poppet, of course I will be delighted to have you. PS. You should have called me for help during your crisis whatever it was. Remember call anytime for anything. Lots of love, Soul Shiner x.

Jack pondered the contents and wondered what possible advice a strong intelligent character like Matt needed. He wasn't surprised that Melanie still hated him so deeply and, finally, he was excited if Harriet was giving him a subtle sexual tease as he had always fancied her but his attention had been on Bridget at the time. He carefully re-read the words and then dismissed the sexual thoughts as his imagination. That was the benefit and downfall of emails as they said everything and nothing. In fact, he thought that they were undoubtedly the worse form of communication that had spread through the whole world like a nasty flu virus; quick and cheap but providing bad communication that pervaded everyone's lives.

The Wednesday morning before the flight to England dawned bitter and grey to match Jack's mood.

He slumped in his wicker chair on the cold red tiles of the patio trying to keep his feet off the ground by resting on his heels. Nursing his cup of coffee with both hands he extracted some physical warmth but his spirit was freezing inside of him. Even the calls of Madre's chickens were subdued and so the normally inspiring start to his day was downcast.

Knowing he was going 'home' to Cheshire was already disturbing his equilibrium. He felt exhausted three days before leaving because his night had been full of waking dreams. No matter what he had done to reassure himself, they still remained vivid and true. He had paced inside the house and then went outside; going around the property a dozen times in the dark, scared of standing on a *niño,* a black poisonous snake. He had put the radio on but was bored by the late night jazz and then he had tried reading his book, *Don Quixote,* but couldn't concentrate on its complexities to put him to sleep.

Eventually, a bottle of beer numbed his senses enough to terminate the avalanche of theoretical thoughts about matters that would probably never be realised. The dreams always started and finished in the same way but were now building into a climax as the weekend loomed. They commenced with how he could survive as a writer with no money and the variation on ways that his ex-wife was trying to obtain more maintenance. He was paying all the bills on the house in Tettenhill and there was no sign of a sale in the current climate. The end of his dream was far more dismal. As his bad back and hip became more painful he struggled to walk and could do no work, exacerbating the money issues, and then he had his heart attack. At the very end he always saw a shotgun being loaded and snapped shut. That was as far as it went. None of it was true, but it took his existing concerns and amplified them a hundredfold, threading different individuals in and out of the dreaming reality.

He decided to follow Manolo's advice on living day to day and walked around the house saying his seven pleas before laying out the contents of his suitcase ready for the trip. This gave him no solace and so he spent the next two hours cleaning everything thoroughly that had been cleaned two days before. This did help; whether it was the physicality of doing it or the satisfaction in his mind that his home was perfect and he could do no more. It contributed to his stability and his 'none' equilibrium was restored for the day. The real key to unlocking his disturbed mind was closure on his old family life, but he hadn't moved on yet as the Law Courts were incredibly slow in resolving both finances and access to Joseph. Guilt about leaving his son reappeared with extra venom and pushed him back to the edge of sanity. He read and re-read the list on his *barraca* window and realised that each of the points were all putting extra pressure on him. They reminded him of how he should behave on his visit but, of course, none of the points resembled how he had behaved in the last two years. Each one required courage and a hardness of character that he didn't possess. That was the crux of the matter, as he knew Melanie was far more streetwise than him. In reality, he was scared of being manipulated by her and so running away to Spain had made it harder for her to influence him.

He sat in his usual seat at the back of the Ryanair 737 as close to the rear emergency exit as possible in order to reduce his anxiety about flying. In reality this was caused by his frustration at not being in control. A middle-aged couple with Manchester accents stood blocking the gangway as they debated why they couldn't see their seat numbers, despite walking the length of the fuselage.

'Bloody Ryanair. They must have changed the type of plane at the last minute, Deidre. That's just typical of these cowboy airlines. Look at that bloody stewardess, lazy cow. She isn't helping anyone, is she?' And so by default they followed the rules explained on their reservations and squeezed their large arses into the seats in front of him. Jack would normally have courteously explained that there were no reserved seats and helpfully resolved their anger. However, he was so stressed by his own return that he just crossed his arms in thought.

'Pfur. Why do Ryanair flights bring out more ignorance than any other aspect in my life? Jesus, they should start charging by a passenger's weight as these two would pay double.' He breathed in deeply, thinking about other sources of ignorance. 'That includes my ex-wife, of course.' He smiled for the first time that day. 'At least I'm going home to see Joseph and that's all that matters.'

Twisting to his left he bent to look out of the window and say goodbye to the green hills above Girona. Immediately, he felt a lump in his throat as his mind roamed. Will he give me a big hug when I see him? The lump grew larger as he doubted the unconditional love that a son gives his dad. He decided he should start calling Spain home with anyone he met in England and then he pictured his lover Bridget lying bloodied in his arms as he slipped back into the memories of his old life in Cheshire. Tightening his lips and blinking his eyes he sat immobile placing his hands on the seat in front to brace himself as the plane roared down the runway on his way home, because it was, and always would be, home, even if he didn't accept it.

Every mile he got closer to Cheshire, he felt happier, because he was nearer his son and, by the time he saw the stunning sight of La Rochelle set in a bright blue sea, he had left his distress on the ground in Catalonia. He stared out of the Perspex window and felt the happiness as he lost himself in the vast expanse of the sky. He got up and left his seat to stand by Deidre and then started to limber up moving his stiff back and hips to the sounds on his iPod. Looking around the plane at the big slumbering *guiris* he smiled as Kool and the Gang sang 'Celebration time, come on', which he mouthed quietly. Then Police crooned 'Every breath you take', and he swayed and danced, and imagined gesturing to his fellow passengers to join in the *funning*. He decided this was his new word and rather than staring sullenly at the madman they would all get up and start to dance with him, smiling as they dumped their conservatism and shared some happiness. But their love for the rest of humankind was drowned by the loud snoring after five cans of Carlsberg and copious mouthfuls of microwave pizza.

This disappointed him for at least thirty seconds before T' Rex allowed him to wriggle his back again whilst riding a White Swan. Unusually for Jack, he maintained his *funning* as they landed at Liverpool. He even smiled as the whole plane erupted in loud clapping and Deidre complained stridently about the rough landing due to the cheap tyres used. She believed this was to do with Ryanair wanting to make extra profit on their £40-return fare. He shook his head and laughed.

Ignorance personified and only in England! But his thoughts were now more intense about seeing his boy and equally as fearful about talking to his ex-wife Melanie.

* * *

It was dark as he drove into the village of Chriseldon, near Tarporley, correctly pronounced 'Tar Poor Lee' by the Cheshire set and he had to search for the welcoming lights of his friend's three-storey, red-brick Edwardian house a few hundred yards after the duck pond. The Fiesta hire car crunched across the pink gravel until it stopped outside the side door. He sat and considered whether staying with them was right for his equilibrium as he slowly collated his valuables, but it was too late. Immediately he opened the car door there was a wave of soulful happiness that overwhelmed him as Harriet rushed to hold him close.

'Jack, it's so fantastic to see you again. You shouldn't have left it for so long as you are always welcome, poppet.' She hugged the breath out of him so it took a moment for him to reply, thus giving him no time to puzzle over the extreme warmth of the welcome.

'Harry, my Soul Shiner. I've missed you too, lovely.' He pinned her arms to her sides and pushed her slightly backwards to bathe in the harsh white floodlight from above the door. Nothing had really changed in his absence. Forty-three-year-old Harriet still had long naturally red hair, streaked with grey around her pretty face and just a few extra lines beneath the eyes. Her purple top barely covered the large breasts and her petite skirt was still too big for her short voluptuous figure. Jack pulled her close and smelled the Allure perfume which immediately reminded him of Bridget.

'You look fantastic, Harriet. Your goodness radiates out of you and that's why I call you Soul Shiner, my beautiful friend.'

'Oh poppet, you writers have such a way with words.' She kissed his cheek and dragged him inside, abandoning his car and luggage.

'Matt!' She called her husband who appeared from the extension that had been used by the nanny before they packed their girls off to boarding school. Matt Diamond, the famous surgeon, was short, stocky and still wore his thick horn-rimmed glasses from the seventies.

'Jack, old chap, how delightful to see you.' They shook hands vigorously as Jack held Matt's shoulder, feeling the genuine sincerity of his welcome.

'How are you, Matthew?'

'All the better for a glass of red, old chap! What do you think?' Jack smiled.

'I think your cellar needs depleting as soon as possible, my friend' and they chuckled together as they examined the wines already set out on the black granite worktop.

'The strange thing, Jack, is when you have a genuine friend you can see them once a year and pick up just where you left off. Isn't that right?'

'True and if I remember the last time I saw you it was also opening a bottle of claret!' All three laughed heartily.

'What a bloody good memory, Jack. I know it's late but do you fancy some Stilton with it?'

'That would be great thanks. I can't get any cheese that compares to it in Catalonia, although we have good wines, my friend, and so cheap too.' Harriet proceeded to source their supper, vainly searching through half a dozen of the blue painted cupboards as nothing was ever organised logically in her skippy house.

They walked through the kitchen that adjoined the snug and sat in the red leather armchairs near the central Aga. Jack was considering Matt who looked worn and tired as he enquired.

'I see nothing has changed with you two. Is she still completely loveable but skippy, Matt? Still losing her diary or mobile between baking all day and supporting a demonstration to save the local badgers?' It was a rhetorical question that didn't warrant an answer but as they turned away from each other and changed the subject it made Jack wonder if they had just argued. They each sank a couple of glasses of red and munched on the blue stinking cheese as they caught up on the more mundane parts of their lives: how their girls had settled in at Packwood School; Harriet's latest project to recycle their waste water through a modified septic tank; her three mornings a week as a classroom assistant at Joseph's school. Nothing much had changed; life was just a repeat on a variety of themes from the previous years, but Jack noticed that each expressed no interest or concerns about the other's conversation. This was a subtle difference compared to the last time he had seen them at a dinner party.

Jack looked Harry up and down when she stood to collect their plates and realised he loved her dearly. They had always been close since their first meeting drinking tea on his patio with Melanie ten years ago. He settled lower in the leather and became comfortable in their company. He always warmed towards Matt as he shared a common intelligent interest in people and how they behave. Jack used his writing about people's thoughts to express himself whilst Matt used his consultancy and surgery on their bodies; both operating on the very essence of all individuals.

As Jack was shown to his room by Harry he felt grateful to have been welcomed into the goodness of their home, as a temporary shelter from the badness that he would experience in the next few days as he was cast back into his old life with Melanie. He heard Harry quietly close her door and go to bed but there was no chatter with Matt. He then heard a distant door bang and realised they slept in separate parts of the house, which disturbed him as he had always genuinely loved them as a couple. Lying in the dark he thought about Soul Shiner alone next door and remembered how attracted he had been through his bad times before his divorce. They had shared their adventures at the local spiritualist meetings and they had become very close, although there was never any explicit sexual attraction. He thought she was still attractive as he lay on his back on the hard single bed with the bedside light off. He slipped his hand onto his cock and started to rub it gently. The 'hard on' had started about an hour earlier and just lying thinking of her and her lingering smell on his neck made him want to wank for the first time in six months. She wasn't the most beautiful person but pheromones and shared ideals incredibly sexed up their friendship and had always drawn them together. As he grunted and came into his hand he felt guilty, but also incredible relief as the dead clotted and yellowed sperm were washed from his hand down the en suite washbasin. Then he slept and had no waking dreams for the first time that week and, more importantly, no thoughts of suicide.

At 7 am, dawn was just breaking through the holes in his curtains as Jack stretched contentedly and contemplated seeing his boy. He glanced at the light beams shimmering on the wall.

Oh, Harriet, you've got holes in your curtains. What a typical skippy thing in a skippy house. Nothing quite works and nothing gets completed. The thought encouraged a huge early morning sigh as he realised it would be a difficult day filling his own emotional holes, but he vowed to keep those feelings away from Joseph and act normally. He looked forward to the mundane Saturday agenda that eight year olds have arranged for them by their mums, and so he dressed, contemplating these happy thoughts and in great anticipation for the day ahead. He went downstairs and into the snug to wait until Matt or Harriet came to the kitchen. On the side worktop above the dishwasher stood a solitary coffee mug but rather than explore to find the perpetrator he waited until he saw that it was Harriet, who came downstairs a few minutes later. She was wearing a typical skippy dressing gown made of flocked printed material covered in garish roses that must have been at least twenty years old. As she moved Matt's mug to the dishwasher Jack commented on her looks.

'Nice taste, Harry. Very sexy. To go with your black negligee no doubt.' She laughed.

'Hello, Jack. How did you sleep, poppet?' Without waiting for an answer she shocked him momentarily by pulling back the front of her gown and, through a yawn, said, 'There you are! Baggy cotton jim-jams with a tie cord. Not what you expected Mister Smoothie!'

'You are a tease, young lady. You wouldn't have done that if Matt was here.'

'Maybe not, Jack, but I think he left at six. It seems he is working a lot more during the weekends in the last year.' She turned her back on him to prevent the obvious question and picked up the whistling pink kettle off the Aga to make them both some filtered coffee through an old jug with a hairline crack down the whole of one side. This was her style; Nothing in the house matched and nothing was thrown away. In fact, everything ended up in a variety of places so water bills covered the spoons in the cutlery drawer and broken torches lived with the cereals.

'Let's take our coffees outside, Harry, It's what I do at home in Spain so that I can welcome the day and say my seven pleas.'

'I suppose it is mild enough. Do you still do that, poppet? I have always admired that generosity in you.'

'Of course I do. It has even more meaning for me now, after all that I have been through and sometimes I also talk to Nim who is my spirit guide.' Accepting his words without question she said.

'In that case let's walk and you can tell me more about this Nim, as I'm intrigued, Jack.' They wandered on the cold dewy lawn and circled the huge Cypress trees that gave the garden and house a grandeur that it deserved as the focal point of the pretty and expensive village. The old rectory was splendid with a gravity endowed by its height and dull red Cheshire bricks. Sipping from their steaming red coffee cups they admired the pale rising sun in silence as it reflected off the lawn and made it look like beaded and shining glass. The trees dripped onto their shoulders as they touched the old trunks in admiration of the soft chestnut-coloured bark and their bare feet ached in the cold dew, but arm in arm they strolled happily in each other's company.

Jack told her about Nim and how his guide had gradually made himself known over the last two years. He moved onto his suicide attempt which he described as an *accident* and that ensured she hugged him close, as she forced him to promise that he would always telephone her if it ever got as bad again.

'Nim wore a white coat signifying purity or was it just Granddad George's cricket whites? It was surreal, Harry, but it happened exactly like some of that spiritualist stuff at the Magic Lamp meetings.' He glanced at her to see if she understood and then continued, satisfied that she could identify with all he said. 'Do you remember the clairvoyant called Mabel? You took notes.'

'Of course, poppet, that was an unbelievable night.'

'Well, Harry, those messages were from Nim, but I didn't believe it then. Now I do, but I have no idea where I am taking all of these thoughts.'

'Don't think too hard about it, Jack, your path will become clear. Just concentrate on Joseph and living for these two weekends at home.'

'Not home, Soul Shiner, my lovely, certainly not home anymore. You are so artistic and soulful and seem to be living in some distant world. I have always admired how you retain that focus to live on a higher plane through the drudgery of our lives. You answer a spiritual need in me, my lovely, and I thank you for that.'

'Poppet, you and I have always been close. It was just that Melanie controlled you all the time and Bridget seemed to be taking all of your attention. So my little friendly voice got lost in the middle somewhere. Do you remember one dinner party when you asked me if I was missing out on the good things in life?'

'Of course I do. It was a serious question,' replied Jack, stopping his pacing and looking at her. She tossed her hair defiantly.

'Well despite all the goodness in my life I have still missed out on the good things in life. I just didn't get upset about it, like you did.'

'You said *didn't*, Harry, so do you get upset now?' She pulled him forward and kissed his cheek.

'Jack, I miss being hot with the wind in my hair, feeling sexy and vibrant with a young man in true early love as he puts a buttercup under my chin, lying on newly mown grass with the gorgeous smell overwhelming my senses.'

'Touché, Harriet, that sounds familiar too.'

'Of course. It is exactly the same as I said at the dinner party, poppet, and it didn't matter then, but now it does.' Jack strolled further, turning occasionally to look down at the tracks they were creating in the dew.

'So what has gone wrong compared to fifteen months ago? I thought you were deep then but not that deep, surely not Harriet?' Tightening her hold on his arm she said.

'I hugged you after that conversation, Jack, do you remember?'

'Yes and you said "Good luck, I hope you find true happiness." I remember now, I was surprised by the emotion in your voice.' She ran away from him on tip toe resembling a nymph with her silly dressing gown flowing behind her like fairy wings and replied lightly with a tease.

'What went wrong was that you showed us all real courage by leaving Melanie and it made the whole group question their own relationships.' She floated past him leaving him gaping behind her. 'Last one in makes the breakfast!'

'Hoy, unfair!' he cried grinning as he ran after her forgetting his bad hips and back in the adrenaline of the chase and real happiness for once.

During breakfast he telephoned Melanie to confirm the collection time. He tried to talk normally and contain his emotions.

'Hi, how are you?'

'Fine,' she replied with hate in her voice.

'I'll collect Joseph at ten and take him to swimming as per the email, and then bring him back about six after I have given him his tea. Is that, okay? No change from normal as agreed, so that it doesn't become a big event seeing his dad again? Okay?' Jack glanced at Harriet who was sat smiling and supportive with a wedge of Warburton's toast in her hand. He had to repeat it. 'Is that okay, Melanie?' This time she deigned to reply.

'Jack, that's not possible. He can't swim this morning as he's got earache.'

'Oh, I'm sorry about that. Can I say hello to him?'

'He's on the toilet so you'll have to ring back.'

'Hold on, hold on I'll still collect him at ten and take him to Cheshire oaks for ten-pin bowling.' Her words were clipped and cold.

'No. Joseph and I have talked and he says he would rather chill in front of the TV so he gets better more quickly. I tell him everything now and treat him like an adult.' She abruptly put the phone down.

'What a fucking arsehole!' He was absolutely furious with his ex-wife. Harry came over and held his arm.

'Jack, calm down tell me what was said.' After the explanation she advised him with a woman's intuition, woman versus woman.

'Ring Joseph in a few minutes and ask him directly if you can collect him at noon and take him bowling after he has chilled out. Ask him how bad the ear is and say you can look after him to make him feel better.' Jack calmed himself and then made the call a quarter of an hour later.

'Hi, Dad. I can't swim today but I am going to watch *Yu Gi Oh* and play Mario Karts on my Nintendo instead.'

'That sounds great mate, so I'll collect you about twelve and we'll go bowling. Okay?'

'Cool, that sounds good, Dad. Hold on.' He shouted through the house.

'Mum! Is it okay for me to go bowling with Dad about twelve?' In the background the evil witch of the north said in a non-committal tone,

'If you are well enough, Joseph, but only if you are. Just remember I've organised that sleepover tonight and you need to be home by four.'

'Okay, Dad, see you later, bye.' The line went dead gradually with three or four 'byes' and 'love yous'.

'That fucking arsehole!' Jack was livid after replacing the receiver. 'She agreed by email that I would have him all day and for tea, and she has gone and arranged something deliberately to fuck me over. Fucking arsehole.' The tears were in his eyes and so Harry quickly came over to hug him tight.

'Don't worry, Jack. We'll work it out. There's no way she can do that. It's morally wrong.'

At midday exactly Jack reversed his Fiesta into the drive of his old house in Tettenhill and turned the engine off. He could scarcely breathe due to the stress as he looked around at the garden that was once his pride and joy. Brambles and weeds had overtaken the beds and the once-pristine grass had grown tufty and tall just like the adjacent farmer's field. He blew frustrated air out in a long breath as he stared at the empty pond and the tall bare roses that had grown wild without pruning.

Sadly, he walked towards the cottage, preparing a smile for his boy. He pressed the doorbell and Melanie came to the door and unlocked it. A door that was never normally locked unless in readiness for an ex-husband's arrival, to make a statement. He kept his mouth tight lipped and thought about whether he would dare use his own keys in the future. Staring at her ugly face he had a momentary nasty thought before immediately regretting it.

I could have let myself in and wanked into your drawer of knickers, you fucking arsehole. Out loud he was more polite. 'Hi! Is he ready?' She replied in a clipped and cold voice to her agenda.

'Next time you ring him, don't agree anything about access without agreeing it with me first.' The only word missing was the usual derogatory *Jack,* emphasising the 'ack'.

Buoyed up by Soul Shiner's earlier advice he said, 'Why?' This was to become his favourite word expressed through rounded lips, questioning and rising in tone with a lingering 'ii' as if he was Chinese.

'Because I have other things arranged for him and he will get confused.' The bad father paused before responding positively.

'That's because you have deliberately arranged things when we had agreed that this and next weekend are for me and Joseph. My time and my arrangements.'

'Well, you never confirmed anything, did you.' Melanie clammed up as Joseph approached leaving Jack in the wrong. His boy was blond, handsome and tall, eight going on ten.

'Hi Dad!' They bear-hugged and Jack lifted him high into the air to look him in the eyes and hug him even tighter. His boy had grown heavier with all the 'chilling' in front of TV instead of shots in the garden with his Dad.

'Hi, mate. How are you feeling, JoJo?'

'I'm good, Dad. The earache has nearly gone now.'

'Well, that's good then. Let's go and have some *funning*.' Joseph turned with his Nintendo in hand and went to fetch his coat allowing her to take a bit of extra flesh.

'I want him back at four.'

'Why?' Asked Jack as trained that morning.

'Because we are going to a friend's house.'

'What time are you going Melanie?' She blanked him.

'We can't be late so he needs to be here at four.' Before he could argue JoJo returned dragging his Man United jacket on the floor. Arms crossed she said to him.

'Pick that up, Joseph. It cost a lot of money.' In his imagination Jack added.

'I know I'm still paying for it. What is even worse is that it's Man U and not Liverpool.' She continued in a cold, flat and hateful tone to a silent poker-faced ex.

'Make sure you have him back at four.' Bending to her son she cuddled and mothered him as if he were leaving on a six-month trip and all for Jack's benefit. She said goodbye to Joseph but not to Jack as she closed the door as fast as possible to keep out the nasty smell. Pointedly she locked it and walked away without waving goodbye. But Joseph was happy and skipped down the drive to jump into his dad's car.

Starting the engine, Jack dumped his ex from his mind and regained some normality with his boy.

'Look, JoJo, it's even got satnav.' Flicking the screen on impressed his son who proceeded to get excited, pointing out the different dials on the hired Fiesta's dashboard. It didn't matter what type of car it was because it was his dad's and the unconditional love flowed between them.

'Where are you off to tonight then, Joseph?'

'Oh just Michael's down the road. We're having supper at about six thirty and then a sleepover so Mum can get drunk again.' Jack logged the content and decided to be late back avoiding the silly curfew. The bowling was great *funning*; the pizza was eaten greedily with extra chips and followed by chocolate brownies accompanied with lashings of 'fat' coke. Suitably stuffed with junk food they browsed in the bookshop and bought Joseph *Yu Gi Oh* magazines and playing cards. At a quarter past five Jack dropped him at home taking him to the locked door and knocking it as hard as the pain in his knuckles allowed.

'See you tomorrow for football training, mate. I'll collect you at ten, okay?'

'Okay, Dad, thanks. Nighty nighty.'

'Pyjamas, pyjamas.' His dad replied lovingly as he turned away and smirked having seen Melanie's thunderous face at the window. Joseph hurried inside wondering what his Mum would say about his being late but she took her vengeance out on Jack not Joseph who received the usual sweetness and light approach. She followed him to the car determined to wipe the smile off his face and held the door open as he tried to close it.

'You bastard. You knew we were going out and you've ruined it. You have to turn up once in a blue moon and take over don't you!' She was hateful and angry.

'I haven't ruined anything Melanie, as you well know. So don't play games with me. And I haven't been around because of two things: one, you have taken all my money and left me none to fly over and see my boy; two, I have personal and private things that you don't know about and never will.' She was vindictive and uncaring in her reply.

'Ah! A new girlfriend is it? Spending your time and money on being selfish as usual.' He had to engage and broke one of his new rules. She was asking for it and therefore he fell into the trap of giving too much detail.

'Actually, I nearly died and then it took me time to move house and get my act together.'

'Humph!' She didn't care and, in fact, would welcome his demise. 'Living in your imagination still, Jack?' This time she did click the 'ack' cynically. 'Living the irresponsible lifestyle. No worries, totally flexible, whilst I have all the problems and look after your son as you can't be bothered.'

'Melanie, I told you from the start that I was going to live in Spain and write my book and that was two years ago. I told you I would support you and I have, but you know *more is truly less* in terms of you and your life. *Doing* changes the mundane and meaningless to exciting and important and you have done nothing in fifteen months except ask for more money and complicate your material life further.' He slammed the car door shut angrily just missing her fingers. She still knew how to take a piece of him and he was even more puzzled as he saw her tears and that made him very uncomfortable. He drove back to Matt and Harriet's home more stressed than when he had arrived the night before, but that was the state of the relationship with his ex-wife.

The three of them sat in the lounge and Jack took a long gulp of his red wine as a concerned Soul Shiner gauged the look on his serious face.

'How was Joseph then?'

'We did some *funning*, Harriet, thanks. He was really happy and no different in his behaviour towards me at all.'

'That's good, Jack,' Matt said relieved that an eight year old wasn't hurt by the divorce. Jack was thoughtful for a moment before sharing his concerns.

'Melanie was crying when I left and I don't understand why.' Harriet smiled at Jack's naivety.

'You don't know women very well, do you poppet? Women cry to divert attention.'

'Do they?' Jack was still puzzled.

'Yes, Jack. Did you arrange your access for tomorrow?' He paused and remembered.

'No, not really.'

'Well, that proves my point then. She will make tomorrow hard for you too and will continue to be difficult for a long time. It just takes time, Jack.'

'Great, that's all I need.' Jack finished his wine and reached for the bottle. Harriet helped to erode his naivety a little further.

'Melanie will cry to make you feel guilty about leaving her. She will cry to extract money from you. She will control and manipulate you as you are too nice, too kind and non-assertive, Jack.'

'Thanks again, that really makes me feel better.' Another slug of wine was required before he commented. 'What have I done to Melanie that is so bad that I deserve such hatred?' Harriet told him bluntly.

'You have taken her lifestyle away, the persona that she projected to all her friends. I tell you what, Jack … she dropped me like she eventually drops everyone if they are not suited to her purpose. She likes to be in control of a relationship and is always looking for something out of it which is to her benefit and that included you, my naive friend. Surely, you know that by now? You can ask any of her ex-friends over the last ten years.'

Jack became more depressed as Matt joined in the psychiatry session.

'You also need to understand about your old friends here in England and what they think. Firstly, you are old news and so they are not interested in you bitching about your ex-wife and, secondly, they are jealous. For example, at soccer training tomorrow they will be jealous of your simple lifestyle. They will be jealous that you had the courage to do what many want to do.'

'So are you two jealous then?' He looked at both of them in turn. Matt carried on.

'No, we are different as we have moved with you and have not stayed the same old acquaintances you knew before as we have also changed. Just remember we are always your true friends.' Jack was too preoccupied with his own position to register the coded nuance about their life and so he didn't query it. Soul Shiner told him about their other old acquaintances Jean and Martin.

'I saw her in Chester today for the first time in ages. I've really lost touch since you left.'

'How are they?' Asked Jack.

'Well they don't have your instability and insecurity. They seem well,' she hesitated, 'boring really. Safe and happy with the basics like most couples. Food, shelter, health, kids. Safe, you know. Don't rock the boat until you die.' Jack didn't like that concept at all.

'Well, I can tell you both that I could never live like that anymore. I need excitement and achievement in my life, not safety. My god, you only live once.' Matt and Harriet were quiet and continued to have separate conversations with Jack. Matt re-emphasised his earlier point.

'Yes and what a nice lifestyle you have. People really are jealous of it. You return from Spain and say you are writing a book. You look great, healthy and unstressed. People secretly envy your freedom, Jack.'

'Okay, Matt, I can see that now, but I left my wife and family just like Buddha.' Matt choked on his wine.

'Bollocks, mate, are you saying you are a god now?'

'No, no, of course not. I am just pointing out that when Buddha truly saw the poor and how they lived, he decided to do something about it and a wife and family were expendable in the greater scheme of things.'

'And what, Jack?'

'So I left mine because I had a spiritual calling which no one will ever believe and as part of that I needed to live in Catalonia and start writing my book, *A Guide to Life*.' Harriet asked,

'Have you started the book?'

'Not really,' he was suddenly defensive, 'but I have everything ready even if it is only in my head because I destroyed the years of notes on my computer that I left in Tettenhill. So on Monday I will buy a netbook in Chester and start.' Matt was laughing at him.

'You know, Jack, if I'm not mistaken it took Buddha six years to find himself and work out how to solve the problems of his perceived world, and he had money as he was a rich prince so you are in the shit, mate.'

'True, Matt, maybe I was pushing the synergy too far, but he did attain full enlightenment. He did save himself first so he could then save the people. Remember the saying, a Lotus flower is a symbol of purity but it grows from stinking mud so good can come from bad.'

'Fuck me! Well that's okay then,' said Matt, laughing at his silly friend, whilst his wife remained quiet and thoughtful. The banter continued until they all went to their separate beds, slightly drunk and worn out by the day's overt and covert emotions that were not equally shared.

Sunday came and went with relatively few problems.

Jack took his boy to football training with strict instructions to put eardrops into his son's ears before and after the game.

'Give Joseph his cough medicine after the session and buy him cough sweets to suck as he runs during it.' Her orders rang in his ears. On the basis that his son didn't cough at all during the day, Jack ignored the instructions and told his son to be tough. As he watched him play soccer Jack emanated a warm loving glow and kicked and tackled every move with him. He lived his son for the whole day and avoided unloading his emotions on the little under-developed persona. Conversations were based on Nintendo games, *Yu Gi Oh* and how good Manchester United was versus Jack's own Liverpool team. All that was needed for their relationship to blossom was to do things as only boys can do together and that was what Jack instigated. Long-distance telephone calls or looking at a photo of JoJo hurt compared to the joy of doing together.

JFDI — Just Flipping Do It — was what truly counted, with flipping changed from the F word normally used by grown-ups.

Joseph and his dad were *funning* and they loved each other. Nothing else mattered.

On the drive home his responsible, focussed and intelligent boy asked a good question.

'Dad, what is circumcision?'

'That's easy. Some people have the end of the skin cut off on Mister Wiggly for religious or medical reasons.'

'Oh Dad, I bet that hurts!'

'No JoJo they use an anaesthetic, so no it isn't painful and is normal and natural for many people. For example, to be Jewish you have it performed as part of a ceremony to confirm yourself into that religion.' The car remained quiet for another two minutes.

'Dad?' said in a drawn-out questioning tone.

'What is female circumcision as it was on TV in a programme about Africa?' Jack didn't hesitate.

'It's a girl thing. Ask your mother about it, mate.' End of conversation as two can play games in a divorce with the child in between. Of course, Jack got the inevitable bollocking when he dropped his son at home. She checked the level of the cough medicine bottle that she had secretly marked with a ballpoint pen. She complained bitterly about the lack of cough sweets and, finally, she asked JoJo directly if they had used eardrops three times in the day.

An unwillingly 'no they hadn't' put his son in the middle of their feud, but Jack was fed up with the crap and said wrongly in front of Joseph.

'When my son is with me he does what I want and not what you demand, Melanie. Stop trying to tell me what to do because we are divorced. So give it up.' He turned and walked away satisfied.

You shouldn't have done that, Jack. Think of the effect on Joseph.

'I'm sorry Nim but she just winds me up so much I have to say something.'

Stay on the higher ground, Jack, and don't let her bring you down to her level.

'Okay, fair enough, but I am only human and not a spirit guide.'

'I don't like Mondays' the Boomtown Rats song seemed appropriate as it repeated in his mind after it was played on the local radio station MFM. Jack slowly drove into Chester and as soon as he hit the outskirts he sat in a queue of cars for half an hour. Unlike his old life he wasn't in a hurry to get anywhere fast and so he relaxed and looked at the stress in the faces of passing drivers and pedestrians. In half an hour he didn't see a single smile. He saw aggression with each other; aggression with wayward children on their way to school and general unhappiness. The weather didn't help with the Gulf Stream pulling in the usual wet and wintry westerlies to dampen any happiness. Harriet and Matt were both out and were briefly seen and bypassed in the morning rush, so he could concentrate on his book. He played on various laptops for half an hour in PC World before choosing the first machine he had tried and then swept home to Chriseldon on a wave of euphoria to start *A Guide to Life*.

He placed his shiny Samsung netbook on the table in the conservatory and typed in the title and then stared at the water dripping from the huge low boughs of the Cypress trees.

'My book, Nim. A record for my son. A guide for my son. Therapy and structure for myself to make up for all that I have missed in the last year.'

*That's good, Jack. All those objectives are excellent
and then we can outline the choices in the Fifth World.*

Half an hour later he typed the first paragraph. Half an hour after that he changed most of it. He then stared at the pouring rain for another hour in between making both tea and coffee.

'Nim, why aren't you helping me?'

It's your story, Jack. I am just a small part in it.

'God this is so hard. I thought anyone can write but I haven't got a clue. All I have is a mish-mash of notes in my head and no storyline.'

*Well, tell the readers who you are, what you believe in
and what I have said. The rest is easy.*

Jack tried again and wrote the start. He then wrote the final few paragraphs until interrupted by the arrival of Soul Shiner.

'Hi poppet, how's it going?'

'Great thanks. do you fancy some tea?'

'Lovely, yes please.' And that was the end of his first intermittent day as a writer, but the hardest part of doing something new is in the first few steps, and at least he had begun to walk along his path.

Teas in hand they sat regarding the miserable weather.

'Jack, look at the wonderful pattern created by the rain trickling down the glass roof. Isn't it fantastic?'

'Everything is fantastic to you, Soul Shiner.' He looked across and smiled at her in her odd assortment of baggy green clothes. 'You look like you have been on a battlefield, Harry.' She wasn't concentrating and misheard.

'You've noticed then?'

'Noticed what, Harry?'

'Matt and I.' Jack placed his tea cup on the floor ready for a serious conversation.

'I've noticed the separate beds and the singular conversations, but I didn't want to ask uninvited.' She grimaced and shrugged her shoulders.

'Always sensitive, that's my friend Jack. You never really know a couple and what goes on behind closed doors, do you?' It was rhetorical as she knew the answer. 'We didn't know one per cent of what you and Melanie said or experienced. We still don't know. We just formed opinions as the months went by and they were just fatuous guesses. Like everyone else, I suppose we were concentrating on ourselves, our girls, schools, work, the usual day-to-day stuff.' She ran her hands through her long gleaming hair and rubbed her temples, pushing her breasts out evocatively. The sexual movement wasn't meant, it just happened and she did notice Jack's interest.

'Yes sex. So important in any marriage and our love life started to dry up in that last year before you ran away, Jack.'

'I didn't run away, Harry. I went to live my dream. I couldn't stand living with Melanie because if we could have nudged along, I would have for Joseph's sake. Leaving him was a terribly hard decision.'

Harriet shifted uncomfortably on the woven banana plant chair that was all the rage that year in Cheshire.

'We don't have that problem, Jack. The girls are away at school and are quite happy to be independent. The fact is our marriage got onto a steadily worse footing in that last year. Seeing your marriage break up pointed out our own deficiencies and, I'm not certain, but I think Matt has found someone else. A woman always knows, Jack. It's the little things like the lack of hugs rather than the excuses to work late.' Jack was defensive for Matt's sake.

'Marriage is about working together, Harriet. Money, trust, respect and work. You have to be focussed on them all and integrate them together for a joint and harmonious view. You mustn't see the combination as what you get out of each other. They are shared things; a true partnership of minds.'

'Well, poppet, I was watching you and Bridget. Don't tell me, but I have my doubts.' She wagged her finger admonishing him. 'I also watched Peter and Jean mess around and who knows what went on there but, in reality, Matt and I met when we were both sixteen and never had a life before each other. So once the girls had left to board, we both started yearning for something more exciting. We were living together but were lonely despite each other's company and every day we disrespected each other more and more and eventually the talking stopped.'

'But surely that's your choice, Harry? You can still make an effort to improve things; you don't just give up after twenty-three years of marriage. Did you know in many countries like China their approach to marriage is much more practical? For example, they never have casual sex. However, starting from very young you have a potential partner and might wait fourteen years before marrying. First of all, you have to find out about the essence of the other person or at least understand and get used to their idiosyncrasies. Then, a year before marriage, you might try sex out a few times and even if the sex is poor, it doesn't stop you getting married. How about that for commitment?'

'It's very good, Jack, and I think I have said enough.' She went off to shower and keep her council. That was the private person that Jack loved. So he sat and kept his questions to himself, respecting her and Matt's privacy and hoping everything would turn out well in the end.

★ ★ ★

Ironically, Matt arrived home very late from work, professing 7 am to 9 pm was normal for a consultant surgeon and that he had already eaten in the hospital canteen. A knowing look was passed from Harriet to Jack to reinforce what had been said that afternoon as she binned her husband's lasagne and quietly walked away to settle in the lounge in front of the TV.

'Do you fancy a beer, Jack? We haven't been to the Pheasant Inn for over a year, mate.'

'I know Matt and I can't think of anything nicer than a pint of Weetwoods after all that shit Spanish lager.' The drive took less than ten minutes in Matt's tank-like Audi Q7 which made Jack appreciate that his Hyundai did everything he needed at a quarter of the price. However, he enjoyed the luxury and praised the car and its owner on its classy feel and performance that made them both feel better than the other people they passed in their less expensive cars.

They settled in the dingy pub with its poor lighting and low-beamed ceiling in a quiet corner away from the bar. As they supped their first lip-smacking pint Jack asked a burning question prompted by memories of the place.

'How's Peter Edam? I do worry about him as he went from being my best mate to an alien in less than two months after the car crash that killed Bridget.'

'He's certainly changed. Remember how he used to be extremely witty and join in the repartee with you? Well, every time I've met him in the garden centre he is completely 'none' to use your new terminology. No humour, no interest, 'none'. In my professional capacity I would say he is depressed and needs to see a shrink.' Jack leaned against the rear of the old pine settle.

'Oh god, poor Peter. After he found out that I was the last one to have seen her alive at the accident site, he wouldn't talk to me.' Jack was disingenuous with the truth and would never reveal the final conversation between him and Peter standing in the field by this very pub. 'I can't understand it. Surely he would want to know if she said anything before her passing? Surely he wanted to know Matt?'

'I doubt it, Jack. He went straight into shock and concentrated on his girls and no one else. I also saw Jean recently and she looked dreadful, mate. I don't know if anything was going on between them, but they were best friends. However, he dropped her too and I think it may tarnish her life forever.' Jack went for the second round and when he sat down he commented on Peter and Jean's relationship.

'I think there was something between them and I know Bridget thought that too, but there again I also thought he was pretty close to Melanie, so I can't judge without facts.'

'He is close to Melanie, Jack, maybe too close and that's another reason why he won't speak to you as he is still supporting her. I know that for a fact from Martin. Just remember … it's your old life.'

'Old life and what happens now are totally separate in my mind, Matt. I have never tried to find out what Melanie says or does, and have always maintained that distance as I think it appropriate because I left her.' They sat and drank, enjoying the warmth of the place which was near deserted on a Monday night. Matt seemed to make up his mind about something and turned to Jack.

'I don't know whether Harriet has said anything, Jack, but we have been going through a pretty ropey year ourselves.'

'That was all she's said, Matt. She maintained your privacy.' Matt sighed and carried on.

'Well,' he hesitated, drawing up his courage from deep within. He cleaned his horn-rimmed glasses with the corner of his shirt to buy some time.

'My marriage is over, Jack. It's my fault, or at least most of it. I just move in different circles with different interests and now the girls are away we don't have a common interest. No more fun dinner parties, no joint friends and the house … well the house is just a house, albeit beautiful. In fact, I stay at work rather than come home as it's easier.'

'Come on, Matt, don't just give up.'

'No really, this has been brewing for over three years and the fact is it was just convenient for us both. I think that's true but I don't know.' The beer was smooth and yeasty. Matt took a few more swigs and continued. 'We were childhood sweethearts and all that. I never lived my youth even when training as a doctor, as she was living with me and at a uni nearby. I have never lived my life how I wanted to, I suppose, and then someone else came along.'

'No, you don't have to tell me, Matt. Keep it to yourself, hey.'

'It will come out anyway, Jack. Her name is Hilary. It's a great rumour that will sweep the Cheshire set for a few months until something more exciting is talked about. The fact is I have been shagging the head of sexual health for this area based in Wilmslow.' He laughed out loud and Jack couldn't help but smile and nudge him.

'Oh god, mate, the stories will be horrific.'

'I know, Jack. Well, Hilary is lovely and different, supportive and exciting and you know, mate, all of those things that I don't have in my marriage. I also never worried that I had copped something like gonorrhoea.' He laughed again, the beer loosening his tongue. 'Extramarital sex is an occupational hazard in hospitals; playing at doctors and nurses like we are still kids. The proliferation of affairs is amazing. I suppose we know bodies so well that we understand life is not a rehearsal and sex is just sex. Basically, we understand the truth of a real relationship.' A third round of Weetwoods was required so Matt fetched them in.

'Any advice Jack? You've been through this twice. You must know the best thing to do.'

'It depends on the couple and the circumstances, mate, it all depends.' Jack was pretty confused due to the beer as he had always been a lightweight at drinking. 'Based on my last failure, I'd say take all the money in every account and just fuck off without telling her. Don't be open and honest and nice or sensitive. Just sit and wait until the court order catches up with you and then go to court. The first appearance is just a nice chat really. Then at the second court appearance, just let the judge decide the split of assets and maintenance if you can't agree. But I can tell you one thing. You are stuffed, mate. Private education, wife with no job, just stuffed!'

Jack knew the frustration of waiting for others to make things happen in a divorce. He had been living in limbo with time to think constantly about all of his action points, without finding any resolution. 'Matt, it's awful you know and never easy or nice. Divorce stops you living your new life as there is no clean break. Time is what you need.' He grabbed his friend's arm and said one last thing. 'Do your best for them, Matt. It will be crap for you but they'll appreciate it in a few years' time, and maybe that will keep you all sane and civil.' The conversation diminished in parallel with the beer left in their glasses, until they were kicked out by the antisocial landlord.

'Well, at least the weather has cleared up.' Jack put his hand on Matt's shoulder as he said it and they walked towards the huge Audi dominating the empty pub car park. The view across to the Dee Valley was enhanced by the bright moon and stars and in the distance they could see the Welsh villages twinkling with their orange lights.

'I'm leaving Harriet tomorrow, Jack, and moving in with Hilary in Wilmslow. I'm sorry to involve you in this but it's fate that you are here. I'm really sorry, but now is the time. I'm going to tell her when we get back home so please keep out of the way mate, okay?'

'I'm so sorry, Matt. Anything you need just ask.'

'Thanks, Jack, I will, but I think she will need your support and not mine. So if you hang around with her I will understand as you get on so well. So just know that I appreciate you supporting her and I won't get jealous or respect you any less, my friend.' Jack could have taken the meaning of this in many different ways so he stayed quiet as they drove back to Chriseldon and the hell that was about to break loose.

'Nim talk to me.' He was lying in bed considering the crisis that was happening in the lounge below and he couldn't sleep.

I'm not a companion Jack; I am your spirit guide.

'That's no good, pal, as I was drinking beer and not spirits.' He turned onto his stomach to ease his aching back. 'Tell me, Nim. How many people's lives have I ruined by my actions in the last two years? Was it my fault that Bridget died, or was it because of some divine retribution?'

Jack your actions and inactions are part of the
path that you chose and therefore there is no fault
attributable as it was on your path.

'So if I hadn't left Melanie then Matt and Harriet might still be together?'

No of course not! They just see your divorce
as a prompt. If not you, it could have been someone
else or another external thing, like Matt moving to
Australia for a job.
The path has many obstacles and each obstacle is a
random event. The path is from A to B but instead
of a straight line it can be snake-like twisting and
turning with false avenues that people go up and then
reverse down to join the main path again.
Most people don't know they are on a path and travel
less than one per cent of it in a lifetime. You have
travelled ninety per cent already and can see it clearly
as you are an old spirit.

'That's as clear as mud Nim or else the beer is affecting my thinking. So why did Bridget die?' He fell asleep before he heard the reply.

You saw the avenue; you went up it knowing it was
a dead end and you caused the accident. Be careful,
Jack; don't make the same mistake again.

The next morning he made his excuses to the white-faced and silent couple and arranged to be away all day. He said a sad goodbye and good luck to Matt and drove towards Leicester to see his mother. Walking into the living room of his brother's house he was shocked by how small and frail she appeared. It wasn't just physical, it was the lack of life shining out of her.

'Hi, Mum. How are you?'

'It's Jack, my lovely boy. Give us a kiss, my lovely.' He leant close and hugged her emotionally as she tried disconcertingly to kiss him on the lips. He presumed it was the way her mind had warped. As he held her close she was looking over his left shoulder at his brother. She whispered in his ear.

'Take me away, Jack, I don't like it here. They are holding me prisoner. Please, Jack; take me home to my bungalow.' He released her scrawny hands from his arms and held them tightly together. 'Your bungalow was sold when you were ill, Mum, and you came to live here, to be looked after. Don't you remember?'

'Was it sold? I can't remember.' She proceeded to cough randomly. A little cough occasionally, a 'put on' type of cough rather than one caused by any illness.

'How are you then, Mum? How do you feel?' He examined her whilst she coughed a few more times. She looked terrible compared to twelve months earlier; thin, old and grey with straggly balding hair.

'I had an operation you know. I've got a new hip. This one.' She pointed to her left hip.

'No, Mum, it was me who had a new hip and it was my right one.'

'Was it? Oh, I don't remember.' His brother sat patiently in the corner of the lounge, allowing Jack time to understand their mother's condition and, therefore, the problems that he and his wife were experiencing. She was whispering but still too loudly.

'They force me to eat things I don't like here. Take me away, Jack.' She belched loudly, a made-up belch and not for any good reason. The belching continued, replacing the coughing. 'See those lorry drivers in the yard over there.' She pointed with a wavering arm at the local factory outside her window. 'They keep bringing prostitutes back in their lorries. I've seen them, Jack. Dirty prostitutes having sex in the cabs.' Jack looked at his brother and got a shake of the head to say no.

'I doubt that, Mother. The factory managers wouldn't allow that, lovey. Just forget about it.'

'I have an enormous scar on my hip, I think it was a shark bite from when your dad and I went to Benidorm.' Jack laughed and rubbed her arm gently.

'A shark, hey? I hope you fought it off.'

'I don't remember. I don't really remember anything now.'

'Don't worry if you can't, but the shark bite story is what I tell the girls on the beach. It's the scar from my hip operation.' Jack dropped his trousers and showed her the scar for the eighth time and his mother was duly impressed as always.

'That's really nasty. Make sure you rub some Germolene on it twice a day.'

'Of course I will, Mum; Germolene is what we always used as children.'

'Ay, it's good stuff but you can't get it in a little round tin now. You were about eight I think when you put your head through our glass front door. Germolene was no use then! Dad had to take you to the doctors for stitches and then collect me from the hairdresser's. You gave me a fright that day, my boy.' Now he could smile as it was all true. He showed her the scar under his chin to prove it. The coughing now replaced the belching and the dog under her feet farted, or at least Jack hoped so, because it was foul. 'Where's Melanie?'

'She's at home in Tettenhill. We're divorced, remember?'

'I don't remember anything anymore. Where are you living then?'

'In Spain, Mother, on the Costa Brava.'

'That's nice. I went skiing there with Tugdual in Benidorm, I think.' Jack didn't reply and talked to his brother to get the family news. Whilst they chatted their mother coughed and belched, the dog farted and she gazed constantly out of the window at the imagined prostitutes but never joined in their conversation.

His brother told him how she had torn up all of her old family photos in the middle of the night and an hour later, realising what she had done, had cried inconsolably. Another night, she had knocked their bedroom door demanding her favourite pillow back, thinking they had stolen it. The Alzheimer's behaviour varied, but was getting much worse. She was refusing food, refusing to get out of bed until late evening, and had become nasty towards them. Jack decided to leave. She wasn't going to miss him.

'Bye, Mum, look after yourself and do what you are told. Don't stay in bed all day and get up and walk outside in the garden. The fresh air will do you good, lovey.'

'I do that, Jack, I love walking with your dad. She never cleans you know. It's really dirty here and they force me to eat disgusting food.' Jack hugged her close and reassured her that Joseph and her other grandchildren were all happy and well, and repeated that he lived in Spain.

'I went skiing there.' He left and felt guilty that he wasn't doing more, but relieved that his brother was looking after her.

'What should I do Nim?'

> *Nothing Jack, do nothing. She doesn't miss you. She*
> *doesn't exist like you. She is truly 'none'.*

As he walked into the old rectory in Chriseldon he felt the sadness and hate in the atmosphere and gathered his courage to listen and give hope for the future.

Soul Shiner flung herself into his arms as he entered the kitchen and sobbed onto his shoulder, shaking and muttering incoherently.

'Gone … another woman … said I made him feel old … nothing in common anymore.' Jack held her tight and let her sob. There was nothing to say whilst she wasn't listening. Guiltily he felt her breasts against him and loved the smell of the Allure perfume as he tried not to feel her soft thighs pushing against his prick. As his dick started to stiffen slightly he pulled her off him and sat her by the Aga whilst he made them both a gin and tonic.

'Here you are, my lovely, take a deep swig and calm down. Just talk slowly and tell me anything you want.' Harry breathed deeply after an intake of the strong gin and started.

'I knew it was bad, Jack, and I thought there was someone else but…' She cried again. 'Sorry, poppet. It's the shock really. I feel rejected and lost and although I knew it was tough between us, I thought we would just carry on.' More tears and Jack hugged her where she sat until they stopped again. He looked at her face and could see pain and tiredness.

'Did you get any sleep last night, lovely?'

'No, Jack, we just talked and he told me that he had some bitch called Hilary in Wilmslow. I should have done something, Jack.'

'But lovely, you implied to me that the marriage was bad anyway, so what could you have done?'

'I would have gone round and seen her and asked her to back off.' He thought privately that was unlikely. 'He said to me that he had never really loved me, that it had been a mistake since we were sixteen.' The sobs grew louder and more intense as he kneeled by her chair and held her hand. 'That fucking bitch has taken my Matt off me.' He let the anger pour over him and murmured all the right answers, but none of it made sense. Her mind was at sixes and sevens in emotional meltdown.

'He wants me to tell the girls as he said it's his fault and they might hate him for it and not want to see him anymore. Oh, Jack. I don't want them to lose their father.' The gin seemed to make matters worse. They sat drinking until late and the crying gradually subsided. He could see that she was tired and made her go to bed, promising to sit in the kitchen until she was asleep. After ten minutes he quietly opened her bedroom door and saw her lying face down, still in her clothes but soundly asleep. He pulled a quilt over her and leant down to move her beautiful red hair to one side and gently peck her cheek. Smiling sadly he turned the light off and hoped the worst day of her life was being dreamed away.

Tuesday followed a similar pattern of alternating despair, hate and self-recrimination but, on Wednesday morning, she appeared in the kitchen in her best clothes having showered and put make-up on for the first time he had ever noticed during the day.

'Hi, Harry. How are you, lovely?'

She gave him a warm cuddle and a light kiss close to his mouth.

'Thank you for being here. I don't know who else I could have talked to so openly in the last few days. You know you're very special to me.' She kissed him delicately again.

'So, Harry, you look beautiful today. Is there a wedding on or something?' She hit him hard on the shoulder.

'No, poppet. I woke up and decided I would make an effort and I suggest that you and I go out for the day. What do you say?'

'That would be great. Where do you fancy going?'

'Chatsworth house in Derbyshire and you are going to be my chauffeur so that I can admire the views all the way there and all the way back! So there.' They laughed together and sped off as soon as breakfast was over. She was determined to have a *fantastic* day and kept saying her favourite word constantly. Early narcissi nodded a greeting to them as they drove into the lush valley harbouring the grey stately home. The coffee and scones in the old coach house were fantastic, the library was fantastic, the walk by the water steps was fantastic and the drive home via The Highwayman pub above Manchester was doubly fantastic. They ran and played like children; they gasped at the views and ate the most perfect steaks in the haunt of the masked robber. The day was an escape from the stresses in both their lives and they forgot everything and everyone else and concentrated on *funning*.

At home in the snug they curled up on the sofa with Harry leaning against him whilst drinking champagne and listening to a CD of Abba's greatest hits.

'You need to buy an iPod, lovely, and download something modern.' Jack slurred slightly, as it was their second bottle of Moet.

'I know, poppet, but that's far too complicated for little skippy me. It took me years to move onto CDs so maybe I'll just wait until the next music invention.'

'Good idea. Save your money. In ten years you'll have a chip inserted behind your ear with a million tunes available, depending on which teeth you tap.' He sang along to 'Mamma Mia'.

'Mum! I'm here.'

'Don't make fun of my music, Jack!'

'I'm not Harry, I love it. I love singing along. "Here we go again, my my, how could I forget you?"' He sang it louder and, pulling her to her feet, twirled her around the Aga nestled in the centre island of the kitchen. She flicked the remote before he let go.

'This pop group is my favourite, Jack, so stop still and listen.' She entangled his hands in hers for a slow dance. The Bee Gees oozed out of the speakers 'How deep is your love, how deep is your love, I really need to learn, 'cos we are living in a world of fools, breaking us down, when they all should let us be.' They danced and looked into each other's eyes.

'This is a wonderful tune, Harry; old but still good, hopefully a bit like me.'

'A lot like you, poppet.' She looked into his eyes. 'A lot like you.' Jack slid his right arm low behind her waist and rested his hand on her soft bum whilst holding her hand on his chest. She cuddled in close and wrapped her legs around his as they swayed to the music. Her fingers moved gently on his chest through a gap in his shirt.

'Soul Shiner, I like my nickname for you as you are, you know.' She just smiled up at him as he continued thoughtfully. 'I remember you at Matt's birthday party when I came dressed all in orange as a follower of Krishna. Do you remember as well? It was not long after Bridget had died.'

'I remember, Jack. You were completely out of order all night but we didn't understand you had so many problems then.'

'It was a wild night; I chatted up all the women as Melanie wasn't there.'

'But you didn't chat me up, did you, Jack?' She tapped her finger on his chest.

'No, Harry you were too special.' He looked at her as he said it and their heads moved closer.

'Jack,' she murmured, 'I haven't had proper sex for more than a year and the last orgasm I had was more than five years ago. We were in separate rooms for a long time. It was all a bit hit and miss, and we ended up having appallingly bad sex two or three times a year.' He knew she wanted to be kissed but Nim was warning him.

Jack, she is on the rebound. Your mate has just walked out. Don't go along the wrong avenue again.

'Well my Soul Shiner, my beautiful friend, it's very sad that a sensual and sexy woman like you had such a bad marriage.' His prick was enormous and stiff pushing against her groin and his breath quickened by the second as she oozed her sex over him. Hot and rampant he could feel it flow like a wave from his head to his toes. He pushed the invisible away instead of the physical and murmured softly.

'I suppose as friends, one kiss wouldn't hurt would it?' She pecked his mouth. 'A proper kiss, please, only to see what it would be like. How much harm can that do?' He didn't remember how they got from the kitchen to her bed, or where the clothes came off, but he knew that the fabulous day and champagne made them happy and the wanton sex ended it to perfection. At some point he knew he had shouted ridiculously.

'Hurry, Harry. Jesus, hurry up, Oh Harry, hurry. Oh God, Oh fuck I've come. Jesus wept, that was awesome' and he carried on riding her, clutched together so tight that they could barely move as he shoved himself hard into her hot wet cunt and listened to her come again and again.

They tried to have normal days before he went home but 'let's go for a walk' became a long fuck. Can I have a hug became a long fuck. Every touch between 5 am and 2 am became an orgy of sex as they dumped their thoughts and grabbed insatiable happiness. Occasional sane moments prevailed, but usually when Jack needed an hour to recover before he could manage another erection.

'You are my knight in shining armour, Jack, riding in to save me locked in this castle. I especially like the riding bit.' He squirmed in the saddle before replying.

'In that case, I think you need a chastity belt, you wanton hussy. No!' He stopped her fingers undoing his flies and repeated. 'No, no, no. I'm not.' He hesitated before he carried on. 'It's just, I'm here in the most difficult circumstances and therefore I seem more wonderful than I am.'

'You are a wonderful lover, poppet.' She opened her flowery dressing gown to show him her flannelette jim-jams.'

'That's so unfair, Harry; you know those turn me on.' He put his hands under her top and moved them upwards to gently caress her nipple with single fingers. 'Funny that, but your nipples are very hard again.'

'I can't think why, poppet.' He tried to keep a deep conversation going as he stroked her breasts but his dick was stiffening again.

'Consciousness is practical, you know. Whether it's meeting someone you love or deep meditation; whatever is your version of consciousness. There is no science that gives consensus to consciousness as an answer to what it is.'

'What's that all about, Jack?' Her hand was stroking his large sore cock.

'I really believe in all that stuff like Buddhism and even feng shui in my new simple house. What do you think?'

'Jack, I do believe in things like that but now I am going through a divorce I only care about my daughters and, quite frankly, even this early I am thinking about how much money I can get and how much I need.' His dick lost some of its stiffness as he replied thoughtfully.

'The money isn't important. Staying highly principled and being nice is more important.'

'But, Jack, money is everything. It is my security and stability for the future. I won't cope with mundane things, DIY-type things and so I must pay for support.'

'Like buying a housekeeper or a slave then?'

'Yes poppet but I know one thing I don't need to buy as I have a new best friend who takes care of my every need.' She bent down and started to suck his cock as he leaned against the Aga and wondered if the back door was locked.

Jack's last weekend with Joseph followed the same manipulative pattern as the first and he resigned himself to the grief Melanie wanted to vent upon him at every opportunity. Communications during the week had proved impossible and every excuse including the weather was used to prevent Jack taking his son on the school run. He managed it once by turning up and asking his son at the door. He asked three times to see his boy's school report and was promised a copy but it failed to materialise. The Saturday night in a bed and breakfast in Llandudno was cancelled because her parents arrived unexpectedly and Joseph was so pleased to see Grandma and Grandpa that he was happier staying at home.

Funny that, he thought more than once, and so Jack used Soul Shiner to support him and she used him to support her.

'I tell you, Harry, if the wicked witch of the north does that again I swear I will get a Liverpudlian hit man involved.' When he did obtain some free time with his boy it was a meagre two hours on the Saturday afternoon when she insisted, in front of Joseph, that he must do his homework as he had no time during the rest of the weekend. The homework was fun for Jack and he loved doing it with his boy, but the manipulation was incessant and subtle, designed to erode his fatherly influence.

Harry told him repeatedly, 'Don't engage with her, Jack. Just say I am coming at this time, this is happening and then zip up.' But Jack was too open for that and believed that if you didn't give information, you wouldn't receive any and then you have bad communications, which he desperately wanted to avoid. He needed to harden up as he played the divorce game, but he treated his relationship with his ex-wife as honestly as two years previously. So the bitter witch took her sweet revenge and deluded the poor little man. She always cried after angry exchanges, whereas in reality only Jack got upset. He was constantly defending himself, trolling out the old phrases.

'People make life not places, Melanie. Work to live; not live to work.' And Melanie thrived on it, turning the knife as often as possible but little realising she had a new opponent in her ex-friend in Chriseldon. Soul Shiner asked Jack how he felt now he had been part of his son's life again. The answer was emphatic.

'"None". I feel "none" because he is here and with her and I am in Spain. If I let myself feel anything except "none" then I would be an emotional wreck.'

The last conversation with JoJo took place in the Fiesta, a poor substitute for a real home.

'I'm writing a book, Joseph.'

'Really, Dad? What is it about?'

'Four tales of love and two tragedies that are intertwined. A book for middle-aged women.'

'Can I read it, Dad?'

'Not yet, son. I've only just started it, but one day you can, when you're older.' Jojo brought tears to his eyes.

'Dad, you know I wanted to be a barrister when I grow up? Well, maybe I want to be a writer now because I'm writing a book too.'

Unconditional love made their lives revolve around each other, no matter what happened or where they were.

Jack felt relief by the time Monday arrived and he could depart.

He hated the control by Melanie, he hated the country and he found it incredibly stressful being with Soul Shiner in her new circumstances, as it reminded him of his old life and that was exactly why he lived in Spain.

Harriet started to cut off from her round of acquaintances the minute she heard the first rumour about Jack and her as an 'item' and his moving in. It was already widespread that Jack had caused her marriage breakdown and was living in the big 'posh' house in Chriseldon. The person who told her the nasty rumour had heard it third-hand from someone who was good friends with Melanie. The daggers were out in the space of a few days and Nim frequently reminded Jack:

> *Hell hath no fury like a woman scorned. You have*
> *enough issues diverting your attention without*
> *ostracising Melanie any further. As for Harriet, just*
> *being in the same house is wrong, Jack. Don't get*
> *caught up in between Matt and Harriet.*

'But it's cheap and convenient being here, Nim, and that's discounting the fabulous sex. It's such a shame that her cooking is rubbish.'

Jack didn't listen and went off down another wrong avenue. That was the way it happened, facts didn't enter into it, mutual support did. Harry hung onto his soulful ways and simple life. The timing was perfect to be together. She asked him plaintively.

'Do you mind if I ring you in Spain for support, poppet?'

'Of course not. Anytime you want to. You can rely on me.'

'Will you be alright back there alone, after the grief and aggravation of the last week?' he replied positively.

'I refuse to be anything except exciting and interesting, and I didn't leave Melanie and all this shit she has given me yet again to be other than that. I am going to live life as I want it to be.' He boarded the plane and switched off Cheshire as if it was the unreality of a bad TV programme, because that was how it felt and, in fact, that was how it was. The TV serial name being, *I was important, now get me out of here.*

In Catalonia, the holiday villages of Bagurr, Kaletta and Yapanc were completely dead during February and March with many shop and bar owners taking well-earned rests before the onslaught of another season.

Jack quickly felt at home and, within three days, the horrors of the trip were left behind, filtered out from the pleasant memories of his son and Harriet. The walk from his home to Yapanc was beautiful on a cold clear day, with the dark green of the pines accentuated by the flat light. But Yapanc was depressing, not because of the lack of people, but the old memories of Karina, Melanie and JoJo. Manolo had moved back into his apartment in town and the *croisanteria* was closed until April, so there were no chance meetings, no life and no boats; just a pretty view with no people. After ten minutes he left as he was disappointed with his negative thoughts. There were also no telephone calls from Harriet as she was visiting the girls at school to break the news, and trying to be brave on her own. And so he telephoned Joseph to reassure him he was safe.

'What's the sun like today, JoJo?'

'It's very bright and very big, really yellow today, Dad.'

'That's funny, Joseph. It's just like that here.'

'Is it, Dad?' Came the innocent reply of an eight year old.

'Yes, mate. Let's share it and love each other, no matter where we are and even if we are not together.'

'Okay, Dad.'

'Love you lots, JoJo.'

'Love you too, Dad. Bye.'

Between his new but sporadic writing, Jack would drive into Palafrio to see his friend and wander around the town enjoying some daily life. Nuria, 'Rent' and 'Sales' were bored sitting in Manolo's office one Wednesday afternoon. The new rentals were almost sorted out for the season and house sales were poor as mortgage lending by the banks was tightened on the second homes that were the agency's main source of income. Jack waltzed in as usual.

'Jack, how are you today?' asked Nuria.

'I'm fantastic. *Hola*, girls.'

'You are always fantastic,' said 'Rent'.

'This is true ladies and wouldn't it be great if everyone walked around and said how fantastic they are all of the time. What a happy place we would live in.' They were also happy to see him as it brightened up their day.

'Did Manolo tell you that I'm a writer now?' The girls were impressed and Jack made a mental note to keep using the line with other women.

'What's your book about?' Nuria was the first to ask.

'Laughter, sex, the spiritual world and tragedy.'

'Really, Mister Edmunson. Your life story then!'

'Of course not, Nuria, it's about life, but not me. It explores paths that have never been touched before.' 'Sales' asked the second question.

'So give us an example of real-life things that it explores.'

'Only if you promise not to tell as it is copyrighted, okay?' After Nuria had explained copyright he gave them some examples.

'So girls, tell me, how do you attract men if you have smelly breath from constantly eating garlic and onions, never shaving under your armpits and never using deodorant? Tell me.'

'Jack!' 'Rent' was critical. 'How did you come to those conclusions about Spanish women?'

'Research, my lovely, but if you want to come out with me to prove me wrong you are always welcome.'

'No way! You are far too white and bald.'

'White? What do you mean white?' 'Rent' explained.

'White means not Latino; not dark and handsome with olive-tinted skin.'

'Fair enough, girls, I can handle that, but tell me why do Spanish women always have thatches and thick and crazy shaped coloured glasses?' Nuria explained thatches which caused a lot of finger wagging by the girls followed by repeated *no's*.

'Jack maybe you need to do more research?'

'I would be glad to, Nuria. When are you free?'

'You are a very bad man, *señor!*' He carried on.

'Okay, some final questions as you haven't helped me at all so far. Why are all Spanish women either blue or brown-eyed with no colours in between, and why do you never wear skirts? Why?' He used his plaintive version of why and raised his arms in the air like a good Spaniard. Luckily, Manolo arrived back from an appointment and warned the girls about the crazy English. He always looked after them when he was at work, acting as a father figure despite wanting to shag all three at the same time. But he was Catalan and business was business.

As Jack went to sit with Manolo he noticed Nuria had three blouse buttons that had come undone, showing all of her left breast and nipple. When he joyfully pointed it out whilst staring closely, he was disappointed with the apparent lack of concern. He was finding out that Spanish girls were never embarrassed about sex and their bodies, unlike the English, and were easy with their sexuality but closeted and inexperienced in practising it.

3
Home is where the girl is

I t was spring in the hills above Yapanc and spring was the time for love and loins for the human beings and twitter-pattering for the animals, and either applied to Jack and Manolo. Despite Jack's good intentions by listening to Nim, he was soon to veer off course again in his new life.

The seasonal flowers on the *barraca's* dirt track were a kaleidoscope of colours, growing themselves into an early summer owing to the full sun on their dry lofty position. Red poppies, purple thistles and tall, yellow osteospermum clashed with the wild grasses that hung heavy-headed in a competition to bloom, seed and whither on the crowded slopes. The yellow-feathered mimosa tree adjacent to the patio smelled divine and shook its golden dust like a magic powder into every crevice of the house. It had grown well with Manolo's father buried beneath the young sapling, but Jack would never know that.

March through April was when the birds and animals lusted for each other in a primal heat that was shared with their human neighbours wandering around Palafrio's renowned Sunday market. Spring accentuated the Spanish cultural need to meet and greet people learned from as young as five and religiously applied until the confines of a grave stopped their wander lust. There was joy in strolling, chatting and drinking coffees or taking early beers in the bustle of their localised humanity.

The blue sky and bright sun warmed the main square as the expats gathered for yet more alcohol at their favourite watering holes, following their brief search of the vegetable stalls for the final end of season produce like artichokes and *calçots*. It was pure fate that Manolo and Jack encountered the drunks as they traversed the plaza on their way to purchase books for Jack's education, about the history of Palafrio and the Spanish Civil War.

'Darlings!' A horsey neigh attracted their attention as Lucy broke away from the other foreigners hidden within the Catalan commotion, and trotted across to them. She gave both of the stallions enthusiastic kisses on each cheek whilst pinning their arms to their sides to prevent any bucking.

'Darlings, how lovely to see you both. In fact it's perfect timing because we are all having dinner together on Easter Sunday and insist that you both join us. Now you can't refuse us, can you? You will have each other for company like two bottom bandits, ya!' Jack explained the term to his puzzled friend and assured Lucy that they were definitely not gay, which gave her more time to plead with them to come.

'So Walter's place at Aguablara ya. 6 pm for drinks and 8 pm for dinner if you find you are short of time ya. We always do drinks at 6 pm every day just to be sociable ya.'

Manolo asked why dinner was so early, as he was used to eating after 10 or even 11 pm.

'Oh, we can't be doing with Spanish timings, darling. Need to keep some of our old customs alive ya. Bye, darlings.' She cantered away excitedly with both her blonde bob and big boobs bobbing under her apricot 'Crew Clothing' sweatshirt and re-joined the others as they disappeared into their usual cheap bar.

'So, Jack, I think it is a good thing we go together yes? Job done.'

'Why?'

Manolo winked at him before replying, 'Safety in numbers.'

Jack's telephone calls to Joseph became happier and more frequent as Melanie merged into the winter and left the two boys alone to chat. Harriet phoned occasionally but kept her dignified council as she tried to be civil with Matt and work out the usual separation issues which revolved around money and the strumpet he had moved in with. Thus Jack's emotional interruptions were minimised, giving a new stability in the spring sun that warmed his heart and made him smile again.

'Hi, Joseph. Did I tell you that I have lizards living under my patio?'

'Really, Dad?'

'Yes really, mate. I was standing outside this morning having a wee on the grass.' He was immediately interrupted.

'Dad! You shouldn't wee outside. Mum would kill you.'

'Well, she can't see and probably wouldn't want to see my Mister Wiggly, mate. So, I was standing putting liquid fertilizer on my lawn and something moved incredibly quickly beneath my feet, startling me so much that I wet my hand.'

'That's disgusting, Dad.'

'I know, JoJo, but when I looked up there was a huge green lizard a few yards away and staring at me hungrily, so I shoved Mister Wiggly back in my pants as quickly as possible in case it jumped up and bit it off!'

'How big was it, Dad?'

'What? Mister Wiggly or the lizard?'

'Stop joking, Dad, you are silly.'

'I know mate, but it's funny, isn't it. It is lovely here and I so want you to come over as soon as possible and see my simple and natural home. My day always starts when I hear the joyful sunrise of dozens of noisy animals and birds and always ends listening happily to the same noises as the sun sets. The only downside is the plague of blooming ants.'

'Where are the ants, Dad?'

'Everywhere, mate, they are a nightmare and no matter how many I kill there's a million more outside queuing to come in. I tell you what, if there was a nuclear explosion the ants would still be there waiting to inherit the earth. Guess what, JoJo?'

'What Dad?'

'I opened the flipping oven this morning and they were inside eating the grease from last night's meal. They have even been in my cereal box, foraging through a tiny nick in the plastic and sometimes, when it rains, they come in through the plug sockets. Can you believe that?'

'They are amazing, Dad. We learned at school that they live in different chambers for different reasons, just like we live in our houses and they even carry away their dead.'

'That's really interesting, JoJo. If you like, you could write and tell me all about what you learned.'

'Okay, Dad. I'll do that.' But no positive encouragement was made by his ex, and no letter followed, so Jack contented himself with laying sticks in front of the trails of ants by his patio and watched them organise a diversion. By the end of the year the ants had become his best and only friends.

On Easter Sunday Manolo excused himself from both the drinks and dinner and asked Jack to make his apologies to the expats because 'they would understand' as if in a coded message.

'So, *amigo,* does that mean you have a new girlfriend to see instead?'

'Of course, *hombre,* I always have a new girlfriend every Sunday.'

'In that case, *amigo* I will pass on your apologies.' But he started to wonder why Manolo was avoiding the group and what exactly there was to 'understand'. He left the *barraca* so as to arrive politely late for the drinks, and wound his way slowly through the pines of Tiramisu. The car window on the off-side was now permanently wound down so that he could catch the spring fragrances which changed with every curve of the steep and narrow road. The cistus, pine, myrtle and rosemary scents gave off a heady Mediterranean mix that cleared the mind between spring and July, after which the heat burned the sappy resins out of the air. On the ridge towering above Aqua Zelida the road dropped steeply towards the beach at Aguablara before rising again into Bagurr. Walter and Freda had built a stunning designer home on the side of this valley, with views past Fornalls and onto the Pyrenees and France.

As he arrived he swung his car around on the hardened red sand of their front yard so that it was ready for a quick exit and also to slowly admire the building's design. He was shocked by the glass pyramid that served as a front door but more so by the Duchess who he saw gliding outside to greet him. She wore a semi-transparent and light blue dress made of silk which was casual but smart and around her neck was a simple string of pale apricot pearls.

'Jack, how wonderful that you could come.' She gave him a warm royal welcome. He admired her from close up.

'It's definitely my pleasure, Duchess, and can I just say how stunning you look, my lovely.' As they delicately kissed cheek to cheek she was gracious in her response.

'Thank you, Jack, I really appreciate that' and held him close a few seconds longer than was polite, allowing him to dwell on the delightful smell of her Chanel No. 5 and to shiver at the gentle touch of fingers as they slid teasingly down his spine.

'*De nada* -You're welcome,' he breathed. Linking arms they walked around the side of the *designabox* and straight onto the terrace that balanced precariously on the huge cliffs that plummeted 200 metres vertically into the Mediterranean. As Jack took the proffered glass of Cordoniu Cava he was welcomed warmly by the other expats and also by the orange sunset slanting straight through the length of the massive living room, as a result of the unencumbered glass walls on three sides.

'Dutch, what an awesome house. I have never seen anything this good. Now I understand why you left Holland.'

'Thank you Jack, it only cost us five million euros which we think is cheap for something so unique, but really we left home as it has become the land of slurry.'

'You are joking, aren't you?' Jack laughed with his uncertain reply.

'Yes and no, my polite English friend. You see there are four million cows, over a hundred million chickens, twelve million pigs and just seventeen million people who are all competing for a little land that has a lot of water. So all that shit and water makes slurry!' The Duchess joined them with canapés.

'He also has a boatyard in Palomost as a little investment to keep him busy, but really it's his first love, Jack.'

'Yes my beautiful and controversial Freda.' He couldn't or wouldn't disagree with his wife as he wiped the sweat off his bald pate, 'but it is just a small shed near the old harbour so we must see if it can be successful.' She stroked her giant of a husband's left arm.

'Let's hope so, my dear, as it keeps you out of my way and stops us going stir crazy with too much togetherness.' Jack pondered the truth and remembered his visit to the astrologer who had predicted his future including a boatyard. As the sun finally set, Jack felt his legs chill below his dark blue Bermudas, but it was still a pleasure to be outside on a platform to heaven. Fairy lights in the shape of Christmas trees were turned on around the edge of the terrace, much to his amusement as they resembled those from an English council estate, but the Cava flowed freely and he was content to make small talk without engaging.

Shortly after dusk a short and pretty Thai woman appeared and announced that Christmas dinner was ready. She informed them that she had prepared *nadal*, Christmas soup, a speciality Catalonian dish consisting of a hotpot of different types of sausage bulked out with potatoes to soak up the alcohol. They walked into the glass lounge and surrounded a square olive-wood table with Jack positioned between the Duchess and Pippa. He stared into the oncoming night, searching for planets and contemplated the irony of a Thai slave cooking Catalan Christmas food on a warm spring evening.

Only with expats in Spain, he thought as they all politely sat at the same time. Pippa wanted to know more about him.

'So *J*,' she touched his bare leg and continued in her upper-class accent, 'What do you do with your time? Do you have a job?'

'Well, Pippa, I have just finished my book.' She sat back amazed.

'That's incredible, Oh how lovely. You must be so proud.'

'Yes Pip, it was an excellent read by Chris Stewart called *Driving Over Lemons.*' He hoped to stop the pretentious chat in its tracks, but failed as she was already half-cut.

'You lemon yourself, *J*,' she squeezed his arm, 'bitter to the taste but you would be lovely in my gin, you know.' She then patted his leg closer to his groin. The Duchess politely tried to save him.

'Jack really is a writer, Pippa, but be careful as he is using us for material. He only tells women that he fancies that he's a writer as a way of impressing them into his bed.' Jack looked coyly at the Duchess before returning his full gaze into Pip's already bloodshot eyes.

'That is true, Pippa, I am a writer,' and left her to make what she wanted of the confirmation as he looked at her with his very clear 'come to bed' eyes. She surprised him with her reply.

'I'm a writer too you know *J*.'

'That's good, so what are you writing, Pip?' He emphasised the last 'p' in her nickname to make a popping sound.

'Well, I sent an article to the *Sunday Times* travel section about expat life here but they weren't keen you know as it is old hat now. The other thing I'm writing, I doubt if you would be interested in, as it's for women, you know.'

'Yes I would be interested actually as I'm writing women's fiction.' Demure Pippa reached for a bottle of Rioja and poured some for herself and then some for her husband Rolly who was sitting to her right. As she did this, she lost eye contact with Jack before saying,

'Rolly is very supportive, Jack, just as I support his art.' Rolly leant across and kissed her lightly on her lips.

'Thank you, Pips, I just love your support. You are stupendous you know. My latest venture, Jack, is to create a catalogue of Catalonia in watercolours. It's just amazing you know.' Jack subtly took the piss.

'That's just great, Rolo, you know but hasn't it be done before by a few famous people?'

'Well maybe, Jack, but I believe in ignoring the past and looking with new eyes at people and places.'

Pippa joined in. 'It means that I can write a commentary for each painting so we work together as a team, you know.'

Jack queried sceptically, 'How many places have you been to so far? You must have a lot of pictures from your last year in the area?'

Rolly replied in his clipped upper-class accent., 'Oh God no, Jack, we spent the winter thinking about the content. You know, the concept in its totality as it were, and I just made a few example sketches in Besalu.' Jack was bored by the half-Greek twat but amused by the way his wife had turned the conversation, confirming the shallow life they shared in the expat pond. Lucy bawled across the table at him.

'So why are you in the Costa Brava, darling?'

Smiling widely at her he said, 'I'm searching for the right woman, darling, my Sun Sharer ya.' The Duchess listened silently and looked coy, whereas big bold Lucy needed a more definitive answer.

'So are you trying out all the women you meet then, darling?'

'No! No of course not, Lucy. There are three billion women in the world and I know that just one of them is right for me. I have even travelled to Japan and China as part of my search.'

'That's great ya. You must be shagged out from the travelling never mind the auditions!' The drunken company laughed as Jack smiled and agreed shamelessly. He was surprised at the aggression in the females and the quietness of the males.

'I went out to the Far East and shagged my tour guides. I went to every massage parlour I saw for ten pounds a pop and all I got was a bit of *funning*.' Quiet Niiige was interested enough to join in.

'What the hell is *funning*? Is it a disease?'

'Having a good time, Niiige, fun-ning, do you get it? I just have a belief that you can't buy time so you should make the most of it ya, Lucy?'

'Ya darling, I can identify with that ya. All I bloody do is think about my business as it is non-stop ya.'

Jack doubted that and so he asked, 'What market do you cater for as a holiday consultant?' Drunken Lucy dribbled slightly and wiped her mouth with the back of her hand.

'Well. I work with other professionals ya, there are loads of companies around here and they focus on the marketing ya.'

As the conversation turned to interest rates and house sales the Duchess leaned close to Jack and whispered bitchily, 'Lucy ferries clients to and from the airport and cleans the houses before they arrive. The consulting is restricted to airport schedules and minimising the cost of the grocery stocks.' He nodded knowingly without looking at Lucy or the Duchess and laughed inwardly. Niiige was having a good whine about high interest rates restricting his market.

'No one in England has any spare cash anymore and the euro is rocketing against the pound which is driving down the expat market for second homes.' He took off his round glasses and rubbed them nervously on his napkin. Dutch asked him how many new properties he was working on at present.

'Well, I have a few in the pipeline, Dutch, but timing is everything in my line to keep the cash flow going.'

The sweet smell of Chanel came close to Jack once again and she whispered, 'He has sold nothing in a year and no one is available now to be ripped off with shoddy work.' Again Jack nodded, but this time he turned to her and looked into her beautiful brown eyes.

'A very interesting night, very interesting indeed.' She was captivating in her physical beauty which took his breath away and so he looked away quickly. It was only 9 pm and all of the expats where completely plastered apart from the hostess who remained in total control of herself and also her Thai slave, who received harsh treatment from her mistress and praise from her master.

Instead of his normally open character Jack had tried not to engage for a couple of hours so that he could retain his privacy. Questions about his old life or statements of dubious fact were answered.

'And your point is?' But there was no fun in that and so he started to open up about his real interests. Demure Pippa talked to him again with her hand on his bare leg, hidden from everyone's view by the huge gnarled table.

'What about your old life, *J*, before you became an expat?'

'Well maybe I'm not an expat, Pip, as I am trying to live like a Catalan?' She stared at him, shocked that a Brit would say such a thing and so he continued telling the truth. 'But I suppose my old life was devoted to my wife, my son and making money to support their lifestyle. Now my life is very flexible and devoted to me only. However that upsets me too.'

'Really *J*?' Her hand moved higher and was now under his Bermuda shorts and nearly halfway to his dick. He tried to speak normally whilst watching her husband who appeared disinterested in his wife.

'Yes Pippa, it's er ...' He hesitated slightly as the hand moved upward again. 'It's as bad in a different way because life becomes selfish. It stretches the time away and you don't feel a sense of achieving or striving. So it makes you feel worthless or at least guilty.'

'I can see why you are a writer, *J*.' Her hand was now stroking his thigh next to Mister Wiggly and she gently pulled some pubic hair making him jump. Rolly looked across and Jack panicked as her hand stilled, but the question from her husband was harmless enough.

'How was your cycling today, Jack?'

'Yes okay thanks, but it's made me a little *rigido*.'

'Oh how lovely,' Pippa said and her hand started to stroke his prick through his cotton briefs causing a deep intake of breath by Jack as he tried to quell his visible excitement. Dutch was talking about the mast on his boat moored in Palomost harbour. Jack immediately and kindly offered to help him.

'I'll come and help erect it so you don't mess it up if you like?' Dutch was pleased with the spontaneous offer.

'Thanks, Jack, I know you have sailed for years but you are so cocky sometimes!'

'No! Not sometimes, Dutch, all the fucking time.' He was having trouble speaking normally as her hand grasped his cock and gently masturbated him.

'Pardon me, I need to stretch, Pippa.' He gave her enough warning so she could disengage before he stood. 'Exercise, Pip; it gets harder as you get older, isn't that right?' He quickly escaped to the toilet to her chagrin and sat on the seat of the marble bowl until his erection subsided.

'I wonder, Nim. How many men have come in her hand at previous dinners and does that include Manolo?'

I am not a sex counsellor, Jack. You are on very dangerous territory here and wasting your precious time. You are chasing pleasure when you have work to do.

'That's not true, my friend, you aren't my conscience. I am researching life so leave me alone.'

His return upstairs to the huge glass box gave him vertigo for a few seconds until he focussed on his new friends who had decamped to the sofas with a view to the hilltop lights of Bagurr. As he went over to them he felt marginally safer away from the cover of the table. The port and cheese were served by the slave as the drunks sat slurring. Niiige was telling everyone about the woman recently murdered in Palafrio.

'They are looking for a man who wears a green jacket like mine. It was terrible apparently; he stabbed her dozens of times.' Jack suggested his theory on all crimes of passion.

'They need to look for someone who is incredibly sexually frustrated, Niiige. They always end up as the murderer, or maybe it was you!' Niiige laughed and replied.

'Oh god, Jack, the motive of sexual frustration would probably include all of us, dammit! Certainly me, old chap, it's so long since I've had sex that I'd actually consider murdering for it.' The Duchess joined in.

'Surely you mean it's murder having sex, Niiige' and they all laughed as she glanced at her husband who deliberately ignored her. Jack was too busy to notice the coded messages between the closed group, as Juicy Lucy had squirmed onto the sofa beside him and was pressing her large boobs as hard as possible against his right chest.

'Do you ski ya?'

'Yes, Juicy, sorry I mean Lucy.' She didn't notice his mistake and so he carried on enthusiastically.

'I ski as much as possible but it gets harder every year.' He gave her his 'come to bed' eyes as he insinuated what was hard and they seemed to encourage her.

'I'll say ya. Hard ya, nice and fucking hard. I like that.' She smiled drunkenly and wantonly, confused somewhere between the two. Jack continued.

'I skied in the Alps at Christmas but I was absolutely knackered.'

'I can't believe that of an athlete like you ya', and she stroked his left chest using her finger to excite his nipple. Jack looked around but nobody seemed to worry about her behaviour.

'It was terrible, Lucy. I was knackered because of the skiing, knackered because it was sex, sex and more sex. The food was full of fat and cholesterol to slow me down and I drank alcohol like water to ease the pain and that included everything from Vin Chaud at 10 am to Leffe Noel beer for some après-ski. I had to use Ibuprofen gel on my back, hips and calves and decided, eventually, that it was also needed on my dick to reduce the pain.' Horsey Lucy barked laughing.

'I don't believe you, darling, I think we need to be bloody careful of your tall stories ya. So why did you call me Juicy?'

She wasn't that drunk, he thought. He ignored her and just smiled so she tried another question pressing her breast harder against his chest so he could feel her erect nipple whilst breathing red wine mist into his face.

'Who was the skiing woman, Jack?' Again he smiled.

'A secret is only a secret if you never tell it and, by the way, my nicknames are usually based on facts.' He tried to stand as Niiige interrupted his wife to save her from embarrassing herself further.

'What car do you run, my friend?'

'A Ferrari,' said Jack.

'Oh really, how stupendous? It's just that I thought I saw a red hatchback pull up earlier.'

'Yes, it was my red Hyundai, but it's a Ferrari special edition model.' Jack ignored the pretentious query and stood pushing Lucy's big boobs to one side whilst Niiige realised he was too drunk to think through a reply about the car. In fact, apart from the Duchess and Jack, the expat group were now completely beyond any reasoned conversation. He walked across to her as she stood alone staring out of the window. He thought he would have a final sensible and serious chat before he left.

'Have you been to see the Josep Pla house in Palafrio?'

'No, Jack, who is he?'

'A great Catalan writer; dead now of course. What about the painting exhibitions in the Cork museum by Tano Pisano or Jofre Mercé?'

'No sorry, Jack, we have been too busy settling in and enjoying the sun for our first three months.' He tried one final time hoping she wasn't really as shallow as the other two women.

'Have you been to Barcelona yet?'

'No sorry. Have you?'

'Yes a few weeks ago, but all I saw were visitors consuming the culture rather than absorbing it; buying up the tourist tack instead of shopping for the free subjective or spiritual wares. How crap is that, Duchess? Barcelona has become a grotesque Gaudi tourist junket and weekend stop for stag and hen parties. It reminded me of when the Brits congregate together in a place like Meribel in the Alps. They stay in their colony to ski, drink beer, eat egg and chips and avoid *pain au chocolat, café au lait* and anyone who is French as they are all snail-eaters. God forbid that Palafrio should get like that.'

She couldn't identify with his issue but as an aside said, 'Palafrio will never be like Meribel, Jack. All the Brits here live in houses like this and are far too middle class to bother going into Palafrio. Goodness me, they have their pools to sit by and their domestics to run to the supermarket. There's no need to visit it apart from an odd drink.'

How fucking true, he thought, and no one in this room has a clue about local life and culture.

The expat women were hard individuals and led all the menial conversations as their husbands whiled away their time drinking and keeping away from anything controversial. The women were all past their children days and remained as forceful as when they had commanded the family. They were strong and in control in any of the pathetic conversations. The wives answered the husbands' mobiles and said he was unavailable if it was inconvenient for their agenda. It appeared that expat life meant the women had grown stronger and the men weaker as a direct contrast to life in England. Pippa was quietly repeating a conspiracy theory from her friend in Bagurr.

'They say Osama Bin Laden has changed his face like in that film *Face Off,* or whatever it was called. That one with John Revolting as the baddy. Anyway, Osama you know, had a recent operation in France and they made him into a Mussulman from Morocco. They say he is living in Palafrio now!' Jack sighed inwardly as no one questioned the truth about anything, but equally they didn't actually believe in much and so dumb and dumber became the norm.

It was high time for Jack to leave without any prompting from his guide and so he took one last look around the company. Niiige sat worrying quietly about his business as credit was getting tight. Dutch wanted an early night so he could be at the harbour by 7 am to be with his beloved boats. Rolly had overheard Jack ask about the two local artists and was slumped in a drunken stupor dreaming of being half as good. Jack turned to the Duchess again.

'I have to go now, lovely. Thank you for an entertaining evening and wonderful food.' He tried to shock her one last time. 'Did you know the Spanish eat loads of garlic and onion in so many dishes that although they never fart they always seem to have bad breath?' Her royal demeanour remained constant.

'I can't say that I have noticed, Jack.'

He carried on. 'That doesn't really matter though because if we all have bad breath you don't notice each other's. For example, I have a *friend girl* in England.' She queried what was meant by the term.

'It's instead of a girlfriend so there's no confusion, okay? You don't shag a *friend girl* and a girlfriend you do.'

'That's a nice expression, Jack, I like that.'

'What *shag?*'

'No,' she said calmly, 'a *friend girl,* just like me.' She smiled and looked deeply into his eyes again which was becoming a disconcerting habit. He finished the story.

'So this *friend girl* in England. All she does is swill constantly with Listerine as she is so paranoid about bad breath and repulsing a potential boyfriend. What is the point in that, Duchess? It's not exactly natural, is it? You either want to kiss someone or you don't want to? Hoy!'

'That is very true, Jack, I don't think a bit of garlic or onion comes into it. When you want it, you just go and get it.' He was shocked as she said it as if she meant him. So he started saying his goodbyes even more puzzled by her royal and aloof persona interjected with sexual interest, but he had enjoyed the night overall. As he said goodnight to Juicy Lucy she insisted in front of everyone that he went horse-riding with her the next day and so he accepted graciously as it was *funning.*

Not to be outdone, Pippa arranged for him to call in at their home and have his auras read and the Duchess requested him as an escort for the full moon due at the end of the week when her husband was away on business in Holland.

'Listen, Jack, I just need you to carry my photographic equipment up that steep hill to the castle in Bagurr and hang around in case there is a murderer about. Is that okay?' He agreed valiantly to do all of their bidding, but looked nervously at their husbands who all appeared relaxed about the 'dates'.

Maybe it was the drink, he thought. Driving away in his Ferrari Hyundai he felt good about himself and he told Nim so.

'They all seem crazy and are definitely boozers, but at least it's a diversion, Nim.'

You need to stay on your path, Jack, and not enter
any avenues or, in this instance, three-lane motorways.

'I will Nim. Don't worry. What harm is there in a bit of *funning*?'

You will see.

* * *

The next morning Robbie Williams was blasting out of the loudspeakers hanging inside the stables near the pretty town of Pals and disturbing the serenity of the spring fields. Jack walked up to an energetic Lucy who was singing extremely loudly. 'It's time to move your body', and swaying alongside the horse. Noticing him from the corner of her eye she stopped strapping the saddle on Trio, the dappled grey that Jack was going to ride.

'Darling, you found us then?' She pecked his cheeks before reapplying herself to preparing the large and rather forbidding horse.

'It was easy thanks. Do the horses like Robbie Williams, Lucy?' He eyed up Trio warily, moving away from the horse's rear legs and any potential kicks.

'No bloody way! Makes them as nervous as you, darling, ya! But I love Robbie for his lack of self-restraint and the balls to be what he is. Doesn't give two fucks ya for what anyone else thinks and lives life to the full, ya.' Jack could smell the horse or Lucy, he couldn't tell which.

'I suppose so but I thought he'd turned gay since shagging that Spice Girl? Geri what's her name.'

'Has he, darling? Good god that has ruined my dreams. Now I'll have bloody nightmares. I can't imagine him in bed with me accompanied by his best mate and poking bums.' She guffawed loudly. 'But thinking about it, I might be able to turn them both around ya!' In fact, everything Lucy did was loud as she kicked Trio in the testicles for not standing still.

Jack you have only been pony trekking a couple of times and that was before your new hip.

'Where's your horse, Lucy?'

'Out the back and already saddled as I went out earlier. Her name is Ana; she's the nice roan one, lovely temper, unlike this bastard.' She kicked Trio again, making Jack even more nervous. She led Jack outside and Trio followed meekly as they navigated around the pile of muck leaning against the old pine shed. It was in an idyllic spot set in a disused allotment with *nespero* trees heavily laden with yellow fruit and unpruned vines running rampant down to the river. Jack stopped and looked at the hill and ramparts of medieval Pals about three miles away. The aged stone town stood proud above the fertile plains that were already sprouting acres of organic rice from mirrored fields.

'We are so lucky living in this area, Lucy; you must be pleased to have your stables here.' She had tied Trio's reins on the olive branch next to Ana's and joined him to look at the view whilst resting her hands on her fulsome hips.

'Ya Jack. This is the best part of my life. No crap about mortgages and remortgages, no pissy clients, just me and my 'orses ya.' Jack genuinely liked Lucy when she was herself and came down from the brash pedestal that she had climbed somewhere earlier in her life.

'Does Niiige ride, lovely?'

'No Jack, darling.' She was dismissive in her voice. 'He couldn't ride anything successfully to save his life, and that includes me ya!' She hit him on his back so hard that he flinched, but she didn't notice as she had turned away to untie Ana. 'Come on, darling; let's see what you are made of, man or mouse ya.'

Jack pretend to have a heart attack or something, you shouldn't get on that horse.

Under his breath he said.

'I'm fine, Nim, it's just like in the cowboy films. You just pull the reins hard left or right and kick the sides.

Which side to go which way, Jack?

'Stop interfering. I'm sure I'll remember when we get moving.'

'Do you often talk to yourself, Jack?' Lucy spoke down to him from the heights of Ana's steady back.

'Only when excited, Lucy, only when excited, lovely. Or nervous,' but he said the last bit under his breath. Jack grabbed the saddle and swung himself upwards but only managed to get a tenuous hold with his heel as he was restricted by his new hip. Using his right hand he grabbed his jeans and lifted his leg over the rest of the way wincing with pain.

'Okay then, darling, let's go.' She turned away smiling to herself and started to walk Ana towards the distant hills of Torreolla, with Jack hoping nervously Trio would just follow. His plan worked so well that he felt comfortable after about a mile and started to enjoy the view towards the cliffs at Estartit, but then she started to trot.

'Fuck me, Nim, that fucking hurts.' He bounced along without matching his rise and fall to the horse and his skinny jeans rubbed his hairy legs making him wince with pain. As his bollocks hit the hard leather saddle he hurt. As his legs took each jarring fall, his hips and back hurt. She looked over her shoulder.

'How is it for you, darling?' He knew she was taking the piss, but gritted his teeth in reply.

'Stupendous Lucy. JFDI.'

'What do you mean Jack?'

'Just Fucking Doing It.' Trio jerked to the left to miss a rabbit running away from the thump of the hooves and Jack nearly fell, wobbling unsteadily to be saved by an unfortunate Lucy.

'Woah Ana. Woah Jack.' Juicy Lucy quickly pulled up and lightly jumped down as Jack admired her arse pulled taut by her jodhpurs. She picked up Ana's front leg.

'Oh no, not again, she's gone lame, Jack. The same problem as last year. Fuck me, poor thing. We'll have to walk back, darling.' Jack quietly congratulated himself.

'Joy Oh fucking Joy, Nim, I told you I'd get away with it.'

It was meant to be.

The lonesome cowboy and experienced cowgirl walked side by side leading the horses back to the stables with Lucy disappointed and Jack exuberant.

'I was just getting back into the swing of it, Lucy. It takes a while when you have been out of the saddle for some time.'

'Don't I know, darling, but that's sex for you ya!' He couldn't work out whether she was giving him the come on or not. Did she want him? Most women in his life had been subservient but the expat women were all bolshy and in control of their men in a variety of ways. 'We'll let them cool off for a while, darling. Tie them under that almond tree over there and I'll fetch some water.'

The horses drank from the pails in the dappled sunlight deflected through the spring leaves whilst Lucy and Jack relaxed sat on a giant cylindrical bale of hay that was the style of the area. It was placed in the entrance to the stable but just undercover of the roof so as to keep it dry which made it an ideal seat set in the shade. Jack wanted to know more about her.

'How did you end up in Catalonia?' She stripped off her pink sweatshirt as she was hot and then replied.

'It's all down to Niiige really. Don't get me wrong. I love it here but I was happy in Broadway, Worcestershire. I had stables and made a good living, but his businesses had a few cash-flow problems and so we came here and brought our money over when the euro was only worth sixty pence. Good timing ya!'

'Very good timing the way things are going now. So do you miss your business?'

'Ya, really badly, darling. It gave me my independence and now he thinks he controls me because of money but, in reality, he still does what I want.'

'How's that, Lucy?' She turned to Jack and leaned closer so that he noticed the sweat marks around her bra and the hard nipples sticking out from her blouse.

'That's easy, darling, I just make him gag for sex and then give it to him when I want something. It gives him no choice as he is too much of a wimp to get it somewhere else ya.'

She leaned closer and kissed him hungrily before pulling back to see his reaction. 'And you know, Jack; I haven't wanted anything off him for a few months so we can finish our ride here.' She pushed him back on the bale kissing him softly and Jack responded as best he could whilst she pinned his arms above his head. Sitting astride him she quickly slipped off her T-shirt and undid her bra to reveal enormous breasts with dark brown and erect nipples that she offered to Jack's mouth.

'Suck my nipples hard, darling, I really like that.' He gently sucked the left one. 'No harder. Make them both hurt.' After he had sucked, she undid his jeans and pulled them and his briefs down just enough to reveal his hard cock. Immediately, she pulled her jodhpurs off with one deft and experienced hand and commanded him to keep sucking as she grabbed his cock and thrust it in her hot wet cunt.

'Jesus, Lucy.' His words were cut off as she rubbed her titties on his chest and tried to eat his mouth.

God this straw hurts your arse, he thought as he thrust upwards. She was groaning and leaking her hot juices all over his bollocks.

'You really are juicy, Lucy,' he managed to say between gasps as she rode him like a stallion. 'My back hurts on this straw, Juicy. Let's change positions hey?' She ignored him as he lay bathed in sweat from the exertions and rode him harder and at a gallop until she shuddered and came, leaning hard backwards so his cock hit the right spot.

'That was fucking good, darling, now you can come on top.' He obliged after taking his jeans off completely and lifting her legs in the air he slid his dick in her and started pumping hard. She came again grunting loudly as he realised she held her riding whip which struck him on the arse in unison with his final thrusts. Pulling out of her without ejaculating seemed the safest bet and so he jumped off the bale and went in search of his jeans that he found in a pile of fresh manure. Quickly he pulled them over the red allergic rash on his legs that he always got from any type of grass. In contrast she nonchalantly dressed as if nothing had happened. Jack was nervous and embarrassed.

'So Juicy Lucy, you lived up to your nickname.' He kissed her tenderly on her closed lips.

'Ya, I enjoyed that, darling. Next time we could do some real riding, more of a point to point rather than a flat race over a few furlongs ya.' She guffawed again.

'I think I prefer a bed to a barn though,' Jack said, 'more comfort and less horse.' He swatted away a horsefly as it bit into him to add to his pains. She didn't look at him as she replied going out to fetch the horses.

'Don't worry, darling, you'll get used to it.'

Driving home he felt used like a stallion brought to a mare in heat. His rash itched more by the minute; his legs were covered in tiny painful rolls of hair where they had been rubbed and matted by the riding and the three weals on his arse demanded an unorthodox seating position as he pushed his arms away from the steering wheel of his 'Ferrari' to wedge his back and lift the weight off his buttocks. He was glad to get home and resume his simple life starting with applying some Germolene.

It was three days later that he pulled up at the old town house in Bagurr that belonged to Pippa and Roland.

As he rang the bell he could hear Robbie Williams singing and Pippa joining in at the top of her voice. He stopped and listened to the chorus amused that Lucy had a common interest.

'I just want to feel real love
Feel the home that I live in
'Cos I got too much life
Running through my veins going to waste.'

He pressed the bell again and waited, whilst examining the old stone wall with its loose mortar and the peeling wooden windows that must have been painted thirty years ago. The place was a wreck which he thought ironic for a successful upper-class artist with an inheritance. She opened the door dressed in old denim dungarees and Scholl sandals but nothing else. He handed her the bouquet of pink chrysanthemums and smiled widely.

'These are for taking the time to give me a reading. Just a small thank you in advance, Pippa.'

'Oh how lovely, *J*. Nobody brings me flowers anymore. That is very special and sensitive of you. It's so nice, you know.' When she hugged him tightly, instead of Spanish kissing he could tell her breasts were riding free under the denim as they gently wobbled against his chest.

'Please come in and we can start immediately.' As she showed him around the house she informed him that Rolly was painting at the Roman amphitheatre at Empuries and would be back for drinks at six.

Jack you need to consider your position here as she is best friends with Juicy Lucy.

'Don't worry, Nim. Girls never share secrets about sex they are much more discrete than men. Anyway, I am here to see if you definitely exist; it's just a little scientific experiment.' Out loud he commented on the wonderful L-shaped balcony that went around the first floor of the house at the rear. It had arched windows every few feet that you could lean through and admire the roses and wisteria climbing into the hot afternoon sun.

'That is so delightful, Pippa, a private garden and a cool balcony for the summer, I would never have known that from the road.'

'It's a splendid old wreck and ripe for development, you know. That is when we have a few investments come through, of course. Come and sit on the patio and we can start.' There were six old wooden chairs that had been painted white many years earlier but now stood peeling in the half-light shaded by the balcony.

'I prefer to read auras here as it's not too bright. Sit there, *J*, and choose any of those coloured ribbons in front of you. Any mind! Any colour that takes your fancy.' An assortment of ribbons was strewn haphazardly across the table as Jack randomly picked a few to show willing.

'Choosing a ribbon if drawn to it, is a form of psychometry. Your energy is attracted to my ribbons, *J*.'

'How many do you want, Pippa?' He asked with an unbeliever's voice.

'As many as you get drawn to and then give them to me to hold throughout the reading.' He finished selecting a handful without thinking too deeply about which ones to choose and passed them over as she continued, 'A reading is based on your personal information, but it may not make sense to you yet and is also based on free will.' Jack thought inwardly.

'Two good *get out* clauses already, Nim.' But Nim was unusually silent. Pippa went very quiet for a few minutes as Jack admired her inner beauty. She wasn't pretty but her demure sensual persona called out to him.

'The colours of your aura, *J*, are complex. I can see yellow showing a logical and analytical mind; you make no rash choices but think things through and you certainly need to do that this year. The blue on top of your head shows you are good at organising work and any home tasks; that is being in charge, not a doer, a decision-maker. You also have green around the head which suggests on-going improvement of your skills and training.' Jack sat and contemplated her and realised things she had said so far were reasonably true and training might include learning his art as a writer.

'You have a green firework coming from your right ear which shows listening and counselling powers. This is usually seen where the person offers advice and, seemingly compassionate, they show strong powers of communication.' Jack shifted uncomfortably and watched her thumb through his ribbons whilst she stared directly at him reading his invisible auras.

'The yellow and orange together show that you could work for yourself successfully and especially on new projects that affect life itself, but not on minor things; remember major ones only. You also have legal matters to attend to. Not minor like home insurance but some major thing again. There is lots of pink too and that shows love and understanding, but you have a strong blue down your left side and that blends with the pink.' She paused and stared through him looking at some unidentifiable thing, but not an aura which made him squirm as he felt uneasy with his feelings. She sounded vague.

'I don't know where to start with this one but sometimes I get the most unexpected visitors so I must say it how it is. I see a fatherly figure who is clean-shaven with a square jaw but he is fat and diabetic with blue eyes and strangely seems linked to cricket somehow as he is wearing white.'

Jack breathed out a loud and deep sigh and took a few moments to regain his breath properly as she had described Nim, just as he had seen him as he started to drown. 'I am hearing someone saying to me "Jim" or something like that. This is someone two below, you understand; two levels down by generation. I hear drums and feel the wind with a smell of wood smoke coming from an open fire. Jim's hair is straight and long and brown and he looks younger now, but that's not how he looked when he passed over. In fact, he is not normal. He must be a spirit guide.' Jack felt cold as he sat mesmerised. 'He is talking to me about your son, a young boy, but you have more than one, don't you? He is saying a J name and he says look out for him and don't abandon all hope as it will all come good eventually. He is also showing me a blank page and writing is starting to flow across it. He's talking to someone else now and I believe it's your father who is saying don't give up on your dreams as dreams can come true if you believe.' She slumped physically and gave him a wan smile before leaning forward and grasping both his knees.

'Was that okay, Jack? You know it was fantastic for me, I have never seen so much before. It was absolutely stupendous you know.' Jack took both of her hands and focussed on her face, but was conscious of her beautiful ivory-coloured breasts rising out of the denim bib.

'That all seemed to be true, Pip, and it reinforces things happening in my life that you have no idea about because you don't know me yet. I was really shocked by it.'

'Good *J*, I am happy for you and so let's look at the ribbons whilst we are on a roll.' She randomly selected one. 'The blue ribbon you have chosen is about your son and his need for your guidance. It tells me that letting him listen to just his mother would be wrong. The pink is for a girl who must be a daughter. She has major financial problems and looks to you for support that you can't give because you will be monetarily poor for a long time, Jack. However, you will be rich in the essentials of life. The maroon ribbon shows you have a strong relationship with someone who is incredibly close to you, but beware as it will end up in disaster so don't give your all.' He wondered about Harriet and then Karina. She continued. 'Trust your intuitive side as there is purple there;

a sixth sense, the third eye. Spend time on your own, *J*, and listen to the angels. Let go of the old guilt and then you can move on.' She relaxed and smiled leaning back on the peeling chair whilst running her hands through her hair.

'Jim is taking your hand and saying everything will work out alright.' She stopped and waited for his comments.

'What can a man say and do when someone has spoken to me like that? I'm still in shock.' She appeared incredibly beautiful as if he could see her aura which was golden but buried deep inside.

'*J*, I suggest the best thing a man can do after a reading like that is to come over here and kiss me as soon as possible.' He stood unsteadily and walked towards her as she stood to meet him and undid the two clips supporting the bib on her baggy dungarees. They slid slowly down her rounded body as Jack gently wrapped his arms around her waist and kissed her delicately. Pecking gently at each other's lips she occasionally licked his with her small darting tongue to tantalise him further and slowly undid his shirt and shorts so they closed naked on each other with an ecstasy that Jack had never experienced before.

'What is it that feels so good, Pippa? The attraction feels like static.' She cupped his cock in both hands and continued to kiss him whilst massaging it into a full erection. Without talking she turned her back on him and bent forward over the table but reaching behind she clasped his hands and quickly tied them using the maroon ribbon so that they were held over her uterus.

'Put your cock in me *J* and fill me with your seed.' Jack inserted his prick and started to push gently as he felt he would burst with every tiny touch. After no more than a minute, she clasped his tied hands to her mouth to stifle the groans as he started to fuck her as hard as possible, thrusting and slapping his balls against her arse until she had come time after time with just seconds to recover. After the eighth or ninth orgasm he filled her with his spunk and juddered to a sweaty halt.

'*J*, take this.' She passed her glass crystal ball from the adjacent seat. 'Take you cock out and put it in my cunt and push it in as hard as you can.'

'Jesus Christ Pippa, are you sure?'

'Just do it and do it now.' So he gently eased the orb into her wet cunt and hoped the spunk would help lubricate its entry. 'Push it in hard, I said. Go on, push it really fucking hard *J*.' As he shoved it in with both hands he watched amazed as her vaginal lips closed around it until she orgasmed with a deep groan that reverberated around the yard. Immediately she squeezed and spat the sphere out to shatter on the floor.

'Fuck me,' said Jack, 'I never ...' but was lost for words. Turning around to face him for the first time in ten minutes he could see she wasn't smiling but appeared to be concentrating on something within herself as she quietly and demurely told him to mind his feet on the glass. Pulling up her dungarees without any endearments she immediately went into the kitchen to make some *Canyella* tea. Jack pulled his clothes on in total embarrassment. It was the first time he had been so controlled by a woman, although Lucy had tried hard. This was exacerbated by his nakedness and her calm silent rejection of him as though he had performed a much needed job. He sat and stared at the lemon and orange trees in the garden and hoped to return in November to see them in fruit, but that was the limit to his thinking because she had shagged his brains out.

All he could do was sit quietly and sip his sweet herbal drink wondering if his bad back and new hip were going to last the week with the constant pain from so much sexual action. She didn't kiss him goodbye but ushered him out before Rolly turned up, and closed the heavy door on him leaving him alone on her ancient doorstep. Still in shock he walked to his car pondering so many disturbed truths from the person he had believed was a fake spiritualist.

It was the end of the week and the night of the full moon. The Duchess collected him from the *barraca* after sunset in her open-topped silver SLK Mercedes.

He could hear her coming as he sat on his patio but it wasn't because of the smooth purring engine it was the CD playing Robbie William's 'Angels' at full blast. 'And through it all she offers me protection, a lot of love and affection, whether I'm right or wrong.' As she came closer to his single and dim outside light, she turned the volume to low and pulled gently onto the grass besides the patio.

'Hello, Jack, what a wonderfully remote place you have. It took me a while to find you, honey.'

'Hi, come in and look around if you like. I think we have time before the moon rises.' She daintily stood on her seat and then sliding her long white legs over the ledge of the door she dropped to the earth in a manner that ensured Jack appreciated her yellow mini skirt. As she kissed his cheeks he felt the slide of her fingers down his spine and her pert bra-less breasts tingle through his thin T-shirt. He hugged her quickly and realised her halter-neck top was completely backless to her waist as he felt the soft skin at the top of her buttocks using his fingertips. Taking his hand she sauntered inside swaying her hips and in complete control of the situation.

'Show me where you sleep, Romeo,' she teased 'I bet all the girls clamour to come and see the simple writer, honey.' She had emphasised the word 'come' facing him and mouthing it slowly so he could follow her large red lips. A dry-mouthed Jack felt overwhelmed by her regal presence and her stunning Duchess type of beauty. It took precisely thirty seconds to show her his truly simple living area before they were outside on the patio again with her delicately grasping his two hands at chest level. She started using a single dainty finger to sensuously rub both of his palms.

'So, Mister Edmunson, are you ready for a night of moon watching?' He realised he wasn't in control but acquiesced.

'Of course I am. The moon is a reflection of the sun and my sun means everything to me. In fact, I can't think of anything more romantic, my lovely.'

'No, not romantic, Jack, it's just art. I am an artist and tonight we will create some beautiful portraits of Luna, the moon goddess, as she rises in the east, released by her cruel captors in the dark omnipotent sea.'

'That's very poetic, Duchess, maybe you should write too.'

'Maybe I should, honey. Maybe I already have.' She talked and tantalised in foreplay before sliding her perfect arse back over the

SLK door and beckoning him to the passenger seat with a curl of her little finger. Dazed by her display he jumped in meekly as she turned Robbie up and started to sing along as they raced down the dirt track bound for Bagurr castle, allowing Jack time to puzzle on whether he had just seen black frilly knickers or pubic hair.

Bagurr Castle is best approached from the road on the eastern side facing the sea and not too distant France rather than the western side where there is no access for cars, but just an old narrow passageway leading from the busy town full of clothes shops and restaurants. In April, the bustling centre was incredibly quiet after nine at night which facilitated their parking and unloading. They quickly started to carry the heavy photographic cases and tall alloy stands up the steep track to the old keep. The castle stood 100 metres above the town so they climbed steadily through the pretty shrubs and trees backlit by yellow sodium lights casting fragmented and constantly changing shadows in front of them. Towering above the path loomed the ancient walls underpinned by steep cliffs that became vertical as they neared the peak. Breathing heavily on arrival they carefully placed the expensive equipment in the north-east corner where it was dark and in a perfect position to photograph the moon when it emerged from the distant watery horizon. They could just see the tip of the Luna disc and therefore they had time to meander to the west side of the small plateau and admire the view of the pretty town in the shadow of the hill below them.

'This is the first time I have been here at night, Duchess.' She replied quietly in sympathy with their surroundings.

'What do you think, honey?' They stood admiring the natural stone houses with arched windows and balconies that partially hid scenes from the sea or mountains painted on their sheltered walls.

'I think it is very pretty and worth a second trip before the *guiris* arrive.' She agreed and added her artistry.

'I love the different shades of light and dark as they are such a beautiful contrast to the haphazard structure of the buildings. But the best thing at this time of night is the silence because the Catalans are all eating dinner and so there is absolutely no one about.' He looked and searched for life but apart from an odd car he saw no one. When he turned the Duchess had picked her way across the uneven ground to set up her equipment and on opening the first steel case she produced a bottle of Dom Perignon champagne and two glasses.

'Here you go, honey, a celebratory drink for a unique night.' Jack popped the cork that disappeared into the scented scrub below and they toasted the moon as she rose gracefully from the horizon. The Duchess started taking photographs every half minute or so using different lenses and settings as the scene constantly changed. At first the giant Luna was apricot and then orange, reflecting back onto the black sea, but as she rose higher the sea became lighter across the whole of the wide horizon and Luna lost her romantic tint and became whiter and purer. Jack leaned on the old ramparts and lost himself in the dark of his thoughts as he watched the distant mountains of Las Gavarras come alive in the moonlight. He played the group called Chamboa on his iPod and danced the flamenco with the Duchess, but only in his mind. He constantly alternated his views from Luna to the mountains followed by the Duchess.

'She's just teasing me, Nim, and is totally different from Lucy and Pippa but still very controlling. In fact, she seems incredibly controlled, almost unnaturally so. Happily married, rich and beautiful; sexy and royal in demeanour and style, but shallow like the others, living in their world of unreality. I have a new word for her and her friends. Instead of living in the Cheshire set's La-La land, I think it more appropriate on the Costa Brava to say they are 'rolling with the waves'.

Appearances are deceptive, Jack. I thought Rolly was the creative artist and she was retired and taking it easy using her husband's money.

She quickly packed everything away as the moon moved high above the sea losing its beauty and then walked across to him hidden in the shadows.

'What did you think of that, Romeo?'

'I thought it was one of the most beautiful moments in my life, Duchess. Why did you call me Romeo?'

'Romeo, Romeo, wherefore art thou, Romeo? If you walk down the path, Jack, you could recite poetry to me as a symbol of your true love.'

'I could indeed but we barely know each other.'

'True, just put your arms around me instead as I am a little chilly.' Jack wrapped his arms and hung his broad shoulders on her petite figure so that she nestled into him, fitting herself into every crevice of his hard body which was pushing backwards against the stone equivalent. She said. 'That's nice, my old friend. It seems like 1,000 years since we hugged on the beach.' Delicately, she kissed the side of his neck under his ear and immediately he felt his prick harden as he appreciated the heady and sensual smell of her Chanel perfume. He murmured to Juliet.

'Of course, in Shakespeare's play there is the inevitable deceit and vanity between human beings that ends in death, thus blighting their true love.' She kissed him delicately under his chin and placed her hand under his shirt to feel his left nipple.

'As I am the Royal Duchess *we* don't have love and definitely not sex. In fact 'we' don't even think about doing things like that as they are beneath us. So maybe Juliet and I have some things in common and maybe we don't.' As she said the last words she pulled his head down to kiss her gently and spin him into a daze; a distant reverie that tasted of strawberries from her lip gloss. Controlling every move she slid her hand inside his jeans and felt his enormous cock before undoing them and pushing them down to his knees. Her head stayed below his waist as she gently sucked the end of his knob moving her lips around the head whilst licking the tip. When she felt he could grow no more she pushed his shoulders down the wall and lifted her mini skirt and sat on his male ego allowing him to rise upwards slightly to lift her onto tip toes and push it in deeper. There was no need for foreplay as she dripped cunt juices on his thighs and, now kissing him deeply, she writhed on him under the full moon. All Jack could do was brace himself against the wall and stay very still. His hands tightly held her small buttocks and pulled her hard onto him as she started to moan and then stopped kissing him as she lost her breath in pure ecstasy. Leaning back she grunted loudly and shuddered as she orgasmed.

'Oh Romeo, Romeo, wherefore did you get so big, my love?' After barely a minute of gentle kissing, sitting on his still-hard cock, she pushed herself off leaving Jack unsatiated and still full of spunk. 'Come on, honey. Let's go as the night has lost its splendour now.' She started to collect the photographic gear with Jack's unwilling help and then walked down the darkened path. Jack silently talked to Nim.

'How frustrated can a man feel with such a beautiful woman?'

The wrong avenue, Jack and you need to watch out for the poison, Romeo.

Jack looked at the Duchess swaying her yellow arse in front of him below the sheen of her naked back.

'Fuck me, Nim, she has just shagged my brains out and now she owns me.'

She always thought she owned you. That will become your decision.

The journey to her house was made in silence and at her glass porch she gently pecked him goodnight and suggested he would enjoy the romantic walk home as she was tired and needed her bed. Without looking back she closed the door on him and his needs. The three-mile walk to his *barraca* was beautiful in the light of the reflected sun and gave Jack a chance to think about the three expat women and their different needs.

Animal sex, spiritual sex and royal sex, but all three had used him for sex and he wondered what they really had in mind for him but, more importantly, for themselves and their lives.

'*Real Life*', Nim, you can't get any more of it than I have experienced this week, can you?'

You can, Jack, because it was just different sex and
nothing clever, nothing spiritual.

You are not helping them as individuals to
understand their disturbed lives. Therefore, it's
definitely not 'Real Life'.

'Hoy … I gave them what they wanted and did a good job, didn't I?'

How do you know that, Jack? Do you have any idea
what you are up against?

He didn't want advice or criticism and marched his way home in front of a trailing Nim, who was pushed to the back of his mind. He was happy on his sexual high, buoyed up by the champagne and constantly looking at his witness, the waning moon.

Something was ringing in his head but the shutters on the windows made his bedroom completely dark so he quickly snapped the light on. It was midday and the telephone rang again.

'*Hola*,' he answered sleepily.

'Poppet you sound half asleep.' Immediately he felt guilty about his date with the Duchess.

'No, just tired, lovely. I was outside and may have nodded off a moment.'

'Fantastic, you sound so much more relaxed and taking an early siesta will be good for you. Be careful with all this sitting around or you'll get fat. I might have to start calling you Tubsy.'

'Tubsy? What an insult, Soul Shiner. I might therefore start calling you wanton hussy.'

'Oh don't say that, poppet, you know I wish you were here; I physically miss you so much. I mean I want you here now if you understand my meaning. It's taken a lot of willpower not to speak to you earlier this week but I must confess I did telephone Monday and you were out.' Jack knew exactly which woman he was with and felt guilty again.

'I must have been out riding, sorry about that.'

'No don't apologise, poppet, I don't want to keep tabs on you or make you wait in for a call. Why shouldn't you get out on your mountain bike? I just feel disappointed when I can't say hello as I rely on our chats to stop me feeling lonely and unloved.' Jack was wide awake now and led her on.

'Well, you can telephone me anytime and I love you dearly, my best friend.'

'That's nice, Jack. Thank you, Tubsy.'

'Or maybe, on second thoughts ...' He left it unsaid as he quite liked the term of endearment.

'Just remember, Jack; home is where the heart is and so you need to make up your mind what you want in your life.' He disagreed.

'Are you sure about that? I thought home is where the girl is?'

'You are terrible, poppet, but I like you being so interesting and exciting as it's a new life for me. I like how focussed you are on your book, I like it that you are sensitive and kind, asking after the girls and Matt. I like how you listen. In fact, I like you more than you know, Mister Edmunson.'

She is falling in love with you from 1,100 miles away,
Jack. You need to be cruel to be kind

'Well, Soul Shiner, you are my best friend and I will always talk to you, my lovely, and try and help at any time.'

'And will you give me hugs, poppet.' He thought about it for a moment.

'It depends what hugs mean in your glossary of terms?' She giggled like a little girl.

'Hugs. The thought makes me breathless even now because I want you to make love to me.' She went quiet and Jack remembered that the best reciprocated sex in the last month was with his Soul-shining friend.

'Do you know why our sex was so good, Harry?'

'No, poppet, I never judged it.'

'Because sex is all in the mind and I think you have a need that I don't understand yet.'

She was breathless as she said, 'I really want you now, Jack, my knight, right here and right now on my kitchen worktop.' He changed the subject as he felt too guilty about his last week never mind last night.

'Write me a glossary of terms so I know what you mean, okay?'

'Okay poppet. What have you been up to this week?' He knew he couldn't tell her one per cent of his reality as she would want more details. Not because of jealousy but because she was a woman and liked enquiring.

'I had an amazing walk up the water tower in the centre of the town. I cycled into Palafrio the other night, at about 11 pm when the place was dead, and hopped over the wrought-iron safety rail guarding the foot of the grey tower. There are a 120 steps to reach the top and the view from there is awesome. You can see the lights of Palomost, the El Far lighthouse near my house and a medieval village on a mound in the plain of the Baix Emporda called Pals. The view is so good because Palafrio was built on a hill for protection from marauding pirates and even had a castle owned by Lord Frio, near where the church currently stands. The palace of Frio do you get it?' She didn't but asked.

'Can I come and see where you live sometime? It sounds lovely when you talk to me about it.'

'Of course you can but you might not like my simple house, as it's very, very basic.'

'Don't worry, poppet, I would just be happy to be there in your arms and cheap is okay by me.'

'No, no, no. Not cheap I never said I wanted cheap, I said simple and that is very different.'

'Okay, poppet I need to go soon. How is your equilibrium at the moment?'

'Up and down, unfortunately. I am not very stable at the moment. I always used to think I tried too hard and was too responsible, believing it was because I lacked confidence, but I think it was because I was just doing the wrong things in the wrong place with the wrong person.' She had registered the points he made and answered.

'You felt trapped then.'

'Of course, trapped in my small world.'

'Well, poppet, just calm down as your life is changing fast and will take years to settle down, just like mine.' He agreed ironically.

'Everyone has different problems. For example, the expats here are preoccupied with visits home and cheap flights, concern for the families that they have run away from, poor pensions and a bad exchange rate. That's life though and so in reality only you can change things, lovely. In their case, taking jobs driving vans or working in a bar would be a good tonic, although a bar might be a bad idea! It's dog eat dog, so remember that and don't rush into anything with Matt and your new life. Just say *mañana* and put it to one side until you are ready.'

'Thank you, my knight. Must dash. Bye. Bye.' She let him replace the receiver first and hung on as long as possible to the call and her loving thoughts.

It took Jack another couple of days to work up the courage to see Manolo because he knew what the topic of conversation would be.

He had neglected his Catalan friend for over a week and, feeling guilty in more ways than one, he went into Palafrio to meet him for lunch in the square.

'*Hombre!*'

'*Amigo!*' They shook hands at head height as if arm wrestling. The sun was out most days now and they had to sit under a parasol to avoid burning. After red wine and *paella* were ordered his friend sat back with a big smile on his face and waited for Jack to tell him about the expat women. He waited and gestured with his hands to indicate *tell me*. Jack sat and leaned his chair backwards whilst closing his eyes so that his head moved out of the shade and into the sun. He said precisely nothing.

'Oh, *amigo*, please … I need to know!' Jack let the seat crash forward and smiled back.

'What wild women hoy!' They smirked at each other before looking around furtively to make sure they weren't overheard.

'What a week, Manolo!'

'Tell me, Jack. How was your horse riding, are you a little saddle sore?' They grinned gormlessly. Manolo punched his arm. 'Are you in awe of your aura?'

'Now don't knock it, *amigo*. I thought she was very good.'

'And the reading?' The friends shook their heads and blew air through rounded lips in appreciation.

Jack queried, 'What about the crystal ball, *amigo*?' Manolo shook his head negatively and so Jack didn't tell him anymore as it must have been unique.

'Which leaves Freda, Jack? Did she keep clicking her shutter?'

'Very funny, Manolo, but she is a very nice person and I have no comment to make about her Royal Highness. Anyway, what do you know about my week or is it guesswork based on experience?'

'Jack, I love them all. They are very beautiful and that is all I will ever say.'

'My problem, Manolo, is the week was so *full on* that my writing suffered and it made me think you can live like that all the time.'

'No, Jack, don't start thinking it is real. Just relax and enjoy life a bit as you have had a very hard time. *Poco poco*. Life takes time my friend so give yourself some of it. Think of your new home and the scents that smell so wonderful and then remember them as part of the happiest of times where tomorrow never came and then you can smell your olives and pines wherever you are in the world to make you happy.'

'That's a nice thought, *hombre*, I must write it down for my book! But seriously what is work and what is *funning*, because I can't separate the two things and it makes me stressed. Then I have the emotional telephone calls that have started to be more frequent from Harry. Although I love her dearly, it's hard work as she is experiencing the unique emotional impact of her own divorce and dragging me back into my old life again. It's been an amazing week and a really sad week all combined. On the one hand, I am a fucking bastard according to Melanie and, on the other, I literally am a fucking bastard to the expat husbands.' Jack shut up and swigged his wine, allowing Manolo to get a word in edgeways.

'*Hombre,* whichever way it is, just say *mañana* and let life come to you. Let's face it, in two years you have done enough towards eliminating your old life gracefully and so enjoy your new life and stop worrying.' He leaned forward towards Jack to ask a serious question and put a hand on his shoulder. 'So my friend, how are you today?'

'None just none.' Jack's reply was quiet. His friend punched his right arm.

'*Amigo,* just focus on practical day-to-day things like me. Black and white. Enjoy some girlfriends and not *friend girls.* Let yourself be irresponsible for a while and forget England. *Vale?*'

'*Vale.* Thanks, Manolo, you give sound advice. I know all the important things are free: nature, love, kindness, but very few people ever concentrate on them. We are all preoccupied with safety and security for us or our family but they both cost money and chasing the money has a price to pay. The expat girls, for example. They have found a new version of the English middle-class women's La-La land. Here in Spain I have christened it 'rolling with the waves.' They seem to be filling in time, no plan, no achievement, just existing. Do you think I am cynical and biased, or is it true?' Manolo replied positively.

'*De verdad* The truth, *amigo,* but let it go for today, let it go for tomorrow, look at the glorious sun and tell me about your dreams What is this CITE business you keep mentioning?'

'Children In The Evolution. Just a dream to teach young children under twelve about the environment so as to make a real difference when they grow up. You know we have an infinite wisdom inside each of us to tackle problems, and that's why technology can be our saviour from global warming. The world has to work together and agree to share technology freely to solve the issues and at least have a budget that can be clearly understood by each country's people or frankly nothing will change. CITE is a great idea, but the motto is to stop talking about it and just do it. It's all topical now but, in fact, it is not real to anyone. There is a problem today and, therefore, we don't need ten years and multiple committees to agree we have a problem, as every day counts. Mark my words; climate change is exponential. Do you know what that means, Manolo?' He rushed on excited by a vision.

'It is not a gradual straight-line increase. It is a rising curve and the shit will happen far faster than anyone can imagine. Have you ever heard of Chaos Theory from the seventies? Little things knock into other things and randomly and accidentally make bigger things and bigger problems. CITE is right. No Talk Do: NTD. Beginnings are always just a continuation of old things. We are beginning to understand global warming. I remember they said that in the seventies and we are still *beginning*, thirty years later.'

'Well, Jack, my friend you have Spanish passion. It seems to me that you need to get the book written and start working on CITE. To use your phrase, NTD, *hombre!*'

The next few days were quiet and normal. Bounced from high to low and back again Jack tried to be stable rather than 'none'. Crazy, wild living to the max one day, and tears of loneliness and insecurity the next made him scared for the future and, without Manolo, there was no one to lean on. He restarted his book and wrote by hand on the yellowing list still stuck on his window: zany, spiritual and meaningful. Two love stories, a marriage failure and two tragedies. It was simple enough and that was what he needed.

Nim supported the new direction and kept him away from the expats who were occasionally seen through the windows of the cheaper Palafrio bars. Jack concentrated on his diet and fitness as they helped to deliver peace of mind. He swam most days in the swimming pool and made a new friend in Esther the middle-aged and very fat cleaner. Jack was amused to see that she cleaned at any time of the day, but none of the Catalan men were concerned about her seeing them naked. This was disconcerting enough but one morning he walked out of the showers to see Esther swishing her mop across the floor around the naked men. He immediately retired to the showers but when eventually he walked out she ambushed him and mopping between his feet she stared directly at Mister Wiggly for what seemed an eternity.

La piscina became his source of amusement and concern. If it wasn't Esther's preoccupation with a white English willy, it was the man in the showers shaving his bollocks in front of everyone. Jack wasn't even safe in the sauna as a Catalan man walked in stroking his gigantic flaccid dick that made Jack gasp with envy before the newcomer's opening line of conversation.

'I need a new boyfriend. How is your life going, *amigo?*'

However, his embarrassing days at the pool reduced because the weather was warming up, enticing him to swim in the sea. He decided a chilly and lonely dip in the Med at eight every morning was much safer and, once braved, was far more spiritually reviving.

4
Men and the art of manipulating women

It was late April before Jack missed his boy's hugs so much that he decided to return to England for a brief reconciliation.

Summoning up all of his courage he rang the Tettenhill number.

'Hi, Melanie. Did you get my emails about next weekend and my coming over to see Joseph?' She left a pregnant pause before her acid response.

'I have told you before. If you want to see him you must ring me. I don't log onto my emails very often.' Jack remembered when he had lived with her and how she used the computer on a daily basis to keep in touch with her multitude of friends. Commendably, he controlled his anger.

'In that case, I am ringing you to ask what Joseph is doing during the early May bank holiday.'

'Nothing as far as I know. Hold on while I check my diary.' Melanie left his call hanging for at least five minutes while she searched for her diary in her handbag by the telephone. She knew it was costing Jack money and liked to play games. Eventually she said nonchalantly, 'We have nothing planned in particular.'

'Does that mean I can have him for the weekend? Yes or no?' There was no response so he continued. 'Do you mind if I take him to Port Merion and stay a night in a B and B?'

'Of course not. Why would I stop you, Jack?' Jack decided to say it.

'Because you are angry over the maintenance money that I haven't paid you.' She sighed as though talking to a small boy who didn't quite understand.

'Of course that doesn't affect Joseph seeing his absent father.' She emphasised the word 'absent' as a punishment. He knew she was angry by her tone. He also knew there was nothing he could do to change her as he quickly confirmed everything.

'I will clarify it all by email once the flights are booked in case you have any issues.'

'Yes yes, Jack. Don't send me emails. I have no issues.' She rang off abruptly without a goodbye. Jack replaced his receiver and considered her negativity but he had no control anymore. He took her agreement as read, trusting her as though they were still married but, of course, that had been his mistake since leaving her.

His second call was to Soul Shiner.

'Hello, Harriet. How are you today?'

'Poppet, how fantastic to hear from you. You never normally ring me. Is everything okay?'

'Yes, good thanks. Look, I'm coming over to see Joseph for the May bank holiday and wondered if you would like a guest?'

'Oh, poppet, you know how much it would mean to me.'

'Thank you, lovely, but this is a quick call as I need to go and sort the flights. So I'll see you Friday evening, if that's okay?'

'Of course it is! I can't wait for your hugs. Don't worry about anything, poppet. I'll make us a fantastic meal to celebrate your homecoming. It will be so good to see you again, it has taken my breath away.'

'Well keep breathing, sexy, it's important! Bye, my lovely.'

'Bye bye, my knight in shining armour. Have a safe journey as I need you in one piece.' Jack gently placed the receiver down on the worn hooks.

'Well Nim it's nice to have one person in my life who really wants to see me.'

*Be careful, Jack. She is building you up in her mind
to be her saviour but you see her as convenient. Don't
use her. You need to make sure she understands your
true intentions.*

'I will make it perfectly clear this weekend, Nim. She is a "*friend
girl*" and not a girlfriend.'

The days passed quickly for the hunter-gatherer as he continued
to write well, buoyed up by his confidence from the expat sex and
the thought of more with Harry. On the Friday evening Ryanair
delivered Jack safely to Manchester and then Avis took him onward
to Chriseldon to be met at the door by Soul Shiner who had been
hovering expectantly for more than an hour.

'Come here, poppet, and give me a big hug.' They slotted
together like the correct pieces in a jigsaw, a one in five thousand
chance. Jack bear hugged her shoulders and squashed her to him
before a brief and gentle kiss became rampant roaming tongues
that immediately made his dick stiffen. She sighed heavily.

'You make me breathless, do you know that?'

'I know, lovely,' he said in a matter-of-fact way without
flattering himself and ushered her inside the house, breaking the
juncture of their passion-filled bodies. Jack explained.

'I was worried that someone else might be in the house.'

'No, poppet, just you and me for a weekend of romance.' He
noted the use of the word *romance* rather than sex as they stood face
to face in the kitchen. He deftly lifted her onto the black granite
worktop placing both his hands on the top of her thighs just below
the hem of her new miniskirt.

'So, my lovely, let me look at you.' He scanned her from bottom
to top. 'Well now, I like your new YFS image Soul Shiner, especially
the high heels, definitely the miniskirt, and is it a new top as well?'

'Of course not, I have had it for ages. What is YFS?'

'It's an old term from a long time ago meaning Young Free and
Single which, of course, you are now. Free and also very sensual.'

He moved his hands up and down the back of her calves as they kissed hungrily. The strong sexual feelings were shared as he slid his hands under her skirt and fingered her panties.

'Poppet,' she said breathless again. 'There's a bottle of champagne in the fridge and two glasses. Let's take them to bed.' He kissed her once again and rubbed his erection against her right knee before whispering in her ear.

'You are very forward, you wanton hussy.'

'That's definitely your influence, Mister Edmunson. I have never felt sexy like this in my life before.' Lifting her off the worktop he let her slide down his taut body and pushed her towards the door. Quickly grabbing the drink he followed her as she swayed her arse in his face going up the stairs, turning and giggling at him occasionally.

'You have the best arse I have ever seen on any women, Harry; it's gorgeous, full and round and …,' he slid his free right hand up her skirt to fondle her buttocks making her pause and turn. He proceeded to lift the hem with his left hand already clutching the champagne bottle and glasses and stared hungrily at her black fishnet tights and the lacy black panties hiding beneath. Jack started to rub the outside of her cunt with his right hand, excited by the friction of the pretty material and making her arch her back with pleasure.

'God, poppet, I want you so bad. You can't believe how much I want you inside of me.' He used his fingers to pull down the front of the tights and pants to see her mound of Venus and leant forward to bite it gently whilst his fingers just managed to touch a very wet cunt.

'Oh, Jack,' she was wriggling her cunt on his finger, 'that feels fantastic.' But abruptly he stopped and pushed her up the stairs again. When they reached the bed he made her sit on the edge facing towards him and proffering both of the champagne glasses towards her she held them out to be filled. He popped the cork clasping the large green bottle in front of his groin and let the foam overflow into the first glass.

'That's what I am going to do to you, Harry. I am going to fill you with my spunk and whip it into foam inside of you.' She used the back of her hands to knead his cock as he filled both glasses.

'I have never wanted sex so badly, poppet.' He made her drink the whole glassful as he greedily followed suit and then took it from her and placed it with his own on the bedside table. Immediately he pushed her firmly onto the mattress and started to gently slide her tights and panties off whilst admiring her soft white thighs. When they were halfway down he leaned forward to lick her clitoris voraciously as she vainly tried to widen her legs, desperate for him to lick more of her red vaginal lips. He pulled the imprisoning lingerie off completely and threw it well away so that he could kneel unencumbered in front of her wide open legs.

She was breathing heavily and lying in complete submission on the duvet waiting for her man. Slowly he pushed two fingers inside of her and then upwards to massage the face of her vagina whilst starting to suck her clitoris as hard as possible. She was already secreting and there was the unique and heady smell of her sex as he started to work every part of her cunt with his fingers. Never before had he smelt something so primal and stimulating. She sat more upright balancing herself on the edge of the bed with her arms behind her.

'Oh God, that is fantastic. You are so good at that, poppet.' She started to writhe and squirm on his hand and he sucked harder before pushing her flat on her back again. It was so intense for her that, within a couple of minutes, she groaned and arched her back shouting loudly, 'Fuck' three times as she came.

Without letting her recover he stood upright so that she could watch as he slowly took his own clothes off. It enabled her to see how enormous and red he had become. As she reached forward to greedily grasp his cock he grabbed both of her hands and manipulated her further onto the bed to give him space to lie on his back with his head raised on the pillows.

'Jack, what are you doing? Let me pleasure you please.'

'Just sit on my cock, Harry, and shut up, okay.' She did what he wanted and he held both of her hands as he arched his groin upwards in unison with her pushing hard down.

'Oh fuck me, poppet, Oh Jesus fucking Christ.' She pushed harder and leaned back using his hands to pull herself forward as his cock worked every part of her. The wanton hussy worked him back and forth remorselessly grinding him with no concept of gentleness. Within a minute she tightened her grip on his hands and had a giant orgasm spurting juice all over his balls. It was so intense that she tried to pull herself away, but Jack grasped her hips and forced her back on and ground her harder and higher. Within a minute she came again and he repeated the process until the fourth time as her face grimaced and she shouted no constantly and collapsed onto his chest.

'My God, you are so hot for my prick. How many orgasms can a woman have?'

'I have never experienced anything like that in my life, my darling, you were so perfect, my knight.' He reached for the champagne as he made her stay on top of his cock that was still huge. This suited her as she didn't want to lose the feeling of it inside. Again he forced her to gulp the glassful and immediately replaced the glasses on the side table.

'Poppet, I hope you are not trying to get me tipsy?'

'Of course not, Harry. Why would I want to fill you with champagne when I have something else you need to taste?' Holding both of her shoulders he started to suck her nipples.

'Suck them hard, poppet, I like you sucking them hard.' He started to thrust upwards again as he clutched and stroked her arse and within a couple of minutes she had a small orgasm.

'Jesus, Jack. What are you doing to me? I have never come so many times before. In fact, in the last few years I have never come at all. You are such a good and unselfish lover.'

'It's not what I do; it's how you feel in your mind, darling. It's what you feel for me that is making it so fantastic.' He forcibly turned her away from him before he put his cock inside of her again. She immediately lifted her knees close to her chest to maximise his penetration and Jack obliged whilst rubbing his hands up and down the curvature of her white back.

'This really does it for me, poppet, Oh God I can't believe how close I am already.' As she got closer he put both hands on her hips and in unison with her frantic jerks he slapped his cock hard in until she came for the eighth or ninth time.

'Stop, please stop, poppet. Let me do something for you as this is so selfish of me.' He wouldn't stop and thrust even harder so that she screamed in passion and shuddered with delight as she came yet again.

'No, no, poppet, stop please. Give me a moment.' He pulled out and turning her on her back he kissed her deeply and squeezed her left breast before fingering the hard nipples. She was still desperate for him and the deep kissing made her want him more. Valiantly, she tried to sit up but he pushed her back to kiss her again and all she could do was attempt to rub his giant prick that was still so hard.

'Please, Jack, let me do something for you. I want you to come.' He let her get up and slide down the bed so that she could suck him, licking her own juices off the red head.

'You know, poppet, I never used to do this but now it really turns me on.'

'What do you think of your own taste, Harry? That is what I love licking and swallowing, my lovely.' He lay and tried to come but felt nowhere near. His cock was stiff and throbbing and she was trying hard for a learner but still he couldn't come. He knew it was guilt and not just because of the expats; it was because she was so wonderful but he couldn't commit. He also knew if he turned her onto her back and closed her legs together under him he would soon orgasm but that was old life and that was the last thing he could do.

Eventually, he pulled her up to slowly quaff the champagne and to talk, losing his negative thoughts by feeling happy for her elation. She was fulfilled and to ensure she felt warm and loved he hugged her tightly to make her feel both safe and wanted. Harry wanted some music so he pressed play on her old CD player by the bed and they both lay listening dreamily to the Bee Gees greatest hits. The first song 'Words' was poetic and beautiful as they lay physically spent under the quilt. 'It's only words and words are all I have to take your heart away'. The music was quiet and the talking was quieter.

'It feels weird coming back to Cheshire as I feel I should still be writing in Spain, but I have a lot of doubts about my new job. Most days I sit and wonder if I can ever be a success.' She tickled his tummy above his now limp prick.

'Well, poppet, you are a writer and I believe in you.' She was emphatic in her support. 'In fact I am very proud of you.' He smiled as she was nearly asleep.

'Thank you, Harry, that's nice to know. Go to sleep, lovely' and he gently stroked her back with his fingertips.

'Night night, my very own knight' and she was gone to the happiest of dreams satiated in both her body and her spirit with her new man. He lay there and talked to Nim.

'Am I happier now?'

> *No, Jack. You have never been so unhappy and you are manipulating a friend who doesn't deserve your disrespect.*

'Would I be happier committing to Soul Shiner and being around her most of the time?'

> *Of course you would as you would feel safe and wanted but …*

'But that is not my path and she is not the one.'

> *Why ask then?*

'Because life is hard and I want to be happy and loved.' He drifted off to sleep, troubled by the amount of love exuded by the woman in his arms.

On Saturday morning the lovers stood close to each other in the kitchen with her arm draped languidly around his neck as he flicked the pages of the *Daily Mail*. She leaned into him and gently kissed his cheek.

'Thank you for being here.' He placed an arm around her waist and kissed her on the lips.

'*De nada*. I am happy to be here.' But he looked away as the telephone rang interrupting the relaxed couple comprising of one. The *one* answered it and passed it over to Jack mouthing, 'It's Joseph.' Discreetly she left the room to go and shower.

'Hi, Dad!'

'Hi, JoJo, how are you?'

'Good, Dad.' His boy had put his handset on loudspeaker so that his mother could listen in. This had been instigated a few months earlier as a clever device to make sure he never came between his warring parents. Jack was excited about seeing him later and instead of asking why he had called he chatted about the midweek soccer match.

'I see you're top of the league above my boys for the first time this season.'

'Yes, I told you we would win the league, Dad.'

'Remember, son, be gracious in defeat and don't gloat when you are winning. Your gain is someone else's pain, in this instance your dad's!'

'Yes, Dad. You always say that.'

'I know, JoJo, but only when Man United are beating us.' Jack laughed with him before Joseph carried on.

'Dad, it's about football that I rang. Mum has bought some tickets to go to Man U today and I have never been before and, Dad ...' he stretched out the endearment. 'it's nearly the end of season so she said I had to ask you Dad.' It was a kick in the balls for Jack, who immediately started to imagine what the conniving Melanie had done to him.

'Of course you should go lovely it will be a wonderful atmosphere and we can go to the beach at Port Merion tomorrow, okay?'

'That's great. Thanks, Dad. Do you want to speak to Mum?'

'Yes please, JoJo, I would be delighted to speak to her, but take it off loudspeaker as it resonates too much in my ear. Bye JoJo. Have a good one, mate.' The line went quiet for a minute leaving Jack to chew on his anger.

'Dad … Mum says she's busy and can you ring her later?'

'Okay, JoJo. Bye, my love, have a great day, mate.' However, whenever he rang later that day the telephone was engaged as if someone had accidentally left it off the hook, and when he rang her mobile instead he found that it was switched off for the first time he could ever remember.

He walked disconsolately up the stairs to talk to Soul Shiner who was wrapped in a dark blue towel and examining her face in front of the mirror in the en suite. He came up behind and put his strong brown arms around her waist watching the red lipstick roll across her full lips. She looked up at his serious reflection.

'What's the matter, poppet?'

'I have just been blown out by Joseph because suddenly Melanie has just happened to get tickets to watch Manchester United and enticed her son away from me again.'

'She can't do that. You arranged to have him all weekend!' Harriet was angry for the first time that he had known her. 'Ring her back and tell her you want him, Jack. No ifs and buts. You have rights!'

'I know that, Harry. Calm down, lovely. Joseph has been manipulated into a situation where I can't say no, and she won't talk to me now which is obviously deliberate.'

'That is disgusting, poppet. I don't believe how low she could sink to use your son against you.'

'I know.' He said it emphatically, 'and now I have to live with that whilst she waltzes off with him.' He was nearly crying and so she turned around to hold him close in a tight hug, lightly kissing his mouth and gently rubbing his back.

'Don't worry, Jack, we will think of something, poppet.' They kissed longer than condolences required and it got hotter as Jack pulled the corner of the towel to one side so that it dropped to the floor. She opened her eyes as if to say no and quickly closed them again as his hands touched her breasts.

'Oh God, Jack, I am wet for you already, darling.'

'Are you? Do you really desire me that badly, Harry?' His hand stretched to her shaven pubic hair and massaged its prickly surface before he forced his forefinger inside of her and pulled some wetness onto her clitoris. 'So you are!' He continued to rub her clitoris as she undid his trousers and grabbed his cock with both hands but Jack wanted to be inside and roughly twisted Harry to face the mirror shoving himself into her so hard that he made her grunt. She looked at him in the mirror before dropping her head and softly saying.

'I can't believe how much …' He was pushing hard and was huge in his frustration as he ran his hand through the back of her gorgeous red hair and grabbed a fistful to raise her head.

'Oh God.' She was panting now but she couldn't look at him for long and was facing down towards the basin which she clutched with both hands to push herself backwards as he thrust. He held onto her shoulders.

'Look at me, Harry. Look at my eyes in the mirror as you come.' He watched her smile break and grimace in ecstasy as she writhed and came and he grunted as he spurted hot spunk again and again.

'Jack, that was so good, Oh god.' He had put his hands onto her titties and was pinching the nipples and thrusting again with his balls slapping against her beautiful arse.

'How do you feel now then, Harriet. Is that good or not?'

'You know it's fucking good. So fucking good.' Her voice was higher pitched and she tried to stay quiet but kept gasping hoarsely as he fucked her. Jack leaned backwards to watch himself slide in and out whilst his hands rested on her buttocks which he suddenly slapped hard with his palm.

'Jesus, Jack what are you doing? No one has ever slapped me.'

'And I have never slapped anyone either so what does it do for you?' As she was so close again he thrust harder and slapped three times in unison with a set of triple thrusts.

'God … Jack, it hurts, but it's making the pleasure unbearable too.' She was crying out in ecstasy and so Jack slapped her continuously until she screamed and came convulsively, with his spunk and her juices dripping down the lovers' thighs and onto the tile floor.

The love session continued on the bed like the night before

with Harriet finally satiated after six orgasms and Jack wondering how sore his cock would be by the time he flew home.

Eventually, their physical hunger took them downstairs and they decided it was warm enough to eat their sandwiches sat outside under the rose arbour that already had a few red solitary blossoms.

She wanted to ease his mental anguish about Joseph and so touching his arm she said, 'Don't feel sad, poppet. Joseph hasn't rejected you. He was put in a bad situation and had to make a choice. At least you supported him in that choice and made sure he didn't feel guilty.'

Jack was silent for a while and then replied. 'If only it wasn't Man U!' He laughed loudly and she could see he was more relaxed after the rampant sex.

'There is always tomorrow, Jack; you can still go to Port Merion.'

'I know. It won't ruin my weekend, as I won't let it.' He stood and smelt the roses nearest to him. 'They smell so good, "Whisky Mac", I think.'

She came alongside linking her arm in his and smelt a bloom before commenting, 'They're fantastic. Is that the variety or the smell?'

'The variety you silly billy, but if it was the smell, I imagine all the drunks would have some in their gardens!' They were happy together in the spring sun and walked past the herbaceous beds hand in hand, stooping occasionally to touch a new shoot or an early flower. She squeezed his hand.

'Why do you call me Soul Shiner? You are always talking about Souls and I don't understand what you mean a lot of the time.'

'I need to ask Nim for an opinion.' She tugged him to one side and stopped.

'Can you really ask a spirit guide for help like that?'

'Of course, lovely. I know it's hard for you to believe, but he does exist. He's telling me things even now. Soul Shiner or Soul mate, the Soul of the world. Where this world ends and a new one begins. Souls are unique and individual. They belong to one person through the reincarnations they undertake during their particular life span, on their individual path. An old soul like mine has accepted that there is more and has not lived as if there is less.' She pulled him gently to start walking again and was silent with her head down.

'That was very beautiful, my knight, very thought provoking but I don't know about Nim. What I do know is that I fancied you so much when we went to those spiritualist meetings and if you had tried something then I would have let you.'

'Why?'

'Because there was a spiritual attraction that means we are aligned.'

'You wanton hussy, if only I had known!' She stopped him again and spoke.

'But I was the faithful wife whilst my faithless husband was screwing that other woman. I also know that when you have a separation or a divorce people turn their backs on you within the first few weeks, especially when it comes down to self-preservation.'

He queried, 'You mean taking sides more like?'

'Yes absolutely, poppet, that's exactly what I'm experiencing. Did you have that in your divorce?' He placed a comforting arm around her shoulders.

'Yes, of course, it happens all the time. I remember the year after separating when my *friends* couldn't help anymore and my acquaintances became busy. Even families start to ignore you as they are too busy in their own lives and own things, being selfish. I would telephone home to England and they were too busy to talk and ignored my plea for support. My elder children, Edima and Rodney never telephone me and never instigate an email. They just reply to mine and then only briefly.

People like Peter Edam never call or send text messages like he used to. In fact, this morning I saw him in his car in your lane but there was no stopping to say "How are you, Jack". Self, self, self but *'Real Life'* is different. It's about listening and helping, and paying attention to detail when people speak to you. Soul Shiner, you need to remember those things, especially this year. They have a need and they want you to satisfy their need; that is why they are talking to you and only you. Try it from today as it makes a difference because it makes you a better person at a time when you are constantly looking inwards.'

'That is so lovely, Jack. Is it in your book?'

'Of course, Harry! Beware, as everything goes in my book and yes I know we are all using each other but how else can life go on? If we use each other nicely and not cynically there's no harm in that, is there? There is no balancing scale for giving and getting friendship, it constantly moves up and down. *Abibajos*; the ups and downs of life.' He stopped and kissed her. 'You are my Soul Shiner because you listen and because you are my best friend.'

She put her hand on his cheek and asked, 'And lover forever, Jack?'

'And lover too, but for how long nobody can say.' He moved forward again, feeling guilty with each step away.

'I hope you stay my lover and best friend for a long time, poppet, as I need you around. You help me live and if I don't speak to you I get very lonely.'

'Well you can speak to me anytime, lovely, and when your small world seems boring doing day-to-day mundane things like thinking about the next three meals or the girls' Christmas presents then just ring me and live on a different planet for a while hey.'

'Thank you, Jack and mentioning the girls they are here tomorrow for the day. Is that okay?'

'Of course. They have known me a long time and your old friend is here as a guest. No worries.' The afternoon drifted into the evening but the deep conversations dried up as they were beyond Harriet's horizons. He explained more about Nim, but he realised she was spiritually shallow and just a good listener rather than truly interested. So he stopped talking about the deeper things that troubled him and was content with her company, hugs and mindless English TV. Fifty candles lit the dining room for a romantic dinner which was when she said she was growing to love him and repeated the phrase she had used when they made love.

'You don't know how you make me feel, Jack.' She didn't solicit a reply or wait for one because she failed to ask him about his emotions towards her.

On Sunday morning, Jack waited reasonably until nine o'clock to ring malevolent Melanie. The telephone was answered after it had slipped onto the recorded message. She definitely knew it was him because she could see the number was Harriet's as it was on the memory from when they were best friends.

'Yes?' Brief and in a nasty tone.

'Hi, it's Jack. How are you today? Was it a good match?'

'I know it's you. What do you want?'

'I'm ringing to tell you that I will collect Joseph at ten to take him to Port Merion as agreed.' Soul Shiner had coached him on positive statements of intent. There was no reply and he thought the line had gone dead. 'Hello, Melanie, are you still there?'

'Of course I am.'

'Did you hear what I said?'

'Yes but Joseph has a cough and wants to chill today so it doesn't get any worse. You know how it gets onto his chest.'

'How bad is this cough because it shouldn't affect his travelling two hours in a warm car.' She didn't answer the question, the master politician. Instead she changed the subject.

'I hear that you and Harriet are a couple now.'

'Melanie, where the hell did you hear that rubbish?' Jack started to lose the plot again.

'Ah you see, you can't keep any secrets around here.'

'So who told you that lie?' She replied with a sarcastic smirk in her voice and he could picture her mouth grimacing as if eating a raw lemon. Twenty years of marriage meant they knew each other's foibles.

'Never you mind, Jack. Many people are telling me. So it is true then?'

'No, it's not true.' He had lost the battle not to engage once again, as she carried on winding him up as only she knew how. Jack was incensed as she was attacking his character, as well as his right to be happy and alone with his son.

'Maybe you and she were having an affair when you left me, Jack. Maybe it's all her fault our marriage broke up.'

'Our marriage broke up because you are such a fucking cow.'

'Don't use that language with me!' Melanie put the receiver down, excused by the use of bad language and that absolutely suited her. Make him angry, make him forget about Joseph.

'You fucking arsehole!' His heart was racing as he stood with clenched fists and shouted at the phone inert in its cradle. Harriet walked in from the conservatory ready to calm him down and asked him what had been said. He explained in full as he stalked around the kitchen agitated by his anger.

'Don't rise to the bait, Jack. Just ring her back and ask to speak to Joseph because he is ill. Then suggest to him that you could take him bowling this afternoon after he has chilled out and if he is feeling better.' He rang the number six times until he finally got a reply and luckily it was Joseph who now answered.

'Hi, Dad!'

'Hi, JoJo. How are you, mate?'

'Okay, Dad. Mum said it was a good idea to chill today because of my cough.' Joseph feigned a weak cough and simultaneously put the telephone on loudspeaker for protection.

'That's bad news mate. I tell you what we can do if you feel a bit better later on. I could pick you up at two o'clock and take you bowling so you are in a nice warm place, hey? Ask your Mum what she thinks?'

In the background he heard her say, 'If you are well enough Joseph but not for long.'

'Okay Dad, see you later.' Jojo replied brightly.

Diplomatic Harriet walked back in.

'And?'

'Partly successful, I can see him later but not for long.'

'Well, if you are having fun and he's not ill, just don't take him back on time. Be assertive with her as she is walking all over you, Jack.'

'I know that but … but JoJo gets caught in the middle.' Harriet came close and looked into his eyes.

'Jack, he is your son and you have rights. She is being a bitch and she shouldn't use him as an emotional crutch. She shouldn't give him choices. She should make positive statements and plans for him to see his father. I really can't believe she has stooped so low.' Jack held her arms and gave her the bad news.

'She is also actively indulging rumours about me living with you.'

'I can understand rumours, poppet, but no one knows anything. I haven't told my friends anything and so it's just vicious gossip at school as usual. If they invent some scandal they can have more fun, but there is a problem though, and I'm sorry because it is my fault for letting you stay here. Any rumour about us has become fact in her head and it will probably complicate your money and your access issues with her. A woman scorned and all that, especially by an ex-girlfriend. It's the ultimate insult to a woman's pride.' He hugged her as she was emotional now.

'Don't worry yourself, Harry. You are worth ten times what she is. I have broad shoulders and can take any shit.' But the truth was out and was to corrupt both of their lives for a long year. As they stood in an embrace about to touch lips the back door suddenly opened and her two girls walked in to see their estranged mother in the arms of a friend's husband. He dropped his hold immediately and went to put the kettle on the Aga leaving a flustered Harriet to greet her girls.

She said at double speed.

'Hello, you two. Jack is over from Spain to see Joseph, and is staying here for a couple of nights.' Outwardly, they seemed unperturbed and went straight to the biscuit tin before disappearing to their rooms. The arrival sequence was fortunate as Matt walked in behind, having taxied them over from Wilmslow where they had met Hilary for the first time. Jack stepped across the kitchen and shook hands warmly before leaving the couple alone and, like the girls, he retreated to the safety of his bedroom but without the comfort food.

Promptly at 2 pm he collected Joseph who came out to the car immediately he pulled in the driveway. This meant he didn't see Melanie, which suited them both. Their bowling was excellent *funning* and strangely enough without any coughing from his little boy. Jack deliberately took him home at the time Joseph had stated and walked him safely to the back door of the cottage. Here he was frozen out by Melanie who used the food in the oven as an excuse not to converse. Left on the doorstep with the door closed in his face he acknowledged it was now war.

'Fair enough, you chicken. If that's your attitude, then so be it.' He grimaced and his heart missed a beat as he turned away without a wave goodbye from his son and, as he walked to the car, he looked sadly at the family home that he was still paying for.

Jack got to Chriseldon ten minutes later to find there were no girls, leaving a lonely Harriet waiting patiently for her knight. She had extracted all the information she needed to know about Hilary and the bitch's house in Wilmslow and was mulling over its ramifications. As the innocents had wanted to see their friends in the village she had agreed they could go off on sleepovers to keep them happy. Only their stability and happiness was important to her now and so she gave them everything they wanted and then some more, spoiling them incessantly.

After a desultory evening where the divorcees sat with their own thoughts, they went to bed early. Jack lay silently under the duvet and snuggled up to her back whilst remaining deep in thought. The weekend with his son was a disaster and his *'friend girl'* wanted to be a girlfriend, or possibly more. She had been happy to pack her two children off as they were in the way of her limited time with Jack and that was the most worrying part of his day.

'Nim, children shouldn't get in the way. They should be loved equally by both parties and not used.'

You have learned a lot today. You can see how your behaviour has affected five other people. Your actions are at the centre of all this.

'That makes me feel guilty, Nim. Surely, I'm not the only one to blame?'

*Who else, Jack? You left Melanie and Joseph and you
started an affair with Soul Shiner, despite my advice.*

Jack closed his eyes to consider it but nodded off immediately.
He was emotionally shattered as always when in England, but he
was also physically tired and literally shagged out. As he cuddled
closer his last sleepy thought was relief that he didn't have to
sexually perform again.

Joseph was genuinely ill with sickness and diarrhoea on the
Monday morning when Jack telephoned to make arrangements and
thus it completely quelled all hopes of any quality time and even the
briefest of beach holidays. After breakfast and more unremitting
sex with his *friend girl,* Jack telephoned his daughter Edima.

'Hi, how are you, lovey? Tell me what's happening in your life.'

'Hi, Dad, where are you?'

'I'm in Cheshire staying at Harriet's house. You met her a
couple of times in Tettenhill; do you remember?'

'Yes, Dad, of course. She must be Melanie's ex-friend by now.'

'Very perceptive, Edima, very clever indeed. I came over to take
Joseph to Port Merion and it all fell apart.' He gave her the detailed
account of the weekend before she interrupted him.

'Dad, I have to go to work soon, but I must tell you one very
strange thing that happened this week to Mum; that is Number
One to you. Well she went to a weird spiritualist in Malvern and
was told her spirit guide is Granddad; I mean your dead father.'

'That's different! Did she believe what she heard?'

'Yes, she was amazed, but it was a complete nightmare
apparently as Granddad George kept interfering and really hacked
off the spiritualist.' Edima was laughing as she told her story, much
to her dad's annoyance because she discredited the truth about
spirit guides.

'Well, lovey, maybe you should believe in things like that too.'

'No way, Dad. What a load of old baloney. Anyway I must go.
Send me an email soon. Bye!'

Edima and Rodney were more distant since Jack's self-imposed isolation in Spain and as he put the phone down he decided he would write each of them a letter to tell them that he loved them dearly. So he sat and wrote long, individual and handwritten letters before walking down to Chriseldon Post Office to send them off. The rest of the afternoon was spent alone thinking about the plot for his book, whilst Soul Shiner shopped in Chester.

He was lonely in someone else's house and longed to be at home in Spain.

Nothing felt right in England anymore.

No children and no Joseph especially.

Life was a study of brief emails rather than far more personal letters.

He truly had no mum anymore and his dad was dead and so all of these things accentuated the love and care experienced with Soul Shiner to a heightened and dangerous level.

After dinner Jack and Soul Shiner sat in front of the television in the lounge and she switched to ITV to watch *Coronation Street* as she cuddled up to him. Jack pushed her gently away and asked politely.

'Do you mind if I go into the kitchen, to see if I can watch something else please?' She clutched his arm.

'No stay with me, poppet, I'd like you here.' He quietly considered his old life and everything he had rejected, including boredom.

'But I don't like *Corrie*, lovely and, in Spain, I never watch TV, especially English crap.' He could see she was hurt about something.

'What's wrong, Harry? Open and honest remember.' She started to cry.

'It's just like my old life. Matt never wanted to sit and watch TV with me. Anything to get out of the same room.'

Disingenuously he thought, 'what about my old life?' But he said, 'Harriet, listen to me. You are over reacting, lovely. It's not like your old life at all.' She continued crying and so he sat back down and pulled her close.

'Look, I will sit and watch with you because you are my best friend and I can't see you upset. But it's just old emotions that have not gone away, okay?' She nodded. He asked teasingly.

'Did you use to have gratuitous sex all over the house?' She shook her head to indicate no. 'So it's not like old life at all is it?' She snuggled lower onto his chest and stayed silent for the duration of the programme. Jack tuned out and talked to Nim.

'Women! I have the Wicked Witch of the North chastising me. I have the Good Fairy in the South imprisoning me. I can't win. I think it's after they have given birth that they change.'

That is correct, Jack.

'Once they have children they become so empowered that they forget the reasons they got married. They feel true all-encompassing love for the first time and realise they don't feel the same way about their husbands.'

And can afford to ditch the one who fertilised them.

'That's a bit strong, Nim, but yes they will do anything, including ditching their man or treating him like shit, to protect their children. Even minor things are seen by us blokes as ridiculous. For example, if a child *needs* a drink of water in the supermarket they can't wait five minutes until the checkout and have to open a bottle off the shelf. Or when they go on a school trip to Wales for a couple of days, the mother has to be there to see them off and stand crying as if they are going to Africa for a month.'

Nothing else comes first, Jack.

'Is it right, Nim? Are they giving too much to their children?'

They have no choice, Jack. It's genetic to be
overprotective; it's their role in life.

'I had never thought about it until tonight.'

So you are still learning and that is good.

Corrie whined itself to an ending with the same antique theme which now meant Harriet deigned to talk to Jack.

'I'm sorry, Jack. I was out of order. It's just … well, I have put so many old emotions in boxes and when the lid is opened it becomes unbearable.'

'Don't worry it's no different to me joining the Collective each day when I make my seven pleas. The world's problems pop out of my boxes too.'

'What do you mean by the Collective?' She waited patiently whilst he gathered his thoughts before he replied.

'The Collective is what my astrologer called a gathering of consciousness. There are many levels of consciousness and this is a fact found in all the old karmic religions. Karma and your karmic debt is part of the Collective. You carry a debt from one life to another and have to reduce it each time you live, in order to reach perfection. The closer you come to perfection the more you are aware of others and join the Collective. Really, it's old-fashioned good versus hidden evil, but most people have no cognisance of any of it.'

She understood nothing, Jack.

'Shall I give you an example?' She quietly nodded yes.

'When I walked across the azure sea with Josep Maria, we stopped to meet his old friends but they weren't necessarily dead. They were just available in the Collective.'

'Is that when you prevented him from dying, poppet?'

'Yes in the hospital in Girona. I really experienced the Collective in the full sense on that day, but that isn't what occurs every day as it takes a special event to reach that level of energy.' She looked confused. 'Is it too deep or is it because you don't believe me, Harry?'

Harriet replied diplomatically.

'It's just not me, poppet, so I don't know what to believe, but I do like you telling me about it, although I prefer you telling me stories about love and romance, like the existence of a Sun Sharer.' Jack was thoughtful, not wanting to lead her on.

You promised you would emphasise 'friend girl' this weekend, Jack.

He ignored Nim and told Harriet a story.

'In Spain one of the most famous novels is called *Don Quixote* by Cervantes.'

'I have heard of it but not read it', she said. He continued.

'In the novel, which is a really difficult read, Sancho Panza is the fat squire of Don Quixote who is a knight like me.' She smiled at that. 'Sancho says in the book "When a wench perceiving he came no longer a-suitoring her, but rather tossed his nose at her, and shunned her, she began to love him and dote on him like anything." Don Quixote the knight of the woeful figure replies. "That is the nature of women, not to love when we love them and to love when we love them not." How true is that, Soul Shiner, when I live 1,100 miles away, which makes you want me more than ever.'

She asked, 'What did this wench do and, by the way, I would like to be called a wench as it feels sexy.' As she lay on her side she was an easy target and so he quickly slapped her arse before replying.

'Well, you wanton wench, you need to read the book and discover the answer for yourself, but remember to count the goats or you will never find out.'

'What goats?' She asked. Jack smiled.

'You have to read the story, my lovely!' Exasperated she went and put the kettle on for some brain-soothing green tea. Shouting from the Aga she said.

'Do you want some, Jack? It's very healthy.'

'No thanks, Harry, I can't stand the stuff but if you have a beer I might be tempted.' She walked in with the beer as the kettle boiled. Partly handing it to him and then withdrawing it she teased him as she said.

'Tempted to do what?'

'Talk some more, lovely, just talk!' She re-joined him on the sofa and turned the TV down before telling him the latest rumour.

'When I was at school today, I saw Melanie who completely blanked me for the first time, but I predict her judgemental attitude will backfire on her, Jack.'

'Why?'

'Because we women work in mysterious ways. I remember your ex was dumped by Bridget's friends after she was killed in the accident. My limited friends have already heard the rumours and closed ranks with me when I'm teaching. Jean has her own problems at home and isn't there for Melanie anymore. That leaves her school friends who just want the excitement of the latest gossip and will dump her after she has told them. Then they will talk behind her back about how she isn't coping and how she has got fatter and, oh look how old and haggard her face has become.' Jack was impressed by the way women politicked.

'I would never have thought of any of that. Women are so different you know. Especially here,' and he stroked her breasts, pushing against the thin flowery blouse. 'Harriet, now I'm divorced I could do anything I want. Have you thought about that?' He pushed his fingers into her bra to touch her hard nipples. 'I could easily go to China and meet a young woman as they desperately want a European husband. I could marry her and live a life of unreality for ten years before she became totally unbearable just like Melanie. At least I would be happy for ten years despite having to drink green tea.' She pushed his hand away indignantly.

'So do it then, Jack!' He kissed her and started to undo her blouse buttons without any protests from his lover.

'You see, I know you better now, Harry, and that was your classic reverse psychology.' She grumped momentarily.

'It's okay for you to be so footloose and fancy free, but I feel trapped and have no one to share my prison with, poppet.' She poked his rounded tummy. The kisses were more frequent and harder now.

'So, my little wench, how do you cope with your terrible incarceration? Maybe you should imagine yourself in my position at fifty-four with no money and no home?' She mused softly.

'I can imagine you in a lot of positions but hadn't thought of chains, my knight.' She didn't say anymore as they were too busy making love on the settee whilst in the background the *News* predicted a deepening financial crisis around the globe so that no one would feel safe anymore.

Jack stood in her en suite after showering to wash away the sweat and sex and was slowly towelling himself down. He looked at the endless upside-down bottles in her bathroom and the dozens of part-used face and body creams, rubs, scrubs and smells. His dick hurt from constant sex and he could see it was sore on the end by the urethra. In the midst of her potions was some spray-on Savlon and so opening the top he directed an orange stream onto the tip.

'Fucking hell, that stings. Fuck me.' Harriet ran in to see what calamity had occurred and immediately burst out laughing as he explained the cause of his pain and showed her the head of his orange cock. He had tears of pain in his eyes as he demanded, 'Stop laughing for God's sake! The nick on my dick hurts like hell. What I need is a little lubrication instead.' She examined the site more closely.

'It looks like a bite, poppet.'

'Well that was probably you downstairs, lovely.'

'I don't think so, poppet, I'd already eaten.' She laughed again before handing him a tube of cream. He read the label. 'For all types of bite.'

'Very apt; hilarious *not*. Why don't you prove your love for me as it's your fault I am in so much pain.' She was still smiling as she delicately cupped his hardening cock.

'How can I prove I love you, my knight? Haven't I done enough already?'

'No, Harry, as recompense and as a gesture of your true love I suggest that we have anal sex or, as a minimum, you let me come in your mouth.' She didn't reject him immediately, but tapped him on his nose with her forefinger.

'No way, Mister Edmunson, I barely know you and I am a good girl.'

'Then you don't love me, Harry, but I agree you are good,' and he started to push her onto the floor.

Eventually it was time to sleep and he sat on the toilet for a last piss and shook his dick vigorously to avoid dripping on the floor tiles and thus disturbing her equilibrium. Jumping into the soft bed he cuddled up to her and commented to a very sleepy Soul Shiner.

'You know, no matter how hard I try, I still can't get the last drop or three to fall in your loo. No matter how long I wait or breathe deeply to relax, I still wet my pants or your floor.' She replied sleepily.

'Go to sleep, poppet.'

'Did you know, Harry, in Spain there are three words for a leak: an *aguero*; hole, an *escape*, or leak of gas or water and also a *gotera*, which is a leak in the roof! What a nightmare!'

'Jack, please stop talking rubbish, I am nearly asleep, my poppet.'

'But, Harriet, I'm wide awake. You know life is always simple to simple people. I don't mean simple-minded but simple-thinking people.'

'Please, Jack; I'm shagged-out, big boy. Life is what you make of it.' Jack wanted the last word.

'No, sometimes it's what life makes of you.'

They both had disturbed sleeps that night for different reasons, but all revolving around the same topic and that was his return home to Spain. Jack was reliving his 'home alone with no money' nightmare and she was dreaming of her 'divorced, alone and lots of money but no one to share her life' equivalent.

A shared pain that was bringing them closer together.

★   ★   ★

Tuesday was the last day before Jack flew home to Catalonia and he was determined to see as much of his son as possible. He telephoned when he knew his boy would be with his Mum having breakfast. He let it ring six times before the answer machine kicked in. He tried again and then a third time.

'That is so rude and so ignorant, Nim. If she saw it was a friend's number it would be picked up immediately in case it was an emergency or something to do with the school run, but not for me hey!' He calmed himself and tried again. Melanie answered.

'Yes?' Jack breathed in.

'Hi, how are you?' No response.

'How about if JoJo stays the night with me today?' A deep sigh from her.

'No.' He had expected as much.

'Why?'

'Well, where is he going to stay?'

'Here.'

'No.'

'But he's stayed here before and he knows Harriet really well.'

'No. Never.'

'I want to see him today, Melanie, come what may.'

'In that case you can come here at five.' She replaced the receiver.

'She is so rude, Nim; I will swing for her yet.'

He arrived at Tettenhill at exactly five and found the door unusually unlocked. A mellow Melanie waited for him in full make-up and sporting a low-cut yellow cardigan that showed her breasts uplifted by a black bra that peaked out at her ex. He moved his eyes.

'Hi, where is he, Melanie? I thought I would take him for tea somewhere.'

'He isn't here. Didn't you get my message?' She asked nicely with half a smile.

'What message?' She continued in the same vein.

'He's at a friend's doing homework and will be here at about six.' He stayed polite whilst swearing under his breath.

'In that case I will come and collect him later.'

'No Jack, don't go, I need to talk to you about a few things. Come and sit at the conservatory table with me.' A suspicious Jack sat and watched her pull up a chair a couple of feet from him so he could smell the White Linen perfume.

Just go and wait in the car, Jack. Listen to some music.

'I know you think I am manipulating you about access to my son but you have to consider Joseph. All I do is put myself in his shoes. Sometimes I think your guilt about running away from him makes you bend things out of all proportion and really, Jack, there is no need as we can still talk and be friends.' His hatred for his wife grew as he listened to what he knew was sanctimonious crap.

'Carry on Melanie; it's nice that you are talking to me in a civilised manner.' She placed her hand on his leg near his groin and leaned forward smiling with red salacious lips.

'I don't want you to feel bad about me.' He didn't as he remembered fucking her arse and his cock got harder as he stared at her rounded breasts.

'I know you better than anyone, Jack, I can imagine your frustration at not having life running how you want it to, but you can't beat the system. You need to give a bit to take a bit. For example, you now owe me £3,000 but I don't want to fall out about it. We just need to agree a new monthly payment.' She leaned forward and put a hand on his cheek and gently rubbed it.

No, no, no. Don't do this.

'I don't want to be enemies, I want to be friends.' They were so close that they both leaned forward and kissed. She put her hand on his prick and undid his jeans as he felt her right breast. As she bent down and started sucking his cock he pulled her head away.

'You were saying?' He did his jeans back up.

'Come on, Jack. Fuck me. I remember how good you were and

I haven't had sex for so long now.' She massaged his cock through the jeans. He held her hand still but left it on his cock. He was very tempted but had a few questions.

'Everything you want is biased towards money and manipulation of access to Joseph. If I get a telephone message to ring you, I then find the phone is off the hook. I telephone and Joseph is not available as he's in the shower or the toilet. Why won't you be normal towards me? Do you hate me so much?' She knew him well enough to take the initiative and stood and took her cardigan off undoing her bra and showing him her huge brown and wide nipples that she pushed towards his mouth. He stood himself and pushed her down on her seat again.

'Joseph is not allowed to send me emails; I get no letters or telephone calls in Spain. Why?'

'Things can change, Jack.' She squirmed on her hot cunt as she wanted him so badly, but only because she wanted to hurt him really bad.

Jack, she is just manipulating you to get money but,
more importantly, to get at Harriet.

'I know you Melanie and after two years I know you even better because I have seen your dark side. I now understand how your female mind works. You have money worries and as all I ever did for you was to support your lifestyle you still want that support. However, I am telling you now that you need to stand on your own two feet. We keep going round in circles about the divorce money, the sale of this house and the Spanish apartment. There are no more answers to your endless questions. Only time will kill them off because I have arranged to give you everything and it is still not enough. There may still be twenty things to consider in your head, but there are twenty answers that are just not answerable. Your mind works through all this in a thousand subjective pathways, linking all the options and the emotive side of everything rather than the practical side of it.' She sat with her arms crossed covering her embarrassment. Her breasts heaved as she responded.

'You think I have no respect for you, even after you left us in the lurch, but I have never talked down to you and I have other interests now as I have moved on. Money isn't everything.' He held his hands flat in front of him and replied.

'This little scene wasn't about money then? It is me that has moved on and not you. You are no longer in my life, Melanie. I don't care about what you are doing and who with. Stop using our son as a bribe to get money from me as it won't work, and neither will you offering sex. You can't hurt me anymore. There has been too much stress but never closure and now we have closure. So dear ex-wife put your clothes back on and cover your flabby little tits. There is no way I am going to fuck you as I am getting more than enough sex elsewhere. When the going gets tough the tough get going. When the green flag drops the bullshit stops.'

'Listen to me Jack and stop interrupting.'

Ignorance from afar, Jack, nothing has changed.

They heard the doorbell which was undoubtedly Joseph as she had locked the door after letting Jack in.

'Are you happy living in Spain, Jack?' Her voice was cold now. He still engaged.

'No. It's not home yet, but in reality I could live anywhere in the world. Remember China, Melanie, I loved it there, but you hated it. The language was the hardest, wasn't it? You have to be careful with any words you speak in China because the same written word can have four intonations and mean four different things. I am going to see *Ma*, might mean going to see my mother or my horse. So you might accidentally say you look just like my mother and get slapped by a young girl as you said she looks like a horse. Do you remember how hard communications were?'

'Of course I remember, Jack.' She had stood up and was adjusting her clothes ready to let Joseph in. He also stood to maintain his ascendance and stared into her eyes from six inches away.

'So let me say this bluntly in English with no intonational meanings. Stop messing me around and fuck off.' He walked away to take Joseph for tea and all she could do was to screech at his back.

'JoJo must eat healthy food. Not chips and pizza; I am trying to reduce his weight.' Jack turned and slagged her off again.

'Then take him running around the village green instead of chilling out every fucking day. He wouldn't get so many colds if he was fitter!' The boys jumped into the car happy to be together again and drove to Christianos in Tarporley and ate a fabulous pizza with chips followed by double portions of rich chocolate ice cream.

He explained the sex show to Harriet just before he left for the airport as he thought it would be easier. Melanie had now made a real enemy and Jack wanted to leave them to fight if they wanted. He didn't need any more stress, but with great sadness he kissed and hugged Soul Shiner goodbye as he genuinely saw her as a best woman friend; a best friend in England. Beautiful South played on her CD in the kitchen and she sang along as she held him. 'For we are going to be forever you and me. You will always keep us flying high in the sky. Love.'

It was a lovely song and lovely words but she wanted to be something that he couldn't accept at least yet … if ever. At the airport he stared at the grey sky and said an emotional and tearful farewell to his son whilst standing well away from his fellow passengers.

The relationship with his boy was being trashed.

Soul Shiner loved him but she was not the right one at the right time.

He had too much living in his new life, but wanted some stability.

The relief as he drove up the dirt track and saw his smiling yellow house was palpable.

He opened a bottle of cheap red wine and took it onto the patio with a tumbler. Sitting looking at the sun as it set, he poured and drank three half tumblers in ten minutes and let the alcohol wash over his tired mind. The view had not been diminished by his absence. In fact, the opposite was true. It was the most beautiful view in the world. The sun set the fields alight and the pheasants and peacocks called their goodnights to their peaceful neighbour who sat and drank his 'bad holiday' away. Half an hour later he was fast asleep, slumped in the cane chair with his feet outstretched, but now he was relaxed and happy for the first time in a week. A man had manipulated the manipulating women and he had closure. What more could he desire other than money, happiness and good health?

★   ★   ★

A solid and sexless sleep refreshed him enormously and after his early morning swim across Yapanc bay he arrived home full of energy to find a pink Post-it note stuck to the centre of his glass patio door.

> *Dinner party tonight. 6 pm for drinks, dinner at*
> *8 pm. PTO for our address.*
> *xxx Juicy.*

He must have just missed Lucy but an invite was nice enough. He relished the thought of an evening of fun as he was extremely glad to be home and away from his responsibilities, which now included Harriet.

Lucy and Niiige lived in Bagurr but away from the ancient centre where he had visited Pippa. He drove up to a boring modern place of three storeys. It had the garage on the ground floor, a living and kitchen area on the top floor to provide a pretty view down to Sa Rera beach and two small bedrooms sandwiched in the middle. Stepping out of his Korean Ferrari he appraised the 'in between a deal' excuse house, where temporary cash flow is everything ya. Rented and unloved it was a statement about the couple's life, where timing was everything as they had problems with cash flow. Deliberately he arrived an hour late for drinks to ensure he stayed sober and in control and so when Niiige let him in he was prepared for everyone to be sloshed already and so they were.

'Niiige, thank you for the invite. I've brought some flowers for the old gal rather than a boring old bottle of wine, ya.' He was taking the piss before he even entered but was warmly received by his new friend and shortly afterwards by everyone upstairs, detecting no change in the way his three fuck buddies behaved towards him. It was as if nothing had happened between them.

Jack stood with a glass of red wine in his right hand whilst looking at the pretty view in the fading light. Quietly he listened to their boring conversations without participating; expat phrases were thrown around with abandon.

'Property prices down blah, fish prices horrific, may as well buy meat, blah, the euro heading to one pound blah …'

But what interested him more were the idiosyncrasies of the dominated males. Dutch remained reserved and in half an hour gave no information about himself, his wife or his business. The only noticeable characteristic was his agreement with the others on the need to minimise spending money and so Jack pigeonholed him as tight. Niiige, the property man, talked constantly about his next big deal, but never appeared optimistic.

'Got this great deal on-going, you know, Jack. You could come in on it if you want. Timing is everything in my game.' Jack politely and truthfully declined by pleading poverty.

That left Rolly, the Greek twat, who was the most despised by the whole group. Whether it was his pretend upper-class accent or his pretend friends in the world of art, was difficult to fathom. The heart of the matter was that none of them had ever seen an example of his amazing talent in the last year and so they despised him for pretending rather than for what he was. He was considered by them all as an untalented, stuck-up arsehole who was clearly living on a rapidly diminishing inheritance.

As usual, the drunken conversation was led by the women who appeared far more assertive than their counterparts in England and any topic veering towards business, politics or children was swiftly discouraged as they had no patience with any of these subjects. Business was boring and so was a husband's job. Politics were pathetic as it was all talk, and children were ticked off as complete and out of their lives. Jack was amused but decided to bend the conversation in his preferred direction as Niiige and Lucy threw an assortment of starters on the dining table with a huge basket of sliced baguettes.

As they all tucked into omelette, fresh Palomost prawns, semi-cured goats' cheeses and a variety of hams he complemented Niiige on the delicious red wine.

'Thanks, Jack. I thought I'd go for the best Rioja but my man at the shop in Bagurr recommended this '98 Valdepeñas called Pata Negra, at only ten euros a throw.'

'It's very nice, Niiige, a very good recommendation, with a big kick after you have swallowed it, ya.' Everyone was enjoying the third bottle, as it went particularly well with the food. Jack continued.

'If you want another Valdepeñas you could try a 2005 Senorío de los Llanos sometime. It's very similar and is very easy to source.' Niiige was enthusiastic about his wines.

'Thanks, Jack, old chap. Where would I get that ya?'

'Oh that's easy. You go to the Caprabo discount supermarket in Palafrio.'

'Is it expensive ya?'

'No Niiige, it's just over two euros a bottle but it tastes fantastic, old chap. However ladies, they say drinking this stuff is very dangerous for your physical health.' Lucy jumped in with both feet.

'Why's that, darling?'

'Because in Spanish it literally means from the valley of the penis and apparently it has special attributes just like Viagra!' Lucy guffawed.

'Well, it doesn't seem to help my husband, darling!'

The Duchess was interested enough to ask Jack, 'Have you tried Viagra then?'

'No Duchess, but maybe I should?' He slipped his foot out of his sandal and slid it gently between her legs right up to her cunt and left it there with his toes moving gently on the outside of her panties. Luckily everyone's attention was on Pippa.

'Rolly and I used Viagra once,' she commented, 'it did no good for my man. He just kept complaining about how uncomfortable it was after his usual three-minute shag.' Jack leaned towards her and surreptitiously put his hand on her thigh before he asked.

'What about you, Pip? Did you insist he carry on and demand sex for a few hours?'

'Of course not *J*. I would have got bored, you know. Anyway, what is the point after you've come once? That's enough for a month or two, isn't it?' Jack thought not in her case, but didn't say so.

Not for a woman who has multiple orgasms and swallows crystal balls in her vagina, I think not! He smirked and let his left hand drift under her napkin to massage her cunt through her thin cotton dress whilst stirring the Duchess with his right foot. He decided to tell them all about an event on his trip to China.

'I was in Beijing airport when this beautiful Chinese girl shouted across her counter from the pharmacy.

"Sir, sir," she said, "you want Biagra?"

No, I don't need it, I replied.

"Belly cheap, sir."

"No thanks I said with a big smirk, I really really don't need it, lovely."

"Ah sir, what about for your farver?"

No, but a good try. My father is dead and probably stiff enough in his box so no Viagra required there.' The expats laughed but Jack hadn't finished.

'"Ah sir, no understand, you no want Biagra, you want EPO? Belly good you, good sportsman, keep you going."'

'What's EPO?' The Duchess asked as she manoeuvred his big toe into her hot cunt.

'I'm not sure, my lovely, something to do with enhancing the blood like Extra Prick Opulence.'

'Belly funny, Jack' said Dutch. 'Did you buy any Viagra?'

'No, I really really don't need it, Dutch,' replied honest Jack as the Duchess's cunt got wetter. By this time they were ready for the main course and Lucy announced it was *paella*, her signature dish. Under his breath Jack groaned.

'Oh Fuck, not a Cheshire set signature dish.' In a panic he left the table to find the toilet on the floor below and hence take a few minutes to try and control himself. He stood above the pan and undid his trousers but hearing a noise he turned to find a smiling Lucy walking in behind him. She leaned over his shoulders pushing her huge breasts into his back and reached around the front of his trousers to grab his prick.

'Go on then. I bet you can't piss now.' As he tried to urinate, she fingered his cock and bollocks so he started to grow.

'Okay, you win; I can't go now, as it's too stiff.'

'Good' she said and bent over with her arse towards him flicking her skirt above her waist to show him her lack of panties. 'Fuck me then, instead.'

When they walked back upstairs no one showed any interest in either their departure or arrival as the group had carried on drinking. Apart from Jack all the expats were pissed out of their heads, slurring and staggering around. The conversation moved between the International Montessori school in Geneva to the quality of the *paella* which they pronounced incorrectly with two hard ls, like Calella near Barcelona further down the coast.

'You mean that horrible tacky English tourist spot? By the way double *l* is pronounced like a *y*,' said Jack as he got more daring, feeling the girls' breasts or arses each time he had an opportunity. Cava was served with puddings, but not just any old cava; it had to be special cava at thirty euros a bottle from the inevitable little shop in Bagurr.

'Niiige?' Jack asked. 'Why didn't we drink white wine with the fish paella, old chap?' A sloshed Niiige replied over his shoulder as he staggered to the kitchen with a pile of dirty plates.

'We never drink white wine in Spain, Jack. We are like the Spanish. Never white wine with fish anymore, only red is good enough ya. That last bottle of Rioja was very prestigious ya and bloody expensive. I bought it from the shop called Serra in Palafrio as it was mentioned in the *Daily Telegraph* ya.'

'But Niiige … it tasted like shit.'

'You are a joker, Jack. I like that in you.' He staggered out under the weight of plates. Lucy cuddled up to Jack in her husband's absence and inched onto his chair with a hand on his leg near his groin.

'How do you feel about marriage, Jack? We don't know anything about your history ya.'

'Well Lucy, if you must know, I've been married four times.'

'No bloody way.'

'Yes four times. Seriously I'm not joking. The first one died and it was very sad. The second and third died but I was used to death by then.'

She asked drunkenly, 'What about the fourth?'

'Oh she is about to die in a really horrific car accident. That's Melanie whom I divorced last year.' The Duchess said in amazement.

'You are joking, right?'

'No sorry, death isn't for joking about.' Jack responded sincerely and then Pippa asked.

'Okay so how did they all die *J*?'

'The first, I call her Number One, she died from electrocution when a hairdryer fell in her bath. The second ...' They all chorused.

'Number Two.'

'Correct. She died when the brakes failed on her car and it went over a cliff. As for Number Three, well she fell off a bridge on our second wedding anniversary.' Lucy punched him on his arm.

'No way, darling,' but none of the girls were laughing and were still listening intently. Pippa punched his other arm that she had previously been clinging to and said,

'I bet you say it was an accident.'

'No Pip, I don't actually, but the police did after a long investigation where I was proved innocent.' The Duchess threw some bread at him.

'You are joking, Jack, aren't you?'

He went quiet before asking his host, 'Lovely cheese this, Niiige. Is it sheep or goat's milk?' Lucy banged the table with her fist.

'Come on Jack, you can't just leave it like that. Who did the servicing on the car?'

'Well me, of course.'

The Duchess asked, 'Who was drying your wife's hair?'

'Well, I suppose I was actually.' All three girls then implied the same.

'I bet you were walking over the bridge with Number Three when she fell off.'

'No, that's definitely untrue. I was far too busy paying the Scouse hit man's brother!'

Everyone enjoyed the story and he felt accepted by the group, including the husbands who were happy to have someone to stand up to their dominant wives.

The Duchess concluded, 'Jack also claims he is looking for Number Five as he is such a romantic.' Jack justified himself.

'Well, they say experience counts, Duchess, and when you have had four wives you learn how to handle them.'

'How's that then Jack?' queried Niiige.

'Only when they ask, Niiige!' The group laughed at the concept, but Pippa wanted to know why he had got married four times as she had completely missed the fact that it was a joke.

'Well, my little pipsqueak, I used to think it was loneliness but you know as I am still lonely, I'm pretty sure that isn't the right answer.' He paused thoughtfully. 'My first wife was really sexy which appealed when I was twenty-two. Sex was vitally important then but not now, of course. I couldn't manage it more than once a month and only for a few minutes. The second marriage was for safety and security; she was just convenient, you know. The third was very rich and when I was thirty-three; money meant more to me than anything else. But the fourth I married purely for social status.'

'Did you really marry for convenience?' asked the inebriated Pippa.

'Of course, lovely, why not? Marriage sums up a man's life and I suppose Number Five will treat me like my mother did, so I can happily regress to being a child in my old age.' Everyone except Pippa laughed and giggled in their drunken stupors and Jack looked at the girls and assessed whether any of them scored any points towards being his Sun Sharer.

*Remember, Jack, death isn't for joking about. Death
comes from unexpected directions.*

'Okay, Nim, back off. It was just a little joke mind.'

At the end of the meal Niiige produced his pièce de résistance, a
single malt Glenfiddich whisky reputedly twenty-eight years old.

Jack was the only one to query, 'I thought whisky had to be
drunk before it was fourteen years old or it went off?'

'No, Jack. The man in the shop in Bagurr assures me this is the
best you can buy at ninety euros ya.' Jack took a small swig of the
whisky and passed it back to Niiige.

'Sorry, old chap, not my cup of tea ya.' It tasted foul and Jack
decided he would go and see the little man in the Bagurr shop to
determine whether he was a fabulous salesman and if Niiige was a
complete plonker about plonk. As they collapsed onto the comfy
settees he ensured he was next to Pippa to give her equal attention
to that shown to the Duchess and Lucy.

'So, my lovely, have they found Osama Bin Laden in Palafrio yet?'

'Oh God knows, Jack. That lot down there are so entranced
with the Pope that they wouldn't notice Osama if he prayed to
Allah in the middle of the square.' Jack tried to be controversial.

'Anyway who is the Pope? He's about as useful as Obama
whatever his name is in the USA.' Pippa poked him in his chest as
a physical comment.

'That black guy will never get in as the yanks are too racist.
Hilary will slaughter him even with that suck cocker as a husband.'

'Cock-sucker, Pippa', he corrected her.

'Whatever,' she slurred. 'They're all bastards, making money
even in the financial crisis thingy.' Jack could see she was more
drunk than he had imagined but he told her something he seriously
believed in.

'Making money in a financial crisis is obligatory as the rich
get richer still because they know about it earlier and sell quicker.
Of course then they buy back earlier and before everyone else as

they are in the know.'

'What is *the know*, Jack?' she asked.

'It's what you have when you are rich. It's privileged information gained before anyone else and it's not in the *Daily Mail*!'

'Oh bugger,' she said. 'That's no good then as we all buy that. What do you feel emotional about *J*?' She tried to smile sexily and failed because of her intoxication.

'You mean apart from you, my lovely?'

'Yes, you devil.'

'I feel emotional about my writing; for example; when my daughter or brother asks me when I am going to get a proper job or join the real world. That is very emotional. Also I get emotional about things that could happen in the future like the prospect of a tsunami of Chinese aggression engulfing the world with their genuine copy attitudes or fanatical Islam and their religious fervour.'

'*J* you think too much.'

'Maybe that's true, Pippa, maybe it is true, lovely.' The girls had drunk more than the boys and were getting aggressive and disrespectful of their husbands in childish ways rather than over any deep emotional feelings, implying they felt nothing for their spouses. Jack couldn't work it all out and sat wondering whether most things were trivial anyway.

He listened and watched the women as they controlled the men's agendas and treated them like six year olds, as if in competition with each other where belittling their husbands was for fun. He realised he was a pawn in a game of human chess and considered the moves as the women demanded things of their men rather than asking for their help. They demanded a renewal of their car insurance and complained about Mapfre or Groupama charging their husbands 1,500 euros for something that Jack had obtained from Linea Directa at half the price, taking into account his English no-claims discount. They demanded and complained rather than queried and suggested. It showed how expats stopped thinking as though things were a problem unique to Spain and thus it was acceptable to accept stupid things. It was the women who complained about the UK recession, lamenting the loss of confidence but purely based on the headlines from the *Daily Mail* or, if lucky, the few random lines scanned below them. It was they who brought doom and gloom to their circle.

Jack went to stand by the Duchess staring out of the window at the pretty yellow lights of Sa Rera.

'Don't your husbands get jealous of your power and freedom?' She half turned and he could see that she had been *pretend* drunk with the group, but was no worse than himself.

'No, Jack, because they respect and trust us, and vice versa.'

'Well surely, Duchess, that doesn't work then?'

'Of course it works, because we all make it work. We meet in the middle. Spain and the life of expats is a direct contrast to that in England or Holland. Life there is lived behind closed doors but here it is always open and honest. Take sex, for example, it is just sex after all. What we really think or know about each other is far more than would ever be disclosed at home.'

As people started to think about leaving, the Duchess offered to pop over and see Jack with a spare DVD player, which he gratefully accepted. Lucy suggested he could join her for a long cross-country ride but before he could decline Niiige interrupted.

'I don't think subjecting Jack to that is a good idea.' Lucy whipped round to face him.

'How can you express an opinion as you never ride with me?' Jack could see his jealousy and politely declined her offer but said she could ride from Pals to his house one day and stop for a light lunch. Finally, Pippa grasping Rolly's hand asked if he would like to come to their small art exhibition in Banyoles and then give her a lift home as Rolly was staying for two nights longer. He politely accepted the invitation to the exhibition and said to Rolly he hoped it would be a great success. As they left, none of the girls drove home but were happy to let their drunken husbands get behind the wheel.

No, no, no, not again Jack. You know what will happen.

'Precisely, Nim, precisely.'

★ ★ ★

A couple of days after the dinner party Jack had a royal visitor accompanied by her permanent footman Robbie Williams. She was getting used to the dirt track and he could see she was having fun accelerating out of the snaking bend to slide the rear of the car until the electronics straightened it out. As she pulled up he walked across to her from his wicker throne and put his hands on the top of the cabriolet's door.

'There's a button you can press if you desperately want to be like the deceased but much-loved Colin McCrae.'

'Really, Jack? Can you lean in and point it out, please?' Innocently he leaned inside the cabriolet whilst scanning the dashboard and anticipated her hand sliding up inside his T-shirt and gently massaging his hairy chest.

'That's nice. To what do I owe the honour of her Royal Highness's visit?'

'Firstly, I was so bored home alone and secondly, I have brought you our spare DVD player.' He helped her out of the car admiring her grey strapless top caressing bare breasts and her tight navy shorts accentuating her lovely arse. They strolled towards his lounge cum everything room and Jack placed the DVD next to the TV and linked up the cables.

'Do you want a DVD to test it with, Jack?'

'Well done, Duchess,' he took the proffered disc but saw it was unlabelled.

'What's it called?'

'There's no title but it's about a painter. It's just a little present Jack to go with the DVD player and to keep you entertained when I'm not around.' They sat next to each other on the settee as it started to play. A pretty young girl was painting by a harbour somewhere in Spain and was approached by a handsome black guy who offered to model for her. Leading him back to her studio flat she started to sketch him whilst pensively holding the brushes in her mouth and imagining him making love to her. Jack turned to the Duchess.

'Let me guess where this is going!'

'Leave it on, Jack, it might change your brush technique.' Within two minutes the pair on the film were both naked and kissing at which point the Duchess had come closer to Jack and started to undo his shorts. She was fascinated by the film and as she started to lick the tip of Jack's erect cock she constantly watched the girl do the same to the huge black guy and copied everything. Jack wasn't allowed to join in but was left out of the foursome. He was stretched back half-naked and no matter how much he tried to move to initiate something she pushed him back harder and sucked or licked him like on the film.

'Duchess', he was watching her not the film, 'I am so close, my lovely, if you carry on like that you will get a mouthful of spunk before I can satisfy you.' She glanced up at him holding his cock upright at right angles to his stomach and then took a long lingering lick.

'But, Jack, you are satisfying me by just doing nothing.' She recommenced sucking and fondling his balls as the actor on the porno movie came onto the actress's face and into her half-open mouth with what appeared to be a litre of white spunk, but before Jack could enjoy the same relief the Duchess stopped touching him and pulled him upright to walk outside. She quickly slipped out of her shorts whilst provocatively showing her delicately rounded arse and then she lay on his white plastic table with her feet on the edge and knees bent up before she invitingly opened her legs.

'Lick me, Jack.' He leaned forward and put his hands on the inside of each white thigh and marvelled at the thin S-shaped pubic hair and red lips that she held open with her left hand. Taking a long lingering lick he had to ask before continuing to run his tongue up and down her labia.

'Why an S?'

'S is for sexy, Jack, can't you tell?' He couldn't reply as his bottom lip was pressed hard onto her cunt beneath her clitoris and he was sucking it higher as she breathed more heavily. He went to insert two fingers but she reached down and pulled them away.

'Just lick and suck and do it harder now, please. in fact, really

really hard.' She convulsed and came and he noticed her juices dripping out the side of her vagina. But when she came she made no sound as though she was desperate to restrain herself. Jack stood upright and held his giant cock ready to penetrate her as he now needed fulfilling but she closed her legs around his waist and reached for him so that they could only kiss. The kiss was different because she licked and sucked his mouth and lips and then inside his mouth and even under his tongue as she tried to taste every bit of her sex that he had sucked out of her. When she was satisfied she pushed him back and slid off the table using him for support.

'That was delightful, Jack. I hope you enjoy watching the DVD.' And she pulled on her shorts and walked to her car. A single royal wave and she sped off down the track leaving both a half-naked Jack and his huge unfulfilled cock standing upright in amazement. There was only one solution and so he went back inside, replayed the last few minutes where the actor came, and wanked himself harder than ever before. She had sexed him up to new heights and then knocked him down to new lows and he wasn't sure whether he liked the experience.

The following day he drove apprehensively towards Girona, via the pottery town of La Bisbal and then, leaving the city to the west, he headed into the hills adjoining the volcanic area of the Garrotxa and searched for the tourist signs to Banyoles Lake.

Although they existed, they were in unfathomable Catalan and he had to stop and ask for directions three times. Jack played Quarenta Principales on the car radio and thought about the reasons why he was so disturbed about the trip. Partly it was because he wanted to be in control of his social and sex life, partly because of the recent experience with the Duchess and, finally, he hoped the arty couple didn't see him as a potential purchaser.

It was nine in the evening by the time he found the small pavilion on the south side of the lake with a solitary notice on the parched lawn. 'Roland Humphries. A sample of Catalonia in water colours.' As Jack walked towards the gallery, he stopped and felt the serene attraction of the waters which were darkening ominously as the sun sank below the wooded hill to his left. A few ducks floated close to the beautiful little summerhouse, surveying its flaking pink paint and half-open shutters, which allowed a dim yellow light to leak out into the rapidly cooling air.

'It's certainly the perfect spot for an artist, Nim. Whether he is an artist we will see.'

It is an imperfect spot, Jack. A place of never-ending
torment where lessons will be learned.

Jack shivered and then crossed himself in appreciation of his life before stepping inside the place. Immediately to his left was a small desk where Rolly was talking earnestly to a very old Catalan lady who was supported by her son. She wore a dark green winter coat to combat the cold of the early evening as the temperature had plummeted to twenty degrees Celsius. Jack watched her as she nodded her grey hair in unison with the points she made to Rolly whilst wagging a solitary finger. The middle-aged son held her arm and tried to calm her down whilst agreeing with her sentiments but, equally, wanting to go home for his dinner. Pippa walked up to a motionless Jack and grasping his arm pulled him to the right side of the single room.

'She is very rich and wants a bargain *J*, but don't we all!'

'What's a bargain?' he whispered back whilst looking at the picture in front of him instead of the negotiation.

'Rolly was asking 1,2000 euros and she wants to pay 200.'

'That would be a bargain. Come on, show me the picture in question, lovely.' Arm in arm she guided him to stand in front of the painting depicting the very pavilion they were standing in but viewed from a boat on the lake.

'Her family used to own this pavilion and see here,' she leaned forward and pointed, 'that is her house and that is why the miserable cow wants it so badly.' Jack stepped back breaking her grip and then stepped left for two paces and then right two paces. Immediately he started nodding his head, pretending to like it and hoping it would put pressure on the potential buyer. In truth, he decided that it was poor and lacked the transparency of the Catalan light that gave everyone a spiritual lift most days of the year. After a few minutes of banal conversation they moved on with a surreptitious glance at the old but dignified hag.

'Show me around, Pippa.' They walked to the next picture and acknowledged the only other couple in the room who were young German tourists bored by the town and happy to have found a free exhibition on their evening stroll.

There were precisely eight paintings on the four walls and all were badly lit by temporary lamps that looked out of place in the grace of the building.

'What do you think *J*? None of the others have seen his work, you know. He must like you a lot.'

'I think they are different and have a certain style, but show me the terrace as the real beauty is outside.' They opened the double doors and stepped onto an old wooden platform built over the lake. It was as big as the room they had left behind and nearly as bright. The lights of the town were to their right and further to the north they could see the Rowing Centre built for the '88 Olympics held in nearby Barcelona. Footsteps attracted their attention as the platform shook slightly.

'Jack, old chap, how lovely to see you.' Rolly couldn't shake hands as they were filled with three glasses and a bottle of red wine. 'I bought some of that wine you recommended from Caprabo and I agree it is excellent for the price ya.'

'Ya Rolly, I liked it too.' As Pippa helped by holding glasses for her husband to pour, Jack asked if the old woman had bought.

'Yes and no. I think she was happy to pay 300 but she decided to think about it. So that's stupendous.' He seemed positive enough and so Jack was pleased for him.

'That's great, Rolly. I like your paintings so thank you for asking me.'

'My pleasure, old chap.' Pippa was also excited about the possible sale.

'Well done, Jack. You arrived at the right time so she thinks there's some competition. How lovely if you sell a painting on the first day, Rolly.' They toasted each other and the sound of the clinking glasses was absorbed by the black waters as they stared silently across them. Pippa broke the false tranquillity.

'This place is very spiritual *J*. Sometimes you can see the stars reflected on the water which reminds me of lost souls captured by the beast that lurks in the depths.'

He turned to her and asked innocently, 'Is there a beast living here?'

'Yes, *J*, there are many old legends of something taking men, women and children down into the depths. In reality, it is incredibly deep in places and because of the volcanic activity over thousands of years there are fissures in the bed and whirlpools above them.'

Rolly moaned like a ghost.

'Don't go in the water at night, Jack, or the beast will get you.' Jack laughed uncomfortably as he heard distant voices from ancient spirits who couldn't escape this world. He shivered again.

'Let's go in. It's turned chilly.' Both of them could see that he was troubled but there wasn't time to ask for reasons as the place needed closing up for the night. All of them helped and within half an hour Rolly's car safely held the eight appalling paintings, ready for him to depart to the local guest house and for Jack to take Pippa back to Bagurr.

'Goodnight, Jack. Thanks for coming out tonight as it's nice to have some moral support.' Rolly shook Jack's hand before driving off with a curt goodbye to his wife and no physical signs of affection.

'Let's go, Jack.' She took control. 'I know the best way home on the basis you got lost so many times on the way here.' Demure Pippa jumped into the passenger side and they headed north.

Jack asked his co-driver, 'I'm not questioning your directions, lovely, but shouldn't we be going south?'

'Of course not, Jack, you haven't seen the best part of the lake yet.' They drove out of the town and after ten minutes she told him to turn down a dirt track which they followed until she instructed him to park under some trees by the shore. He turned the engine off and they walked side by side to the water's edge to admire the most amazing vista. Far to the south they could see the distant twinkling town of Banyoles and in front they had the reflection of a crescent moon as pretty as the moon itself that smiled twice at the two lovers.

'Isn't that wonderful *J*? Do you believe in the legends now?'

'Actually, I always believed, lovely, from the moment we walked onto the terrace and I heard the voices.'

'I knew you heard them as well. You are hiding a lot from me *J*.' She cuddled into him with her arms around his waist and looked up to be kissed. It was a long and tender kiss made special by the location. Pulling away she undid her blouse and bra and dropped them on the floor with a serious demanding look at him. She slipped out of her skirt revealing no knickers and leaving her Crocs on, she pushed him away.

'Catch me if you can Soul Snarer!' Running away down the edge of the lake she waved frantically shouting. 'Take your clothes off first!'

'Fuck me, Nim, what am I supposed to do?'

This is a bad place, Jack. The spirits are unhappy and you should drive away as quickly as possible.

Jack stripped quickly and then slipped his sandals back on before chasing after her. He was exhilarated by the night and the spice of the terror held deep in the depths. As he closed on her he could see that she had stopped and was facing the moonlight with her arms high in the air and her head held back. The soft light threw shadows over her plump curves accentuating her beauty as she stepped forward into the wet mirror and slowly sank from view.

'Fuck me Nim, what the fuck is going on.'

Quickly, Jack, or she will be lost forever.

Within ten seconds he dived towards the spot where she had disappeared and searched with his hands as he kicked down towards hell and found no bottom. It was no use opening his eyes as the acidic water would have burned like fire. Frantically he swam to his left until at last he felt her hand and grasping tightly he kicked upwards towards heaven. Again he kicked and using his free right hand he had to pull hard to reach the surface whilst his lungs were bursting. They emerged gasping, sending ripples for lonely miles until they were absorbed by the soft muddy shore. Still breathless they paddled towards the shallows and soon managed to stand and clasp each other with the water safely at chest level.

'What were you doing, Pippa? I thought you were going to drown?'

'Oh *J*, it was awful, I went forward thinking it was shallow and shelving and suddenly I dropped into a hole. It was terrifying because it was full of weed that clung onto my whole body pulling me down.' They hugged tightly and gradually calmed down. 'There's nothing to worry about *J*, it was a silly accident. There are no ghosts here you know. Look at the moon and its change of colour. Oh how lovely *J*.'

She splashed him before coming back to kiss him hungrily. As they clung to each other, their hands sank downwards and touched, excited by the danger. He grasped her hair with both hands and pulled it back behind her head to make a rope that he held tightly in one whilst he used the other to massage her breasts and hard nipples.

'*J*, turn me round and put your cock in me quickly.' He leaned her forward and entered her gently before thrusting in hard with a grunt. Grasping her hips, he leaned backwards and stared at the moon like a man possessed, riding her until she gasped and came.

'Jesus *J*, that was so fucking good. Put a finger in my arsehole and keep fucking me.' He slipped a finger into her and used it to press against the head of his penis, exciting her as it touched a sensitive spot. She was very close again and breathing heavily as the water washed backwards and forwards in their frenzy.

'Take your cock out now quickly and shove your fist in me.'

'My whole fist?' Jack was incredulous.

'Just fucking do it and do it now and ....' her words were now moans 'and shove it in. Fuck me with your whole fist as hard as you can ...' She came howling like a wolf whose cry reverberated off the nearby cliffs and bounced back at them.

Get out of the lake, Jack; get out and save her sanity.
Do it now.

He needed no second bidding and walked her back towards their clothes, with Pippa leaning on him needing a crutch as if she had run a marathon.

'That was so lovely *J*. Can we go back in the water and do it again?' She lurched towards the darkness but he yanked her forcibly away. Pulled from whatever called her they arrived back at the car and he made her dress quickly before driving silently home.

It was a few days later that Jack's equilibrium was disturbed by an expat.

Behind the *barraca* stood a group of small hills no more than 100 metres high with the house lying halfway up their wooded slopes. The shade of the pine trees predominated at Jack's level but as you climbed higher the land supported more quercus and corks in a sunnier, more open disposition. Meandering across the hills was a set of ancient dirt tracks that linked Yapanc to many old villages, including Palafrio and Bagurr with their ancient castles and it was across these tracks that Lucy had to come. He knew she might arrive at lunchtime because of the phone call the previous evening, but he didn't know *if* she would arrive as the method of navigation seemed slightly hit and miss.

'Darling, I know the track across the plain towards Palafrio leaving Bagurr on my left and then as the ground rises I'll head towards an old village called Esclanya where I had a wonderful lunch last year. If I can get there at midday ya, I'll head directly for the sun which must be in the south and get to the top of a ridge and have a look around ya.'

'What do you mean look around Lucy?'

'Well darling, you are on the way to the lighthouse and if I'm high enough, I'll recognise the headland and make a beeline towards it.'

'Okay.' Jack paused. 'What if it's raining and the visibility is poor?'

'I'll get bloody wet ya!'

'No, I mean in terms of the right direction?'

'Don't worry, darling I'll just ask people.'

'But Lucy, there are no people to ask and also, my lovely, you don't speak Spanish never mind Catalan.'

'Good point ya, but it's no use getting a map as I can't tell the difference between the crack of an arse and the inside of an elbow, never mind the contours and the tracks.'

'Well in that case, Lucy, you are buggered.'

'Darling, trust me because I know what I'm doing, so I'll see you tomorrow ya.' He heard the steady walk of a horse coming down the hill and walked behind the *barraca* to see if it was her. Threading his way through the olive plantation was Trio with a despondent Lucy on his back.

'Hiya, why are you coming from that direction? It's the opposite of where you have your stable.' She jumped down and tied the horse to a branch.

'It was the weather that caused me problems, darling.' Jack surveyed the clear blue sky and sun in the south high above Yapanc bay.

'Really? How was that?' She kissed him quickly on the lips.

'It was the heat, darling, I haven't had a drink in three hours and all I could see was mirage after mirage of the same wooded hill.'

'You mean all the countryside looked the same?'

'Exactly, darling, so how about a drink for the horse first and then one for me.' Jack fetched a bucket of water and placed it by Trio's nose as the stallion snuffled around the foot of the olive trunk in search of some grass, but even in May it was starting to dry up and go crackly brown. They walked to the side of the house and she sat on the terrace whilst Jack fetched two beers.

'You have a wonderful view here, darling, and these fields in front are perfect for riding.'

'They were perfect for all sorts of wild flowers too, but the local farmer came last week and mowed them for hay.' She was thirsty and asked for another beer after a couple of minutes so Jack fetched another can of San Miguel which she quickly consumed.

'Right, darling, off we go ya.'

'Pardon lovely?' He was incredulous; she had ridden for three hours, got lost and drunk nearly a litre of beer and now she wanted to move again.

'Let's explore! You can come with me on the back of Trio.'

'Won't the horse need a rest?'

Good excuse, Jack.

'Bugger me, he's a big strong thing and could go for ages. In fact, look at that.' She walked up to Trio whose knob was hanging limply a foot below his balls.

'You can't beat a massive dick, darling, can you?' She bent down and gently stroked the horse's knob making it grow another six inches and stiffen.

'Fuck me, Nim. I can't believe she's doing that.'

'Fuck' being the operative word, Jack.

Juicy Lucy was now very juicy as she was excited by the horse. Still stroking the enormous 'hard on' she smiled up at Jack.

'How about holding him still whilst I see if I can crouch underneath.'

'No, no, no Lucy there is no way I am going to help you get a horse's dick inside of you. God how dangerous is that. Trio could get frisky and split you in half for God's sake and think of the germs!' She stopped playing with the horse and sidled up to him. Pushing her big boobs in his chest she started to lick his lips with her tongue gently forcing his mouth apart and carrying on licking his mouth on the inside of the lips. She reached down inside the waist of his thin shorts, but he pulled her away from his exposed cock.

'Right, I suggest you go and wash your hands before we go and explore.' Disappointedly she walked to his outside tap and rinsed her hands cupping them to throw water over her face to cool herself down both physically and sexually. The water glistened in the air as she sprinkled it over her making a pretty fountain in the sun. She came back with her breasts bursting through her now see-through shirt and trying to escape the black bra under the wet pink cotton. She looked beautiful with water glistening on her face and beads rolling off her blonde hair as she tossed it side to side. Swinging herself up on the horse she then leaned over to offer a strong brown hand to Jack and he was duly thrown up behind her. Kicking the tired beast on, they headed across the mown fields towards El Far with Jack desperately unsafe despite clenching his feet into the sides of Trio and wrapping his arms tightly around her waist.

'Don't worry, darling, I won't gallop. I know you're scared to death of horses. I knew the first time out that you weren't a horse rider.'

'Really, Lucy, and I thought I gave you a really good ride, my lovely.' They grinned together as they went into the shade of a copse of pine.

'You were okay, darling, but you need to do better than that first attempt.'

'What at? Sex or horse riding?'

'Both together,' she said as she stopped Trio and lifted one leg over the horse's neck so that she could turn to Jack and kiss him. She desperately wanted him as she had been excited by Trio's prick as opposed to her new lover, who was sat facing her on her favourite horse. It was her ultimate dream to have two stallions together. Jack unbuttoned her shirt and slipped his hands under her bra to fondle her wonderful breasts as she kissed him hungrily.

'My fanny is so wet, Jack, stay where you are ya.' She slid down off the horse and placed her hands on his bare leg.

'How tight are your shorts darling?'

'Very loose, why?'

'Can you take your cock out of them and keep it out?'

'Yes but why?' She didn't answer; instead she stripped off her boots, jodhpurs and panties and left them on the ground but sexily she put the boots back on. Jack searched the wood for onlookers.

'Someone might see, Lucy. Do you want me to get down now?'

'No, stay there, I said.' She climbed back on Trio facing

away from Jack presenting her arse and open cunt to him as she mounted.

'Pull your shorts to one side darling and come onto the saddle so that I can sit on your prick.' He slid forward onto the saddle as she lifted her arse and then lowered herself onto his erect prick guided by his hand.

'Oh God, darling, that feels good' and she kicked Trio into a walk tracing a circle between the trees.

'Jesus, Juicy Lucy you are living up to your nickname.' Her wetness dripped onto his thighs and was soaked up by the hot leather saddle.

'Hold onto my hips, darling, and pull me onto you.' She urged Trio to move faster and they trotted in unison as Jack desperately clung to her strong thighs. She forced him harder into her cunt with each bounce. 'Push, darling, push ya ... come on ya.' The 'ya's' spread into a primal scream and then she grunted through an enormous orgasm finally sitting hard on him ensuring they both tumbled heavily onto the ground. Trio wandered unconcerned into the wood whilst Jack lay on his back trying to work out which bits of him were broken. She raised herself and laid her breasts on his chest to kiss him.

'That is the best orgasm I have ever had ya. Bloody brilliant, darling. You did much better this time.' As she said this, she pulled Mister Wiggly out of his hiding place and levered herself on top of him to start riding him with her hands on his chest. Jack couldn't say a word; his cock was still stiff enough for her but he was winded from the fall. So he just lay still deciding he may as well die like this as she fucked him harder than any other women in his life until she came once again. Immediately she pushed herself up using his chest and caused him to scream silently as it hurt his bruised ribcage. He watched her arse as she walked to her jodhpurs and started to dress, leaving him desperate to come but hurting too much to contemplate asking her to favour him.

'Trio, Trio come here, you stupid man.' Jack finally moved as he felt the red ants starting to bite his buttocks and brushing them off, he valiantly and quietly started the walk back to the *barraca*.

* * *

A few days after the expat women had tried to outdo each other's abnormal and controlling sexual antics, Jack decided to consult Manolo, the ultimate Lothario, and ask why the women insisted on total control as it disturbed him. He drove gently down his track with his windows open whilst admiring the banks of flowers and listening to the breeze rattling the giant bamboos. At the tarmac road he turned westwards towards Palafrio to be confronted by a red sky that burnt his eyes with its beauty.

The girls in the office greeted him kindly and wanted to chat as there were no clients in sight, it being midweek and relatively late. He leaned over the counter and looked openly at 'Rent'. She was a Castilian blonde with light blue eyes and a harsh, manly voice. He was always amazed at her hair which had natural highlights of silver and gold indented within the blonde.

'So tell me, my lovely, why do Spanish girls only ever have one boyfriend?'

'*Señor* Jack, we can have more if we want but we are careful to select someone from our pool of friends so we know the person before they become our boyfriend.'

'That's very different from the English because we don't have that large pool of friends and if we have a pool we jump in too early. But tell me, lovely, why do all Spanish women smoke as it's so disgusting; just like kissing an ashtray.' Her friend 'Sales' had an opinion.

'That is unfair, Jack, none of us here in the office smoke.'

'True, but surely if you consider your friends it seems rife.' Nuria translated the word 'rife' before answering on their behalf.

'We agree you are correct, *señor*, and maybe it is a Spanish statistic but we do not know the answer.'

'I have an answer.' Jack wanted some controversy. 'It's because it makes them more assertive and more manly in a man's world, because the Spanish man rules the woman, agreed?' He was lucky they only threw pens and rulers at him.

'I take it all three of you disagree, but I also bet you are looking to marry and have babies soon to join that hierarchy.' Nuria was the only one to reply.

'Well, Mister Edmunson, you can be very perceptive sometimes, but also this is cruel as we want to be independent women until, of course, we catch our man!' They all laughed and knew it was true, but Spain was different from England in this respect. Jack felt he was onto a winner with the topic and so he asked a final question as their boss walked in.

'Spanish girls never walk around without bras especially here in town. Also they rarely go topless on the beach and so they are totally different from the *guiri* girls, agreed?' Manolo slapped him on the shoulders.

'Agreed, *amigo,* that is why I love the *guiri* women and the summer is coming my friend, this is good yes!'

'Yes *hombre*, yes, yes, yes!' As Jack said it, he noticed Nuria with her head down but definitely listening and could see her boss's antics hurt his loyal retainer. Manolo completed his thinking.

'On the beach, the local girls are good Catholics, modest and sensible but this is in direct contrast to the girls in the newspapers where you see so many legal adverts for bizarre forms of prostitution. So what is the truth about Spanish women, Jack?'

'The truth, Manolo, is your girls are all wonderful, beautiful and sensitive and deserve to find equally wonderful husbands.' A chorus of grateful cries came from the three young women and this made him beam. 'Also, because none of them smoke, they are all eligible for a date with me!' A similar chorus of opposition resulted.

'No way. Too old and not rich enough.' This helped him on his way out of the door and across the plaza to the Bar Fun Fun.

Two glasses of red wine were ordered as the friends relaxed on their stools and listened to the birds roosting in the trees.

'Manolo, revealing all your secrets if you want, please tell me why are the expat women such total control freaks?' His friend took a sip of wine and then some time to consider his answer.

'They appear to be working together but they also operate solo. I keep out of their way because they like you to believe they lead simple lives but I found that they are very devious behind your back. For example, whilst it appears to be a fun competition with a new plaything, they are also terribly jealous of each other. As individuals they must have unique issues with their husbands, but also with their own roles out here. They act as if on holiday but of course they are not. It's as if they are torn between their old independent lives with structure and their new dependent ones without structure. Basically, be careful as they are very volatile my friend and could be dangerous.' Jack stretched his back whilst sat on his stool and quietly absorbed the sound advice.

'Thank you *hombre*. I will remember that and make sure I am *funning* and only *funning*.' They sat and admired the pretty girls who strolled by, with many stopping to kiss Manolo, the Catalan Casanova. This was appreciated by Jack because when they were introduced they also kissed him. The kisses were always tender and gentle yet the experience was exhilarating as each woman had a different scent and touch. Not a perfumed scent but a more primitive and genetic vapour that exuded from their skins and alternatively excited or disappointed him. He asked Manolo whether he could feel these dissimilarities.

'*Hombre*! You crazy English. What can you do with a smell? I only look at their teeth and their titties.' At least five times Manolo performed an introduction using the same words.

'Jack, this woman is the most beautiful in Palafrio, but she is the only one who will not take me as her lover.' After the young lady had blushed or giggled he would hold her close and say to his friend.

'I love her, Jack.' All the women knew and accepted Manolo for what he was and enjoyed the praise because it was always genuine. Jack asked his enticing friend another serious question.

'As you have so many *friend girls*, why don't you settle down and get married *hombre*?'

'Because, *amigo*, none of the hundreds of women that I dated have ever told me that they love me. Until someone says those words, how can I know my reaction? If someone says it then they will give themselves 100 per cent and only then can you decide if you want to give everything in return.'

'Manolo that is prophetic and also very sad. I think you only find the perfect woman by having several wives, as they will all give you something different. In fact, I thought monogamy was a South American hardwood and I had married three different women at the same time before someone explained it to me.'

'Jack, this is good yes! Three wives. One to make love, one to cook and one to clean. Each can alternate to prevent boredom for you.'

'What about their needs, *amigo*?'

'Pfur. They should be happy to have a man and a home yes?'

'No! Maybe that is why no one has said they love you!'

Another beauty stopped to say hello.

She asked Manolo in Catalan, 'Who is the *guiri*?' She used Catalan so that Jack didn't understand the rudeness associated with the term. She could tell he was a *guiri* as he was dressed differently from the rest of the men in the square. He wore black sports socks, Jesus sandals, blue and white check shorts, a pink T-shirt and a straw trilby hat. One of their drinking companions in the bar was a Dutchman, nicknamed Pieter the pig, who worked with 1,200 sows in nearby Mont Raz. One evening Pieter called him Pata Negra, the black foot, just like Niiige's favourite wine. Jack had a defence though.

'Pieter you must understand that I am the fashion icon of the Baix Emporda and I dress like this because I want to be different.' Blunt Pieter who was eloquent in the English language actually agreed.

'You certainly are different, you fucking prat.' Undaunted, Jack expressed his individuality.

'It is easiest to be weak as a group, my piggy friend. For example, drinking too much booze and grossly overeating and hence being fat like you, it is acceptable, so you can let yourself go, Pieter, and follow my fashion to be in my peer group.' Pieter took his glasses off to wipe the tears of laughter from his eyes before replying.

'But who sets the standards for the peer group, Englishman?'

'Point taken, Pieter, but you know that my words are true. It's also easy to be strong as a group. For example, if you are threatened in your country with something like war then belonging and enjoying the group's protection are vital. Politicians form their own peer group. Do you remember recently when President Bush said in a speech about the economic crisis, "We don't fear the rise of the Asian economies, we welcome it". You have to read between the lines and you must interpret the opposite. The way he said it was in fear and was a covert message to other politicians. So, my friend, you may laugh at my fashion but really you want to dress like me.'

Pieter knocked him off his stool and as the *guiri* staggered he said,

'I would rather live like one of my pigs and wear pink everyday!'

Manolo and Jack had been *funning* for nearly two hours and despite the general acceptance in Spain that you can sit in a bar and nurse a single drink, they had participated in five *copas* apiece and were in serious need of some food to soak it up. They moved from their perches on the stools by the bar window to a table set on the plaza and ordered bread rubbed with raw tomato and garlic with a plate of the finest Iberian cured ham. The night was black above them and the reflections and glare of the plaza lights hurt their eyes. Jack had returned to serious mode, firstly because he was drunk and secondly, the nice girls had gone home to eat their dinners. The square was already deserted at nine-thirty as the summer fun that extended the opening hours wouldn't really commence until mid-July. Then it would last a frenetic six weeks before the Spanish decided it was too cold and retreated into their winter working lives. Jack nudged Manolo who was concentrating on eating his food which he treated as an appetiser before going home to eat properly at eleven.

'You see all the posters in the windows around here.' He waved wildly around the perimeter.

'I'm fed up with their lies in our society *amigo*. Whether it's posters or TV ads that tell you to spend 50 euros with a company to revive your ugly face.'

'What is the lie, *hombre?*' Manolo sat back as he munched on.

'The lie is how they show close-ups of perfect skin on beautiful models and highlight the removal of non-existent wrinkles generated by computer graphics. It's not real anymore! I am fed up with violent films and fucking swearing in fucking everything. I'm fed up with adverts for food implying it's good for you when in fact it's not natural anymore, and is 100 per cent processed crap. I abhor weight-loss pills that defy exercise and eating a good diet. The reality for fast weight loss by eating a pill and not changing your lifestyle is an impossibility. It's all lies, all rubbish, *amigo*. The TV, radio and newspapers predict and promote the impossible and we are happy to let them do it and worst of all we believe it.'

'You crazy English'. A little Rioja and you think you can change the world!'

'I do want to change the world! I'm fed up with pollution and I don't mean belching smoke from the exhausts of lorries although that is bad. No, I mean spiritual pollution not physical pollution, the constant cacophony of demeaning attitudes which are materialistic and dumb. Unwanted interference in my life and demands on me to make decisions that are becoming faster and faster.'

'You crazy English, so crazy!' Manolo had eaten two thirds of the shared food taking advantage of his friend's talkative abstinence.

'Yes! I am Crazy Jack; the man who believes you can do anything you want to, if you truly believe and I believe I can change the world. Look at mobiles. What a terrible affliction on our society hey, a disease just like a virus and a virus for which we have no cure. Electronic AIDS, passed from user to non-user and multiplying beyond our control. Text after text, call by call, it's all changing our genetic code. Now is a time of plenty in our little world that we take for granted and forget about nature. Forget our basic genetic need to eat, drink and live by multiplying and fighting over our being. I want to dominate my world in my way, sowing my seed as I am the king!' A very loud Jack had attracted Lluis the bar owner's attention and he swiftly gave the pair the bill and ushered them away so he could close up and go home.

As the month of May flowed towards June, Jack rolled with the waves and lived his life like the expats. The only regression into old life was the weekly telephone conversation with Joseph and the more frequent and more dependent calls from Soul Shiner. The more they talked, the more he depended on her and he would wait on her calls late into the evening and vice versa. The problem was one of circumstances combined with distance. She knew nothing about his extra-curricular activities with the expat women, but he did tell her about the odd trip to bars with Manolo. Just giving a tiny amount of detail meant she wanted more. He didn't believe she was jealous but she was inquisitive, like women are; whereas blokes can't envisage and don't need to be bothered about details, never mind understand them. One night she rang him at one in the morning.

'Poppet, are you awake?' He had turned on the torch kept by the side of his single bed and looked at his watch.

'Yes, lovely, of course I am; it's only one in the morning.' He collapsed back on the pillow and wondered why she wanted to talk.

'Sorry, poppet, but I was lying in bed thinking of you and I didn't know whether you were out or not.'

'That's okay. You know I'm usually in but came home late after a beer or three with Manolo in Hotel Yapanc.'

'Did you have fun, poppet?'

'Yes thank you.'

'Who was there?'

'Oh, just the usual crowd.'

'What does that mean?'

'The people who normally go in the same bar every Thursday evening.'

'Are you hiding something from me, Jack?'

'No why should I? The basketball was on TV with Barcelona playing a league game, the beer was good and I just went to relax with my friends.'

'So why won't you tell me who was there?'

'I will, if you don't get so stressed about it.' An exact tone was used for her reply.

'I won't. I'm not stressed at all.'

'Well that's good then, Harry.'

'So who was there?'

'There was Ferran the harbourmaster, Maria from Barcelona.'

'Who's Maria?'

'She's a woman who works there every weekend but is on holiday this week.'

'Is she nice?'

'She's a very nice and normal person. What's the matter tonight? Why have you rung me?' The line went quiet and he could hear her crying.

'Come on, lovely, what is it?' She gasped between sentences.

'I just feel so lonely poppet, I'm sorry. Just a bit pre-menstrual as well and you're there and I just thought of lots of things and it screwed me up, okay?'

'Okay, Harry, don't worry about anything. I'm still there for you, lovely. You can ring me anytime and say what you like.'

'I'm sorry, poppet, I don't want to seem weak, but life is hard on your own.'

'That's okay, don't worry about me. I'm writing my book and have to go out or I would go stir crazy.'

'Do you need someone else to have sex with Jack? I know how horny you can be.'

'Why do you ask?'

'Why don't you answer the question?'

'Okay, woah Harry, just slow down hey. God, you are touchy tonight. I am not looking to have sex with anyone, okay?'

'Okay, I'm sorry.'

'And stop saying I'm sorry all the time, you don't need to be sorry, just be you!' Soul Shiner twisted and turned every word he said and was also reading between the lines and then jumping to the wrong conclusions. If she knew about the expat women, she wouldn't bother ringing him. Jack knew her anxiety was dangerous to their friendship because they lived in different circumstances, but he would never let his friend down as she needed him.

'You see, Harry, we have a similar problem, you and I.'

'What do you mean, poppet?'

'I mean we both have a life but they are poles apart. Yours has a structure but mine doesn't. You have family and friends and therefore some form of commitment everyday, and I have none of those things. So we see life differently from different perspectives.'

'I suppose so, my knight. I miss you so much, Jack.'

'I miss you too, lovely.' Jack paused and picked up his manuscript.

'Listen to this, lovely; it's an excerpt from my book written today. "Western culture assumes God in a human form but in Chinese philosophy the Tao or *way* is the closest to an overall deity and in their culture it is formless. Taoism cultivates a philosophical awareness of life but in our culture it has to take a material form, something to worship, something solid, something like a person who in the West we absolutely need for our thought process. A person to talk to and to rely on in our small-mindedness but, now, in developing countries like China, they want to be capitalists. They want to be Western adopting our materialistic values. They want Prada, Rolex, KFC and Baskin Robbins and are rapidly junking their old values for material things. What silly fools."'

'That's nice poppet. I am proud of you, you know.'

'Thank you, lovely, but the point is, don't think solid and material in our relationship, but think instead of life and be philosophical about it.'

'Okay, poppet, but I suppose absence has made our relationship intensify and each of our perceptions of the true depth of our feelings increases all those emotional things around love.' Jack was shocked by the use of the 'love' word and quickly changed the subject back to uplifting spiritual topics.

'Symbols are also important in life. Did you know, in China a square is the earth and a circle is heaven?' She didn't. 'Also, the reverse image of the Nazi swastika represents brightness for Buddhists and, if you look at it,' Jack drew it on his notes, 'you have six lines and a centre making the magic seven.'

'Jack, it's so nice to hear you talk about all these things.' They wafted over Soul Shiner's head as Jack got more engrossed at 1:30 am.

'There are seven steps to becoming a Buddhist.'

'Jack, poppet, tell me you still want me.'

'I still want you, lovely.'

'And would you tell me if you didn't and if you found someone else?'

'Of course, Soul Shiner, remember I have always said I would be open and honest. I have always said that, haven't I?'

'Yes, my knight. You are a fantastic person and you are right. If you tell the truth you can get through anything. Night night, my knight, I just needed a chat.'

'Night Harry, sleep tight.' Jack replaced the receiver and immediately felt guilty. At 8 am the next morning she rang again after a brief six hours sleep. Jack couldn't see the time as the shutters effectively kept the night in and the daylight out. He was so tired he just picked up the phone without a light.

'*Hola?*'

'Small friendly voice here.' Soul Shiner sounded happier.

'I'm just ringing to apologise for last night, poppet. Really, I was out of order.'

'No you were fine, lovely; the time of the month doesn't help, does it?'

'No, but sorry, poppet. How are you today?'

'I have no idea yet, lovely.'

'Oh sorry, poppet, were you still asleep?'

'Yes but don't worry I normally get up at this time *mas ou menos.*'

'What does that mean? Is it Spanish?'

'Yes, lovely, it's commonly used to mean more or less, as an expression about how they live. It normally means twenty minutes either way or, in my case today, more like two hours.'

'I'm sorry, poppet; I just wanted to talk to you.'

'Don't worry, Harriet you can ring me any time.'

'The last few days have been dreadful, Jack, I can't get used to single life and I seem to be more forgetful.'

'That's normal, lovely, you're under a lot of stress. What's gone wrong this week?'

'Oh just little things really but they all add up and make me scared of life on my own.'

'Give me some examples.' Jack yawned as she started.

'Well I got home yesterday and I couldn't find my mobile so I looked everywhere and had to ring it in the end. I had only gone and left the thing in M&S in Chester so I had to drive all the way back in. Then, when I got home, I couldn't find my diary so I immediately presumed I had left that in the same place and went to the store a third time and, of course, they didn't have it!'

'Where was it then, lovely?'

'Under my car seat, it must have slid out of my handbag.'

'That's funny, you silly billy, but none of it is important.'

'I know they are little things to you, poppet, but they drive me mad. I can't turn the central heating off and so every night I wake up pouring sweat and I keep getting letters threatening to cut off the water and electric.'

'Why? You have standing orders or direct debits, don't you?' There was a pause.

'Well no, poppet, because if you give the Government all that information they can take your identity away.'

'You silly billy, it's not the government. They're only bills, lovely, you need to set up direct debits.'

'No I can't. I'm sorry. I just don't trust banks or computers, especially things like Internet shopping. I would never do that.'

'Soul Shiner you are living in the eighties and you need to get up to date. You must remember how slow and archaic everything was then? The closest you got to rudeness on the radio was when they said someone was a Dinky.'

'I remember, poppet; double income no kids yet. That applied to Matt and I then.' She didn't elaborate so Jack carried on.

'Now they need some new phrases like that. Linky and stinky come to mind to reflect what we have created and contradicts the rush towards money and material things. "Lost if not kind yourself" or "stupid if not kind yourself." How about it, Harry? Giving not taking, not all me, but all them. Does it work?'

'Yes I like the sentiments, Jack but I need to emphasise that I'm not a technophobe. I just don't use technology much.'

'You used the Internet last week lovely and lost all your technophobia.' She went shy remembering what Jack had enticed her into. She had stood in front of her Apple PC and used the webcam to video talk to Jack on Skype. When he had taken his shirt off to show her his chest he had refused to take his trousers off unless she joined in. Wanting to impress him, the prudish Harry had stripped revealing brand new bright red underwear.

'What have you got on?' Jack said in an incredulous voice that totally ruined her confidence and any plans he had for joint masturbation. Soul Shiner changed the subject to mundane day-to-day life and, after an hour of chat, she finally left him to get out of bed and think about his day starting with the inevitable coffee on the patio looking at his view.

Jack, Soul Shiner complicates your new life and you
are too sensitive to tell her. You need to leave her alone.
She is not on your path and she is not your Sun
Sharer so just let go.
You have to be cruel to be kind.

But he was too weak to let go and kept ignoring Nim. He realised she was pulling him back into his old life and could see his weakness but she was a good fall-back position; rich, pretty, great sex and seemingly spiritual, but he already had doubts on that score.

Saturday nights in Spain at the end of May gave an early indication of the crazy summer in store. Hotel Yapanc was renowned for its disco which started at midnight and always finished promptly at three-thirty, allowing the privileged guests some sleep after the revellers had 'de-partied' into the night. It was Manolo's territory, a place he called heaven. The women previously introduced to

Jack in Palafrio square would sidle up to Manolo and accept his comforting complements until eventually he settled on one to take into his house across the road and shag the night away. Jack chatted up some English girls from Sheffield who were too drunk to do anything with the man they nicknamed 'Spanish Jack', except to use him to hold them upright but, thankfully, they only vomited copiously when outside. They were the very antithesis of the Spanish girls who drank little alcohol and were always polite but not interested as he was too old. However, he was still young enough to enjoy watching their sensual dances on the bar whilst being sprayed with water by one of the owners. After a couple of hours there was only so much sexual frustration he could stand even when pissed and after arranging to meet Manolo he staggered out to walk the two miles home and recover some equilibrium in the peace of the moonlight.

The next day they met at midday and sat on the now pristine and quiet hotel terrace for their first beer. Jack asked about Manolo's latest beautiful companion.

'So what was she like and where is she now, *amigo*?'

'*Hombre*, she was magnificent and now she sleeps the deep sleep of a woman satiated by a truly great lover!'

'Modest too, *hombre*.' Smirking and clinking their bottles of Voll Damm beer in mutual appreciation they watched as a fight started on the beach. An old Spanish couple were in conflict with a handicapped women in a wheelchair, who was desperate to get to the sea near the end of the specialist wooden ramp that ran from the promenade. The couple wanted to spread their towels in the same location and so they were arguing loudly in the Spanish style. There was much gesticulating, back turning and returning to shout something else but after a few raw minutes it was all over and forgotten with each side settled happily alongside each other.

'It would never end like that in England, Manolo. Our rows are calm and controlled and as they intensify people deliberately use words that are more hurtful so the parties bear a grudge for the rest of the day and let it rankle.'

'You English are all the same, *hombre*. You rush to the beach to argue with your families. Then you sit and go bright red. In the Far East they use their umbrellas during the sunny days wherever they go and put on face-whitening cream. In Australia they have public areas where they spray you with factor-forty sun oil.'

'What about the Catalans then?' Asked Jack.

'That is easy, *amigo*, we tell you English to protect yourself with sun cream and then we go and sit out without bothering to do anything except take lunch for three hours when the UVA is at its peak.'

'Very astute, Manolo.' Jack surveyed the beach and could see it was true but he knew that after May they would also take precautions. He pointed up the promenade.

'Look at these women coming our way. They are so pretentious. Look at their deportment and how they look at the people they pass. They are ignoring them, not welcoming and open, but trying to be superior which is something they are not. They have this requirement to give them their self-esteem and maintain their equilibrium. Look at them Manolo, strolling on the Yapanc prom with their designer sunglasses and compare them to their children who are open and have a purity of spirit that is unrestrained with a simple intent.'

'I agree Jack, but it applies to many people here, especially in the summer. Notice the smart BMWs and Mercedes that you never see during the rest of the year. Look at the influx of the middle classes who identify each other by their appearance, the way they speak and the things they speak about. They talk pseudo intelligently about many things but fundamentally they accept the differences in each other's bad opinions.' Jack argued from a different point of view.

'I can see the outward symbols but they are just badges of honour in a crazy world at civil war. Whether it be over cars, houses or even their type of job. Their position in life must be visible to all to maintain it. It's about competition and not any subjective hidden traits. Physical things make a nice person in their world but anyone can make money, it's easy.'

'Hoy Jack! How can you say that? Making money is hard.' Jack tapped his friend's chest with a single finger.

'That's why you will always be poor, Manolo. Listen to me. Making money is easy. Firstly, work for yourself, then buy something and sell it for more than you paid. You know you can do it, but you don't have to think about it, you just have to do it. In fact, you don't even need to be intelligent to make money. You just need to be intelligent about *how* to make money.' Manolo was puzzled by Jack's view on business as he was only used to selling a simple service that he found easy by being nice. He wanted to understand more.

'What would you buy and sell in this world of easy money?' Jack knew the answer immediately.

'Anything, *amigo*. Anything that you are interested in and already exists, but you must do it better than someone else. I saw true capitalism, true buying and selling in China. Communism in China is a myth now. They dumped their history and culture sixty years ago when Chairman Mao started the Cultural Revolution and threw the teachers into the fields to work. They then decided twenty years ago that they needed capitalism and now they control half the world's Gross Domestic Product. So it's simple; buy and sell well. There are 1.2 billion Chinese and they're all fighting to make money anyhow and without strict rules. They don't have our self-restraint and they don't have their history holding them back. The real shame is you see all the wealth in their fabulous shops and banks but where has all the profit gone? To the people? Bollocks! To a select few as it is dog eat dog, *hombre,* and you find the same rules about making money in different countries, with different politicians and ruling classes. It's obscene but equally it's real life. Japan takes Western inventions and makes them better; China copies them and makes them worse.' Manolo watched a beautiful woman walk by wearing a bikini and a semi-transparent beach dress.

'Look Jack, this is real life. My God, what a beautiful woman. You need an afternoon in bed with someone like that to knock the shit out of your head!'

'Find me one that cares and it might work, but just shagging is no use to me, *hombre*. I am far too sensitive.' Jack was frustrated as he watched her swaying arse and so he returned to philosophising as a substitute for sex.

'The Chinese never admit "I don't know", they prefer to lie and tell you anything so as not to lose face. I loved The Far East but Melanie hated "all those nasty little people". She missed the point that they were entitled to be different, are different and will stay different through our generation. All she could see was how people ignored each other in Japan, standing back to back on the subway, and then she hated the mandatory spitting on the floor in China. You see, she missed the fucking point. The dignity and politeness of Japanese culture, coupled with the need to be perfect and work sixteen hours a day if necessary. The open friendliness in China, coupled with their laziness and happiness to live in shit and the imperfect.' Manolo loved it when Jack talked like this.

'*Hombre*, you crazy English. I think you need to write to let your imagination flow. If you worked in a normal job you would suffer, penned into a life of drudgery, but most people are happy with that. This is good yes?'

'Of course it's good, as it suits most people, but really the environment interests me more than anything as nearly half the world's jobs depend on forests and agriculture. That is an amazing figure in itself. There are new diseases and a resurgence of old ones flaring up again, and all induced by how we use the land and also by climate change. Did you know eleven out of the last twelve years rank amongst the warmest since records began in 1850, and so it could be an exponential problem that follows the chaos theory? We are already fucked and can't do anything about it. Our only solution is technology to help us reduce greenhouse gases, to allow us to live safely in the terrible environment we are creating. It's like the world recession, it just needs a little spark to set it all off, like the current lack of confidence. A crisis in environmental terms will be triggered by a volcano or something, a simple natural disaster that sends dirt into the atmosphere and changes our world.'

Manolo asked, 'Did your spirit guide tell you this, *hombre*?'

'No, of course not, but I see and hear things that others don't and and if I am right then I am a saviour and if I am wrong, you can carry on calling me the crazy English.' Manolo grunted with disbelief and so Jack leaned forward. 'You need to think about things like that and simplify your life.'

'How can I simplify my life, *amigo*, I am an estate agent and I like women. What is simpler than that?' Jack was exasperated as his friend was a great listener but he really wanted an argument.

'A simple life? You? Dump your three mobiles and stop the constant communications, *hombre*. They require you to make constant decisions so fast without all the facts that you can easily be wrong. You work hard and pay to improve your life but isn't it a false pretence? Most people work harder and see their children less. They pay to listen to someone else's opinions on fifty TV programmes, pay to communicate more frequently about nothing and learn some unimportant information quicker. There is no anticipation or joy in waiting for real information of real value. There is no excitement, no forward planning, and no thinking, so it all gets dumb and dumber. Really all this crap is cheating people of their humanity!'

'Bravo, Jack, please go and write your book now and get it all down before you forget it.' They laughed into the sun and asked for the bill as Jack went quiet whilst staring at the horizon.

'Nim, I have lived my dream since my marriage failure, but dreams aren't real, are they? I have lived my dream but dreams aren't reality.'

> *That's not true Jack. You can make your dreams come true. Everything you have told Manolo can come true and your path is to tell that truth to the world.*

He finished his reverie dumping a five-euro bill on the silver platter and stood to go.

'One last tale from the Far East that reminds me of you, Manolo. The Chinese emperors had their concubines delivered to their bedroom rolled in a carpet. What choice an Emperor had, as the number of concubines in the palace varied from 80 to 3,000, depending on how much money he had to keep them all happy in the shops and at the hairdressers. Imagine the arguments and fights between all of those women so they could earn the honour of being shagged and then imagine the gloating afterwards. But his eunuch would always ask him if he wanted to keep the "seed of the dragon", i.e. the spunk. If he said no, then the girl would have to endure a host of herbal remedies and acupuncture to get rid of the baby dragon.

'An evening in Beijing would have been like you last night as the Emperor walked around a room full of girls. "Hello, darling, do you fancy a bit of seed? Do you fancy licking a dragon tonight?" He must have been constantly tired like you today, *amigo*, and imagine how desperate were some of the concubines as they would never get a crack at him. Although I suppose a nice life, shopping, loads of friends and no sex might actually appeal to a lot of women!'

'Was his penis the dragon, Jack?'

'No, he was symbolically the dragon, not his dick. Find a nice Chinese girl, Manolo, and put a new slant on things. Hoy!' As they slowly shook hands Manolo made a parting comment.

'Jack you can't stand small living, that is, living small; you want to be part of something bigger, *amigo*.'

'That is very apt, *hombre*. How did I manage to become a big man in a small world before I walked away? Going to England brings all the hurt back and crushes me. I don't think I can do that again.'

They parted with a friendly slap on each other's shoulders. Practical Manolo went to have a sexy siesta with a woman who was also a new paying client, whilst spiritual Jack went to continue his writing but, of course, that wasn't real work in most people's eyes.

Real Life established itself once again, far away from the madness of Cheshire and the expat women and Jack started to relax as the heat of summer encroached into the nights.

Occasionally, he saw Manolo's lonely mother whiling away her time in her allotment and he would walk across a tiny bridge made of railway sleepers to keep her company. One perfect morning under a clear blue sky, he prevented the eighty year old from climbing some tall wooden step ladders to pick *nesperos,* a sweet small yellow fruit that resembled a plum. He went up instead under the hot sun, competing with the ants and the birds for the tasty crop. Although she held up a basket in wavering arms he couldn't reach down to drop in the fruit and so he squeezed them into the pockets of his shorts and ran up and down the ladder.

Jack would sit outside his simple home every morning and talk to her peacocks, pheasants and cockerels by imitating their calls and they would talk back as he said his seven pleas. He kept to his ideal simple life by walking to Palafrio across the fields, stopping to admire centuries-old terebinth trees and enjoy the delicate and fragrant smell of their resin. They had been used to mark ancient roads to sacred spots, as mentioned in the book of Genesis and had been valued for turpentine and soothing balms for over 7,000 years, but now they appeared to be indicating Jack's true path.

He used the time that nobody can buy, to chat to fish market girl and the Post Office clerk, because that was real life. They wanted and had time to chat and not rush you through your purchase. He still used the Internet to buy things like tickets to the Cap Roig concert festival to see the hip-hop group Facto Delafe y las Flores Azules, but was happy wasting twenty minutes to collect them in the bank, showing his passport and credit card before giving a signature just to collect some tickets.

'Only in Spain,' he thought.

When he handed over some of the tickets to Manolo's three staff, they gave him the money immediately which was a pleasant surprise as he was used to women taking money rather than giving it.

In the evenings he choose to drive into the town centre to avoid a dangerously dark walk home, but he still needed to take care after a few *copas* to avoid the extraordinarily high kerbs that were found everywhere. These were seemingly designed just high enough to trash the front spoiler on your car and to total your alloy wheels. He would stop and watch groups of men playing Toss the Peg, *trobada de bitlles* in the sandy, dusty squares as the sun set through the trees, and he compared it to skittles played in the alleys of country pubs in England. The centre of town itself was an entertainment if you took the time to sit and watch from the stool of the Bar Fun Fun. A boy of three sat on his manic brother's bicycle crossbar, gripping the handlebars in abject fear as they raced through the plaza, narrowly avoiding the evening wanderers. He watched children skipping down a steep street, happy to be carried away by the slope and knew that adults could never skip in such total abandon, enjoying the inertia of their emotions. At least once a week the older people of the town gathered in the square to listen to traditional bands playing Catalan folk songs or ball music. They waltzed and twirled gaily, excited and rejuvenated in the summer atmosphere, a spiritual happiness giving them new youth for a few fleeting hours. The cheap Centre Fraternal bar was swollen by holiday visitors at the weekends who pledged their allegiance to the institute by paying 100 euros for a two-year membership and then a further 25 euros a year to be served cheap food and drink at half the price of the other bars. What was gained in the discounted friendship of the same acquaintances every night, was lost in the lack of flexibility to explore. Ideal for a man ten or more years older than Jack but too slow for his tastes as they sat playing chess or cards and cheering the Barcelona basketball team to yet another easy victory.

He enjoyed the Fun Fun bar the most, eyeing up and challenging the demure women who would remain shy but really wanted to return his look and smile for a bit of fun in their lives. In the main they were unable to participate in his games and were afraid of their hostile husbands' reactions. He would order *pipas de calabeza*, pumpkin seeds, and tell his drinking partners how they reputedly put 'lead in your pencil' whilst downing three-eighths of a bottle of red, because that was the unit of sale instead of a half.

Finally, the heat and dust took its toll on the level of customer service received in many establishments as it came to the holiday season. Many times it reached an appalling state as they seemingly couldn't be bothered about anything as the *mañana* principle applied more frequently. He had a car problem with his satnav and so he took it to the nearest garage thirty miles away in Vic. After waiting four hours he drove it home to discover on arrival that his lights and indicators wouldn't work anymore. As for the satnav, well he still drove a hundred yards to the side of the road according to his LCD display.

So summer approached, the dust thickened and Spanish life dawdled to a standstill.

'*Real Life*' established itself again and the refrain 'only in Spain' was used more frequently.

5
Living the dream

oco is a very useful word in Spanish as it means crazy. Crazy drivers, crazy *guiris* and the start of a crazy summer where thirty-three degrees Centigrade is normal, but the effect of this torrid heat drives the locals a little abnormal, a *poco loco*.

Refreshing cold showers are obligatory three times a day as an attempt to remain reasonably normal mentally and reasonably fresh physically. The first is taken in the morning following a hot and sweaty night's sleep. The second is after a siesta to wash the mind awake before going back to work and the third is in the evening before an aperitif with your true friends, followed by a very late dinner any time after ten. The tripartite soldier's daily routine of showering, shitting and shaving is ignored as they are governed by the weather. Trips to the toilet reduce as less food is eaten to drop one's body heat and avoid competing with the air temperature. The shaving increases as a hard and coarse beard proliferates under the sun bolstered by the calcium in the water.

Even the English had to follow the Mediterranean rules to survive the summer, adapting both their body clock and their mental attitude whilst their physical self changed of its own accord. Nobody really stirred until ten in the morning after which all their activities were compressed into the three and a half hours before it was time for lunch and a siesta. The place then slumbered the heat away, apart from the *guiris* on the beaches and in the restaurants, but even the *guiris* took an involuntary and relaxing siesta lying on the burning sands as they turned pinky-red and became affectionately known as *gambas,* prawns by the locals. After 6:30 pm, everywhere would gradually wake again, building to a crescendo of activity throughout the evening as the Catalans came alive in a wonderful mix of over-emotive happiness and pure gratitude for life.

This lifestyle left English Jack with too much time on his hands, leading to too much thinking.

That cerebral emotion had terrified him for quite a few months until he came to terms with it by realising you don't have to be scared of dropping out of a fast English lifestyle. In the interim, it meant that he became more *loco* than the locals, experimenting with outrageous behaviour to truly discover who and what he was, as he wallowed in the heat of time. After swimming naked near the solitary El Castille beach, he would drive home without drying or dressing and enjoy the feel of the breeze on his body through his wide open car windows and the freedom of spirit as he rebelled. Once parked at his *barraca* he would find a private spot under the pine trees to take a shit, revelling in standing with his legs open and squeezing it out, unencumbered by a toilet and happy to be part of nature again that took him back a thousand years. As he defecated, he listened to the onshore sea breeze as it began to build in the treetops and rattle the needles searching for the rising heat eddying off the red earth. He was content that he had fed the ants before washing his arse with the hosepipe and swilling the dry and white sea salt off his brown and now thin body. He felt at one with nature for the first time in his life and listened to the winds as his behaviour took stranger twists and turns pushed by the messages held in the air.

Most of the day he walked around naked, confident that visitors couldn't creep up on his exposed spot and occasionally he shaved another pattern on his hairy body as a talking point with the women he looked to shag. First it was an S on his left chest copied from the Duchess's thatch and then the whole of the right calf. More visibly he used his hair clippers to create a thin line down the left side of his head that bent its way an inch above the ear following the contours of the normal but receded hairline. He even shaved his pubic hair making an exact square above his cock that was short and spiky to the touch. As the heat increased during the day he desperately wanted sex and feeling deprived he would wank himself with baby oil whilst standing in front of the bathroom mirror and thinking of the time he had fucked Soul Shiner leaning on the sink. His problem was not a lack of sex but irregular sex compressed into a solitary week in the month with the expats.

Soul Shiner, the small friendly voice, rang him most days to relieve her loneliness and share her problems about the divorce with Matt, otherwise known as 'the bastard', or to chat about the girls' demands for independent summer holidays at a camp in the USA. The conversations started to follow a turgid pattern.

'Hello, my knight, how are you today?'

'I'm excellent thanks, just a bit lonely.'

'Don't be lonely, poppet. I can pop over to see you if you like. Pop and see my poppet!' Jack thought carefully about involving her in his Spanish life even if she was lonely too.

'That's very kind of you, my lovely, but I'm thinking of coming back to see Joseph and so I hope to see you soon anyway.' She was disappointed as always but rarely pushed it any further and so she gave him her news.

'Matt has asked if I want to stay in the house, so what should I do, my knight?' Again Jack remained non-committal.

'Firstly, you silly billy, go and get yourself a solicitor because you'll need one eventually, even if it's only to file your divorce papers. Secondly, find out the maximum amount of money you could get if you sold all the assets, including his shares and things, and then take him to court. Finally, be nice but at the same time be extremely hard.' She was worried about the social stigma of divorcing because she was now ostracised by her ex-friends, with Melanie in the background stirring up the odd rumour about her and Jack. Being 'divorced' was not the 'done' thing in her mind, and so she had started to say she was single if asked.

'Poppet, I feel like a social leper nowadays and when I bump into someone downtown, I feel that I have to justify my life all of the time.'

'That's perfectly normal, Harry. Stop worrying about it as the feeling will go away after a few years. Trust me; it is just a phase you have to go through.'

'A few years? My God, Jack, that's a terrible stigma to live with.'

'But it's in your mind, Harriet, and not how people see you or talk behind your back. It's in your mind only, my lovely.'

After half an hour of unstinting support Jack would hint at the lateness of the call as it usually commenced at midnight his time as she went to bed at eleven her time and that was when she felt the most vulnerable. Curled up and comfortable under her duvet, it was the perfect moment for Harriet to speak to her poppet, her love and selfishly ensure an untroubled night's sleep. Her longing for his company became more needy as the weeks passed by and the depths of her imagined love increased dramatically, enhanced by the need for all-embracing sex again.

'I really miss you, poppet. I could talk for hours about nothing. It's so good that I found a telephone company to give me such cheap call charges.' Jack stifled many yawns during the conversations, but resolved to be available for his best friend in England whilst cursing the previous late-night drinking session when he had mutually supported his best friend in Spain. He was caught between the caring friendships of two wonderful people and it was making him incredibly fatigued. Sometimes she would ask very pertinent questions from afar as if reading his mind.

'Poppet why don't you *woo* me anymore?'

'I do *woo* you, Harry; I sent you a postcard last week, didn't I?'

'I mean really woo me, by talking nicely to me. Remember like in May when you stayed here and spoke romantically about love and life. You know how much I love and miss your romantic words.' Jack carried the 'love' dilemma with a joke rather than a blunt and honest answer.

'Woo woo,' he cried down the telephone, imitating the owl that hunted around his house every night.

'Not that sort of wooing, poppet. You know how much I want you. Can I please come and see you, Jack? I get so lonely, poppet.' He tried to put off the inevitable visit.

'You can, but I am really busy with the book. I'm on a roll, Harry, and so it would upset my rhythm if you came across just now.' He emphasised *just now*.

'Please, poppet, just for a weekend, so I can see where you live.' He knew he couldn't resist much longer, but desperately needed to keep his local life private.

'Maybe next month, Harry, if you really want to, but I suggest we stay in the hilly plain above the airport so that we don't waste any time travelling all the way here. It will also be better as we can avoid some of the heat if we are high up in the hills and away from the busy beaches.' She was overjoyed.

'That would be fantastic, so long as I can see you. That is all that matters, poppet. Can I go and book the flights please?' Now he had no more excuses.

'Of course you can, Harry. I wasn't being awkward. I will be absolutely delighted to see you and I'll take you up to a beautiful place called Rupit in the Collsacabra.'

'Thank you, poppet, I love you and miss you so much.' The love word worried him again but he replied positively so that he could get some sleep.

'JFDI and send me an email to tell me which weekend it is. Any will do during July as I have no plans and all the time in the world for you, my lovely.' Soul Shiner thanked him continuously until she rang off leaving Jack lying on his back in the dark justifying her trip to himself. He did love her and her company as they had so much in common and, of course, the sex was fantastic. However, he knew deep down that his love was never going to be strong enough to match hers and then he drifted off to sleep before Nim could tell him where he was going wrong. In fact, Nim was forcibly kept from his thoughts as the heat and craziness increased during the month and the guide's previous good advice was pushed to the lowest of priorities in Jack's life.

Just like Nim, Karina now seemed a distant dream but remained a constant longing deep inside of him. Joseph he spoke to once a week and he resigned himself to losing the close relationship with his junior Sun Sharer. So the four protagonists for his emotions and spirit were kept at bay as the practicalities of *loco* life took over.

Jack always ensured he had a long siesta every Saturday afternoon now that the weekenders from Barcelona had returned to throng Hotel Yapanc's disco. His old and constant refrain of *fifty down, fifty to go,* was wearing thin even in his own mind, as Sunday was always a write-off as he tried to recover from the lack of sleep and excess alcohol. Even if he left the weekly party to go to bed at a reasonable time, his body clock made him wake up early as he had lost the habit of youth and was unable to sleep into the afternoon.

'*Hombre!*'

'*Amigo!*' They could barely hear each other above the Latino music, even with their heads bent close together.

'Jack, why don't you stay at my house across the square tonight? Don't drink and drive, *amigo.*'

'Thank you, Manolo, but if I stayed with you I wouldn't be able to sleep at all with all that thumping of the bed against the wall and I would lie awake feeling frustrated for an hour.'

'*Hombre,* you mean three hours not one.' They were grinning and excited as the place filled up so that by one in the morning you had to force your way out and escape to the exterior summer bars where you could catch your breath and buy a drink in the relative coolness. Jack homed in on a couple of forty-year-old English women and managed to chat up the prettier one called Amanda above the beat of the music. He knew she was interested by her body language; the casual arm around his neck as they talked, the hands around his waist to stop herself staggering from the excess booze and, after a slow and sweaty dance to fast music, there was an inevitable kiss and tentative movement of hands close to breasts and groins. He told her he was a writer which was the best chat-up line he had ever used and gravely showed her the S on his chest which he swore was the symbol of a secret society he couldn't reveal on risk of death. He shouted above the thumping din.

'Shall we walk around the harbour to cool down, my lovely?' She turned away momentarily to converse with her best, and soon to be lonely, friend before slightly slurring her response.

'Okay, Jack, I trust you to escort me but you mustn't do anything that I wouldn't do!' He kissed her again and put his hand on her right breast as he pushed his hard cock against her groin.

'Well, Amanda, that's about everything then!' She giggled and grabbing his hand she led him swaying through the pack and into the relatively cold night air at a mere twenty-five degrees.

'God, Jack, is it always so hot in there?' She welcomed the walk to cool down as her body was sexually warming up. They were walking with arms held around each other along the elevated harbour wall and staring across at the bright lights illuminating the heaving pile of people a few hundred yards away.

His left hand drifted onto her arse as he replied, 'I know the heat is incredible, isn't it? Not that I come down to the disco very often, of course.'

She turned and kissed him slowly before strolling on and commenting, 'I bet you come here all the time, to chat up the tourists. In fact, you're probably the local Casanova.' Her hand slid up inside the back of his T-shirt to test his muscles.

'No, of course not. You misjudge me totally! My best friend Manolo is the local Casanova. I sadly have no women in my life; I'm a writer and am still looking for my Sun Sharer.' She stopped and turned him towards her bringing her hand around inside his shirt and onto his hairy chest. Kissing him deeply for a few minutes she wrapped her tongue around his and then dropped her hand down to his trousers and started undoing his flies.

'You are so nice, Jack, and also so big!' She had his cock in her hand with her confidence buoyed up by the drink. Jack wanted her and took control.

'Come with me onto these big rocks on the seaward side. I promise you a very special view.' They clambered onto the rocks where they were now hidden and settled into a dark cleft. Immediately he started to strip her.

'My God, Jack, I have never had sex outside before and certainly never in Spain.' She was giggling drunkenly. He had her cunt in his hand and a nipple in his mouth and therefore couldn't comment but just wanted her wet enough to put his cock in as soon as possible. As he attempted to insert it she pulled away and lay back on the rock but then she pulled him forward and started to rub his prick against her clitoris.

'Use your hand to hold your cock, Jack, and rub it against my clitty, but kiss me as you do it.' He obliged and hoped the foreplay would end quickly as he needed to fuck her brains out and loose his load of semen and with it his pent-up frustrations. She was getting excited and wet so he tried to put his prick in her again.

'No don't, please, I have problems with penetration. I'm sorry, but can you just rub your knob really hard against my clitty.' He didn't want to but he was a gentleman and could foresee that a rape charge wouldn't be particularly nice with the hardened local police who adopted harsh Fascist tactics. So he got her more excited and purely by chance he slapped his knob hard against her clitoris and the area immediately below it.

'Oh Jesus Christ, Jack, please slap it hard again that was incredible.' So he held his cock and slapped her cunt with it and the harder he did, it turned her on more, whilst it turned him off completely. However, it worked as she gasped and came, jerking upright and clutching onto him in ecstasy.

'You're so good Jack; I have never come so well before.'

'That's great Amanda but shall I put it inside now?'

'No, just slap it against me again.' So he continued to rub and slap and she had two more orgasms before deciding the rough rock was cutting into her chubby arse and demanded to go back to the disco. He had failed to have an orgasm which was getting into a bad habit after experiencing the same problem with Soul Shiner and the expats on many occasions. They walked quickly back to the thrumming hotel as they were now unencumbered by arms or kisses and with a brief peck on arrival she went off to find her friend leaving Jack feeling grossly used as he slumped in a blue cane chair on the terrace.

Nuria glided up, still dancing to the tune blasting away inside before she too collapsed on a chair next to him.

'Hello, Jack. Did I see you arrive with a girl?'

'No, lovely, not any girl it was my friend Dutch's sister. You know Dutch, don't you. We were just chatting in the cool out here.' He gently touched her arm. 'How about your luck tonight? Have you *copped* yet? Or are you still saving yourself for Manolo?'

'What is *copped*, Jack?'

'It's when someone leans over to talk in your ear like this and then accidentally kisses you.' He kissed her lightly on the lips and was surprised that she didn't pull away.

'Is that all it means, Jack? It seems a strange word for something so insignificant.'

'No, lovely, there is more to *copping* than that, but more importantly you need to explain why a kiss is so insignificant.' He looked up to see Manolo rolling his way towards them.

'Before we can discuss it privately, here comes your boss so I'll have to show you more *copping* later.' She immediately deferred to the Catalan male by offering him her seat and then took herself off towards the nearest bar where she could keep a surreptitious eye on them both.

'*Hombre*, where did you take that fat English woman? I saw you going out towards the harbour.'

'Nowhere, *amigo*, and she was chubby not fat. You know how bad the light is inside; it makes everything seem more beautiful hey. Anyway, we just needed to get a breath of air.'

'And did you give her a breath of air, *amigo*?'

'Unfortunately not. She breathed out a lot but I was not allowed to breathe in.' He punched his friend's arm and pointed to a dazzlingly beautiful blonde squeezing out of the door in a short and tight black dress. 'What about her, *amigo*?'

'So, you have seen my new Swedish date, Jack? I cannot lie,

hombre, she is already my lover.'

'That makes one hell of a change; you have never said that before. When did you meet her?'

'Today at lunchtime and then she came to see me in my office after work.' Jack was very confused by how sudden it all seemed.

'So when did you make love to her?'

'I fucked her on the photocopier after work tonight. No one else knows as my girls had all gone home!'

'You dirty bastard, Manolo. That is definitely fast reproduction *amigo*!' A happy Manolo stood and went to escort the Swedish bombshell to his house and as soon as he had departed Nuria returned again to sit next to jealous Jack. He could see she was upset as her gaze followed the couple past the front of the restaurant and across the square.

'I suppose he is taking her to his house for sex again, Jack?' He shifted uncomfortably wanting to defend the indefensible but she didn't need an answer. 'I went back to the office tonight as I had forgotten my mobile and saw him fucking her.' She had tears in her eyes. 'He doesn't care about me, Jack. I try so hard for him and he doesn't notice.' Jack put his arms around her for the first time and smelt the pungent sweat from the dancing.

'I'm sorry Nuria. One day he will wake up and realise what a wonderful woman you are and regret his past and maybe then he will only want one person in his life. But it will take an extraordinary event to change his current path.' She sniffed and traced the thin shaved line above his left ear.

'Why have you done this to your hair, Jack?'

'It's just for fashion but ever since the shark attacked me I use it as a reminder to make the most of my life as I can see it every hour of every day.'

'No! When were you bitten by a shark?'

'Last year Nuria, it was a terrible shock. I can show you the scar if you would like me to prove it.' She put her hands on his chest and smiled from very close.

'So is seeing your shark bite part of this crazy English ritual called *copping?*' He kissed her gently.

'You are a beautiful sensitive woman Nuria and you should trust me because *copping* is much more sensual than looking at a huge scar.' She returned the kiss, tasting sweet and pushing her little tongue delicately into his mouth. He continued to probe with his own tongue whilst holding her hands and linking their fingers in a sexual way to resemble their bodies joining together in love. He whispered in her ear. 'In England we say "trust me I'm an estate agent".' She didn't realise that he meant the opposite as she could only see the positives of a sexy man who wanted her when the untrustworthy Manolo had mocked her again.

'*Señor* Jack, why don't you show me your beautiful *barraca* and tell me more about *copping?*' They kissed again and quickly he pulled her to her feet to walk hand in hand to his car, watched surreptitiously by Manolo who was closing his shutters. In the space of five minutes they walked into Jack's house and she went to stand in the dim lounge, lit by a single yellow side lamp, to admire the view into the tunnel of the night.

'Jack, I never knew that something could be so beautiful.' He walked up behind her and slid his hands up to her breasts.

'Are we talking about the view or about you, Nuria?' He turned her around and looked for a reaction. She coyly dropped her head ever so slightly and so he lifted her chin with two fingers and then slid them across her olive-coloured cheek to stroke her mousey grey hair.

'Jack, you must know a Spanish woman does not give herself lightly. No *juegas* my friend because I have no boyfriend and I am always very serious about sex. I don't commit to anyone, you know. In fact I don't do this very often, if at all.' He totally ignored her seriousness and started to undress her, quickly dragging her onto the settee as his single bed was too old and dank to entertain on. She gave way to everything he did as revenge against Manolo and although Jack realised it, he could only think about coming inside her. They were both frustrated so they physically fucked each other without shame or remorse, but it was totally unsatisfactory in their minds. Once he had come, Jack could only think of getting rid of her but she lay under him as his cock grew smaller and started to talk about her mundane and strict Catholic life.

'No one understands me, Jack, especially your friend Manolo. He thinks I will wait for him forever.'

'Did you and he make love?'

'Yes, it was wonderful as he was such a beautiful lover. I was in heaven.' Jack shifted uncomfortably with shame, but also at his own lack of performance and selfishness. Nuria was stroking his back with her fingers as he had his face in her breasts gently licking a nipple to pass the time and seem interested. She felt a lump on his shoulder and because of the position of his body she could see to squeeze the large black head. Immediately his erection subsided and he pushed himself angrily onto his side.

'Stop please. It's just like monkeys behave for God's sake.' He went quiet as she sat up shocked by his reaction. He needed to explain.

'I'm sorry, really I am. It took me back to my old marriage and I used to hate that.'

Nuria struggled silently to her feet and started to dress quietly. As she moved he smelt her; a nasty sweaty odour from her armpits and the thatch of pubic hair that he now found distasteful.

Throwing on his own clothes, he politely rushed her out as she started saying, 'No one understands me, Jack, especially Manolo,' but that was the last thing he needed to hear, and so he drove her quickly and silently back to her car in Yapanc, giving her a cursory peck goodnight before returning to Manolo's *barraca* to fall into a guilty and uneasy sleep.

On the Sunday night an ashen-faced Jack was so tired that he retired to bed at nine as the locals promenaded in Yapanc before drinks at ten with dinner at eleven. At the same time the English tourists duly finished their *postres* and gazed in amazement at the crazy Spanish. It was therefore about midnight and after three hours solid sleep when the telephone rang.

'Fuck me, Harriet. Give a man a break, please.'

'*Hola J*, is that you? You sound strange. Are you upset about something? It's Pippa speaking.'

'Sorry, I was fast asleep, lovely, but I admit that I am strange.'

'*J*! It's only midnight. What are you doing in bed so early? You haven't *copped* have you?'

'No! Pippa I am absolutely physically knackered because of all my swimming and cycling today and also because I'm so emotionally drained from writing my book.' As he turned onto his side he was also thinking, and the shagging and booze doesn't help.

'Why, Pip? Are you jealous?'

'No, Jack, of course not. I'm happily married.' He took this as a sign that Roland was hanging around at the other end and so he talked more carefully.

'Good. That's very good, Pipsqueak, happily married is good.' Jack yawned and wondered what was the point of the call so that he could go back to sleep.

'Jack, don't go to sleep on me, I heard you yawn. Listen, the weather tomorrow is supposed to hit forty degrees and we are due to have a heatwave all week. Something about the Sahara you know. Anyway, I'm having a barbecue on Tuesday so we want to invite you to come and join us.' He took it that Rolly was definitely listening and politely asked.

'Who will be there?'

'You know who *J*, our friends as usual. So can you come?'

'I would be delighted and thank you for your kind invitation. Is it six for drinks by any chance?'

'Of course! You really are half asleep.' She missed the sarcasm. 'See you Tuesday *J*. Bye, darling. See you soon.' *J* collapsed onto the bed and threw a sheet over himself now that it had gone cooler.

'Forty degrees. Fuck me. I hate the fucking heat.' But before he could fall back asleep he had a visitor.

Jack this is becoming a pattern. Once a month you are invited to meet the expats and once a month you are invited to meet each woman individually. How many other men have they taken into their circle?

'Nim, fuck off. I just want to go to sleep. You should be telling me about their other lovers as you see and know everything, so goodnight.' He slipped into sleep within a few minutes and was jerked sharply out of it as the telephone rang again.

'For fuck's sake, fuck off will you!' He said this to the dark room before flicking the light on. Wide awake and angry now, he picked up the telephone and answered much more politely.

'Yes, Pippa … what did you forget to tell me?' A small friendly voice said.

'Who's Pippa, Jack?' The warning bells rang because she had called him Jack. She rarely called him that.

'Hello Harry, my lovely, how are you today? Was it a good one?'

Don't engage, Jack.

'Who's Pippa, Jack?'

'Answer my question first, my lovely, and then I'll tell you.' He was thinking fast but needed more time.

'I'm fine, Jack, and today was fine.'

Oh fuck, he thought, everything's fine. She said it again.

'And Pippa?'

'Don't worry about Pippa. You might just meet her in a couple of weeks when you come over. It all depends on whether we come here to the *barraca* or go to a hotel in Rupit and I keep changing my mind about what is best for you, lovely.' Soul Shiner liked the idea of visiting his home and so she was reassured that he had nothing to hide. Less aggressively she said.

'Why would I meet Pippa, my poppet?' He breathed a sigh of relief as the danger was over and crossed his fingers behind his back as he lied to her for the first time.

'Because, Harry, she is Manolo's mother and lives next door. She rang earlier to remind me I have to feed her birds for the next few days whilst she visits her sister and then I thought it was her ringing back about some tiny forgotten detail, as old people do. They never get everything right first time, do they? That applies to me when talking to you, of course!'

He made her laugh and relax and so she proceeded to talk for another hour and a half about nothing. However, he felt that he couldn't shorten the conversation because of his earlier mistake. At 1:30 am he fell asleep again and was glad that he had Monday night to recover fully before the celebratory barbecue to herald the arrival of a heatwave. The one dream he remembered that night was pouring sweat whilst cooking a thousand *butiffaras*.

He had not returned to the house in Bagurr since his spiritual reading and when he stood outside, he felt a terrible urge to walk away. The exterior was grim and cold and still not welcoming despite the unbearable heat. He rang the bell and was greeted warmly by Rolly within the dark hallway. As he walked further inside the spell of evil was broken by lively laughter from the expats on the balcony. The girls ignored him as usual with perfunctory kisses but the men were pleased to see their ally. Rolly pointed to the chair where he had sat for his reading.

'Take a seat, old chap, and I'll pour you some of your favourite Valdepeñas.'

'Do you mind if I sit on the other side by the balcony. I just need some air. It's so stifling.'

'Of course, Jack, wherever you feel *comfortable.*' Rolly pulled the other chair around for him so that he was still part of the group.

He knows Jack. Listen to his tone and the use of the word comfortable. They are playing a game with you.

'Rubbish,' he said to Nim in his mind. 'I'm just feeling guilty. There's no way she would have told him.'

You are wrong, Jack. This is a bad place and you shouldn't be in this group. They have no morals or principles and they invite evil.

'That's rubbish, Nim. They are just a bunch of expats with loose morals who get pissed all the time.' The expats were on gin and tonics with three slugs of gin in a tall glass of tonic and, as they had already drunk two each, it was remarkable that there was no effect on their outward physical behaviour. Jack was delighted as it made it easier to listen and relax because by now they didn't care what they were saying. The general chit-chat reflected the Cheshire set with the wives sharing their shallow and unhappy lives. A trip to La Roca the outlet village brought Dior and Versace into the conversation as they frantically saved their husband's money in the sales whilst blowing 500 euros. The husbands remained stony-faced but Jack laughed and teased the women that they had bought cheap rubbish, especially the brand new skimpy tops at 100 euros each that they all modelled, showing their breasts and partly obscured nipples.

The women seemed hell-bent on finding a 'fab' kitchen for Pippa when she really needed a carpenter and bricklayer to make the house weatherproof and then they got bored enough to discuss which brands of expensive Spanish Cava were dryer than the others. Names, names, names … just like in Cheshire.

Jack couldn't be bothered with such mundane conversations anymore but he was shocked by the quiet acceptance of it all by their men. It was as if the women had some power over them that he couldn't understand. As they drifted onto brave Prince Harry, shown on the BBC shooting his machine gun in Afghanistan, he had to join in and be controversial especially when Lucy said, 'He has been such a good Prince since his dear mother died.' This was Jack's opportunity.

'I'm sorry, girls, but everything he did on that film was edited and controlled to make us all believe there's a war we need to be involved in and, quite frankly, that's bollocks, isn't it?' Lucy leapt to the Prince's defence.

'You can't say that, darling. He travelled home with dead bodies for God's sake. I saw him arrive at RAF Northolt on Sky TV.'

'Lucy, it is all about control and manipulation. He never got near the enemy whilst he was there because everywhere he went he was chaperoned by the SAS. It was also deliberate that they showed the bodies and the weeping relatives with all that sad music at the same time. It was stage-managed just to make you proud to be involved. Good old Great Britain fighting the baddies and winning, whereas of course we are being thrashed by an Islamic enemy who own the country and will never give up.'

'Bravo, Jack,' Dutch joined in. 'We don't have the same level of Nationalism on TV in Holland and so we get more of the truth, but it is still very manipulated.' The girls descended to the kitchen to prepare some food leaving the men to talk on their own for a change. Jack looked around and could see they were happier to be alone without their wives. He leaned forward conspiratorially so the girls wouldn't hear from immediately below.

'I couldn't believe what they bought at La Roca. Us men have a single wardrobe full of clothes and always pick the same three things to wear each week and the women have three wardrobes full of clothes and yet still have nothing to wear.'

'I agree Jack, old chap,' said Rolly happy with his new friend who had liked his art exhibition in Banyoles.

'I told Pippa when she came home that all the purchases needed to be returned.' Jack was impressed.

'And did she agree, Rolly?'

'Oh no, not at all. She said because they were in the sales she wasn't allowed to take any of them back.' Jack grabbed and shook his shoulder and tried to stiffen his resolve.

'Be a completer finisher, Rolly, either you are or you are not. Tell her again and follow it through. Remember to repeat this to yourself. *What I say is what I do and what I do is what I say.*' Rolly looked doubtful but Dutch liked the concept.

'I like those sayings, Jack, but for business, my friend, and not for wives, or especially not for my wife.' Jack remonstrated with him.

'If you want a nice life, don't suggest practical solutions to your wife when she throws her issues at you. Just sit back and listen and then throw the query back in a dozen different ways and that will make her happy. If you're really lucky, she'll go off and discuss it with all her girlfriends and you can get on with being a bloke for a few days.' Niiige wanted to know why he shouldn't give a practical solution to Lucy. Jack wagged a knowing finger at him and checked that no girls had sneaked upstairs unnoticed.

'Look Niiige. If you suggest that you know better than them, they won't like it because they know that it's totally untrue. It makes you look more of a twat.' The three expat men sat back in amazement as their teacher continued the lesson. 'Remember they are shopping as a form of greed and this is no different to the base level motivation to eat and then overeat, to store up reserves of fat for bad times in the future. Their lives revolve around *sexo, poder, y dinero.*'

Rolly asked first. 'What's that, Jack? We don't speak Spanish, old chap.'

'Sex, power and money and a combination of all three allows them to control us right?'

'Right,' they all agreed, but were puzzled before he told them some more home truths.

'I suppose around here you could change that saying into sun, sea and sex but in the end, boys, so long as you can find their a spot, g spot, f and e spots inside of their vaginas you will keep them happy and under control.'

'Right' they all agreed. He looked at their faces.

'You haven't got a clue where those are inside a woman, have you?'

'No.' At least they were united in their ignorance and Jack realised why he could fuck their wives at will. He quietly pondered that for a few seconds and then corrected it in his mind to their wives could fuck *him* at will.

'Jack, can you tell us...' He cut Niiige off before the full question came out.

'No. I can't explain at all. You have to experience them to truly know. So go and buy a sex guide and try it out, or if that doesn't work go to a girlie bar and pay seventy euros to be shown the practicalities. Remember ... practice makes perfect.' The girls were returning so he left them with one final thought as the women clattered up the stairs.

'Look, you need to change your whole attitude. For example, a Catalan man loves three things in his life. Barcelona football club, Rioja and work. Whereas a typical Englishman loves football, beer and the occasional, but rare, sex.' Dutch jumped in.

'Sorry, Jack, I don't understand as I am not English.'

'It's the contrast in lifestyles out here as you two poor Englishmen try to go native but find it impossible to achieve. You still enjoy watching kick and run English soccer on Sky, you hate the fizzy pop that they call beer, and you can't really be arsed about work.' There were peals of laughter as the women arrived and they realised they needed to keep their plaything on a tighter lead. His final whisper to the boys was poignant.

'Remember, behind every strong man there is a strong woman.' They leaned closer to know why. 'So make sure she stays behind you and doesn't get the urge to go in front.'

Rolly was despatched to the barbecue and was accompanied by Dutch and Niiige as it always takes three men to cook a few *butiffaras* and pieces of chicken leaving the plaything to be played with.

As the women placed rice, salad and bread on the table they quizzed him about his past. They had witnessed his bravado and thought it was a lack of confidence or a defence mechanism but they had never bothered to understand his true character and so had made the wrong assumptions. Pippa started the inquisition.

'So what is the truth about your last wife *J*?'

'Melanie manipulated me just like you three, but her type of manipulation wasn't as pleasurable. She took all of my money and keeps trying to hurt me through my son Joseph.'

The Duchess queried, 'But what did you do wrong, Jack. You must have hurt her to change her love for you?' He sat back and drank some wine.

'I don't think I did. I was open and honest and ended up being taken for a ride.' The answer was disingenuous and avoided his own guilt as he continued to justify himself. 'The sex was bad and then stopped. She spent money like water on any amount of fripperies and she controlled me as if I was six years old.' He bent the truth to make himself look good and admitted nothing was his fault.

Lucy reprimanded him.

'Every marriage fails because of the faults in two people, darling, so you must have been to blame as well. Look at us three. Everything you just implied that was wrong in your marriage, equally applies to ours.'

'Precisely!' He agreed without any clarification, but looking around at their faces he realised their marriages were truthfully failing. Pippa confided in him.

'We expat women have our own revenge mechanisms *J*, and nobody should cross us as we always win.' He laughed out loud at her threats ensuring that she wagged a reprimanding finger at him.

'Beware *J*, don't mock now. I have found that a hairgrip in the ear at three in the morning causes considerable pain with a burst eardrum and cannot be attributed to me at all.' Jack grimaced.

'In that case if I ever slept next to you, I would put my swimming earplugs in, with the added advantage of reducing the noise from your snoring.' Pippa clipped him hard over the head with the palm of her hand, which hurt as she was unable to judge her own strength as she was so pissed. It was the Duchess's turn to reveal one of her control methods.

'If you have long hair like me, when you have sex you can take a few strands and wind it around your man's cock and in his sexual ecstasy you pull it tight as if by accident. This cuts his foreskin just like a scalpel and forces him into an embarrassing trip to the doctors in Palafrio. Not only does he have to explain how it happened, it then takes the sore wound a few weeks for the stitches to heal so whenever Dutch got excited it hurt him like hell. Serves him right, the silly old bastard, chatting up the young Catalan girls and thinking I don't know. I know everything including his trips to the Eclipse bar in Palafrio for a quick Polish shag.'

The only one who didn't comment was Lucy but Jack already knew she used sex to control her husband who returned shortly with the others holding a large platter of mouth-watering meat. After they had gorged themselves Jack suggested a game for the drunks.

'Right, listen. This is a competition between the women.' He sat them in a row on the balcony and explained the rules. 'I am going to stand by your side with this bottle of Cava and then you have to tilt your head back and open your mouth so I can pour it in.' A chorus of 'fantastics' and 'oh how lovely' came from the girls.

'But it is a competition so, as you drink, the boys have to count out loud to see who can drink the longest before giving in. Okay?'

'Okay, Jack' said Pippa. 'Me first please, I just love Cava you know.' Jack stood beside her and poured the foaming drink into her pretty mouth whilst the boys counted loudly. After three seconds she gagged and spat the overflow onto her pink blouse to loud clapping.

'Who wants to go next?'

'Me, me, me!' The Duchess beckoned him to her side and steadied herself holding his waist and tilted her head back highlighting her beautiful white throat.

'Are you ready?' He looked into her mouth and could see her red tongue that gave him so much pleasure.

'Ready, Jack, but be gentle with me, please.'

'Trust me, Duchess, I am always gentle.' He poured twice the amount of Cava into her throat compared to Pippa, creating a foaming torrent soaking her neck and face. She gulped and hit him in the groin with her fist.

'That was unfair, you horrible man.' Dutch applauded and reminded her that she had only lasted one second. Now Lucy sat expectantly with a drunken grin on her face and her head already resting on the chair back. She slumped waiting for Jack to metaphorically fill her.

'Come on then, darling, give me a gobful ya!' Jack poured a little less avidly into her huge mouth and the boys counted. Juicy Lucy easily beat the others and could have carried on glugging it down without stopping. Jack was impressed and clapped too before announcing the results.

'This competition, boys, is a measure of a woman's ability to perform a blow job.' The men all cheered manically. 'So the Duchess at one second never bothers. Pipsqueak at three seconds sometimes gives it a go but then spits it out, and Lucy constantly loves to do it and always swallows.' Wild clapping and laughing greeted the result and they all searched for their glasses to keep up the momentum towards oblivion.

The evening went steadily downhill as squirty cream was slurped across three bald heads in an eight-inch line and then licked off by three women in a race. Pippa was the fastest, licking sweating Dutch and complaining it tasted salty. The Duchess licked Jack and forgot about the time as she gently and sensually licked his whole head from front to back avoiding the cream that was bad for her figure, which left Rolly and Licking Lucy who was slow because she tried to avoid the odd sharp spikes of hair, and complained bitterly that he had lacerated her tongue.

After the games, they all drifted down to the garden and moved into separate groups again. They were making the most of the excessively hot night which squeezed every possible scent from the plants giving a heady mix dominated by English roses.

The girls walked arm in arm and passing Jack, who was smelling the giant purple bougainvillaea, they started to giggle uncontrollably bending backwards and forwards whilst supporting each other in case one should collapse. He watched their breasts rise and fall before addressing them seriously using his daughter's favourite expression.

'You lot are nightmare. Expats rolling with the waves.' Eventually a sensible comment was returned and understood.

'Agreed, Jack!' Then they strolled on chattering about nothing, leaving Jack to enjoy the night sky and garden with its enchanting scents which included the women's perfumes. Niiige had disappeared, reputedly to vomit, and Dutch was reading a sailing magazine on the balcony whilst Rolly was clearing the debris in the old-fashioned kitchen, with its stone sink and standalone painted cupboards from fifty years earlier. The women passed Jack again and the Duchess asked him a question on behalf of them all.

'Do you have any principles, Jack?' He appraised his drunken fuck buddies before answering.

'Yes, of course I have. For example, I never shag someone's wife unless their marriage has already broken down.' A chorus of 'mmms' came from the gaggle of smirking girls. She asked for another example.

'I never take drugs; never have and never will as it is a taboo subject. Have you seen how rife cocaine is in Yapanc each weekend, with the young and rich from Barcelona?'

'No,' said Pippa, 'but why would you never try drugs?' He wondered if they had experimented when they had enough money.

'Because, Pippa, I couldn't afford it if I got hooked.' Lucy admonished him.

'That is a poor answer and I don't believe it, so tell the truth, Jack. Why not?' He looked at the stars in the black sky and remembered his friend in Liverpool.

'My best friend at University was completely stoned one Saturday night and when we were staggering to our hall of residence in Penny Lane he walked in front of a bus and was killed instantly.'

'Is that true?' She was aghast.

'True,' he said, and they gathered round and gave him a giant and genuine three-woman hug. Jack went inside to the toilet and carefully locked the door not wanting to be disturbed like at the previous party. When he finished he crept silently into Pippa and Rolly's darkened bedroom and watched the girls walking below whilst masturbating. As he got close, he opened her knickers drawer and used a set of black lacy ones to rub his hot cock and spurted loads of white spunk over the rest of them. He didn't understand why, but he felt compelled by something and walked away satisfied after carefully closing the drawer for her to find his gift the next morning.

It was midnight and everyone in the garden stopped to listen to the chime of the Bagurr church bells in respectful silence before making their way to the table and chairs on the balcony for a last whisky. Pippa wasn't talking to anyone in the group as she stared into night. After a few minutes her strange disembodied voice broke the silence.

'I think you can actually touch emotion when you are with someone who is sad and distraught, or even someone who is the opposite and incredibly happy. You can feel emotion in the air like an electric force around people you know.'

Jack, go home now. Pippa is dangerous for everyone around her as she is a focal point in the continuum and is fighting against the Collective. Go home, Jack, and hurry.

But Jack was too interested in this exotic creature to take any notice. She carried on but looked at Jack with a terribly serious face as though in pain.

'What was it at Banyoles that you heard or saw? I know you did, so don't deny it *J*.'

'I don't deny anything I experience, especially to myself, but I am always very careful about telling other people in case they think I am completely bonkers.' She asked again.

'What was it?'

'I heard voices, very ancient voices calling from the depths of the lake and they were in pain because they hadn't passed on.' The other expats sipped their whiskies and passed no comment, alternating looks between Jack and Pippa, entranced by something between the two that they sensed but couldn't see. She stirred rolling her head three times anticlockwise in wide circles before placing her hands flat on the table and taking a deep breath. A soft voice emanated from deep within her and gave a message to them all.

'Friends and friendships last but for a fleeting moment and as quickly as they start they can also end.' She looked at Jack normally as if nothing had happened and asked him about his previous premonitions.

'I sometimes see and hear things. For example, a few years ago in Ludlow, I had a premonition in an old house just like this and later someone died there by hanging themselves.' Pippa asked the question that no one else dared.

'Do you have any premonitions now?' He glanced around at

each serious face in turn and told the truth about what he felt.

'I can see death. All I know is that an old friend of yours Dutch will die soon. In fact, I see more than one death. I don't know any more details. I never know, I just feel.' No one moved and no one commented as they were all captivated by the unreality of the moment. It was Jack who finally stood and clapped his hands dispelling the evil.

'Come on. This is all too serious and not a topic to be discussed at midnight. Who wants another Scotch?' Everyone had their tumblers refilled and drank quickly. Pippa had returned to normality and wanted closure on Jack's wives.

'I still believe there is an element of truth in your wild stories about Numbers One to Five but tell us; why are you here? Why are you living in this area?'

'That's easy to answer and to answer seriously. I am searching for my *Alma gemella;* my Soul mate or what I call my Sun Sharer. The thing is, and you may not believe me, but I know she is here and I know our past lives have something to do with this area.' The subject wasn't interesting and so the boys started to talk about football and Lucy disappeared to the toilet leaving the spiritual Pippa to chastise Jack.

'So *J*, talk to me!' She leaned across and pulling his shirt open she extracted his jade necklace supported by the band of thin silver chain. Jack couldn't understand how she knew he was wearing it, as he always kept it a secret. Fingering it gently in her right hand she watched the candlelight refract off the mineral surface.

'This is very special *J*, it has a spiritual quality. I can feel it, you know.' Jack repossessed it from her reluctant fingers thinking she was like Gollum in *Lord of the Rings*.

'Pippa, this is something that I was given in China and when I need protection I always wear it.' She asked.

'Do you need protection here *J*?'

'Yes, it seems that way, but I don't wear it very often as it's very precious. Jade can be damaged by light, sweat, chemicals and bumps, so I am very careful with it as it means so much to me.' She knew how special it was as she had touched it and felt heat travel all the way up her arm.

'What is so special about jade?' It was the Duchess who had returned and reached into his shirt forcibly taking hold of the magical stone. He replied whilst watching her face screwed up in intense thought as she rolled it in the fingers of her left hand to stop it burning her.

'In 4,000 years jade has been considered better than gold or diamonds in China because it is supposed to be animated with Soul. This stone is in the shape of a peach which is a symbol of longevity and the fruit of celestial beings. Jade has always been considered as a spiritual mineral representing merit, morality, grace and dignity.' He positively snatched it from the Duchess's hand as she staggered slightly and quickly tucked it back into his shirt to be hidden from the expat women. Lucy had re-joined them after scenting the stone and jealously queried.

'Did a woman give it to you, darling? I bet it was a woman ya.' He clammed up as the atmosphere seemed all wrong. It was if they were surrounding and threatening him.

'Why?'

'I'm intrigued, darling, nothing more.' He watched the three of them hovering around him as the hairs on the back of his head prickled. They seemed scared to touch him or the magic talisman that he had been told could keep evil at bay.

'Yes, our tour guide called Charity gave me her most prized possession.' Lucy asked again.

'The necklace?'

Jack laughed to break the tension. 'No, her virginity! Maybe I did bring on my marriage failure ... well just a little. My behaviour certainly pissed off my ex-wife Melanie on that trip.' He stood and started to kiss the girls goodbye and shook hands with the semi-comatose men and then left as quickly as possible. Pippa insisted on showing him to the door and kissed him longingly on his lips at the doorstep. He wanted to give her some advice before she went back into the ancient stone house. He held her arm gently.

'Think of good versus bad, not good versus evil as bad resides inside all of us just like good. That is now and every single day and sometimes you can't differentiate between the two things. Bad doesn't come and go like in the Apocalypse. It's there all the time living amongst us and we all practise bad sometime. I know these things, Pippa. I know an expat from around here and she seems good, but evil resides in her.' He looked at her face but she didn't associate what he said with herself as she pushed him away both mentally and physically.

'Goodnight *J*. Keep your jade close.'

The Duchess was the first to telephone him the next day for her monthly appointment before each of the other two women followed suit, as if he was bookable like their favourite hairdresser.

'Hello, Jack, Dutch is away on Thursday and as it's a full moon again I fancied a picnic on the beach. Would you like to come with me?' He pondered the invite for at least two seconds whilst listening to Robbie Williams in her background.

'I would be delighted, lovely.'

'Come to my house about nine and we can walk down the hill to the little secluded beach past Fornalls. Bye!' And she had dismissed him.

Pippa telephoned a minute later.

'Hi *J*. I'm going to the Roman ruins at Empuries. Do you fancy a day out exploring on Saturday? Rolly is at an art exhibition in Barcelona, so I'm free all day.' The same Robbie song shouted out his love.

'I would be delighted, lovely.'

'Collect me at my house at ten, bye!'

Lucy phoned immediately after.

'Hello, darling.' Jack replied.

'Hello, Robbie Williams speaking. Can I be of service?'

'You can service me anytime, Robbie.' She giggled at his joke so Jack continued playfully.

'I would be delighted, lovely.'

'Sorry, darling, delighted to do what?' Robbie crooned on the background.

'I will pick you up at your house at the time and date you select.'

'Okay ya, darling, well done, you are so clever. Sunday at 9 am, but I'm driving as we have to take the horsebox.'

'Why?'

'You do say why in a strange way, darling, as if you were Chinese. Because we are taking Trio to a competition at Figueres.'

'Is Niiige coming or has he a got a deal on where timing is everything ya?'

'Spot on, darling. You're learning ya. Bye.' She put the telephone down.

They used the same telephone, Jack. It's all a game
and you are being played.

'I understand that, Nim, but what harm can it do to have a bit of *funning*?' But Jack didn't need an answer anymore as he needed an escape route instead.

The Aguablara house was in darkness as he arrived and he considered whether it was the wrong evening as he knew it was unusual not to have some external security lighting turned on.

'I suppose a full moon makes lights obsolete to some extent, but either there's a power cut or she is practising witchcraft in the dark.' However, as soon as he pulled up the Duchess beckoned him from the pyramid porch where he found she had stacked all manner of things for the picnic; a gas Tilley lamp, a freezer bag containing two bottles of Dom Perignon, a large red blanket with a waterproof surface on one side and another bag with the actual picnic. Kissing her lightly on each cheek he complimented her foresight.

'Well done, Duchess, but there's a lot to carry.'

'That's why you're here, Jack. You do come in useful on such occasions. More of a horse than a man.' He pondered the truth about whether he was a pack horse or just a horse to be ridden. He had a vague recollection about horses and ancient gods but it passed. She laughed and loaded him up, leaving one item for herself and then they commenced the short walk down the incredibly steep hill. The weight was killing him but he decided he couldn't complain, so he soldiered on, trying to concentrate on breathing instead of talking. They passed above the beautiful harbour of Fornalls with its quaint fishermen's houses and wended their way to the small beach lying under two giant holiday homes which were in darkness and therefore unoccupied.

Using the gathering moonlight they easily found their way to an outcrop of rocks close to the sea that was as remote as possible from any unwanted visitors. Within a few minutes they were sitting side by side on the blanket making small talk and sipping the exquisite champagne as they watched Luna slowly climb into the sky, accompanied by a sighing swish of the gently lapping sea on the pebbles.

Jack wondered if Karina was also watching Luna and yearned to be with her and not the Duchess. Immediately he felt guilty as he also knew Soul Shiner would like to be there enjoying the spectacle, but the reality was present with the beautiful woman who wanted him to share something she loved and he quietly respected that too. The reality was in the now, not in the if.

The huge orange disc was more magnificent than when they had seen it from the Castle as the lower perspective made it seem bigger. However, it was partly obscured by a yacht mast as the vessel bobbed at anchor a few hundred yards out. The Duchess hugged her knees and stared at the giant full moon that faded from orange to white as it rose above the ocean's black straight horizon.

'Jack, I'm surprised you don't know more about the moon with your interest in spiritual things.'

'I avoid the moon, Duchess, and only think about it reflecting the sun because light and day is good and dark and night is evil.'

'Maybe it isn't, Jack. In many myths, Luna is the female archetype controlling birth and death and as part of the cycle of the universe she therefore controls all living matter. We are all affected by the moon but women especially. Even our menstrual cycle is linked to the celestial body. It certainly affects my emotions and can even trigger my fertile time so it is in my blood and in my soul. The moon can teach us many things, Jack. You should get to know her better.'

'Her? You keep suggesting Luna is female.' He was impressed by her spirituality as she softly spoke about her love.

'Yes of course, she is a woman's friend.'

'In that case, I will definitely keep out of her way as I want a simple life and don't want to get caught up between moonstruck women.' She laughed and pointed to the myriad of lights of the ghostly cruise ship that had appeared a couple of miles offshore. Jack hypothesised.

'It must be out of Barcelona or Palomost on the overnight run before the next port. Look, it must be a ghost ship as it's fading away.' Sure enough within a minute the lights mysteriously disappeared.

'Maybe it is a ghost ship, Jack, or maybe it turned towards Majorca and is now stern on to us! Come on, let's swim.' She stood and pulled off her apricot T-shirt and slipped out of her blue shorts proving she had nothing on underneath and then started to gingerly tip-toe across the rounded stones. She was the most beautiful woman Jack had ever seen and, framed by the moon, she looked like a Goddess.

'Come on, Jack, you can help me. These stones really hurt my feet.' Jack stripped quickly and moving close behind he whisked her up in his arms and waded into the sea sending moonshine-tinted ripples to battle the small lapping waves. Before she was christened in Luna's waters, he looked deeply into her eyes and kissed her hard and then he examined her perfect body.

'You do know you are the most beautiful woman in the world, don't you?'

'Thank you, Jack, but it doesn't make me any happier or any better a person.' She kissed him again as he let her slip down his body and gently she swam away from him on her back so she could see his Luna-white face. They bobbed silently making as little noise and as few splashes as possible and gently moved with the waves as the moon got higher and whiter. The silence was broken by some fishermen clambering onto the rocks on the headland 300 metres away and so, laughing at a possible discovery, they lurched up the beach to the safety of their blanket which they gently wrapped around each other.

'The Chinese Emperor used to have his concubine delivered for the night rolled in a carpet.'

'Did he, Jack? And did he make love to her very slowly and very gently whilst watching the moon?'

'No, but I can do that for you if you want me to?' Their bodies were intertwined under cover of the rug and she answered his question by sliding his prick into her hot wet cunt and gently moving up and down. They stayed like that for a couple of hours, barely moving, having tantric sex. Their feelings were in their human togetherness and not their animal desires as they lay and watched the bats circling like vampires above them, but the only bites they received were from the mosquitoes slipping between their bodies and the woollen protection. As she orgasmed she cried painfully, holding him tighter and Jack knew in his heart that this would be the last time they would make love.

A loud crunching came closer from further down the beach.

'Excuse us. We're just trying to find our tender to get out to the bloody yacht.' An English family of four scrunched by, delicately directing the torch away from the lovers but the magic was gone, and so had Luna as she climbed higher behind the enormous headland of Aguablara leaving them in near darkness.

As they slowly walked back up the long hill she clasped his hand feeling safe and secure and he felt sorry for her as if she were his sister. Whatever she was experiencing, she refused to discuss. Stopping to catch her breath she asked him a direct and embarrassing question.

'Is Lucy better at sex than me?' He decided to be direct with his reply too.

'So you and Lucy have decided that you two are better than Pippa, but want to know who wins?'

'Yes all three of us want to know that, but you knew it was a competition, didn't you? You realised ten times faster than the previous playmates, but still carried on. In fact, Jack, you have been fabulous.' She leaned across and kissed him.

'Any extra kissing doesn't earn more points, you know.' She punched him in the stomach and dragged him upward again. She wanted to tell him more but couldn't because of the strict rules of the game.

'You have to imagine it's like golf; some days the grip on the club is better than others.'

She turned expectantly. 'So you won't say then?'

He was adamant. 'No. Why do you want to know?'

'Because Lucy has no finesse. She is just an animal and horsey with no sensitivity.'

'That's very bitchy!'

'We are not best friends, Jack, just competitors. Pip claims she can have multiple orgasms, but I can't can I? So is that you or is it because of me?'

'It's neither of us, my lovely, well not physically anyway. It all depends on what's in your mind and maybe you have more guilt about Dutch or something like that?'

'Okay, Jack, that's okay, I can see that. Maybe the guilt is to do with you and your spiritual goodness instead.' She went quiet as she thought about her life until Jack told her how beautiful she was again and what a wonderful night it had been because of her. At the door she turned before entering and shouted across to his car.

'Did I see you with a woman in your car on the way to Bagurr last night?'

'I doubt it,' he replied feeling evasive.

'I'm sure it was your car, Jack, with a woman in the front seat.'

'Maybe it was me, with Manolo's mother, as I took her to see her sister in Esclanya.'

He drove away quickly as he needed to sleep but on the way home he realised how complicated his life was now, made worse by the jealousies from these worldly wise women.

★ ★ ★

A few days later, Pippa and Jack were driving towards Escala and the Greek and Roman ruins of Empuries when she asked the same embarrassing question.

'Are the Duchess and Lucy better at sex than me *J*? Tell me straight. I just need to know.' Jack concentrated on the road thinking quickly.

Oh no not again. He abruptly said, 'Pardon?'

'Shagging. Fucking.' She replied coarsely.

'Er … what do you mean, Pipsqueak?'

'Come off it *J*, we girls talk. Are they really a better shag than me? They claim they are, as you well know.' His answer was lost in his hesitation. He needed to understand more and asked.

'How much do you talk?'

She replied openly. 'We talk about everything. We are expats.' This let him off the hook and he said emphatically discouraging any new questions.

'Well, in that case, you can judge for yourself, can't you, if you know so much.' The rest of the journey was made in silence as she digested the thought.

They stood on a low hill with a sea breeze whipping Pippa's brown hair behind her as she gazed towards the old harbour in awe of the ancient site. Jack read out loud from the guidebook but she somehow knew its history.

'The ancient city of Empuries near Escala was founded 600 years before Christ by the Greeks and, in the third century BC, after the Romans beat Hannibal, it grew into an important Roman City. Sited at the end of the River Fluvia it gathered in the richness of the area from the local rice to the minerals from the distant mountains and became one of the most important ports in the Mediterranean. Julius Caesar expanded the city tenfold as a place of rest and reward for his war veterans but, by the ninth century, it had been devastated by the Vikings.'

Jack looked at his quiet companion who made no comment and so he joined her looking at the stunning view. The sea stretched from the headland of Escala to the larger one above Rosas and, apart from the protruding hill of Empuries, now called Sant

Martin, you could see the beach, a line of coastal pines and a hint of the rich alluvial plains behind. The wind seemed alive like an invisible being as it gusted and made her fall towards him, and so he pulled her close and kissed her.

'Penny for your thoughts, my lovely.' She gave him a giant hug before replying.

'You don't need my thoughts, Jack. You will know them soon, as this was our place.'

She wouldn't expand on the comment and so he remained puzzled as they examined the old roads and buildings. This included the communal toilets where the Roman men and women sat side by side with their togas lifted, enjoying a good chat. Jack poked his head down an ancient toilet and admired the wide and deep stone drains beneath.

'How did they get rid of the shit then?' It was rhetorical but she knew the answer.

'Slaves from North Africa crouched in the troughs down there and shovelled it out towards the sea.' She was an amazing historian as she talked about the lives of everyday people who had lived in the different streets of the town and then, as they walked into the ruined amphitheatre, she went totally silent.

This is a wicked place, Jack. There were many
bad deaths here dedicated to the Temple virgins and
she remembers.

'Shut up, Nim. She can't possibly remember anything. Go away.' They stooped to enter a small tunnel far from the tiny numbers of the general public that roamed the site and she turned to hold him tight and then kissed him.

'Do you remember, my Jack?' He pushed his hands under her T-shirt and started to stroke her nipples as he grew hard and kissed her again. Jack vaguely remembered their last love-making as if it was in a different era, a different time, but it was a confused memory. She opened his jeans and pulling up her skirt she made him push his prick into her.

'Slow down, Pippa. There's no need to rush. There's no one about.' But she couldn't reply and started to grind onto him without kissing or making any eye contact, remaining aloof with her head turned away. She shouted a strange word out loud as she came.

'Centurion,' and made Jack laugh as he joined in the game of Roman history. He said in jest.

'Who are you, my lovely?'

'I am Phippalis, vestal virgin of the Temple of Artemis and now you have violated an instrument of Zeus you will be cursed forever.'

'No I won't be cursed, Pippa, but if you want to improve your score compared to the others, why don't you give me a blow job?' She immediately crouched and started sucking and fondling him as he reminded her of the game with the champagne, but as he got closer he started to panic as she seemed to want to carry it through to the foaming end.

'Okay, lovely, I can put it back inside you now.' But she was like a woman possessed and pushing him against the hard stone wall she manipulated his cock until he cried with an anguished scream as he came into her mouth and she greedily gulped down his semen. After he had finished jerking she stood and kissed him sharing the spunk in her mouth and writhing her tongue around his. She sat on his cock again and started to grind him harder than before until she orgasmed again and screamed. The event was so surreal, all he could do was joke about it.

'You have just gone into first place in the league against your expat friends, Pip. You were fantastic.' But she didn't reply and seemed dazed and so he tidied their clothing and supported her out of the dank dark tunnel and into the light of the arena. 'Are you okay, Pippa? You look really pale.' She clung to him and as he watched her eyes they rolled to their whites as she collapsed onto the windswept dirt of the arena which had been bloodstained 1,000 years before by the innocents martyred in the name of Artemis. Immediately he shouted for help from some German tourists nearby who telephoned for an ambulance. She was given oxygen as she lay inert clutching handfuls of sandy soil and was then taken to the hospital at Palomost to be met by Rolly who was on his way home from Barcelona.

Jack stayed at the site seemingly routed to the spot as he listened to the wind moan around him, trying to tell him his history before the attendants asked him to leave so they could close up. He received a call from Rolly explaining that she had been discharged and that they could find nothing wrong with her and so he made his way back to his car.

You also met, Pippa here in a previous life, just like your Sun Sharer Karina. You lived right here in Empuries as a Roman Centurion, and that is why she wanted you to come today.

But the evil is growing inside of her and she is jealous now; just as she was jealous of you then, hundreds of years ago.

She would have you believe that she committed suicide with a dagger in her heart and her blood flowing into the cracks of the very stones you walked on today. You felt guilty about her death and you have carried this burden through many lives but now it must stop. You must listen to the winds and follow your true path.

The air was cold as he gazed across the pines lining the beach, standing to attention as the Roman soldiers embarked in the harbour for their long journey home. He could smell them on the wind; the sweat and leather from a hard day's march and, as he pictured the boat riding out on the choppy sea, he remembered waving to his Sun Sharer who was standing outside the Temple on the hill of Sant Martin.

He remembered he had visited the beautiful city many times and worshipped the Goddess Artemis through her vestal virgins. The vision dispersed as a scurry of mini tornadoes swept through the tall trees and threw grit into his eyes, blinding him from the truth. He drove home slowly, scared of meeting his past and not understanding the complicated depths of the story.

Which still left one person in the competition.

Jack arrived at Lucy's modern monstrosity of a house to find an old Landrover and horsebox pulled up outside and a big buxom horsewoman slapping her riding whip against her black boots in frustration. They kissed Spanish style in front of possible witnesses.

'What is wrong with you, my lovely, you seem frustrated to say the least.' She flashed her eyes at him.

'I am not frustrated, Jack, I am fucking angry with nasty Nigel, who is a fucking lying, thieving cheat.' Jack stepped back slightly from the flailing whip, but also because he didn't need or want any details.

'The fucking bastard has only been re-mortgaging our properties without telling me.' Jack calmed her down by patting her shoulder and holding her whip hand.

'What do you mean, lovely? Stay calm and tell me.' She sighed.

'Jump in the Landie and let's have some *funning*. I can't tell you anymore as I don't know the full story and, in fact, if I hadn't intercepted one of his phone calls, I wouldn't know anything. The fucking bastard. No wonder he does all his so-called business on his mobile and away from me. I'll give him "timing is everything", right up his fucking arse.' Jack stayed quiet and let her rant, but after half an hour she asked him to keep a secret.

'Promise you won't mention this conversation to anyone, Jack. Promise?'

'I promise and in fact I have already forgotten it, Lucy.'

'Especially our friends ya!' He pictured his fuck buddies rather than the husbands.

'No one will know, friends or enemies.'

'Thank you, darling, but if you want you can tell me your secrets about sex with the Duchess and Pippa. In fact, all I want to know is who is the best among us.' Now she was smiling and reached to squeeze his bare leg below the shorts.

'What makes you think I have sexual secrets with those two happily married women?' She ran her hand under his shorts to feel Mister Wiggly and told him why.

'Don't even think of giving me a condescending answer as you gave Pip and the Duchess or I will thrash you with my whip.'

'Fantastic, lovely. Shall we stop around this bend?' But he rushed on quickly as that was the last thing he wanted. 'How do you know what I said to them?'

'Texts, Jack, simple texting.' She paused for the knowledge to sink in. 'So who is the best shag then?' He pulled her hand away from his dick and placed it on the steering wheel before replying.

'Why?' It was a great phrase for not engaging. She answered.

'Because we don't have what we want in our own men and so we invented a competition to see who can get the missing ingredients from someone else and I don't just mean sex. I mean things connected with the body and soul.'

'And your point is?' An equally good phrase to avoid engaging.

'The point is … if our partners are failing at many and various things, we attempt to extract any absent elements from elsewhere, and although we are looking for different contributions from you the only common one is sex.' He turned to her as she crashed the gears in the Landie that must have been at least thirty years old.

'So what else … what missing ingredients did you want from me?'

'I will never tell you, darling, but an example could be my husband's financial, ineptitude which you know a bit about from my earlier outburst ya.' He didn't really understand the game so he asked more.

'Okay, so if I prove to you that I used to be financially successful as an IT consultant then you can offset that against Niiige's stupidity with the debts on your properties?'

'Correct, darling. You are so clever. I told the others you were the best. We take your attributes and use them to compensate in our lives elsewhere.'

'What a weird game, Lucy. You and the other two really are rolling with the waves.'

'But that is the point, Jack. It isn't a game.' He stared ahead at the road and wondered what essence of being each was trying to extract and that worried him.

They pulled into the showground at Figueres in Salvador Dali country and slowly crossed the brown burnt grass to park. The place teemed with horses and riders stinking in the sun, exciting the visitors and riders alike. All seemed eager to impress and as Lucy was now focussed on her preparations for the showjumping he arranged to meet her five hours later, after the event. After faithfully promising to watch, he slipped away and straight out of the pedestrian entrance close to the town. He had no intention of looking at horses for five hours under a scorching sun and headed instead to the air-conditioned Dali museum, which he could see in the distance crowned with its golden eggs. After a delightful and entertaining visit and wonderful *tapas* with two beers he could truthfully tell her how enjoyable his day had been.

'Did you see my showjumping when Trio hit the third fence and I managed to stay onboard?'

'Yes, my lovely, you were excellent. Where did you come?'

'Biased Spanish judging, darling. Didn't get placed but I had a great day ya.' They sat and let most people leave whilst they drank beer sat on the bench seat of the Landie and relaxed looking at the distant hills towards Cadaques.

'Right, come on, darling let's get the horse in the box ya?'

'Ya Lucy, what do you want me to do?'

'Take his bridle and walk him in and I'll come behind and kick him up the arse.'

'Oh great, well don't kick the poor thing too hard or he may take it out on me.' He looked down.

'Fuck me, what do you feed Trio, is he on Viagra? Look at the size of his hard on.' Lucy bent down and stroked the horse's prick and was excited touching it.

'Jesus, Lucy. It's a horse for God's sake. What planet are you on?'

'Calm down, darling, horses are our best friends and have been for 1,000 years. Stop being so jealous and lead him inside.' As Jack reached the front of the horsebox she closed the three-quarters door and locked it. He thought he knew what was coming but was proven wrong. Walking up to him she kissed him just once before pulling her boots and jodhpurs off and undoing his jeans. Without saying a word she turned her arse to him and helped his cock inside of her.

'My God, you are so wet, Juicy.'

'It's the riding darling it makes me really horny ya.' Jack rode her as she leaned with her hands against the wall of the horsebox and placed his hand over her mouth as she was moaning so loudly.

'Sssh, Lucy, someone will hear for God's sake.' But she was hotter, wetter and hornier than he had ever seen in a woman in his life and she couldn't stay quiet. As they poured sweat in the enclosed space, Jack ejaculated and she orgasmed with him shuddering and breathless. She turned around and kissed him feeling his wet cock.

'Will you do one last thing for me darling?'

'Of course, anything gorgeous. What do you want?'

'Just hold the horse's head and keep him quiet ya?'

'No problem.' Jack pulled his jeans together and zipped them up before grabbing Trio's bridle and stroking his muzzle. He expected her to unlock the door and fetch some water or her riding gear but in the half-light he watched in amazement as she crouched under the horse and put Trio's cock into her spunk lubricated cunt. Jack had never been speechless in his life before but now he was dumbstruck as he watched her work Trio's huge prick as far as she could push it into her swollen vagina. Grunting and moaning she told him to hold Trio still as the stallion started to buck in excitement.

'Fuck me, Nim, she isn't going to try and get the fucking horse to fucking come inside her, is she?' He just couldn't say anything to Juicy as what was there to say? Three bangs on the door announced an official ready to leave for his home. She stopped moving and moaning, leaving Trio to stamp noisily. Jack told the official they were sorting out a major problem with the horse that had a little stiffness and that they would be gone very soon. When she heard the man move away she started pumping under the horse again and within a minute she had come loudly before pulling herself out from under the agitated beast that was left frustrated and stamping around them.

'Fuck me,' she leaned her head on Trio's haunch. 'That was so fucking good, my baby. Much better than little Jack, my big horsey boy. You deserve a present.' Leaning down she started to masturbate the horse and lick the end of its cock. He had heard of the Romans doing something similar but couldn't believe his eyes.

'Nim, please. Nim. For fuck's sake get me out of here.' But Nim didn't have the key and whilst Jack silently gawped at the monstrous sight, the horse spurted a pint of spunk onto the straw on the trailer floor, splashing Lucy's face. She wiped it off on her T-shirt and licked a bit from her finger.

'Tastes a bit saltier than yours, darling.' No comment came from Jack who wanted to be outside and alone whilst vomiting. She could see his shock and smiled, wagging a sticky finger at his disbelief.

'Beat the others ya.' And she came closer and wacked him hard on his arse with her whip.

'Fuck me, Lucy. Did you beat the others or what. I would certainly fucking say so!'

The evening after the horse show, Jack met Manolo at the Bar Fun Fun and entertained him with the sexual events of the last few days before asking his advice about the expat women again.

'*Hombre*, my advice is simple. You should never have got involved with them. I did warn you, *amigo*.'

'You did Manolo, but you weren't exactly explicit were you. You just gave me a few innuendos!'

'No, *amigo*, I didn't give you details but my experiences with them were nothing compared to what you have done. Madre Mia, if only I had the same opportunities! Mother of Jesus forgive me, please, as I would like to sin as badly as Jack and say Hail Marys for a whole week. This would be good yes! But some of the things that happened seem bad, almost evil. Is that right?' Jack lolled on his stool searching the square for women.

'Hear no evil, speak no evil, and see no evil. That's a very old Chinese expression enacted by three monkeys sculpted on the front of a Temple in the World Heritage site in Nikko, Japan. I agree with the saying but I'm not sure about speaking no evil. I can avoid bad things by closing my eyes or putting my fingers in my ears but I don't know how to judge what's bad in what I say.'

'Come on, *hombre*, make life simple, this is too philosophical. Tell me more about the horse.'

Jack continued, 'No listen, bear with me and drink up. For example, if I say the Pope is a fraud is that evil? No one can judge evil. If you take a gun and kill a multiple child murderer is that evil or is it good?'

'It is good, of course.'

'No, Manolo, it is evil as you become a murderer. You see, you can't tell the difference and I certainly don't know if the expats say good or evil things.' They were too drunk to carry on the philosophising and so they concentrated on Manolo's specialist subject; women. Manolo told him a secret, whispering conspiratorially so the old ladies sat nearby couldn't overhear.

'I have a favourite chat-up line and it works every time.'

'Tell me *hombre*; I need some tips from the master.' Manolo whispered again.

'I ask a woman what are the three favourite things in their life.'

'Is that it, Manolo? It sounds like rubbish to me.'

'No *hombre*, trust me as it works every time. You then have an opportunity to bend the conversation towards men and women, love and pleasure. One night a woman said to me, "I like sex, chocolate and red wine". So I said, do you mean all together? She immediately laughed and so I followed up the opening.'

'How?'

'I see you are drinking the red wine and so we can go to my apartment for some chocolate and then if you like we can make love.'

'And did she fall for something that simple?'

'Of course, *amigo*, she wanted me and needed an excuse. She only had to make two easy decisions that inevitably led to the sex. Most women just need to justify it in their heads and they are yours for the taking. Never forget that, *amigo,* as it is the truth.'

'Manolo, I bow down to you, *señor*. You are the master.' Jack swayed slightly as he asked Casanova something new.

'Is it true that if a Spanish man offers to take a woman to dinner and she goes, then it's wham bang, thank you man, afterwards as there is an expectation of sex no matter what?'

'Of course! Why would you spend good money on a woman it she wasn't going to give you a good wham at the end of the evening?'

'My god, Manolo, that is terribly male chauvinistic. Is it really true?' Jack couldn't believe the Spanish attitude.

'*De Verdad!*'

'Every time?'

'Ninety per cent.'

'In that case I need to become more Spanish in my attitude and not so English.'

Manolo was emphatic about his dominant male culture. They talked openly that evening about girls but it was the first time they had shared any detail. They compared how they felt about nymphomaniacs and the lack of achievement or disappointment in not satisfying them. The cock-teasers were given short shrift as were the girls who were unable to come unless rubbing a knee on their clitoris for an hour or two. They compared notes on sex with battery-powered tongues and vibrators, no oils or too much oil, and the women's complaints about washing the sheets afterwards. Smelly armpits, hairy arses, hairy thatches or shaved mounds, too much penetration, too little penetration, only clitty, wanting hot gel, wanting cold gel and every component in between. By the time Lluis kicked the inebriated pair out of his bar they had covered the whole sexual spectrum experienced in their lives over the last thirty years and were truly intimate friends.

Jack ended the night by confiding in Manolo.

'Illicit sex, like with the expat women gives me confidence but that's all. A moment of fun and a confidence boost. I don't feel guilty if they are married as they wanted it to happen and it's their lives they are ruining even when their husband doesn't find out.'

'What do you mean even if not found out?'

'Well, they are eroding the respect in their marriage and every little bit destroys it. Don't you agree, *hombre*?'

'Agreed, *amigo*.'

The pair rolled across the plaza and searched for a taxi as they were too pissed to find their cars, never mind drive them.

The best and least crazy parts of June were the early morning fishing trips in Manolo's *menorquina* as they touched the rising sun and dwelt on the sea.

Jack was a Piscean and therefore drawn to the waters, spiritually delivered from the waters and, in every life, he had also lived by water.

They would meet at Yapanc harbour at six in the morning and crank up the old diesel engine to rumble out of the bay, disturbing only their fellow fishermen who left at that perfect hour. Manolo chose to turn left or right and head towards Tiramisu or Palomost based on his unique and local knowledge of the best places to fish for the time of year.

'Why are we going this way today, *amigo*?'

'*Hombre*, trust me I know these things.' Jack pushed him further.

'What type of fish are we trying to catch?'

'You will see, *amigo*, we have great prospects today. I feel it in my Catalan bones.'

'What are we using for bait?'

'The same as usual, *hombre*, the dead fish is good for anything.' Jack leaned back and admired his friend.

'You haven't got a clue, have you, Manolo?' The Catalan smiled at the crazy English.

'I know everything about the sea and fishing but my friend, you are too exact in your life. It isn't what you catch or even how much that's important. What is more fundamental is watching the sun rise, to see the perfect place that we live in and say thank you to God.'

'Amen,' said Jack in total agreement.

By seven o'clock the sun would start to burn as they sat rolling at anchor off a small beach. Their simple nylon lines and multiple hooks hung motionless off a piece of old wood on the white deck. Manolo never put sun cream on and was chastised by the white-skinned Englishman.

'You recommended I wear factor forty which makes me look almost ghostly with its whiteness and then, blow me down, you use nothing. Why?'

'I am Spanish, *amigo*; I have naturally resistant olive-coloured skin.' Jack sat and thought before commenting sarcastically.

'Have you seen baked olives on top of a pizza, *hombre*?' But they stayed out of the ultraviolet some of the time when they leapt off the stern of the boat to swim amidst the rocks and stare at the scarce fish through their scuba masks.

One day at the beautiful beach of Aqua Zelida Jack watched a shark swim lethargically past him and in a blind panic he swam to the sea bottom and faced it . The shark slipped away and Jack returned to the boat to tell Manolo.

'Fucking four-foot fucking shark. This close to me.' He had his arms outstretched as his chest heaved trying to draw breath.

'Jack, I have never seen sharks here, *amigo*. Maybe it was a dolphin or a big tuna yes?' Jack sat shaking his head.

'No one ever believes me about sharks. This has happened before and no one believed me then.' He contemplated the lies he had told women about his shark bite in order to drop his trousers and show them his scar from his hip operation to see if they were interested. He remembered JoJo refusing to swim in the deeper parts of Yapanc bay and he pictured the sightings of sharks on the yacht trip with Karina and from his upturned dinghy.

'Manolo, listen to me. There are sharks here and if they are not dangerous fine, but if they are, they only seem to be after me!' He vowed never again to take sharks in vain.

Motoring back to the harbour they always saw the same two light aeroplanes flying overhead towing banners. During the month there appeared to be a battle of wills in the early morning skies. The first plane was bright red and would fly close to the beach with a trailing sign saying 'Come to Torres Disco.' Manolo told Jack the owner was a businessman called Torres from Madrid who was disliked in the area.

Within a few days they noticed a white Cessna giving a Catalan response 'Come to Gonzalez Nightclub.' As the month hotted up so did the competition in the air. 'Support Real Madrid FC' said the red plane for a few days. 'Support Barcelona FC' said the white plane in response.

By the end of June the competition was personalised. 'Independence for Catalonia' said the white Cessna. 'One Spain,' said the red plane, until finally they were both grounded by the local police for the personal insults made 300 metres in the air as the two planes buzzed around each other up and down a few miles of coast. 'Torres is a Fascist.' 'Gonzalez fucks Chickens.'

Jack wasn't totally sure about Manolo's translations but he enjoyed the *funning* in the sky.

Nuria bumped into Jack just once that month after his fatuous liaison with her.

They stood in the square outside the office and regarded each other, with neither willing to comment first. The strong woman had to tell him exactly what she thought in a calm and dignified way.

'Sometimes you need to use alternative types of tyre when you are on a different road surface, *señor*.' After delivering the secret code, she turned away with her head held high and happy that she had put the matter right in her mind.

'What, Nim? What the fuck was that?' Out loud he said.

'Nuria, please wait. I'm so sorry, but I don't understand.' She regarded the stupid man with a critical eye.

'It means, Mister Edmunson, that when you go down a road

in a bulldozer it damages the tarmac, but the same machine on a building site does a perfect job. So maybe when you drive again you must start with a bicycle and build up to a scooter before using a car.' Now she had really finished with him and strode away satisfied that he understood everything ever said between them, and also for their foreseeable future. Jack stood in amazement and was still puzzled at her Eric Cantona type statements.

> *She is saying you have hurt her. Next time you meet someone who is kind and sensitive you should be gentler and take their feelings into account instead of purely your own.*

'Oh right, Nim, I get it now. I'm a bastard and she didn't use me to get back at my best friend Manolo. Fucking typical fucking woman who always talk in riddles and think they are always fucking right. Well fuck her.'

> *That's the problem Jack, you did. That is exactly what you did.*

But the month of June weighed heavily on his conscience and as his friend Manolo was out for dinner with a woman client, he had no choice except to buy a twelve pack of San Miguel beer and head home. He sat in his chair in the warm night air and ignored the view as he slowly and purposefully went through the box, bottle by bottle, until with the last one in his hand he wandered from the house and into the middle of the field so that he could survey the stars. He squinted upwards at their brightness as he swayed and then fell backwards to lie in a self-inflicted stupor that he had used to punish himself.

At seven thirty the next morning he felt the already hot sun beating down on his face and ants crawling up his back, thus enticing him to move back to civilisation.

*Why are you doing this, Jack? You seem to be in
self-destruct mode.*

He felt too ill to answer but, in reality, there was none as he grabbed his mountain bike and headed for the sea at Yapanc where he plunged into the water to wash away the beer. Dragging himself onto the beach he let the sun dry him before cycling towards the Torre headland where he could stare at Karina's house, with the subterranean boathouse in particular giving him an awareness of the future foretold two years before.

He stared and remembered and then he glimpsed Karina in a window. He hoped she would wave and run out to say 'Hiya', just like she used to but she slowly and deliberately turned away, leaving him distraught.

'That's why I'm doing this, Nim. Running amok with other women as I was rejected by my Sun Sharer. If I can't have the real one why can't I have them all?' He shuddered. 'No one listens to me … ' The shout dispersed across the empty sea to reach Nim alone. 'I am lonely and unhappy in this pretend new life. There is no structure, no money and no JoJo.' He threw his bike to the ground and stood on the sea wall holding the sides of his head as the tears fell to the dusty ground.

*Try again, Jack, and try harder. I'm listening
my friend.*

Jack looked at the sun and told Joseph that he loved him and he pointed to the horizon as he repeated wider than the sky and bigger than the sea. There were no pleas for others that day, the Collective needed to help him instead.

Crazy June drew to a close on the 'crazy English as he rode away from his Sun Sharer who had also been contemplating the same sun glinting across the exact same sea.

He cycled slowly back to his simple but lonely home and

deliberately diverted away from Yapanc where his best friend Manolo remained oblivious to the true love of Nuria.

He remembered Nuria's words of admonishment and realised his wanton action had betrayed his *amigo* as he sat in his simple gifted house and that made him feel guilty.

He constantly deceived his Soul Shiner who loved him dearly and he felt even worse as he loved her … but not enough.

> *A man takes nothing into account; even when nothing*
> *is everything. You have disturbed the continuum of*
> *your path and now you will have to live with the*
> *repercussions.*

Todo es un poco loco, everything was a little crazy and June was over.

6
Complications

The fundamental basis of any reality resides within reality itself.

The unrealities of June became the unforgettable realities of July starting, ironically, with the ever-increasing unrealities of Mother. Jack telephoned her from his *Barraca*.

'Hi, Mum. How are you?'

'Who's that?' She said in a disinterested and flat tone.

'It's Jack, Mum.'

'Jack who?'

'Your son, lovey.'

'My son is here. What do you mean my son?'

'It's your younger son, Jack, who went to live in Spain. Do you remember? It was after my divorce. Stop and think about it for a moment and ask my elder brother who just gave you the telephone so you could speak to me.'

'Oh yes, you must be my son, otherwise he wouldn't have given me the telephone, would he? What's your name again?'

'It's Jack. There you go then, Mum. Yes it is me, your son Jack. How are you today?'

'Why are you in Spain, son?'

'I live here now, remember?'

'Do you?' She coughed before continuing croakily.

'Are you on holiday? I've been to Spain on a skiing holiday.'

'No, Mum, I live here remember. I left Melanie and came to live here and you went skiing once, but it was in France.'

'Did I? I don't remember going to France, I don't remember anything really.'

'Can you remember the name of my best friend and his family in France?'

'Yes of course I can, I remember now. They are called Rodney and Edima. I went to their wedding in Spain, didn't I? That was horrible, your brother forced me to go on an aeroplane, but I don't like flying and when I got there they made me eat snails and hot chocolate.' She giggled. 'Wriggly snails swimming in the chocolate and they served it all in a big cereal bowl. Your dad didn't like the chocolate but he ate the snails. Is your dad there? Is he on holiday with you in France?' The line went silent as she thought about something before coughing again.

'No. Mum, Dad's not here.' He hadn't the heart to remind her that Dad was dead and his stomach turned over thinking about them both. With a heavy heart he carried on the pointless conversation. 'How are you feeling today?'

'Your brother is holding me prisoner and made me eat snails yesterday. I'm not going to eat anything he gives me as I think they are putting poison in it to try and kill me and take my money. Everyone is stealing it, Rodney.'

'No, it's your son Jack speaking, not your grandson, Mum. Don't worry about your money no one is trying to steal it.'

'I thought you committed suicide?'

'No Mum, if I had I wouldn't be talking to you, lovey. I promise you I won't attempt suicide again. Life is too precious and the more I talk to you, the more I realise that. Remember I love you, so never forget it. Write it down on the inside cover of your glasses case. Jack my son loves me forever. Okay?'

'Okay, Jack. I miss your smile, son. You were always a lovely boy, but far too sensitive.'

'Thank you, Mum. Have you been walking today?' His mother lost her rational thoughts again.

'Your brother is terrible to me. They lock me in my room and feed me chocolate. You know that dark stuff and I only like milk chocolate from Easter eggs. Did you send me an Easter egg?'

'I'm sure he is very kind and looks after you, Mum. Love you lots, lovey. Please put my brother on the phone. Bye!' She didn't say goodbye for the first time ever and that saddened him further.

'Hi, how are you, Bro?'

'Terrible.'

'What do you mean terrible?'

'You ring up every few weeks and you miss out on all the mess, don't you.'

'I know how bad it is, Bro, because you tell me every time I ring and you tell me in your emails. So I know and understand and I feel sorry for you and always thank you for being there for Mum.'

'But Jack, the point is *you* are not there for her.' He emphasised his displeasure and then repeated the exercise several times.

'*You* don't have to cope with her not eating and making up any excuse possible. *You* don't have to cope with her refusing to get out of bed. *You* don't have to cope with anything as you are living it up in the sun.'

Jack remonstrated. 'You know why I live here in Spain. I'm writing my book and changing my life. You know that. What's got into you today?'

His brother was upset as he replied. 'It's not enough, Jack. You're being irresponsible. You've left your mum and your son, and you've let your wife down.'

An irresponsible but hurt Jack replied, 'So has she been on the phone stirring it up again, on the pretence of caring about Mum's condition?'

'You just see your side of everything, Jack. You have hurt a lot of people with your selfishness.'

Jack replied quietly as the argument was getting out of hand.

'I have never been selfish and have tried to keep everybody happy whilst I suffer and try to write my book.'

'You're in Spain. You are not paying your dues. You only care about you. Mum is a liability and we have had enough.'

'Well at least you are being honest about your feelings.'

'She's going into a home and as you aren't here taking responsibility, I have to and so the decision has been made.'

His brother replaced the receiver leaving Jack to stare at the burnt grass leading towards the green pines without seeing any of it. He didn't feel sorry for his mum as he knew she didn't live in the real world anymore, but he was angry with his brother for walking away from the problem.

You cannot feel anger, Jack. He and his wife have done their best and they feel you have walked away from your responsibilities to your mum and to them. They feel you have let your son down, as her son has let them down. Don't feel angry at them.

How would you react? You never talk about the real thoughts in your life with any of your family and therefore they don't understand you. So they make up their own versions of the truth.

Only Soul Shiner knows the truth behind all of your thoughts and your actions, but she doesn't believe.

The Llevant wind blew pieces of thin stick, brown pine needles and blades of grass across the patio as Jack pulled his chair off the edge of the red quarry tiles and dragged it fifty yards into the field in front of the ochre house. He dropped his body onto the rough and rickety cane and slumped watching the sun descend towards the west setting the sky on fire. Over the next hour the wind whispered her secrets brought from the coast of North Africa. She told him that guilt is like the spices of the Moorish markets, piled high and loose with an enticing and intoxicating aroma that people loved, but could only stand so much of in their daily diet. She compared life to the sand dunes that changed shape through both her force and her direction, so that no one could find a path through the desert. She taught him the realities of his existence, but gave him no answers as the remnants of the red sun illuminated the traces of sand and spices in the air.

And then she was gone, whispering herself to silence through his humanity that crept into the depths of the night.

When the telephone bell sounded its old-fashioned ring, he knew it was Harriet and welcomed the warmth and love of the small friendly voice.

'Hello, poppet, how are you today? I can't wait to get a big hug from you next week.' He smiled lying on his back in his single bed and placed Cervantes' *Don Quixote* on the side table. He read it most nights to still his mind and as it was written in Spanish, it guaranteed sleep after he had struggled to translate a couple of pages. He couldn't wait for a big hug either and matched the warmth in her voice.

'Hello, Harry, how did I guess it was you?'

'Because nobody else ever telephones you, my shining knight, and because you know I am lying in bed in my pink floral pyjamas wanting you here with me now.' His hand was already on his cock as he listened to her voice. She repeated.

'So how are you?' He explained that his writing had gone badly during the day and so he had resorted to an early beer or three at five that afternoon. Then he told her about the conversation with his mother and brother that had ruined an already bad day.

'Your brother is within his rights, isn't he?'

'Of course, Harry. He controls her and her money and so I have no say in anything that happens. I accept my irresponsibility. There is no dual power of attorney and he and his wife are very stressed with the situation.'

'You are responsible and kind, poppet, but you are trying to change your life and no one will ever understand your deeper motives.' He pondered her version of the truth before agreeing.

'Why don't people believe me? It's as if everyone is jealous of my freedom and my single-mindedness to make a different life.' She told him the obvious truth.

'We are all jealous, poppet; even I envy you your freedom.' He sighed.

'But freedom has a price to pay as you become more insecure. You have no structure and less money to do things which, ironically, contradicts the time you gain. Then you can't use all this new time as you need more money to pay for things to fill it! Sometimes I think that working in a real job so you that can't spend money or think too much is a better option.'

He had shocked Soul Shiner who chastised him.

'You shouldn't say that. It sounds as if you regret all the hard work and all the bad times you experienced to create your new life. You should never say that, Jack, as you are doing so much to improve yourself.'

'Maybe, Harry. I know most people don't have the courage to do it but when you do, well, you're fighting the world because it's seen as abnormal or selfish by your friends. It would be easier to come home and get a job, pay my debts to Melanie and see Joseph every weekend.'

'Well do it then, Jack. Just do it. You can come and stay with me, so pack up now and come home, poppet.' He had heard this reverse psychology used a few times during the years that he had known her but was dubious about whether she really meant it. Therefore, he was careful with his reply.

'Maybe and maybe not. *Mañana* as we say here. Give it another day and life will have changed again no doubt. If I don't write my book, I will see myself as a failure. If I come home, any money I earn will go straight to Melanie to pay my debts. So I'm stuffed every way you look at it.'

'You can stuff me anytime, poppet. In fact, you are already in my mind doing just that.' He imagined her lying in her warm bed and asked slyly.

'Are you being wanton again?'

'I just want you so bad tonight, poppet, and I get so embarrassed thinking about you sexually.' He took control as his prick started to ache.

'Put your hand down your pyjama bottoms and then start to

gently rub your clitoris.'

'I can't, poppet, I'm too embarrassed.'

'Don't argue, just do it.' He paused. 'Are you doing it, sexy? That's me lying next to you with my hand fondling your breast and now I'm kissing you very gently.'

She spoke quietly. 'I can feel your kisses and my cunt is so wet for you. I can't believe I'm doing this.' He comforted her to give her confidence.

'Listen, lovely, don't be embarrassed. Just close your eyes and imagine my smell as I kiss you deeply and feel my finger as I slip it into your wet cunt and then back up onto your clitty. Can you feel it?'

'Oh god, I want you so bad.' She was murmuring already in the pleasure of her imagination.

'Now I have undone your pyjama buttons and I am pushing back your top so I can see your beautiful titties and hard nipples. Can you feel me as I am sucking your right nipple?'

'Oh Jesus, poppet, suck them both and suck them hard. I am so close.'

'And now I've moved down your beautiful body, sliding my tongue over your tummy and I am licking your clitoris. Can you feel my tongue moving faster and faster as I push two fingers up and down inside of you? What does it feel like, lovely?'

'Oh no, my god, you are a fantastic lover and right here by me now.' Her voice was high-pitched and the words shortened as she got closer to her orgasm whilst Jack rubbed his cock in anticipation of her coming.

'And now I'm sucking your clitoris really hard with my bottom lip pressed hard underneath it and my fingers are rubbing that spot you love so much on the front of your vagina.'

'Oh god, yes oh god.' She forced her words out and grunted as she came. Jack stopped rubbing himself frustrated that he couldn't feel the same level of emotion.

In a very quiet voice she said, 'Thank you, poppet, but now I feel really embarrassed as I've never done that before in my life.'

His reply was disingenuous. 'Don't feel embarrassed; be happy and relieved. It's just a way of staying close to me, okay?'

'Okay, Jack, but it's not the same as the real you and I really can't wait until I come over. I'm going now, but have you heard about Joseph yet and whether he can travel with me to Spain? Or if not, he could possibly fly with me in August?'

'No I haven't asked yet, but I will talk to Melanie and see if she'll let him come.'

'It would be really good for him to see your home, Jack. He's just a child. He needs to see it and know that he can come there at any time.'

'I know, lovely. Leave it with me and I will ask her when the time is right, but she is using him to hurt me.'

'Don't worry, Jack. Night night, my knight.'

'Goodnight lovely, sleep well.'

The following evening Jack sat patiently in Bar Fun Fun waiting for Manolo. He saw Nuria leave the estate agency and deliberately ignore him, making Jack feel guilty but then 'Rent' and 'Sales' left with a good-natured wave as so far they had not been corrupted by the crazy English.

Manolo strolled across the plaza with a dark-haired beauty on his arm.

'Jack, let me introduce my latest girl or as I call her my cock-holder.'

'Jesus, *hombre*, I trust she doesn't speak English? I also presume you mean cuckold yes?'

'Of course not, *amigo*, and yes to whatever that word is!' Jack smiled widely into her green eyes and introduced himself.

'In that case, my dear beautiful woman, I hope you enjoy your penal service with the Casanova of Yapanc.' Jack continued to letch as he kissed her cheeks and then she left, summarily dismissed by Manolo who would practise his technique on her later, but only after she had cooked his favourite dinner. Jack handed over a beer and quizzed him.

'How the hell do you get away with it, *amigo*? You must have something extraordinary for the girls to run around you in such a frenzy?'

'I just love them all, *hombre*. Each girl feels special and then I move on to another, but never insult the last by telling them there is someone new. Job done. This is good yes!'

'You are unbelievable, my friend, the master indeed, but where did you meet her?'

'I went to a French client's house for lunch today and she was the *canguro.*'

'What do you mean a kangaroo? Was she hopping around the garden?'

'Hoy, *hombre*, your Castellano gets worse. Not a *kangorro*, a *canguro*, the babysitter for their three children. But my client is a very bad man and owes me much money and so I decided I would fuck him up by stealing his woman.'

'You mean babysitter right?'

'No, *hombre*, my client was also fucking her so I wanted to let him know he must give me my money. Now she has told me the details about his affair, I know he will pay up or unfortunately I will tell his wife. Job done. This is good yes!'

'Manolo, you really are unbelievable. How much does he owe you?'

'40,000 euros which is all black, no tax, no tell, for renting the biggest house on the sea front in Sa Rera for a year. He is a bad man, Jack, and next year we will rent to someone new, I think. If he still pays me no money, then I will visit him again and drop an electric toaster in the swimming pool when he is in it!'

'*Amigo*, you wouldn't stoop so low?'

'Yes, *hombre*, I would indeed and then the whole of Sa Rera can eat French fries.' The little boys giggled together but it was a salutary lesson to Jack on how hard his friend could be when it came to money. They ordered another San Miguel from Lluis the barman and watched the girls stroll by. Jack told his friend about his day.

'I went to the Hotel Yevant in Yapanc for coffee this morning because it has a lot of middle-class customers like me and I was lonely and wanted to chat. I was sitting watching the sea roll gently into the bay when a slight and intelligent looking brunette sat down beside me and started to read Jorge Bucay's book called the *Tres Preguntas*, The Three Questions. Have you read it, *hombre?*' Manolo supped more beer and slowly shook his head to indicate no.

'I asked her what were the three questions and she said in sexy Spanish, 'Who am I? Where am I going? And who with?' So we were having an intelligent and interesting conversation that I hoped would lead to a date when a middle aged, fat Brit came over and sat on my left. She then decided she could interrupt us because we were speaking English. She didn't join in the conversation, she just wanted to talk about herself and her life to try and impress us. Can you believe how rude that is? For example, she said she had bought her apartment in Yapanc twelve years ago before the property boom and she said she prefers it here rather than La Manga in the south. She said not to go there as it's so downmarket compared to here, talking down at me, as if I didn't know this area at all. She was so fucking pretentious, false and uninteresting and didn't listen once. It was amazing how rude and positively boring she was and it really summed up the contrast in the expat versus local culture.'

'So you didn't like Amelia then?' Jack smiled at his friend. 'Don't tell me, you sold her the apartment.'

'Of course, *amigo*, at twenty-five per cent more than she should have paid and black, no tax, no tell. A good deal, yes, but a stupid woman and only here because her husband has money. Mind you, she was very beautiful a few years ago.' Jack pondered his smirking friend's morals.

'So you are bribing the Frenchman and scamming the English woman who you probably shagged as well. I thought you had the decency of a staunch Catholic, *hombre?*'

'I do have morals, *amigo*, and follow the code of my Church. That is all you need to do. Follow our code and join us, Jack.'

'*Hombre*, if you practised your faith you might persuade me to join in but I don't believe that you do.'

'So what do you believe in, Jack? Your reality this summer is unreal, yes? You shagged Nuria and now I would never want her. You shagged the expats in many sordid ways and duped their husbands, or so you think. In fact, your behaviour has changed radically since January when I pulled you back from the brink. So I repeat, what do you believe in?' A non-plussed Jack sat and considered silently that Manolo knew about Nuria before changing the direction of the conversation.

'I could believe in the Catholic faith but you would have to persuade me. So go on, tell me about the core doctrines.' The drunken challenge was accepted by his Spanish friend.

'We believe in the immaculate conception. That the Blessed Virgin Mary was free from original sin at the conception of Jesus and this was a grace bestowed on her by God and has never been given to anyone else.' Jack breathed out.

'Pfur, *hombre*, there is no biblical support of this doctrine and there's nothing in the scriptures either. Surely she was just an ordinary woman and not a virgin at all. Even the scriptures say she had two other children called Joseph and Mary. Do you believe her husband gave her one or God 'magicked' a baby?' Manolo rolled his eyes at his friend.

'You miss the point, crazy English. It isn't a physical question. It is the fact that she was free from sin!' He continued unabashed onto the next doctrine. 'The Apostles creed is used at mass and before you tell me, yes I know it didn't come from the Apostles. It's the Nicene Creed from a few hundred years after Jesus died and it says I believe in one God who made heaven and earth. One Jesus Christ, God of God, light of light and he will come again and judge the quick and the dead.' Jack was shaking his head from side to side in disbelief and drinking the remains of his fourth large beer.

'Quick? What is meant by quick and why judge the dead? If you're dead you are dead hey!' Manolo didn't know but added.

'*Vale* maybe it is my error in the translation.'

'But you believe in Nim and all I look for is resurrection of the dead.'

'You see, *hombre* how can I believe in that? Where is the proof about physical resurrection? If it's spiritual only, then fine but tell me, why do you pray to saints? You have a different one every day.' Manolo replied in a serious voice and with a solemn look.

'It's linked to the resurrection. You must believe in life after death and also that your relationship with others doesn't end with death. We pray to saints to recognise this communion. Job done. So if you picture a saint as a friend or a member of your family, you can ask a saint for help in exactly the same way.'

Jack slurred his words.

'So you pray *with* saints not *to* them. They are a go-between to your god.' His friend nodded yes. 'Why bother then, Manolo? Why not have a direct line? You keep saying life after death but no one can prove it, can they? And then you have the Papacy, that huge bureaucratic nightmare. What use is that then?' Manolo was happier answering something practical instead of metaphysical.

'That is easy, *hombre*. It was instituted directly by Jesus to Saint Peter when he said "on this rock I will build my church". Did you know that Peter was the first Pope until AD 67, before he was crucified near the Vatican hill in Rome where his body lies under the current basilica?'

'No I didn't know, but that is fascinating.' Jack liked the realities of religion as Manolo completed the tale.

'And his best *amigo*, Saint Paul, was beheaded on the same day because of his faith.' Jack was sorry for the world that killed people for their beliefs, but asked again.

'So what does the Papacy do? Does it keep evil at bay? Does it make your daily life any better? Does it stop wars or famine or Aids? All I am saying, *hombre,* is what is the point of it if it doesn't use its incredible riches and power? It has two out of three things that make the world go round, although I suppose it tries to influence sex too by advocating no birth control.'

Manolo waved his hands about vaguely as he was unaccustomed to serious discussions with Jack, and was unprepared for his friend's controversial views on his religion. 'Finally, Manolo, you have the seven sacraments at the heart of your life. Actually, I do believe the number seven is meaningful in many religions and through the centuries, but why did they invent the sacraments! Why is it reinforced into you as a Catholic to follow them religiously?' Manolo smiled drunkenly at his friend and patted his knee gently.

'*Amigo*, this is why you have no structure in your life, but I have because I have a way of showing my belief. Religion has to be followed religiously. Firstly, baptism opens the door to the church and, secondly, at confirmation your baptism is perfected.'

'*Hombre*, why a second attempt? Why not get it right in the water? Follow my philosophy of keeping it super simple?' Manolo ignored him.

'Then we have the Holy Communion, which is simultaneous with stage two of initiation into the church and we do this at a minimum once a year.' Jack didn't like the structure and told him so.

'Why so many stages and why minimums? Either you believe and are in the Church, or you don't believe and you are out.'

'Listen, Jack. Let me finish the whole seven. Next, we have confession which is a penance or reconciliation although it can come earlier.' Jack interrupted again.

'A downward slide to hell is reversed by saying sorry and you're righteous again, just like in a game of snakes and ladders?'

'No, *amigo*, open your mind. Confession is the forgiveness of sins, which is an outward grace and a reconciliation with God which is an inward grace. You must do it at a minimum once a year and on Easter Sunday to coincide with the resurrection.' Jack humped and pfurred his lips in disbelief at the concept as Manolo doggedly continued.

'Listen and learn. "For those whose sins you forgive, they are forgiven. For those whose sins you retain, they are retained."'

'Look, Manolo, if you were a true Catholic you would practise all this, a lot more than you do. It seems that you use your religion on occasion just in case there is a heaven and hell.' Manolo wagged a finger at him.

'No, *amigo*, it is not convenient and not an insurance policy, but some things are hard to understand 2,000 years on. For example, the next sacrament is marriage and hoy! The world has gone mad on that one, I agree. Leaving ordination, which is for a very limited few and definitely not for me, finally, the last sacrament is the anointing of sickness or as you call it the last rites.'

'The last one I can understand, but the whole thing is anathema to the majority of the population so you may as well give up, *hombre*.' Manolo was emphatic.

'Never! It's institutional and not very alive, but that is the point. It gives me structure and structure is what you do not have Jack George Edmunson.' Controversial Jack finished his beer and banged the glass down on the table.

'I don't really disagree with any of it or in fact any religion really. Good on you, good on the Catholics, Hindus, Buddhists etcetera, for following a code of conduct, a structure in life that is a great way to live with others. What I do worry about is if eighty per cent of the population don't give a toss we are all down the pan, and we have no better morals or principles than 2,000 years ago. Or does our instant media coverage make it easier to judge good and bad events so we see evil earlier and condemn it, or we see good and applaud it ... there's a thought *hombre*!'

The two friends had put the world to rights again and bumped shoulders as they trundled across the square to find their cars and take the local dirt tracks to avoid the police as they drove home to Yapanc.

The reality of the first weekend in early July was the arrival of Soul Shiner to audit Jack's life in his simple house. Before collecting her late that Friday evening at Girona airport he telephoned Joseph.

'Hi, Dad!'

'How are you, JoJo?'

'Great Dad, it's really hot here and we are having a barbecue tomorrow with my friends staying for a sleepover.'

'Fantastic, mate, and what else have you got planned?'

'We have a huge new pool in the garden that we put up last night. It's really cool, Dad, about ten metres across and nearly two deep, just like a real swimming pool.'

'That's great, mate, I hope you enjoy it. Was it expensive?'

'No Dad, it was only about £500 and will last us for ages. Maybe you can come in it when you see me in August?'

'Maybe I can, JoJo, but we would need to ask your mother. In fact, I need to ask her about you coming to see me in Spain. What do you think? Would you like to come over?'

'That would be great, Dad. She's here now so do you want to speak to her?'

'Yes please, JoJo. Thanks and bye! Have a great time tomorrow! Bye!' He waited patiently for his ex to say something, but as there was no greeting he started.

'Hi how are you?'

'I told you Jack,' the 'ack' clicked ominously before the real conversation had even started. 'I told you that any access must be agreed with me before talking to Joseph correct?'

'And your point is?'

'You just mentioned to him about coming to Spain before talking to me.'

'Yes I mentioned it. What's the harm in that? I also said that I was going to talk to you about it. So the point is when can he fly out with Harriet to see me? Any dates will do between mid-July and the end of August.' She left him hanging again whilst she thought of some excuses.

'There's no way he can come to Yapanc unless you come and fetch him. If he were to die on a plane with someone other than you or me I would never forgive myself.'

'Hold on, Melanie. He could die crossing the road with a friend of yours in Chester, so what planet are you on?'

'We have other plans to consider too, so I couldn't commit to any dates for you to come and fetch him. We are trying to stay flexible and match in with other people who are in *our* lives.' The 'in our lives' was pointed.

'I want him to see where I live and enjoy himself with his dad. So give me some dates please. Even four days would be enough for him to visit me. I'll even do the absurd and come and get him, although it's crazy.'

'It all depends on the weather, Jack. I also need to wait until my friend confirms when we are camping.'

'So you won't give me any dates then?'

'I have just told you why not. Don't you listen to me? You aren't here taking responsibility for anything, and you are not even paying me my rights.' She put the telephone down before she could hear his angry response.

'You fucking arsehole! I'm paying for everything whilst you are sat in our house doing fuck all.' Frustrated by her ignorance and fearful for his relationship with his son he jumped in his car to collect Soul Shiner and drove as fast as the traffic allowed, ignoring all the speed limits.

Soul Shiner drifted through arrivals wearing pink shorts and a bright green top. She hugged him hard but kissed his lips gently.

'I have missed you so much, my knight. I'm so excited to see where you live, poppet.' Jack was genuinely happy to see her again.

'I have missed you more than you can imagine, Harry. Come on, lovely. Let me take you to my simple home.' He held her hand until they reached the car and only then did he let it go to open the passenger side door.

'That was nice, poppet, I like being wooed!'

'Well I am going to look after you all weekend. I will cook for you and take you to beautiful places, ply you with alcohol and make passionate love to you. Is that enough wooing for a weekend?'

'Woo woo!' She smiled as she hooted and he started the hatchback Ferrari. Settling happily into her seat she sat staring at him.

'You look nice, poppet. Thank you for letting me come over. I really missed you.' As they drove, he told her about the conversation with Melanie and she promised she would think how they could overcome the negativity, but the matter was shelved for the weekend as it was purely reserved for *funning*.

★ ★ ★

Harriet stood in silence on the field outside the *barraca* and looked around her for a third time before drawing a deep breath.

'Well, Jack. I never would have imagined something so fantastic in a million years.' She pulled him towards her and looking deeply into his eyes she leaned in and delicately kissed him.

'You have done so well, poppet, it's such a spiritual place. It really is an ideal spot to start your new life away from the Cheshire set and all those problems in your past. Well done you. It's absolutely fantastic.'

Jack had been relatively quiet on the drive home and had let her talk about her divorce and the girls. His equilibrium was disturbed by letting an old life reality into the unreality of his new one. He didn't know whether it was the right thing to do, despite genuinely loving her, but not enough of course. However, he couldn't admit how he felt and so would only comment on the practicalities to his best friend in England.

'Simplifying my life is incredibly difficult, but living here helps as I can appreciate the simple things that are important. I wanted to give up everything, to start a clean slate. To get rid of all those things that clog up one's life so that I could start to be me. It's almost purification in itself but instead of disappearing up a mountain and living as a hermit I chose to stay in modern life and start again. Some days I can feel quite negative about wasting time in this style of life and get terribly frustrated when the words don't flow.'

'I can see all of that, poppet, but you missed some important things out.'

'What are they, lovely?'

'Firstly I am incredibly proud of you, for staying so focussed and writing a book. I am impressed by your life, achievements and desires. Secondly, and most importantly, you need to make a cup of tea for your best friend, using Typhoo of course as I have brought you some of your favourite tea bags.'

'In that case sit down and look at the view and I will serve your every need, My Lady.'

'Thank you, my shining knight, and does that mean every

need?' He didn't need to answer as he grabbed her hand and hurried her inside to make love before any tea was brewed.

The weekend started with fantastic sex which continued during the night and on into the next morning. After a late breakfast of tortilla on wholemeal bread in a Palafrio café they went to the prettiest beach in the area between Kaletta and El Castille. In the summer the single-lane dirt track for cars was closed, otherwise hordes of tourists would have used it and then the beach would have been spoilt. So they parked near Cap Roig and walked two miles through the heat before descending the path to the three small bays where no more than thirty people relaxed. Offshore a few boats bobbed at anchor so their occupants could take leisurely dips before participating in a waterborne lunch.

'Goodness me, Jack, you keep showing me such beautiful places. Just look at the clear water and rocks, they are so pretty.' They progressed slowly sinking into the damp sand until they neared the second small bay where they encountered fewer bodies, but now they were all naked.

'No!' She had stopped as she remonstrated.

'Yes! What are you scared about?' He teased her again. 'Who knows you're here, Harry? Are you ashamed of your body?'

'No! I am not but I've never done it before.'

'Well let's try it to expand our knowledge. You always said we should try different things. Wasn't it you who wanted to look on the Ann Summer's website?'

'Okay, poppet, but if I don't like it, I want to go somewhere else? Okay?'

'Okay!' They spread their towels a hundred yards from the nearest couple then Jack ripped his clothes off with bravado and threw them to one side whilst Soul Shiner sat with her top off and hesitated about removing her shorts. He stretched himself back and showed his manhood putting his arms above his head.

'That feels amazing, what freedom it gives you.' She whipped her shorts and pants off and turned on her side towards him, coiled up like a foetus.

'I can't believe I let you bring me here you devil.' They started giggling and carried on uncontrollably as he smeared suncream on her breasts and then when she turned over he used the lubricant to massage her arse and caress her cunt.

'I could get used to this, poppet. It really turns me on.'

'Really, lovely? I dare you to go for a walk then.' She looked at him defiantly and rose to stand above him, flaunting herself deliberately. He watched her walk away in total admiration, but he felt increasingly uncomfortable as she relaxed and enjoyed the sensation of nudity. As a man started to walk towards her she turned adeptly stepping a metre into the sea and kicking the small waves as they rolled passed her. Harriet was smiling with delight as she got closer to her lover whilst the man caught up from behind. It was Jack who was now worried and all he could think of was to place his Fernando Alonso baseball cap over Mister Wiggly to hide his erection. She knelt on their towels and teased.

'Do you want some factor thirty on your todger, Sir Gotalot?' Lovingly she smeared sun cream on his cock, enjoying his unease when a woman walked by and he reverted to using his cap to cover up. The only time he felt reasonably comfortable was when he was in the sea but even then he was on the lookout for jellyfish and so eventually it was Jack who instigated an early departure. As they walked under the shade of the tall green pines she asked a taunting question.

'So my, poppet, why did you feel so uncomfortable when it was your idea, in fact your sexual fantasy to do it?' He shrugged.

'I felt really strange. It wasn't being nude; there was something deeper. Maybe a lack of confidence in myself, or the fact that I was with a woman and felt protective? I don't know. We spent three hours on a nudist beach and as you became happier I got more uncomfortable.'

'Why, poppet?'

'I know why, Harry. It's because I spent three hours trying not to get an erection and failed.'

'How could that disturb your so called equilibrium, my big poppet. Poppet in and poppet out!'

'Very funny, Harry. It disturbed me because I kept looking at the other men!' They held hands and swayed their beach bags as they walked and were quietly happy apart from an odd tease by the newly liberated Soul Shiner.

'Can we come back tomorrow?' Jack growled.

'The second word is off!' She giggled the rest of the way home.

Jack showed her around his new life between the bouts of sex, but avoided Bagurr and Aguablara. He took her for aperitifs in medieval Pals so they could watch the sun go down across the paddy fields and treated her to a typical Catalan meal at the village nearby called La Boada, although she refused the *caracoles*, snails, despite the restaurateur professing to sell 10,000 a week. During the meal she asked the only question about his new life that constantly worried her.

'Have you got another woman, Jack? I need to know because I can't give you all my love and open up my heart if you have got someone else.'

'I have no other woman in my life, Harry. You are my best friend and lover and I don't need another girlfriend or sorry *friend girl*.' His slip of the tongue meant everything to her. Her eyes were dancing as she teased him.

'Am I your girlfriend then? Did you mean that?'

'You are my best friend and lover. Isn't that enough? Just remember I have never promised you anything and I have never said that I would be faithful. In fact, I have never asked you to be faithful to me either.'

Now she looked disappointed as he was withdrawing his commitment. He reached across and held her hand to reassure her. 'But I am ninety-five per cent faithful and love you dearly. In the last year I have shagged you ninety five times and the others only five. That's almost perfect love, isn't it?' His little joke made her laugh and she felt happy that he used the word girlfriend and love, but she didn't know the truth about his life and never would.

* * *

So the weekend passed happily. It was hot and torpid and after twelve noon it drained the body until it naturally revived as the sun dropped lower. They ate copious amounts of ham and cheese with the high fat content worrying Jack for two minutes, until he decided he would be Catalan and pop a pill to lower his cholesterol whilst retaining the bad but enjoyable diet. They drank red wine served cold by most bars, thus allowing the drink to quickly warm to the best temperature to maximise the taste. They walked the hills behind the *barraca* watching the grasshoppers fly away from their feet in a blue blur through the dusty air, and debated where the swifts went after eight in the morning as the jays and the butterflies arrived to dance across the shimmering heat of the day.

Soul Shiner loved Catalonia and she loved Jack.

She was delighted to witness the plastic bags that leaked and confessed she ate chocolate if Jack wasn't around. She loved the Spanish tradition that you only eat it when you have no kisses, and demanded to know all the other things that he loved in his new life. As the long weekend drew to a close, they were happy as they lay in his bed for a final time. Soul Shiner sang him her favourite Bee Gees song 'Massachusetts' in a wavering falsetto.

'I feel I'm going back to awful England,

Something's telling me I must go home.

And the lights all went out in Catalonia,

The day I left you standing on your own.'

Jack answered with his own piece of music by her other favourite, Abba.

'Money money money, all I need is money, in my poor man's world.'

'How true, poppet, you need to stay focussed on that book and make it happen. I believe in you no matter what happens.' She lifted his left palm and saw his life line was broken about half an inch away from the wrist.

'Oh god, Jack, you're going to die soon.'

His first thought was unkind. How shallow you are. His answer was kinder.

'No I'm not, lovely. That was where a kid at school dug his pencil into my hand when I was eight years old. Anyway to be safe, I did technically die in the sea.' She collapsed with relief onto his chest and stroked his rough brown face that needed a shave again.

'Can I come and see you again this month, poppet. The girls are at camp in America and I just get so lonely.' She had him pinned down and he was off guard after rampant sex.

'Yes, of course, but not July, wait until August, and I will try again for some access to Joseph.'

'That will be fantastic. Thank you!' She was in heaven and fell back on the bed in delight.

Jack tried several times to persuade Melanie to let Joseph travel to Spain and whether it was with Soul Shiner or any other of their ex joint friends the answer was always no. He failed miserably and her reasons for JoJo not travelling became more obscure, but she was teaching him a lesson about shagging her ex-friend and not paying his maintenance, and she knew the way to punish him was through his son.

He wasn't happy to spend double the money to fetch and carry Joseph. The time they would have together would be too short and also the flights very relatively expensive. So he decided to fly home to see his son and Harriet for a couple of midweek days. After treble-checking that he could see his son he was reasonably confident when he arrived in Tettenhill in the Hertz hire car. He rang the bell and got no answer. He walked around the outside the cottage and could see no sign of life. He decided to telephone Melanie's mother, who claimed she didn't know where her daughter was, and eventually he called personally on her close friend in the next village, who admitted Melanie and Joseph had gone away. The friend refused to tell him where, so he wasn't able to go and tear his ex-wife's heart out.

* * *

Soul Shiner was his only friend left in England and when he arrived in Chriseldon he was overwhelmed with her love and support which helped to soothe his stress and anxiety.

'Sit down, poppet, let me get you some red wine to help calm you down.'

'Can you believe what the fucking arsehole has done? How can she stoop so low as to use my son's relationship with his father? I never thought it would come to this, Harriet, and I tell you now it's war. Access, maintenance the whole fucking lot can go back to court and, if necessary, I will come and live here so that I can legitimately demand access for half a week. What a fucking arsehole.'

Soul Shiner was rather pleased with the thought he might return home but was careful not to show it in her answer.

'Calm down, Jack. There is nothing that you can do now and we can think about what can be done tomorrow.' She was right, but it took a bottle of wine to calm him down and slow the pounding in his brain before he cried. He sobbed his heart out on her shoulder and kept repeating.

'I love him, Harry. It's not fair you know.' But the damage achieved by Melanie was far deeper than his relationship with Joseph as he unhappily cast around for answers to all of his issues in the vacant two days before his return home.

The next morning they were sat eating bacon sandwiches for breakfast when he shocked Harriet.

'You know that Nelly Furtado song about how a lover can become best friends. Do you know it?' She warily nodded yes.

'Can you be both lover and best friend like you are now or is it one or the other? Could you let go of being my lover and just be my best friend?' She wondered why he was pulling away from her.

'Why do you ask, poppet? Is it because I bring you back to your old life and so I am associated with your fear of returning to it? Or is it because you don't love me?' She held back her tears and stayed strong as she knew he was still in a mess over not seeing Joseph. He answered seriously.

'If I don't engage with you, Harry, and don't tell you how I feel or what I am doing then I can't get hurt because I don't have to think. Do you understand?'

'No, Jack. Why would I, when I give everything I have to you and never hold back.' He breathed deeply before he replied.

'If we are just best friends then I can never hurt you. You can never have any emotional material to work on. No ammunition to fire at me for not committing to you.'

'Do you intend hurting me then?' She started to cry and so he put his arm around her.

'Don't cry, lovely. I love you more than my previous wives, but I question if it's enough, and so because of all those issues in my mind I want to play safe and not hurt you.'

Snuffling she asked., 'So, poppet, you want to stop being my lover, is that right?'

'No lovely, that's not right. Our sex life is fantastic, isn't it? Why would I want to stop it? I just feel that circumstances are going to get in our way and I don't want to hurt you.'

'I'm sorry, poppet, I don't know what you mean by *circumstances*.' She forced the last word out as Jack continued.

'I mean, I live 1,100 miles away and don't want to live in England. I have no money but you have your life, your friends and your family all living here. Things like that worry me.'

Whilst she prepared her reply he also thought, And just fantastic sex and not making real love is also a problem.

The night before the pattern had been the same as he marvelled at her mind that let her have multiple orgasms, but again he couldn't come. There was too much shit in his head. She stroked his arm.

'Jack, my fantastic shining knight, you make me happy and support me and if you want to stop being a lover and just be my best friend then I can live with that. I just need you there for me, as I never feel lonely because I can talk to you about everything in my life.'

'Let's see what happens, Harry; I'm not jumping to conclusions, but I just needed to talk about it as I am screwed up, okay?'

'Okay, talking is good, poppet. Keep talking. By the way do you really love me more than your two ex-wives?' He avoided an answer by making some more Italian coffee which they took outside to sit on a bench under the nearest giant Cypress tree. Staring at the sun he opened his thoughts to his best friend.

'I know I have told you a bit about Nim and my path, but there is something driving me and I can't help thinking that things are meant to be. However, the world is full of falsehoods and I need to understand the truth. For example, the universe is a single atom according to the Dalai Lama. Bollocks! He also says he will make Tibet independent again, which is more bollocks, and he even says that Prince Charles is a wonderful man.' She joined in.

'Bollocks!' He talked some more.

'Well maybe Charlie is wonderful but the fact is I am fascinated by old wisdom, old spiritual sayings and acts, as I think we can learn from people who have thought about life in different ways and over thousands of years. For example, I might love some parts of Zen Buddhism but I don't accept it as a whole.'

'Give me an example, Jack, as it makes it easier for me.'

'Well, there's a garden in Kyoto, the old capital of Japan, and set amongst the small stones of the grey raked gravel are fifteen large rocks. The designer predicted that you have reach perfection if you can see them all. So you sit there looking at a sea of flat gravel, penetrated by amazingly shaped rocks and search your heart. If you see fifteen, which is a number based on the moon's cycle, you either believe in Zen or you have found the perfect angle. Practicalities versus spiritualism, so which is the truth, Harriet?'

She clutched his hand tighter, leaving him to roam around his mind as her thoughts would never reach that far as they were grounded in the day to day practicalities of life. He turned and looked at her knowingly, realising she had no concepts to share and so he carried on philosophising.

'There's also a shrine and temple in the same place as the Zen rock garden, with a simple stone washbasin that was used for water to service the tea ceremony. Inscribed on the basin is

"I learn only to be contented". It's when you are contented that you are spiritually rich, that is, calm and contented, like me today as opposed to yesterday. But if you don't learn and you are not contented, you are spiritually poor and wealth doesn't alleviate this. That is important in Zen philosophy. So what are you Soul Shiner, poor or rich?'

'I am poor, Jack. Well actually, I'm confused between money and spirit. I'm sorry but your mind is on a different plane to mine, poppet.' He considered her answer and then carried on.

'It doesn't really matter to most people either, but most people are not on a quest to find their true path like me. Shall I tell you more, lovely, or are you bored?'

'No tell me. Please continue as it makes me very peaceful whilst looking at the beauty in the garden.' He thought some more before he continued.

'In Shinto shrines they have fortune papers that you can buy for £3.00 each. If it reads "very good" or "excellent" you do nothing, but anything less and you have to tie it to a fortune tree, which is a real tree nearby and this will improve your luck. So you give money to have a *bad* fortune paper as they are written and therefore carefully manipulated by the monks. Then you feel content by spending more money as they charge you to tie it to the fortune tree. What is that all about? Do you know what it says on these fortune papers?'

'No, poppet, what did yours say when you tried it?' She was smiling at his serious face.

'A wish. You'll be successful owing to others' help.

An expected visitor. He or she will hardly ever come.

Love. Take your time.

Removal. Move now, it is high time.

Missing thing. It will be found behind other things.

'So, lovely, I can take the meanings in any way my mind bends them. *Others' help* is finding a literary agent. *No visitor* could be my son Joseph. *Love* means shag slowly or wait until a rich pretty girl turns up. *Removal* is my rent is due, and so I had better get out quick. *Missing thing* could be a person I will discover.

'What I am saying in a roundabout way is I have a lot to learn because this year I know I have to interpret things I hear and see, and if I'm strange with you, it is not, I repeat not, because I don't love you, but because I do, as you are my bestest friend.' She hugged him close so he couldn't see the tears in her eyes. He would never know the true love in her heart as she hid her determination to keep hold of him, no matter how much he pushed her away.

On his way back to Catalonia he allowed Nim back into his consciousness, missing the coincidence of the plane flying closer to heaven and also that his spiritual home was coming closer by the minute.

He was reading a handwritten poem in his author's notebook by a Chinaman named Zheng Ruo Xu called *'Chun jiang hua yue ye'*. The theme was about complications in life.

'It can't get more complicated, can it, Nim?'

> *Of course it can, Jack. I can only repeat that you*
> *should live life to my values.*

'Remind me what they are?'

> *A way of life not an existence.*
> *Never give up.*
> *Work hard play hard.*
> *All the things you keep ignoring, Jack but you*
> *know all that.*

'I know, I know, I know.'

> *You've got no money, so why don't you marry*
> *Soul Shiner? She's rich, especially after she screws*
> *her ex-husband.*

'Your language has become really coarse for a spirit guide.'

No it hasn't, Jack, as it is your voice. The voice of
your conscience.

'Anyway, I wouldn't marry her because I know what it would be like after ten years, just like Numbers One and Two with the same recriminations. Why would I want to ruin her life? When I married Number One, I was convinced that it was true love that led to marriage, but I remember twenty years later my ex-friends telling me they knew she wasn't any good for me. So why didn't they say that before I got married? Obviously they were not true friends!

So what, Jack? You could feel safe and secure and
have fun with her. Give up your path as it is too hard
and run away from your reality. Run back to easy
old England.

'It's usually only Harriet who uses reverse psychology, Nim, so you are learning my friend, but you never solve my problems or give me solutions. Just like a woman, you give me options and play them back to me in a hundred different ways. Are you really a woman, Nim?'

I said you see who you expect to see and you chose
Granddad George.

'There you go again. Finding it impossible to say yes or no.'

You have your problems but also you know the
solutions, and unless you make the right decisions you
cannot move forward in this Karma.

So the salutary two days in the reality of England were over and he gladly ran back to the unreality of Spain, faced with Harriet and her eternal love visiting him a few days later.

His deep conversations with her confirmed she was a young soul rooted in the practicalities of daily life, but that suited him although he knew he was using her. She was convenient and luckily lived in England. So he re-emphasised the advantages of visiting the hills above Girona in a place called Rupit rather than disturb his equilibrium in his simple home with its secret life. He could cope with this as if it were a holiday, albeit taken grudgingly. So sooner rather than later Jack collected Soul Shiner at Girona airport again.

She breezed through arrivals wearing a baggy misshapen dress totally unsuitable for her figure and resembling a flowery marquee tent. This was the height of Monsoon fashion but Jack laughed inwardly at her fashion sense.

'Hello, Harry, what a beautiful, floral, multi-coloured thingy you have on, my lovely.'

'Isn't it fantastic, poppet? I bought it especially for this weekend and even had my hair dyed and cut for my new image. What do you think?'

'Your new hair style makes you look younger; it's kind of wispy like a cat and flicked back ... well sort of. I love it and it reminds me of one of those young female pop stars. As for the dress it is wild, just like you.' He kissed her hard and grasped her bum in front of the arriving passengers before leading her to an especially cleaned red Ferrari with its unique diesel engine and split rear seats.

As they drove towards Vic he told her about Rupit and the village nearby called Tavertet where Matthew Parris set his delightful book called *A Castle in Spain*.

'You will love Rupit, Soul Shiner. It's one of the wonders of the world.'

'Why is it called Rupit?'

'Rupes means rock in Latin and you will see the place to belongs to the rocks.' They rose through the wooded hills which she said were *fantastic* and then headed back towards the coast to climb onto the high plateau of the Collsacabra, which overlooked the giant reservoirs that fed Girona. The meadows and distinct rocky outcrops were populated with unique species of cows and goats and were equally as *fantastic*, but the word was used more

270

than once as they walked into pedestrianised Rupit. After wobbling over the swaying chain bridge they wended their way to the Hostal Estrella located in the centre of the ancient stone town. As soon as they were in their garret room with views to the tumbling river, she took him and then she took him again, desperate for his body to curb her insatiable sexuality.

Jack lay naked and exhausted in the hot room that stank of their sex and wondered if life was to Harry's agenda and therefore she was no different from Melanie. She returned from the bathroom and lay on his chest and traced around his eyes with her forefinger.

'Am I irresponsible, poppet? Flying out here for a dirty weekend?'

'No, of course not. We will have a wonderful time that we will always remember. The only person who is irresponsible is me and my lifestyle, leaving the Wicked Witch of the North to bring up Joseph on her own.' She tapped his nose.

'You're not irresponsible. You make me happy and support me.' He sat up slowly on the pillows cuddling her shoulders with his left arm.

'My problem is, I don't understand my new role in life yet and, more importantly, why it's so different.'

'Don't think too much, poppet, just make love to me again. Forget the world and all of its problems. I want to give you what you want, Jack. I know that sometimes you can't come. Is it something I'm doing wrong?'

'It's not you, Harry. You are a wonderful lover and every time we make love you are losing more inhibitions and becoming an even better one. I think my issues are all in my mind and to do with my past life.'

'Don't you mean your old life with Melanie?'

'No, lovely, I mean something in previous lives too, but don't ask me to explain as nothing is clear. I know my old life also comes into it. Guilt for a start and also wanting to give you multiple orgasms and probably overcompensating for everything. You're intelligent, lovely. Maybe you can work it out for me.' She sat up and kissed him gently before pulling back and thanking him.

'No one has ever said I was intelligent before. That was a fantastic thing to say. Thank you, poppet.' She snuggled down again and was content as he pondered his lack of orgasms until she started to fiddle with his limp cock again. The sex was never-ending. They kissed and transferred chocolate and wine between their mouths, dribbling brown liquid down each other's chins and licking the juice away hungrily. Jack took a long piece of the dark Lindt chocolate and slowly eased it into her cunt and then proceeded to suck and lick it with her sensual parts until it disappeared and she had come again. As she lay happily in his arms he asked her a question.

'For how many years do men and women continue to have sex? What do you think and when do you stop? Does the woman give up first as she loses her self-confidence and gets fat and wrinkled, or does she see it all subjectively and emotionally rather than physically?'

'Oh, Jack, I don't know. Let me help you come. That's all I want today.' Harry started to suck his cock and lying with his eyes closed he allowed himself to come in her mouth for the first and last time. After her ultimate act of giving he felt nothing extra and so the guilt overtook his mind again.

'Was that good, poppet?' She was smiling up at him.

'To use your favourite word, it was *fantastic*.' Happy Harry started to list all the sexual things she wanted to try with him from dressing up, role play, oil massages and whipping.

'But not this weekend, Harry. Save the fantasies for another day, especially the whipping.' He lay back with his eyes closed remembering Lucy and questioned how he had released so many sexual desires in Soul Shiner. She challenged him again.

'Is it because you feel you are growing too old to try new sexual things, Jack? Is that part of the problem about having an orgasm too? Tell me, poppet, do you need to accept you are growing older?'

'I never accept that I am growing old.'

'Come on, Jack, look at yourself. Some days you are a physical wreck with a bad hip and a bad back. Remember, I know you now and see when you can barely stand in the morning until you loosen up.'

'That's true, lovely, but usually because you have shagged me silly all night. I still don't accept growing old but I do realise that I am. I have no hair worth talking about apart from in my ears and poking out of my nose. I'm also as blind as a bat trying to read, whether it's in books or on cans of baked beans.' She poked fun at him some more.

'Come on accept it, at your age.' His reply was loud.

'No. No. No. I hate that phrase "at your age". It's like a death knell.'

'You are with a woman who is ten years younger and you are scared to admit to growing old, Mister Edmunson! Why not just accept it and move on?'

'Pfur.' He breathed out. 'Because as soon as you do, you would start to give up. Fifty-three down and forty-seven to go. It's a question of willpower, of non-acceptance and of thinking young.' She was laughing at his fervour but pleased with his attitude.

'Ah, so nothing to do with you eating high anti-oxygenating foods including gallons of red wine?' Jack corrected her.

'Antioxidant I think you will find, lovely. I am not pond life, although you may think that. No, it's not just food and drink that counts. It helps if you are swimming or cycling daily, using wrinkle-free face cream and talking like a thirty year old.' She rolled off the bed to dress for dinner.

'Touché, my love, touché.'

'But hear what I say, Harriet, as what I say is what I do. I am going to stay young and I never give up. Not ever!' He said this to her disappearing back as she waved bye bye entering the bathroom, swinging her arse to tempt him in the shower with her.

'Fuck me, Nim, maybe I am too old as I'd rather have a nap.' But he had excluded Nim to avoid some home truths about his wayward summer of *funning*.

They did walk after lunch on Saturday, following the river downstream to the 200 metre waterfall. As they searched the small square for the correct signposts Jack waved a map in her face.

'You do realise we can't just go for a walk. We have to have a plan; a start and a beginning and preferably a round trip with a purpose. Just going out for a stroll has no objective and retracing the same route is bad for the mind.'

'It's fantastic to have a personal project manager. I love it when you take control!' She came close and put her tongue in his ear. 'Do we really have to walk? We could have a little stroll in our room, poppet.'

'No! I want to show you the waterfall.' So they walked in the shade of the trees along the river bank until three-quarters of an hour later they reached the soaring cliffs high above the valley that cupped the silvery reservoirs and the Sallent waterfall. Watching the depleted summer waters tumble over the enormous drop took their breath away and no number of *fantastics* could describe the natural beauty of the sight. As their long round trip came to an end, they could see the 1,000-year-old castle opposite them and on the same level. Below its walls was a yellow stone village, strung along the edge of the steep river valley that had been eroded over thousands of years. Holding hands they were hot, tired and contented as they strolled along Rupit's main street. It was already twilight owing to the brewing thunderstorm that suddenly cascaded rain down the streets. The happy couple ran for shelter escorted by rolling thunder and jagged lightning but were soaked within seconds. Once in their bedroom, they stripped and towelled themselves dry before leaning out of the window to marvel at the storm lashing the province all the way to the distant coast with its halo of lightning.

'Fantastic! she said and pulled his towel away before leading Jack to the bed to make love again.

The problem with Sunday was they were both thinking about Soul Shiner going home and for very different reasons. She would have stayed another week but he wanted to resume a simple, cheap life and try to write. In the afternoon they drove back to the airport via the lake at Banyoles and sat sunbathing in the grounds of the municipal pool which utilised part of the magnificent lake. The cordoned-off waters were invitingly shallow and free of weeds and holes on the lake bed, unlike the area that Jack had experienced with Pippa. They slid into the wet mineral warmth dazzled by the bright sun reflecting off the surface and amazed by the vivid blue green waters coloured by the miniscule volcanic algae.

'Jack, you haven't just farted have you?' The stench of sulphur was off-putting. He answered honestly.

'A fart isn't very complimentary is it and the answer is no. When your feet touch the bottom they release gases and that awful smell, but think how good the water is for your skin.' As they floated on their backs, a beer belly swaggered along the shore, lolling from side to side, sporting short cropped hair, diamond earrings and tattoos. Jack laughed and signed for Harriet to look.

'That's just the English women who are here in the summer. You should see the men!' He dived under the surface to avoid the sight and cleanse himself of his guilt as the crazy English. His irresponsibility hung heavily on him like a lead diver's belt as he worried how he was perceived by people from his old life. It was Soul Shiner who was the catalyst to drag his morose thoughts home, but he couldn't wash his guilt away. After an emotional farewell, he drove back slowly to Yapanc, depressed by the happiness he had experienced over the weekend with his best friend and lover, but knowing it wasn't right.

★　★　★

Upper-class Rolly decided the best way to celebrate Pippa's fiftieth birthday was an all-day party for their friends, starting with breakfast and ending with a late supper at the tumbledown house in Bagurr. The lower classes were expected to attend when summoned by formal invitation, but Jack didn't play at social niceties anymore and decided he would only go in the evening.

He stood on the doorstep talking to Nim.

'Straight in, dinner, straight out. Is that okay?'

*Of course Jack but don't stay. Eat and run. These are
bad people and this is a bad place. I warned you last
time and now it's worse.
She took you to Empuries to relive your past and
submerge you in her power.*

*You have to be here as it is on your path. Learn the
truth in this karma by facing up to your history.*

He proffered the flowers to a radiant Pippa, who swayed as she opened the door.

'Happy birthday, my lovely.' He kissed her on the lips and could taste the booze.

'*J*! Oh how lovely. Thank you. We have nearly finished the Cava but you only drink red wine anyway, don't you?' She placed the flowers haphazardly on the sideboard in the dark hall and as Jack followed her in, he rescued them as they started to roll off.

'You haven't drunk much today then?' It was rhetorical but she didn't notice.

'Of course! We all have, silly.' He said hello to the expat gang who were more inebriated than he had ever seen and sat watching their antics whilst slowly sipping his red wine. Lucy slumped heavily onto his knees.

'Hello, darling. God you have bony knees ya.' She put her hand in his shirt and felt a nipple but no one seemed to care as she stuck her tongue in his ear.

'You missed some great nosh ya. It was all themed on good old Blighty.'

'Really, Lucy, how surprising ya.' He took her hand out of his shirt as he wanted to keep the jade necklace private.

'Tell me what you've eaten today, Juicy?'

'Well, Pip and Rolly drove the Range Rover all the way to Waitrose in Dover ya, to buy the food. Fourteen bloody hours each way ya, and they even used the Chunnel for speed ya even though it is so bloody expensive.'

'Ya, Lucy and that's before the petrol and tolls ya. Hardly *green* ya?' He was taking the piss but no one cared or noticed.

'So for breakfast, we had English smoked bacon and free-range eggs with the best Warbies bread for toast, baked beans of course and delicious black pudding.'

'Sounds great' replied Jack gently moving his knees as they hurt from the weight of her muscular body. 'And for lunch?'

Niiige piped in. 'It was wonderful, Jacko. Breaded ham, Cheddar and Stilton, English Spitfire beer, followed by strawberries and cream. They did so well with everything ya but timing is everything, Jacko. Imagine driving twenty-eight hours and keeping it all fresh ya.'

'Ya Niiigo, fucking unbelievable really.' The waste of time and money shocked Jack more than the concept. Rejecting everything Spanish to stay English was as bad as their clinging to their middle-class English cars and watching Sky TV all day.

Dinner was served as Niiigo tried to persuade him to join in a little property adventure and so he used its arrival as an excuse to escape to the toilet. Lucy immediately followed him in and grabbed his cock from behind.

'No!' He kept pissing as she fondled and sprayed the floor and then the wall.

'I didn't mean it when I said Tiro was better than you ya.'

'No way, horsey!' He was following Nim's advice rigidly and not engaging. Quickly he finished pissing and pushed away the lusty swaying woman to escape upstairs. Jack sat by the Duchess for safety and praised the host and hostess on the finest Scottish beef, roasties made using King Edward potatoes, Waitrose Yorkshire puddings, horseradish sauce and cabbage. This was swiftly followed by rhubarb crumble and Waitrose's best custard which he wolfed down before disappearing to the toilet again. As he walked out, it was a drunken Pippa who accosted him this time.

'Come back inside *J* and fuck my brains out. It would be so lovely, you know. A *big,*' she extended the word, 'a really *giant* birthday present for me *J.*' He was tempted, but stuck with the plan and politely refused, manhandling her towards the toilet and closing the door after pushing her in. He regained his seat by the

Duchess, who leaned into his ear.

'Not taken the bait then, Jack?' He smiled and nodded his head before starting an aimless conversation prompted by the British 'nosh'.

'National pride has been lost by we Brits. It's okay serving this food but we are trying to retain something we haven't got? We're influenced by so many things like Indian or Chinese food and have lost our identity, don't you think?' She expressed no interest and drunkenly gazed at him without uttering a sound. 'We have no interest in our national anthem and the national flag. In fact, England is more popular than Great Britain, just like Catalonia instead of Spain.' The Duchess never got drunk, but this time she lolled against him without any wandering hands.

She managed to say, 'Yes, Jack, how true.' Encouraged he continued.

'We don't have freedom of expression anymore, just a narrowness of mind to live faster. Agreed?' Rolly shouted across the table.

'Agreed, old chap.' Jack turned his attention that way as the Duchess now appeared to be asleep.

'Rolly, have you noticed how all Spanish girls have those thick glasses with brightly coloured frames? Aren't they as ugly as hell?' Rolly raised a glass.

'Ugly, yes, Jacko.'

'So Rollo …' Irreverent Jack was bored, 'Now you are nearly fifty, do you get seepages when uncontrollability of the penis afflicts you in the middle of the night, and when you have to piss four or five times?'

'Stupendous, really stupendous seepages. I keep pissing in my pyjamas or on the toilet floor, old chap.'

'Told you so, Rollo, it's an age thing. Do you really wear pyjamas? My god! Anyway, take the Spanish word *esperar*, to wait and to hope. Do you *hope* to have sex with Pip or are you *waiting* to have sex with her? Hoping it will happen positively or waiting for it negatively?' Rollo was trying to keep up with him and failed and so sober Jack continued.

'Decipher this. "Hello, I am waiting in the queue". Or is it, "Hello I am hoping in the queue"? Waiting has an objective but hoping is not definitive about what or when?'

'What are you queuing for, Jack?' Rolly's eyes were unfocussed as he asked.

'Nothing Rolly, I am just pleased to be a Pisces, my friend.' He didn't expect anyone to question why and so he told them. 'It stands for Perhaps I Should Count on Extraordinary Sex!' No one stirred and no one heard the quieter words, '... with your wives, pissheads.'

Dutch tried to make some banal conversation with Niiige.

'Went to Els Tinars restaurant at Sant Faliu. Thirty euros each... best meal ever had.'

Jack was perturbed as it was a repeat of the Cheshire set comments. Dutch continued to bore boring Niiige. 'You have to take the C31 Girona road unfortunately. It's awful; terribly busy at peak period about seven-thirty at night and even worse when all the tourists are around. Jack realised the C31 Palamost to Girona road was no different from the infamous A51 of his Cheshire set days. It was a sad dawning that living in Catalonia could be similar to Cheshire and the Spanish hype for a better lifestyle was in the unrealities of his mind. The only difference he had created was in living more simply.

He looked up and saw Pippa and Lucy stood in the shadows of the long balcony, positioned where only he could see them. They had turned the CD on and deliberately chosen 'I kissed a girl and I liked it' by Katie Berry. The two expat wives started to kiss and fondle each other's breasts to try and entice Jack into some *funning*. He was shocked at first and then excited, but had promised Nim not to get involved. So he just waved as they pushed hands under skirts trying harder to seduce him. Despite his erection, he genuinely hated the song as it was constant and repetitive on the radio. There were a million good songs in the world but only the new and limited few made it onto the pop stations.

'So we are all going along the same path, Nim, and that doesn't include dual lesbian fun in front of expat husbands.'

You are learning quickly, Jack. Eat and run. Resist
the temptations and grow stronger in your resolve.

The Duchess had woken and so Jack explained his writing, comparing himself to Josep Pla.

'Who is that?' She asked vaguely.

'He has a foundation, a charity in Palafrio. Have you never seen it?' She nodded. 'He came from a local wealthy family and became a great writer with passionate narratives of the closest reality, poetical subjectivism. He was also an extensive traveller.'

She was unimpressed and still silent.

'After the politics of the European war he took up an inner exile in this area just like me. He chose a simple life and walked and talked with the farmers and fishermen in the beautiful countryside. It was a meditation, a search for his identity, which is no different from mine.' He shoved her shoulder for a response.

'I would like to read some of his work, Jack.'

'I don't think you would, lovely, as the *Complete Work,* which is the best known, contains forty-six volumes and can only be read in Catalan.' She smiled at him sweetly as he added. 'Or just read my book, lovely, if I ever finish it.'

Jack stood to leave before anything bad happened and took the opportunity to reprimand them all.

'Don't you think we all use our money to protect ourselves from reality? We fill in our time at the cinema or pub and anaesthetise ourselves in our big houses with a wall or fence to stay in our little perceived worlds.'

No one cared to answer. 'Expats hey? Who would think it? We invent a board game, dream about opening a bar or having a little shop or we end up doing decorating and gardening. Making the leap to real jobs is impossible here, don't you think? You need to have money to live well or just make do and survive. So which cohort are we all in then?'

Nobody responded but at least Rolly managed to wave goodnight. The Duchess slept with her head on the table and the rest stayed pleasantly quiet.

'Goodnight all.' Jack walked out alone.

The day after the party, Jack expected the three women to contact him to renew their game but he only received two calls and they were made separately and privately. The first was from Lucy who asked him to meet her at 11 am in the square in the heart of Pals. They sat under the olive trees and sipped *cortados*, small white coffees, with an expectant Jack prepared to wait for her to do the talking.

'Well, darling, you know we had a little game with you which, of course, I won. Well you don't know *why* I had sex with you.' Jack pondered who had been the best before he replied.

'I thought that was the game.'

'Initially ya, darling, but you were more serious than our previous flings and therefore it changed the dynamics with our husbands.'

'They knew Lucy?' He was incredulous.

I told you, Jack.
I told you repeatedly it was more than a game and
this isn't the end.
Hear the words and listen to the silences. Examine the
meaning and take the opposite.

'Ya, silly little Niiige knew because I told him and then I used you to beat him over the head ya.'

'Why?'

'That is a very good word and you say it so well, Jack.' She thought for a minute before carrying on. 'The truth is, he's a wimp and is living a dream, but didn't tell me his nightmares. I went to his office making sure he was out on a wild goose chase ya, and read all his accounts. He has made no property sales in the last two years, darling. As you know, I had a suspicion about him re-mortgaging and I found all the evidence there to prove it. We have no money now, just debt. He didn't tell me, but we have nothing left since the property crash and I think we actually owe hundreds of thousands, but I can't be sure.' Jack leaned over and hugged her tightly.

'I'm so sorry for you, Lucy, that's not fair.' She started to cry and whimpered with her head tucked onto his shoulder. He asked bluntly.

'So what have you done? How have you left things with him?' She sat up and dried her eyes on her napkin watched by the tourists on the next table.

'I asked him for the truth last night and he lied to me, so I told him what I know and that I am leaving him at my convenience.'

'Do you need some money? I could help if you want.'

'Thank you, darling, you are kind, but I have some secreted in England to get through six months or more. I'll sell the horses and of course the Landie and horsebox and take what I can make back home.' She sighed deeply and smiled at him.

'Thank you for listening, Jack. I know you won't tell anyone ya.'

'Of course not, lovely.' She pushed the metal chair back and put a hand on his shoulder to say goodbye.

'I certainly beat the others ya!'

'Ya Lucy, you certainly did, lovely.' She turned and walked away down the old cobbled street, leaving Jack to pay the bill after he had recovered from the shock.

When he arrived home he took a second call but this time it was Pippa who asked him to meet her in Palomost for a drink at three that afternoon. She couldn't miss his inimitable style as he sat in a café on the front looking at the fishing boats in the old harbour. He was dressed like a *guiri* with blue shorts covered in yellow fish, a pink T-shirt and his bright red Liverpool football club baseball hat.

'Hello *J*, you are nice and bright today.' They Spanish kissed and ordered beers. *J* decided to adopt the same tactic as he had in the morning and sat not engaging behind his dark sunglasses.

'Have you seen Lucy or the Duchess *J*?' He took a sip of his beer.

'No.' He added nothing.

'I just wondered if you'd been chatting to them.'

'Why?' He delivered the word and drank some more beer, content to wait.

'*J* you know we have been playing a game, don't you?' He nodded yes. 'Well it's over, but there have been a few repercussions, you know.'

'No sorry, Pippa, I don't know.'

'Well, I only joined in the games a couple of years ago because Rolly was becoming a pain as he ran out of money. As you were a serious contender he got more jealous than normal and things have been getting out of hand.'

'And your point is?'

'I suppose *J*,' she looked around and her lips were trembling as a tear slid from her left eye, 'I suppose my personality has changed since you've been around. You know how weird things have happened. I don't understand it really, but Rolly got angrier with me instead of letting things pass.' She stopped to cry, hugging a napkin to her face whilst Jack hugged her.

'Come on, Pippa, tell me everything.'

'It was always fun when he and I started it you know.'

'Started what lovely?'

'The games. Dressing up, handcuffs and then he started on other weird things with leather and bondage and I let him because he controls me through his inheritance.' Jack waited patiently. 'He started to go too far you know and whipping me fucking hurts *J*. I don't know why it's so extreme, but it coincided with you arriving and now he won't stop.'

'Just say no, Pippa. If he won't stop, well you need to leave. Say no or I will come round and beat the shit out of him.' She pulled her skirt above her knees and showed him the bruises from the night before.

'My back is also a mess *J*. I hurt so much.' She burst into tears again and he comforted her by taking her for a walk towards the harbour. He could only repeat his sensible advice before she drove off, but he couldn't see that it would help, so he worried about her safety and sanity as he drove slowly home.

✫ ✫ ✫

Much later that afternoon, Jack was writing sat at his desk in the *barraca* when he noticed a car hurtling up his track. As it came closer, he realised it was the Duchess and he recalled the lovemaking lit by Luna which had been tender and loving, in direct contrast to his encounters with Juicy Lucy and Spiritual Pippa. As she pulled up and slid over the door he was shocked to see she was completely naked.

'Have you driven naked all the way here?'

'That would be telling, Jack.' She walked up to him, a goddess in her power and beauty and wrapping her hands around his head she kissed him deeply before holding tight to his shoulders and jumping up on him for a frontal piggy back.

'Take me inside and fuck me, Jack, but be quick.' He held her soft white bum cupped in his brown hands and walked awkwardly inside to lay her on his settee. Dropping his shorts he was about to enter her when she pushed him on his back and sat on his cock and started to fuck him. She writhed hard and bent him backwards as she took total control and as he got closer she inserted a wet finger up his arse. She forced him to stay on his back as they orgasmed simultaneously with him moaning in delight as she possessed him. Without moving off his still stiff cock she pushed his wayward hands away from her breasts and held them together on his chest.

'What was that all about, Duchess?'

'I wanted you to know that I could fuck you how and when I wanted.'

'Why?' He expected another shock.

'Revenge, Jack. Revenge on men and in particular my husband who has been shagging our Thai maid and also the Polish girls at the Eclipse bar. I wanted to fuck you before I go home naked, dripping your spunk and tell him I have decided to leave him.'

'But you intimated to me that you knew about his behaviour?'

'Firstly, you came along, Jack, and became our plaything. Secondly, my private detective in Holland exposed his fraudulent business dealings in child pornography and explained the dirty money that built the glass house in Aguablara. So now I have completed my own book, my lovely writer, friend and sold it to the Dutch *Hello* magazine. Now I can return to Holland, free and independent and within a week he will be extradited and go to jail. So revenge is sweet, Jack, and I wanted to say goodbye in my inimitable own way.'

She jumped off him and ran outside to slide over the car door leaving a trail of sperm on the plastic. Jack stood open-mouthed on his patio, his shorts around his ankles and the smile wiped off his face. All he could think was that his arsehole hurt.

'But Duchess … I don't understand my part in this.' She reversed the car and as she gently pulled away she told him the truth.

'You see Jack, I could have loved you.' There was a pregnant pause before she said. 'But I saw what you did with the other two.' He looked at her quizzically and his jaw dropped trying to get his words out.

'You saw?'

'That was in the rules of the game and now the game has ended. Goodbye, Centurion.' She waved languidly before driving off at speed leaving him to watch the dust as her Merc disappeared down the drive.

7
It's not what the astrologer predicted

The Spanish holidaymakers always disappeared on 1st September, leaving a few Dutch and Brits to the empty beach and warm sea. During the fortnight that followed the boats moored in Yapanc Bay were brought to the harbour and trundled, by a succession of endless lorries, to their winter bases. Hidden away in the burnt-out fields or dusty boatyards, they remained landlocked for nine months as their owners forgot their babies.

September to October was a time for reflection after the torrid and manic summer. Each morning was heralded by crickets starting a cacophony of noise at precisely 10:30 am and finishing precisely at 7 pm. It was when the jellyfish arrived in huge numbers, keeping the locals out of the warm sea but stinging the tourists who now had no lifeguards to administer the acidic antidote. Inland, a less painful pest multiplied as a million flies buzzed through the tops of the pine trees from first light. Even a giant owl joined in this period of natural relaxation when caught between Manolo's mother's wire fence and a deep trench on Jack's property. Barking like a fox at the inconvenience, it alerted Jack who had taken his torch to investigate and found a two-foot high bird staring at him beadily with a giant yellow eye.

As he tried to get closer, the sharp beak and neck twirled to face him from whichever direction he approached until, taking off his sweatshirt, he tossed it over the owl's head and grabbed the vicious bird to his chest. Restraining the flapping wings he struggled up the bank of the ditch and threw the bird onto the open ground beneath the pines. The pink sweatshirt fell off the bird's head and it sat moodily staring at him before gliding off majestically into the night. It was an amazing sight that reminded him of the pleasures of a simple natural life.

At the end of September, six of Manolo's family, including the Catalan Casanova, joined together to harvest the grapes in his mother's field. Apart from his friend, the men were all over sixty years old and arrived in a variety of equally ancient battered cars. Two of the family clan could barely walk but as they all moved painstakingly slowly, it seemed to make no difference to the quantity of grapes picked. They slowly criss-crossed the adjacent hillside, throwing the juicy fruit into dirty and torn baskets that had been used for a generation.

As Jack watched, he could barely see the vines as the leaves were brown to match the sandy burnt out hillside. Randomness appeared the norm, but occasionally the men came together as a group to chat and advise each other on the state of the harvest before starting afresh and typically three rows away from where they were before. Jack was mesmerised by the ballet performed in various shades of blue overalls which seemed as old and as tired as the men with their washed-out hats matching the clear sky. It was a true celebration of living as the traditional family effort spread across the three-acre field producing at best its 600 bottles of red wine for their private use.

It was also a time to adapt to the seasonal foods in the peaceful market, which was now devoid of the *guiris*. He bought tomatoes which were still on the vine, eye-stinging onions and the newly picked aubergines to make fresh and tasty ratatouille throughout the whole of September. In October, he would change allegiance and purchase delicious *setas*, field mushrooms, which had been hooked out of the dewy mountain grass beneath small pines in the foothills of the Pyrenees. However, he yearned for November each time he went down his dirt track as he paused to admire the pomegranates hanging red and hard on the small stunted and semi-leaved tree. They were covered in ants and still too bitter to eat for both the ants and the humans, who were vying to be the first to taste the delicious red interiors.

This only left the wild pigs to join in each evening. Driven down from the isolated hills in search of food, they rooted around in any area fed by sprinklers so that they could gobble up the juicy worms until a car's headlights would scatter them towards shelter. One evening a 300-kilo boar charged past Jack's patio at what appeared to be ninety miles an hour. On the basis that pigs can't fly he climbed to safety on the patio table and shouted his many cowardly insults.

'I'm going to put pork on the barbecue tomorrow, you bastard.' He stared into the night to see if it was safe to get down and decided to stay put.

'I need a new paintbrush, lumpy bum, so come a little closer if you want your bristles plucked.'

He hoped to scare any clever pig away but, in fact, the boar seemed to enjoy a playmate and returned nightly. Therefore, it was Jack who nervously scouted his wet patch of land from behind his windows before venturing to sit outside with a certain trepidation. It was there that he mulled over considerations of great magnitude, usually after half a bottle of Rioja, when feeling his lack of responsibilities weighing him down.

'Nim, why do I feel guilty about having so much time? I understand now why people fill in their spare time and don't use it to think. They process junk from the TV, Hi Fi or PC. They want and need to do something but stay paralysed and unable to think as they can only fill. That is the curse of modern life. Thoughtless filling.'

Being alone achieves a purity of spirit, Jack. You
needed this time especially without the corruption of
the expats.

'Expats twats, who needs them hoy! Who first used that term, Nim? Does it mean ExPecting Awesome TimeS? Is that what they crave on arrival abroad? The people I know are not truly expats as they are still in part of Europe and are Europeans in their European home. A bit of Britain, Brittany or Belgium. In fact, anything they want from *home* they can obtain here. But tell me, Nim, is it right that I should try filling in my time now that I have time on my hands? Should I adopt a more normal or more socially acceptable pattern? Start with breakfast, wash up, and then go off on the school run equivalent before work? Shop on the way home, go to the gym or meet my friends at the pub? Is that normal or have we created a lifestyle that fills in time? If everyone sat like me and did nothing, would they experience a different set of thoughts and a different perspective on life? Would most people use the luxury of free time to think, presuming they would learn to stop filling in their time first. Then it's easy to sit and let time wash over you and only then can you really think.

But only after a few months and not hours, Jack.
Even then most people wouldn't think as they
couldn't. They are not capable of thinking about what
is essential and important in life.

Jack sat with his daily view for hours on end and did nothing except look at the odd remaining flowers and listen to his neighbour's birds. Occasionally, he talked back to them which made them stop their randomness and return his imitated calls. He was learning to live alone for the first time, coping with the peace and stability within him and that was a hard lesson.

'Nim, my simple vista to the sea and El Far is wonderful but if I shared it would it improve?

Two people sharing can increase the pleasure tenfold.
But on your own, Jack? It's not the same and not
as good.

'You know the best thing about this view was sharing it with someone like Soul Shiner.

*If you share it with a lover, the pleasure increases
twentyfold. But with your Sun Sharer that joy
becomes infinitesimal.*

Jack sat and pondered every day and took time to heal and understand himself. He gave up on healthy eating and stuffed himself with deliciously fatty meats and cheeses, washed down with endless red wine costing a third of a euro for a litre from the local *bodega*.

But he missed people and questioned the point of living if you couldn't communicate person to person. He had his odd emails and telephone calls but realised how dysfunctional he had become and so he drifted towards nothingness. There was no expat *funning* anymore and so he would telephone his boy more frequently to keep his sanity. But even his beloved son lived in a different reality and was always happy with some day-to-day ritual with friends orchestrated by his mother. There was very little JoJo could tell him to help reduce his dad's isolation and as school and football occupied his boy's time it was anathema to his distant father. Nim sometimes prompted Jack into action, but only when allowed access into his imagination.

*Jack, this is the year of the horse in Japan and China.
You should look it up on the Internet.*

Jack sneezed three times.

'Bless me, Nim. I could I suppose. Why are you telling me about it?'

Have a look.

'Did you know in China they say if you sneeze once someone is missing you? Sneeze twice and they are saying dirty words behind your back, and thrice means people are talking about you.'

*Of course I know that and I know who is talking
about you.*

'Know all. So who is?'

The Duchess and Lucy are talking about you.

'But have they excluded Pippa?'

*In their plans they have. She was ensnared into
their game.
But you told her she is good and has evil fighting
within her and now she understands.*

*Pippa is the good one in the triumvirate and can be
sacrificed to satisfy the others.*

Jack didn't understand and so he dismissed Nim and Googled
the year of the horse.

*'People born in one of the twelve cyclical lunar
years identified by different animals have similar
idiosyncrasies. Those from the year of the horse
always have positive hope. They are sharp-minded
and dress fashionably. They have gifted silver
tongues and an acute insight, but they don't
adhere to old habits and like to show off. They fall
easily in and out of love and have a passion for
intellectual activities, an immense good humour
and although well liked are also very wilful.'*

'That is me I guess, but I don't think my summer clothes are
truly fashionable. Having said that, I do of course set the fashion
within my peer group.'

I don't think so, Señor Pata Negra.

'Fuck off, Nim.' He turned his computer off and standing
unsteadily flicked the radio on instead and started to dance

haphazardly to the Latino music. Everyone needs to fill in some time but, in his case, he also needed to relieve his stress and depression as he flexed his stiff back and hips to the beat.

Manolo appeared to distance himself from Jack and in Jack's imagination it was because his friend resented him shagging Nuria and taking advantage of their friendship. After a couple of weeks they needed each other's company and agreed to meet in Bar Fun Fun that evening. The locals were celebrating a fiesta with a rock band near the sports arena and more traditional music in the plaza, and so parking close to the centre of town proved impossible. Jack drove past Coqui Park, the thriving children's amusement centre, and laughed at the huge green illuminated dick that announced it was open. As he walked the mile into Palafrio he saw the local businesses were closing behind the giant decrepit wooden doors that hid acres of space containing metal works, carpenter shops and large boatyards. He perched on his stool and sipped his red wine in the pleasant evening atmosphere about an hour before the sun disappeared and took away the heat. He had too much time and no company until Manolo finished work and so he continued to ponder the big questions in his life with Nim.

'Nim, talk to me, please. Am I happy and what makes me happy?'

You still can't answer those questions and so you have not found your true path. Just know that you are close to it and can reach it with a strength of will that is within your new powers.

'I have nothing anymore. No house, no money, a car that the bailiffs want to seize to pay my maintenance and so this global crisis is such an irony for me.'

But material possessions mean nothing, Jack. Why worry about the world's finances when you have more important things to achieve?

'It's not a crisis you know. Most people still have exactly the same as they always have but because we have no confidence in each other we think we have forty per cent less. But that's a joke, Nim, as we all have an imagined forty per cent less, apart from me as I still have nothing. What crisis is affecting my ex-acquaintances? They are still sitting in Cheshire with their Mercs and fab houses, their kids are still in private schools and they still use private hospitals. Even simple normal people here in Spain are devoid from reality when they panic after reading the newspapers' dire warnings that the Gross Domestic Product reduced by a fifth of a per cent in three months. What crisis is that then? That's barely a statistical error. It's paranoia about losing their material possessions after all those years of spending beyond their means.'

Manolo arrived and shook his hand before grabbing the stool alongside him and ordering a beer.

'Who were you talking to, *amigo*? Not your imaginary guide again?' Manolo smiled at his crazy friend who replied apologetically.

'Come on, *hombre*! I was just thinking aloud about the crisis. Mark my words, Manolo, it's the start of war out there. This financial crisis is a tsunami that will overwhelm more than just the banks It will set people against people and countries against countries, as if at war. Attitudes will harden towards protecting their country and their people and the leaders will harden their stance. Mark my words, the world will change over the next few years and there will be more real wars and more protecting of interests in a less open world.'

'I agree, *amigo,* but no one wants to face up to that now, they hope to ride it all out. However, think positively as you should survive better than anyone else, Jack, with all your simple living in your spiritual harmony.'

'That's true, *hombre,* but I still need money to live on.' Manolo asked him about their earlier telephone conversation when Jack was struggling with his novel.

'What is this *ling* stuff you were putting in your book. Is that important in your spirit world?'

'Yes, but the word is "spiritual", *hombre;* a way of life and not a disembodied entity.'

'You crazy English', you do talk some *basura, amigo,* the only ling you understand is in cunnilingus if my English is correct. You must practise ling a lot with all those girls you keep shagging.'

'True, very true, Manolo, the physical features of my house or the daily trip to the beach channel the, *qi,* or energy, straight into my dick ready for some ling. I must remember the term "lingalot" as it sounds like a good chat-up line. Excuse me, madam, but do you lingalot?' The second glasses of San Miguel beer were already half-empty and they started to relax in each other's company once again. Jack asked him why he had never travelled outside Catalonia.

'I never see the need, *amigo.* All my friends live here. It's a beautiful country and it makes me happy every day that I wake.'

'But, Manolo, there are nice people everywhere in the world. You need to stop being so insular on the peninsular and leave Spain and see the world. Go somewhere you see on the news like the Middle East and see real people in nightmare situations.' Manolo just shrugged his shoulders as he wasn't bothered about others, just himself. Jack disapproved of his attitude and told him so.

'No don't shrug at me. You need to be more worldly in your thinking. For example, I support 750,000 refugees in Gaza by giving the United Nations a £10 a month donation. That means they receive 100 per cent food aid, unless the Israelis stop it going across their border of course.'

Manolo congratulated him. '*Hombre,* this is good yes! Very good, but still thousands die in other places like Africa just because they are not on a political agenda like the oil in the Middle East.' Jack had to agree and nodded sagely as he drank before answering.

'How sick is power and manipulation in our world and we supposedly live in a democracy. Like hell we do. We have no control over anything. A mere handful of people tell us what is good for us as it meets their objectives, the truth of which we can't even contemplate. Politics is just a way of people formally taking advantage of each other, and then each country politics with each other but not with true understanding. You have to know the language to even have a chance of understanding the people as there are over six billion opinions out there and every single one is subtly different.'

'True, *hombre,* but like me and my love for Catalonia, many are very opinionated about key questions like the environment, tax or education, and many opinions are wrong. People have little or no knowledge and base their opinions on ignorance or spurious TV or newspaper reports. In fact, just like me!' Manolo laughed at his joke and asked Jack a serious question with a punch on the arm.

'Are you advocating Communism or Fascism because you seem to believe that only you have the answers and, therefore, you need an extreme political system to be in control!'

'That's probably true, but actually I am advocating thought not ignorance and I don't really care what system is used to control the people. However, you do need some control or you have a knee-trembler situation.' Manolo was perplexed.

'Is this a political term I have never heard of?'

'Not usually, it's a certain position when you have sex that you personally will never experience as you always lie on your back, *amigo.*' They laughed in the twilight as a band called Pa d'Angel started to play a waltz for couples of all ages, including their children and grandchildren who filled the plaza with some *funning.* 'That's really nice to see, Manolo, and so different from England.' They both admired how sociable everyone seemed as the dancers chatted away whilst moving and twirling past each other. Jack changed the topic but still remained on the subject of control.

'Look around at the adverts on the shop windows, *hombre.* Some adverts are bollocks too. Fifty per cent off a new item just arrived from China that still gives the shopkeeper the same profit margin. It's not a real bargain. It's just lies to get you inside. Isn't it a shame that you can never say what you mean in today's society? It's like my satnav that tells me politely that there's a *safety* camera ahead. Why not just say a speed trap? Do you ever think about adverts on TV and stop to repeat them out loud to yourself, instead of just letting them wash over you?' His friend shrugged as he replied.

'Of course not, *amigo,* what is the point in that?' Jack was more emphatic.

'Because *then* you would question their validity. I have loads of examples but can't comment on the veracity of the products.'

'Why?'

'Because you might own half of their goods and get upset, that's why!' Manolo asked him for some examples.

'Okay, brain in gear my Catalan shopaholic. Adidas: Impossible is nothing. You can't actually achieve the impossible by definition, impossible is impossible. Nike: Just do it. I actually agree with that one and it's very apt hey?' Manolo was interested and gave his own in return.

'Hyatt hotels: You're more than welcome. That's good isn't it, Jack?' He agreed and replied.

'But sometimes it takes you three days to work out the meanings. For example, Landrover: Go beyond, rather than saying boost CO_2 on the school run or roll around a lot on bends. Beyond what? It makes it sound like you can reach Mars in a 4x4.' Manolo was struggling to catch the English double meanings and so Jack continued.

'The Olympics: One world one dream. Now that was really good, it's just a shame that the world saw everything on TV after a twenty-second delay instigated by the authorities. That's a bit like some of the products themselves in China. You want a North Face jacket, genuine copy, only twenty dollars. Impossible, of course, but what a great term "genuine copy". Much better than complete rip off.' Manolo had one for Jack.

'Toyota: Moving forward. That is funny isn't it, *hombre*? It's a car. Of course it moves forward by default for the vast majority of its life.'

'Nice one, Manolo, it's as bad as that film *Back to the Future,* clever and meaningless at the same time. How about; Hitachi: Inspire the next. What is that? They only want you to buy a TV or a radio, don't they? Do you get inspired by a microwave, *amigo*? And what is *the next?* The next purchase of their product no doubt. I don't know.' It was Manolo's turn.

'Kia: The power to surprise. Absolute crap and noisy with a total lack of sophistication.'

'Manolo you can't say that! You are totally bigoted by your middle-class preference for Audis! But what about perfume advertising? Jesus wept, how bad is that on Spanish TV which vies with the adverts about tooth care for god's sake. Entranced: Possess him, rather than smell better or hide your BO. Nothing is truthful anymore. We live in a world of lies; a false world, a world of unreality and it's getting worse year by year.' Manolo was enjoying the conversation as it wasn't the usual spiritual stuff.

'Jack have you noticed that the adverts are always spoken in an American accent, as if by a hero in a Marine uniform. Even on television in Spain! And why American, *hombre*? Why look up to them? They got us all into a war in Iraq twice, and all the shit that's coming from terrorism as a direct response. They have screwed up the world economy. They are not as intelligent or cultured as us; they have no history and are war-mongering, junk-food eating, fat and thick. Look at what else they give us. Most of the films are violent and shallow like *Hellboy Two*, *Babylon AD* and what terrible messages they give out! Go and kill someone, live in unreality, make it hurt.' Jack fell off his stool.

'Good god, Manolo, what did I say to provoke that? Whenever you travel abroad just make sure you don't go to America!' They ordered Vichy Catalan water, sourced locally at Caldes de la Maldeva thermal springs, in order to purify their spirits, and also to prevent arrest for drunken driving by the numerous police on fiesta duty. After a toilet break, Manolo reminded Jack that the bottled water was full of salts and at his age he should be careful in case he had a heart attack.

'*Amigo*, you are the one with the failing business and want to be careful about having a heart attack!' Manolo agreed his profits were plummeting due to zero sales.

'Think positive, Manolo, you are just losing some money. In China if someone steals your money they say that they have taken away your bad luck. So feel lucky instead of gloomy.' The Catalan Casanova sat glumly watching the quick stepping couples who were now casting long gyrating shadows from the excessively bright lighting in the square. He asked Jack a more personal question.

'Did you find a girlfriend in China or Japan, despite Melanie being with you?'

'No, well not really. All I found was a quick and unsatisfactory shag with a guide in a hotel room, but you should see the girls, Manolo. They are so beautiful and so different from European women, positively dainty in comparison.' He had to explain the word dainty before Manolo commented.

'But if you don't speak the language of the three billion women you are testing out to find your Sun Sharer you cannot be successful, *amigo*. How can you really know someone whom you can't speak to?'

'Love has no boundaries *hombre*. I travelled around the world to find my Sun Sharer.'

'Really, Jack? In that case I take back every bad thing I have ever said about you, as you are certainly a hard worker.' Jack smiled in reply.

'Well you see, *amigo* I work at my vocation. In fact, as a poor man, now I am thinking about selling this body and was contemplating 50 euros a go. What do you think?'

'Is that black, no tax, no tell? Because if not, it is too cheap, *hombre*. You will get extra if you take your clothes off rather than just unzipping your jeans.' Jack was mortified and told him why.

'But I include a good quality condom, *amigo*.' An unimpressed Catalan replied.

'Maybe you are just after the sex and not the money. Remember to charge extra if they *chupar*.'

'What do you mean *chupar*?'

'Suck, Jack. Chupa chupa are the lollies for the kids in the shop. You must have bought some for Joseph. Anyway, charge more as it is dangerous.'

'Why?'

'Because the younger the person the more they chew the stick.'

'Very funny, Manolo, and I suppose you also like using Facebook on the Internet?' It was the Catalan's turn to question why.

'Because when you see someone online, they usually show the most beautiful photo they have ever had taken and you can give them a *poke*. Hoy! What a strange term? Looking at pretty photographs of girls and wanting to *poke* your friend's teenage children. That is weird or perhaps I'm just becoming a dirty old man.'

'Becoming, Jack? Anyway, I hate the Internet. It is all too young for me. I would rather watch a DVD of a Barcelona FC soccer match from ten years ago.' Jack spluttered into his drink.

'What's the point in that? Why watch past glories? You should live for now and not the past.'

'The point is, Jack, that it makes me happy, unlike you, and remember you live for now and have forgotten all the good things in your past. So, as you become more frustrated with dumb and dumber, you could be listening to the Eagles or Joe Walsh and enjoying your music.'

'*Hombre*, I give in. Maybe I should try it for a while but I couldn't adopt the same principle with cars. My weakness is having to drive the latest car; simple and economical but up to date.' Manolo had a dream and told him about it.

'I want to own a Bugatti Veyron one day, *amigo*.' Jack was nonplussed.

'You've been watching *Top Gear* on Dave TV again. That is so much drivel and over £800,000 for a car is ridiculous. It's like worshipping a new heathen god and its acolyte Jeremy Clarkson. Save the world and go electric as all you need to do is get from A to B. You would be like the expats who are terribly eco-unfriendly with their car use. Using four-wheel-drive gas guzzlers to pop from Aguablara to Palafrio four times a day for nothing. A just-do exercise to fill in time as they don't need to plan as they have so much time to waste. I even had to explain the ESP button in the Duchess's Merc.'

'What is ESP, *amigo*?'

'Manolo! Every man should know that. ESP is the button you have to press as you cross the border from France into Spain. You know when that is yes? It's when the speed cameras are all clearly marked by a sign a mile ahead rather than in England where they are painted yellow, half-hidden and have a policeman with a camera straight after. Tell me how many times have you seen a policeman with a radar detector around here?' Manolo thought for a moment whilst sipping his salty water.

'Once in five years, but we still have terrible traffic problems on the C31.'

'*Hombre*. Don't mention the C31! That takes me back to my old life. Tell me about positive solutions not problems. At the Beijing Olympics they banned half the cars each day and put everyone else on bikes to cut pollution during the games. We could tunnel like moles and drive under the earth sucking the CO_2 into giant underground scrubbers before releasing pure air into the atmosphere. Solutions, Manolo, not complaints please.'

'So who is your hero, Jack? The head of the Spanish Traffic Ministry or Mister Greenpeace? Who do you want to be like, you crazy English?'

'I want to be like James Bond, suave and sophisticated, a real man driving an Aston Martin. Definitely not the short-arse Tom Cruise, too smiley, too godly, American, and so full of shit. What about you?'

'I want to be me. This is good yes? I am happy but you are not, as you contradict yourself. You want a simple life and a fast expensive car. You want a Sun Sharer and a dozen *friend girls*. Are you truly happier now, Jack?'

The crazy English shook his head negatively and then answered honestly after a short pause.

'Having all this time to think hasn't resolved anything in my mind, Manolo. I'm not happier, or unhappier, but stable.' Lluis had brought them some free tapas to celebrate the festival and warned them the tortilla contained very hot chillies to remind his expat customer of Indian food from England.

'No pain no gain' Jack said as he took an enormous wedge of tortilla, chewed, swallowed and choked spitting it out onto the pavement.

'Fuck me, Lluis, are you trying to fucking kill me?' His friends Lluis and Manolo cried with laughter at their trusting friend and it took a couple of hours before Jack's mouth had recovered. And that was the highlight of the evening as they forgave each other.

Casanova was out of luck that night as no women had passed to be chatted into bed. He said disconsolately.

'Time to go home, Jack, there is no more *funning* to be had now. I am sorry about the food joke. Lluis and I thought it would make you happier. Job done.' As they left Bar Fun Fun most people had also departed the square and were eating at home leaving the two chums desolate and alone except for each other and a smirking Lluis. Manolo shook his best friend's hand and promised to see him later in the week.

'Jack, *amigo*, what is the most important thing you want in your life?' His friend gazed at the dark sky searching for the stars.

'To be happy.' Manolo joined his search as he agreed.

'And me, *hombre*, and me.'

Jack emailed Soul Shiner the next day as he sat playing a CD by Will Young, and he quoted the words to tell her how he felt at that precise moment.

'Who am I to tell you, that I would never let you down, no one else could love you half as much as I do now.'

The problem with instant communications on the spur of emotional loneliness is that someone who believes you are their Soul mate or supposed Sun Sharer can instantly draw the wrong and very serious conclusion. Modern life allows you to make an instant decision and therefore more wrong conclusions quicker. Jack was wallowing in the emotional depths and making promises, but it was all talk and wrong of him. It was also evidence of his over-serious approach in his thinking and his introverted lifestyle.

Nim kept warning him of the implications but was ignored because Jack had no one else to rely on. No family, no son, no girlfriend or *friend girl* in Spain. She telephoned him the same night.

'Hello, my knight, thank you for my lovely email today, it meant a lot to me. Tell me how is that fantastic book coming on?'

'Better this week, thank you. Now I'm writing what I think about my thoughts and not what my thoughts are. Does that make sense?'

'No!'

'Well, lovely, everyone has thoughts. For example, I miss you but then I would write about why I was thinking that I was missing you. Do you understand?'

'Frankly, poppet, you have just lost me. What about telling me something simple like some local colour in your day-to day-life?' He obliged.

'I discovered that Girona is called the City of love.'

'You need to take me there, poppet.'

'Indeed I do, *friend girl.*'

'Don't call me that, you know how much I hate it.'

'Sorry but it's a term I wrote in my book after meeting two lesbians holding hands walking down my dirt track. "*Friend girl*" is an open and honest term.'

'Jack,' she remonstrated, 'how do you know they were lesbians? Holding hands is harmless.'

'I know they were lesbians because I was chatting them up as I do with every woman I meet and I just know. The walk down to Yapanc in the afternoon was wonderful though. It was so pretty. Tell me, Soul Shiner, how many times in the last year have you sat in your window and looked at the sky for half an hour, watched it's multiplicity of changes or walked outside and seen 500 swifts zooming from high to low over a field in front of your house.'

'Never, poppet. That is something I love about your life; the way you embrace nature.' He considered that as he felt he was still leading a complicated life and so he told her a story based on something he had heard years ago on the Chris Evans show on Radio One.

'There was a man sitting happily under the shade of a large oak tree in Cheshire and his ex-colleague rushed by on his way to work, barely having time to say hello and without even a "how are you?" So this is the exact opposite of Spanish life, okay? About ten years later the worker passed by the same tree again having been so busy he had never been back that way in all those years. His old colleague was still sitting, smiling happily under the tree and saying good morning to people he knew who passed every day. The worker said to the tree man. "What have you been doing for ten years?" The tree man replied. "I have been sitting under the tree talking to my real friends, shitting, eating, drinking and being very happy. How about you?"

The worker rubbed his face with both hands as if to relieve the stress. "I have rushed around the UK to earn good money, bought a fabulous car and house, had a heart attack and got a divorce, so I barely see my kids and feel stressed and unhappy." The tree man was puzzled. "Why don't you lead a simple life? Take some time for pleasure with true friends and have a Real Life?"

The worker looked at the tree man and said one word. "Why?" That summarises most peoples' lives, Harriet. Modern life makes you paranoid about doing. For example, you are paranoid about your diet; I know you are, so don't deny it. You try and reduce your cholesterol by eating Flora proactive cling film and gorge on Soya Bifidus drinks. You listen to the news ten times a day as if you can influence it and, when someone mentions the word *crisis*, you jump on the bandwagon. True or untrue?'

'True but ...'

'But what, lovely?' She answered.

'Life is complicated, poppet, as I think my problems take on the magnitude of what I put into them. I mean, I think about them and therefore I make the problems bigger. For example, can lovers become best friends? No, not until they both have a new lover so they can forgive and forget. In fact, it's no different from marriage really. But women take longer to forgive as they are more emotional than men.' Jack sighed deeply.

'Listen to me, Harry. You need to stand in the sea and paddle your feet. You need to feel the heat of the sun on your back and the cool water on your toes.'

'You don't have to justify everything, Jack' she said quietly. 'I know what a wonderful spiritual place you live in and I want to be there too, okay?'

'Okay, Harry I'm sorry if I rub salt in the wound. Really I am sorry, but are you living or existing? You see, I think I am *living* in Spain and you are *existing* in England, but to do this I had to reject your world and society.' Harriet asked about his court case for non-payment of maintenance.

'Have you any news, poppet?'

'Yes it was great this morning. I received three emails about it whilst I sat relaxing in sunny Spain. The first was from Melanie telling me I am a bastard and totally irresponsible. The second was copied to me by my solicitor and was from him to Melanie and her solicitor agreeing I am a bastard and irresponsible, and the third was from my solicitor to me alone asking me what I want to do about being an irresponsible bastard.' He laughed for a good minute.

'Really?' she asked.

'Really, but summarised of course!' She missed him and the Will Young words had upset her earlier in the day. He could tell she was out of sorts and so he asked what she was worried about.

'You always say open and honest, Jack, so can I ask something please?'

'Of course, lovely, just ask.'

'Well, I know you say you want to be there for me when you are in Spain but I think you might drop me sometime in the near future.'

'Soul Shiner, listen carefully. It's not that I don't love you, it's just circumstances. They get in the way of relationships no matter what you or I do. You and your divorce and your two girls. You have more money. You lead a different life from me and it is more sophisticated.'

'I can change, Jack. I can be like you want me to be.'

'No you can't change and that is the point. You will never change your lifestyle and you have to be you. That's before we talk about subjective things like shared thoughts and ambitions. We have touched each other and may or may not move apart as it is out of my hands and it is in our fates.' She was silent for a minute and he could hear the Bee Gees playing in the background, he could have sworn it was 'Words'. She queried.

'Do you really think you can change this world?'

'Yes, as long as I think I can, does anything else really matter? But you can't do anything without your health and I haven't got my health so, in fact, I haven't got anything. We are back to circumstances. I haven't got any money, a house or real friends except for you and Manolo, so I really know what it is to have nothing.'

'Nothing is a strong term, Jack; you have got me and a rented house. You have also got a fantastic red Ferrari.'

'That's true, lovely. I have something and should be positive about it, but it really is dog eat dog in the world, and is getting worse because of this crisis. You know there are three million children a year who get pneumonia in the Philippines and 900 of them die. It's dog eat dog in Afghanistan, the Congo, Gaza, Zimbabwe and no one has the moral courage, and by that I really mean governments, to put out a joint statement just saying no to bad things. Real people, real problems, *'Real Life'* ... and these are not in war zones but within civilised society, within relatively rich countries. In Kenya, you get a political protest that then becomes a riot and the soldiers are brought in and they use live rounds. Sometimes I think the only things we truly share with other countries is music; pop music, easy listening stuff. You can sit in a hotel in China, the USA or Colombia and listen to Il Divo or Lionel Richie. I tell you, anything else must be seriously disguised as I can't think what is truly common.' She answered for him.

'How about family values? But I suppose sometimes they are stronger or weaker so you could argue against that. The approach to death is different, don't you think? Here in England we think about burial for a couple of weeks and plan the funeral around the family's appointments, but the Spanish bury people in twenty-four hours?'

'Yes, Harry, and so we should. How sick is the English approach to make death convenient for the living? It's bloody inconvenient for whoever died.' She gave him another example.

'How about the approach to birth?'

'No way, Harry, life is very cheap in some parts of the world. Greed no, even that is different. Recession hits the West and you dump twenty per cent of the workforce who then earn nothing and people say thank god it wasn't me. But in the Far East they say I know what we can do. Let's take a pay cut and keep everyone employed. Money is different, food is different, physically the places, the towns, the country are different. Governments are different but their people in mind and soul … well, you could say, deep down, we are all the same, but who gets that deep? We do have the same needs the same thoughts I suppose and of course wherever you go two per cent of the population control and own everything. Treat the symptoms not the illness and solve some issues.'

'Jack, you think too much about everyone and everything and need to look after yourself, poppet. If you carry on sleeping badly just think, come over to my side and stop drinking so much red wine. Say it to yourself and imagine me there and use it to stop those bad thoughts in the middle of night. Okay, my knight?'

'Okay, Harry, goodnight.'

'Night night, my knight.' He put the phone down thoughtfully and realised again that they were on a different path.

The expats had always found it difficult to contact Jack as he refused to have a mobile. However, Manolo always found it easy by calling in after checking on his mother because he was a true friend. So Manolo and Jack shared their *mañana* attitude as a matter of how they viewed their lives and enjoyed their freedom. The expats had never let go of the English rat race and were annoyed by Jack's *can't be arsed* style instead of seeing it as a simpler life, and so it was Manolo who called in to tell him that Dutch would like to speak to him as soon as possible. Jack explained *simple* to his friend.

'Simple means controlling your communications, *amigo*. No mobile. I contact my friends. Receive an email, action it, then press delete. It's very easy if you try it. I contact who I want, when I want.'

'Well *hombre*, I think you should contact Dutch as it sounded important, but he wouldn't explain.' Jack contemplated why Dutch would need to speak to him and could only imagine it was about the Duchess and their affair.

Telephone him, Jack, and have some moral courage.

He rang the glass house that night. Dutch seemed happy to speak to him and immediately made Jack feel more comfortable.

'Jack, my friend, how are you?'

'Great thanks and you?'

'Not too bad considering, but I think you know the Duchess has left me to go to Holland?'

'I'm sorry to hear that. You wanted me for something?'

'Yes in fact we, that is Niiige, Rolly and I would like to meet up with you.'

'Why?' He waited patiently, his heart beating faster.

'We want to arrange a peaceful meeting in the bar by the church in Bagurr at say two tomorrow. Can you come, my friend?' Jack couldn't understand what was happening here and hesitated.

Agree to go, Jack. There are things you need to know.

Dutch could sense his difficulty in accepting.

'Trust us please, Jack. Life is not all black and white, there are shades of grey ... we want to put things straight about the last few months, as we believe it is only fair to you.'

'I'll be there at two. Bye.' Jack replaced the receiver and puzzled further until the next day when he arrived to see them sitting calmly in the bar. The welcomes were warm and friendly and so he relaxed and ordered a beer waiting to see what was said after the small talk. Rolly started.

'Well I may as well get the ball rolling you know. Have you heard the bad news, Jack?'

'I'm sorry, Rolly, what bad news do you mean?' They all breathed in sharply and a single tear welled from Rolly's right eye.

'I'm sorry to have to tell you, my friend, but Pippa died last weekend at the aerodrome near Escala.' Jack was unable to speak and so Rolly continued whilst the others sat drinking grimly.

'It was horrific Jack. Dutch's friend had flown his six-seater down from Holland and was kind enough to offer to take us for a free trip.' He paused and summoned up his courage remembering how it happened.

'She was very vague all day and was the last out of the flying club offices as she said she needed the toilet. So we were all waiting for her with the engines running under test. It was surreal, Jack. She walked towards the aircraft and instead of coming towards the door, it was as if something controlled her and she walked straight into the propeller.'

'Oh fuck, Rolly. I can't believe it. That is awful. Was there no chance?'

'No, Jack, it was horrific.' Rolly broke down and cried leaving Dutch to explain further.

'There were bits of her everywhere, Jack. It was the worst thing you can imagine, but it seemed like she allowed it to happen.'

Niiige expressed an opinion. 'We think she was made to do it. There were so many weird and bad things happening in the last six months and we think something evil took her.' They all drank heavily in silence. Jack broke it first.

'I don't understand, sorry. You think something evil made it happen?' Dutch answered him.

'We have arranged for a special blessing with a priest at three. Just here in the church and that's why we asked for you to join us.'

'Hold on. Slow down, boys, this is all a bit unreal. I know the women's behaviour was strange, especially Pippa's, but evil …? I can't believe that, sorry.' All three of the expats glanced at each other and Dutch volunteered to be spokesman.

'Jack, my friend, the three of them were very close and they played you along. We knew most of what was happening but we couldn't help you as our own positions were fragmented and dangerous. In any event, you would never have believed us although you had a premonition of Pippa's death at one of the dinner parties.' Jack decided they were being open and honest and told them three things.

'The Duchess said that you, Dutch, set up a child porn site and had fled from the police to hide here. Lucy told me you had hocked the property business, Niiige, and Pippa … well, she was very affected by spirits and I could see that, but she claimed you beat her unmercifully, Rolly.'

Dutch got the other twos' nodded acknowledgements before answering.

'The truth is why you are here talking with us, Jack. The Duchess used my legitimate porn empire in Holland to set up trafficking in child prostitution and is now in custody there. Lucy siphoned off all of Niiige's money and is somewhere in South America, leaving Pippa, who you know was very disturbed. Pippa has been in several mental hospitals over the years, claiming a past life in Empuries near here. She abused herself in every way possible and always claimed Rolly beat her.' Rolly said.

'I never hit her once in her life, Jack. I loved her and supported her during her mental illness.'

'Fuck me, boys, this is all a bit much to take in. I knew they were playing games with me, but what you are saying defies belief.' Dutch placed a hand on his shoulder and looked him directly in the eyes.

'Jack, we want you to come to see the priest for your protection. We want to help you.'

'No, sorry, Dutch, I believe in many things but protection by a Catholic priest blessing me isn't one of my beliefs. Why do you need to get this blessing?' The big man was sweating heavily on the top of his bald head.

'Jack, we know over the last three years that they formed a witches' coven, although we believe they roped Pippa in as some sort of sacrifice.' He let it sink in.

'We used to meet in the church here to combat it and pray for their souls. They were crucial evil in their group of three. You don't know about the black magic they used to practise. It was as if they were scared of your powers for good and had taken on the wrong plaything this time. The last two lovers just disappeared, Jack. That was how seriously evil we believe they were.' Jack was flabbergasted.

'I'm sorry, I won't come to the church, but I do believe you.' Dutch was tapped on the shoulder by Rolly, who was unable to speak, but prompted his friend to tell Jack the worst part by holding out his hands towards Jack.

'Jack, you should know that Pippa was also pregnant and it must have been your baby. We think it was best the baby died in the accident because of the evil inside her but we feel guilty as it means we deserted her and the good side of her spirit.' All four sat drinking without talking. Jack thought quickly.

'Nim, I need your help. Is any of this true?'

Why would they lie, my friend? I warned you but I
can never be explicit. They were witches after your
soul but I fought them to save you.

The church bell sounded three times, clear and beautiful, releasing them from their stupor. They stood and hugged each other and Jack queried what each would do now. Dutch told him he would stay in the most beautiful house in the world.

'I can't go home yet, Jack, I want to as I am lonely and I want to see my family, but the lawyers need to sort it all out first. At least I'm safe here until they have done that.' Rolly was taking his paints and travelling in Italy and Greece where he could stay free of charge in his family's properties. Niiige told him he was undecided.

'Timing is everything, Jack …' He left it open and walked away a broken man. As they turned towards the Church Jack wished them all good luck. He also said he was sorry, truly sorry …

Niiige was found later that day having committed suicide in an old monastery near the castle at Toreolla by hanging a rope through an ancient hook where they used to slaughter the pigs.

The blessing had not prevented the evil winning in the old dank house of the monks.

Early the same evening Jack took a call from Harriet but the momentous events of the day still hung over him and pervaded his mood. He had never shared any expat stories with her and certainly couldn't start now. That made the conversation more charged than it should have been.

'Hello, my knight, how are you today. Have you enjoyed all that lovely freedom, poppet?'

'Hi, lovely, it's been a strange day. The weather feels like there's electricity in the air as if something is waiting to break. Apart from that I glanced at the English newspapers and the crap headlines like the kidnapped child sighting, hurricane on its way next week, a £70 charge for emptying your bin. Really all this crap is cheating people of their humanity. We don't have freedom of expression anymore we are just out to go faster now and believe anyone.'

'Calm down, poppet, life's not that bad. Why are you so stressed?'

'Just the usual things stress me and it's because I am writing about them. For example, why do we all want to shop and buy new things all of the time? Why the faster turnover of our gadgets and the must-have attitude to buy the latest thing.'

'I don't know, Jack.'

'Sorry, lovely, it was rhetorical. I was going to give you a suggestion. It's because it plays to our self-esteem, plays to our confidence and fulfils our self-need when we justify ourselves to other people. It doesn't matter what it is. For example, we need a mobile so friends can telephone us and boost our confidence. So everything is about self-need. Colleagues use a mobile to share work problems and their worries, or to reassure you or themselves. You dump on people more now as a modern day self-crisis. Really it is a crisis of self that has turned into a craving for something better and more luxurious.' Harriet interrupted.

'But, Jack, you say you think simple, like when you are sat in a simple bar, but really you are happier going next door to an upmarket one.'

'I agree, but I am trying to change that attitude. Why cleaner, smarter, better? It can be applied to anything. More food choice or just a more expensive way to brag to my friends that I have more and am therefore superior. It makes me feel better about myself and more comfortable when mixing with other richer people in my tribe, and satisfies my satisfaction.'

'Goodness me, Jack, you are thoughtful today. Is this all in your book?'

'Some of it, but not everything otherwise the hero would sound like a crackpot who has lost his marbles. I think I have so much time to listen and think that I get all of these ideas because of that void. For example, people don't like to say no. I bet you don't either. No. I don't know the answer. Why is that? Children say no really well. But adults can't. And if they don't know the answer, they make it up. You must have noticed that. They will cover themselves and say "Oh yes, it's about ten miles", whereas, in fact, it's twenty and they just guessed it. Adults make something up rather than say no, because you have to appear knowledgeable as an adult. Kids just say "I don't know", or "no". Adults learn to cover up their inadequacies, especially in front of other adults.' She replied thoughtfully.

'I do that all the time. It makes the conversation go around in circles sometimes. I might be at lunch with my friends and we all have an opinion but none of us know the truth. We don't know the facts about something but we can natter for ages about the subject.' He waxed lyrical again.

'The other thing I wrote in my book today was how, when you are over forty, you start making little noises when you do things like getting out of a car. You might grunt, expressing to others how you feel. It means I'm old now and you need to look after me better. Please take more care of me by asking if I am okay. You lift a sack of potatoes and snort but you don't need to. Or that gritted sucking of air through your teeth as you turn your spanner on a blocked u-pipe.'

'You are funny, poppet. I can't wait to read your book.'

'We shall see, lovely. Maybe no one will ever get to read it so they can't see themselves in the pages, and that especially applies to you.'

'Is Soul Shiner in your book, Jack?'

'Yes there is a character called that. Why?'

'Because I don't want to read about things between you and me.'

'Why?'

'Because they are private and it upsets me.'

'But, Harriet, only you and I know what was said between us and so not even our closest friends will read it and see you or me in the book. In fact, it won't even get published in my name, if it ever is published.' She wasn't happy and he could tell.

'What else is in the book, Jack?' She sounded like Melanie which annoyed him.

'The hero shaves all the hair off his body including his scrotum and the painful little nicks hurt! This is to shock people on the beach. He also grows his hair on his head very long and slicks it back to form a silver grey mini ponytail, just to rebel.'

'You've done that, haven't you? You have actually done it since I last saw you.'

'Yes, I wanted to experience it before I wrote about it.'

'And does this hero in your book have sex with other women?'

'Yes.'

'And you've tried that too, haven't you, Jack?' He decided to avoid the direct question and her anger.

'Listen, lovely, I value people who see their lives as living the extraordinary not the ordinary. By the way, thinking that you are one of *my* characters in *my* book can be a terrible form of vanity and self-indulgence.' She was quiet and felt insulted whilst he was thinking about his cowardice with her and whether he was using her as a fallback position, leading her on and not really wanting her.

The silence continued and he wondered if he had said too much. Was he waiting for something better but latching on to her for safety and security a place to go when visiting Joseph? She had started to cry.

'Why are you crying, Harry? There really is no need to cry, lovely. Are you pre-menstrual?'

'Yes, Jack, but being pre-menstrual doesn't change what you said about having other women.'

'I have not said that, Harry, stop making things up. Your hormones are making you overreact.'

'No they are not!'

'Yes they are!'

'No they are not!' She shouted down the phone and he stopped her with a few words.

'So why are you arguing so loudly then? Remember, Harriet, there is no *maybe*, only *there is*.' He repeated it slowly and clearly. 'There is no maybe; only there is. Maybe I will dump you or maybe you had an affair. Accusations are not acceptable in my new world. I know how people react and fight and threaten through fear, emotion and jealousy and I will not be party to that sort of life, okay?' She slammed the telephone down on him.

'Fuck you then.' He said out loud. 'The daily telephone calls were pissing me off anyway.' He knew his best *friend girl* wanted to come to live in Spain and was chasing him. He knew he was pushing her away and remembered his relationship with Bridget. He thought if that hadn't worked, neither would he and Soul Shiner. The telephone rang.

'Jack, you really don't know people.'

'Yes I do.'

'No you really don't. The way things are, it seems I am just convenient for you, Jack. Is that correct?' He didn't answer and she replaced the receiver again. There were no more telephone calls as she knew how to be hard. After all, she was going through a divorce and had learned a lot from Jack.

'Jesus Nim, what is it with women? All over a draft book. But that's my problem, isn't it. I trust people not on what they say, not on what they do but on what they would have done. That's why, with my outlook on life, I get taken advantage of all the time.'

Do you include Harriet in that?

'No. It's not that I am the cause of her pain it's the fact that I share her pain. She will never see that.'

As they say in the CIA, if you have problems and pain, just suck it up.

That's what you think isn't it, Jack?

Jack was furious with Harriet and her attitude and momentarily gave up on her. So he stormed out of the house and raced down the track to reach Bar Fun Fun before Manolo finished work.

Casanova walked across the square with the world on his

shoulders. Jack looked at him and thought he had aged a lot in the last few months as he wasn't the same effervescent self.

'What's wrong, *amigo*, you look exhausted?'

'*Hombre*, thank you for the beer.' He slurped back half the glass before wiping his mouth with the back of his hand and telling Jack his problems.

'In just four days Jack, we have had thirty per cent of clients cancel their rentals; all because of the TV news about the crisis. This is not about real money, it is about confidence and all the news programmes and newspapers are scaring people. In fact, many of my clients have safe jobs, but still they feel the need to plunge into the crisis as if they have been left out! Hoy!' Jack ordered two more large beers.

'I'm sorry about your work, *hombre*, but in any given rental apartment how many steps does it take to put an elephant in the fridge?' The serious Catalan man looked askance at his best friend who repeated the question.

'I have no idea, *amigo*, how many steps?'

'Three. You have to open door, put the elephant in and close the door. Job done.' Manolo was still puzzled by the crazy English who asked another question.

'How many steps for a lion then?' Manolo thought and answered 'Three'.

'No, *amigo*, not three. The answer is four.'

'Why four, *hombre*?' He was more puzzled now and taking it very seriously.

'It is obvious, you silly Catalan man. You have to open the door and take the elephant out first.' Jack made him smile which was the objective. 'Continuing the animal theme, *amigo*. At the zoo there was a conference for all the species of animals both large and small, mammals, insects, reptiles everybody, but who didn't come?'

'*Que?*' He was very confused.

'The elephant, of course, as he was still inside the fridge.' A worried and stressed Manolo was relaxing now as Jack gave him a final thought to test his maths skills.

'What is one plus two times three?'

'Easy, *amigo*, the answer is nine.' Jack punched him on the arm.

'Wrong. The answer is seven. One, plus two times three. Don't you listen *hombre*? I will give you one last chance. I have twenty sick sheep and twenty die how many are left?' Manolo was completely bewildered but answered.

'If you have twenty-six sheep and twenty die you have six left, correct?'

'Wrong, *amigo*. Do the Spanish schools not teach maths? The answer is none and he explained the joke to his poor friend as the third beer arrived on their tall table. Maths and language skills were put aside to talk about the essentials in life: women. Jack queried Manolo's psychology of shagging everything that moved and getting no satisfaction whilst eschewing all responsibilities. He asked directly.

'How do you know if the woman you are taking out is the right one for you? Answer three questions and you will know. Firstly, would you like to be marooned on a desert island with her?'

'Yes I would find her work to do.'

'That is a typical Catalan answer. In my eyes, if I didn't have sufficient Durex I wouldn't bother with a woman as they talk too much. Just some baby oil for a wank would suffice. Right, concentrate now. What do you think of her mother in both mind and body? As your girlfriend gets older she will look like her mother and be like her.' Manolo was smirking as he replied.

'I see her as the matriarch, the rock in the family and I can get my sex by paying for it on another island reached in my *menorquina*.'

'You are so Catalan Manolo. That is a disgraceful attitude. In my case, as they all grow hairy after the menopause, I suppose the answer is to get rid of her and buy a younger model. Now the third and final question. Is she rich enough?'

'*Amigo*, that is too easy. In Catalan law what you put into the marriage remains yours and so she can be rich and stay rich after I have kicked her out of my home.' Now it was Jack who was perturbed.

'In that case, *hombre*, I would definitely marry a rich woman in England!'

'Don't marry anyone, Jack, stay single like me. If a woman gets too close, I run like that Olympic sprinter what is his name? Boult? And then I turn and celebrate to the cameras after the affair is eighty per cent complete, but still win.'

'Manolo, you are truly like the fastest man in the world as all your girls have told me.'

'Really?'

'Yes the fastest at coming too soon.'

'Very funny, crazy English, but sex is just like a game of football and not athletics and I am an aficionado.' Jack asked.

'You mean you can hit the bar or miss an open goal when you are having sex?'

'No, Jack, not sex. I am talking about love, which is like the Champions League of all games versus mere sex in Spanish Division Two.'

'Why?'

'Make one mistake in the Champions League and you are completely fucked.'

'Just so, Manolo. Just so. But my sexual problems are all physical not emotional like love. My ceramic hip squeaks when I have sex, and I have to put my reading glasses on to suck a woman's clitoris in case I miss. The problem then is that I can then see all their imperfections and there is nothing worse than nipple hair to turn you off a woman.'

'Fuck me, Jack, that is so fucking sad.'

'You never swear, *amigo*. Life must be tough for you. Come on; tell me some swear words in Spanish?' Manolo replied.

'Jotan de puta.'

'What does that mean? I thought *Jotan* is a paint manufacturer?' Manolo refused to tell him but offered advice.

'Try translating it on the Internet. But the best way to swear is different from in England. Try something like: I shit on your mother's grave. That will get you into some serious fights, *hombre*.'

The night was drawing to a close and the irreverent chat dried up. Manolo returned to his original problems and commented on his friend's thoughts about business.

'The financial crisis has made people realise that they rely on each other now.' Jack replied.

'No way, I disagree. They are just as greedy and self-centred and are still in denial until their confidence returns. Only then will they resume the same material-orientated lives. Mark my words, the tsunami is coming. Did you see that recent Obama speech about the crisis? No? He said we must all do what we can individually to overcome the financial difficulties.'

'Really?'

'Really. He said in my case I can't wait for my inauguration in January when I get my free houses, free cars and a huge salary increase!' The frivolity for another night died in the chill of the October evening. Jack had one last but serious thing to tell his best friend in Spain.

'I saw the three expat husbands in Bagurr today. Dutch asked me to meet up with them so they could tell me the truth.' Manolo grasped his shoulder as he could see Jack was sad inside.

'What is the truth, *amigo?*' Jack told him everything they had said.

'Jack, my best friend. You get into some terrible jams. You saw the men and you got the truth. But did you really, Jack?' They stood and walked soberly down the narrow side streets to find their cars.

The *barraca* was a lonely spot for the weak-minded. Jack made pasta and took it outside to sit on his wicker chair sat on the edge of the patio. He looked at the view and placing his food on the floor he called to Nim.

'When I went to Empuries with Pippa I could hear and see spirits, Nim, and I knew they were calling to her, which is why she passed out, but I couldn't hear everything because their voices were for her alone. I knew I was involved somehow. I knew Pippa from a past life and I felt Karina at my side, but pushed the thoughts away.'

> *You have always been close to Yapanc, Jack, and have*
> *always heard voices in every life for nearly 1,600*
> *years. This is the area you always come home to and*

every time you search and meet Karina again, and
every time you lose the love of your life.

That is your challenge in this karma, to win her or
lose her forever, as there will never be another chance.

'I believe that now. I also feel that Pippa was a friend in the past but took her own life and I blamed myself for her loss as it has always been on my conscience. But, Nim, I can't see the future.' Jack sighed and closing his eyes he started to cough uncontrollably as if drowning. He talked to Nim in his mind as he gasped for breath. 'I can only see bad things. There is a car accident and it plummets over a cliff avoiding a beautiful woman in a white dress and there is a man drowning.'

Jack, everything you have seen and done were cul de
sacs off your path and you took them, but came back
down to re-join the central way.

You must follow this singularity and, although the
spirits accepted your reasons for deviating, they will not
accept anymore. You have been critical of life and all the
cynical sides to it and were duped by a coven of witches.

He felt light and floated upwards seeing his body slumped in his chair, but he felt calm in the transcendental experience. He was closer now to the crescent moon with the conjunction of Venus and Jupiter forming a face in the sky which was Nim. His guide reassured and calmed him as his father drifted by blowing his breath across him as a zephyr on the cool night air.

Listen to me, Jack. I will tell you your history and
how you know Karina.

You lived in Empuries with Karina and also Pippa
1,600 years ago.

You were already an old spirit then and they were both drawn to you as they were vestal virgins serving in the Temple of Artemis. It stood on the headland where the main fortress looked over the harbour and is where you see the village of Sant Martin. The Acropolis had this temple dedicated to Artemis, who was the daughter of Zeus, king of all the gods on Mount Olympus, and as a Hellenic goddess she had her following in Empuries, even when the Romans drove the Greek army away.

Old gods never die and she was still worshipped by many. She helped all women through childbirth, virginity and fertility, but dearer to your heart she was also the goddess of the fortress and the hills full of wild animals, as she was a huntress on her horse. But Artemis had asked Zeus to grant her eternal virginity and through the centuries she became known for her possessiveness. In the temple, serving the goddess, were two friends and you know them in this time as Karina and Pippa. They knew you as a brave and strong Centurion who worshipped at their temple each day to guarantee good hunting, but you did more than worship as you met them in their disguises in the city and took them sexually, making them want you more and Artemis less. Pippa adopted all the idiosyncrasies of her mistress goddess and became jealous of her friend. So when the Vikings sailed into the harbour you went to the temple to protect them both and the Vikings slew you in a lovers' embrace with Karina.

That is why you have searched for centuries and never been together, but now is your time, Jack. She cannot see it as she is possessive of Josep Maria and protecting her virginity in the murkiness of her ancient spirit.

'What about Pippa, Nim?'

She wanted you and was jealous of Karina, but it was she who betrayed the city to the Vikings, by telling them when the garrison was weakest.

'Why?'

Always why, Jack, I have taught you well. For the love of a Viking, a king indeed who met and took her as he reconnoitred the rich but decaying city, and promised her she could be his Queen.

The high priestess of the temple had seen this liaison but too late to stop the treason. As the Vikings invaded she took her revenge on the traitorous Pippa and stabbed her to death, but made it look like suicide to protect the religion.

That is the memory you have just before you and your Sun Sharer died.

Jack shuddered as he regained his body to sleep soundly.

At midnight after Nim's extraordinary revelation Jack had an equally extraordinary dream, but the fine line between dreaming and waking was indistinguishable. He was still slumped on his cane chair on the patio, lit by the bright crescent moon and the planets that cast deep shadows in the trees, with long tenuous arms reaching across the field and to his very feet. He was dreaming of a giant wild boar running towards him. Foam came from the mouth of the beast as the beady red eyes bored into Jack's closed ones.

Dancing in front of him were his expat *friend girls*, including a deathly white Pippa strung together with stitches that oozed blood as she smiled across at him. The Duchess was intoning a prayer to the moon, wanting to communicate with the goddess Luna and invoke her spirit to force Jack to fertilise all three of them with devil babies.

As the wild boar grew larger in his dream it got closer to the coven. The last fling of the expats was them symbolically running away across his beautiful field, avoiding the realities of their lives and Jack, their spiritual lover, who broke up their witches' circle with his goodness.

In his dream he knew he would never see them again. It was all too complicated and he didn't know who or what to believe. As they ran away he saw a baby's head appear between Pippa's legs just like the glass orb she had sucked inside herself and then spat out.

The Duchess pointed at him and mouthed 'I loved you' and Juicy Lucy imitated a cantering horse, whipping her arse with her hand and shouting 'I fucking won ya', at the top of her voice. They told him they had someone new to play with, a black Mussulman who would give them something Jack couldn't, and he realised they were all swingers, with their husbands seeing him as a plaything too.

But the last scene was a grotesque Pippa turning towards him and in her hands she held a silver platter on which sat the black man's head with a screaming mouth and staring eyes.

As Jack jerked awake and stood up terrified, the friendly and satisfied boar trotted away from the dish of pasta that lay at Jack's feet. A haunting wind whistled through the trees before blowing him off his feet and onto his stomach in the field and, as he lay, he watched in fear as the expats waved goodbye in the distance, promising to visit him again.

'Are simple life and 'Real Life' incompatible?

Although it was November in Spain it felt like a spring day in England.

Thirty fat grey pigeons sat in the skeleton branches of the tree immediately outside Jack's compact yellow house. They watched him greedily eating a bocadillo made with *queso*, cheese and *membrillo*, apple jelly and relished where the crumbs fell. He munched away, steadily digesting his thoughts about what he was doing in Spain, and whether to give up on his dreams and return to England as a consultant.

*Jack, you are just lacking in confidence and your
recent experiences have exacerbated it.*

'The book is crap, Nim, even my best friend, Harriet, was too busy, or too bored, to read more than twenty pages after promising she would read it properly and give me some feedback. She's too polite to say it but I know it's crap. My Spanish is also crap as I have no motivation to learn it if I'm returning to England and, quite frankly, it doesn't help anyway as they all insist on speaking Catalan.' He pointed his sandwich at the gaunt tree with its plump occupants. 'Unlike that lazy lot, I don't have my simple and *'Real Life'* after all this time.

Redefine simple life, Jack?

'That's easy I wrote it in my book,' but he hesitated before replying. 'A book on fish, flowers and birds, for the area where I am living. A real log fire set in a large room of a house which is in a beautiful spot where you can eat, sleep, talk and be. A comfortable chair to look at a natural view made up of rocks, trees and plants, with a vista out to the horizon so you can watch the sky as the shape of the clouds and the colour changes every hour of every day. A radio with a battery pack so you can sit anywhere and listen quietly to the Latino music in the sigh of the breeze as you relax under an olive tree, shaded from the hot sun whilst falling in and out of sleep.'

I hate to interrupt your dreaming, but you have all of
that and yet you are still complaining.

'True but I want someone who loves me, Nim, for what I am and not what I *seem* to be; someone to listen and accept, not question and change. Who loves me for my smile, my conversation and not my achievements; for my trying and failing, but supports my trying. To share my hurt and pain, and joy and laughter, in equal measure, without question or complaint. To do things with me that I love; to climb a mountain, sail a sea, plant a garden or write a book. To live simply, not obscenely, and embrace all people without prejudice and without criticism. To share my reality, my realism that what we have on today's earth should be cherished, nurtured and loved because life is not a rehearsal. It's here and now.'

So it's easy then. You are missing your Sun Sharer,
Karina, and you know Harriet is not the one for you.
Most people never try to find a simple life because it's
too hard to contemplate, never mind achieve the change.

They are not old souls like you; they are too
entrenched in reality to contemplate more subjective

> *matters about life itself. Have confidence, Jack, and*
> *believe in what you are doing. Now is the wrong time*
> *to start questioning all that you have achieved.*

Jack scraped his cane chair backwards and stretched as he stood emptying the plateful of crumbs onto the edge of the patio for the pigeons and the ants. He walked inside, placing his plate in the sink, and continued to the yellowed list stuck inside the front window which described his priorities in life ten months earlier. Tearing the paper off the glass left glue marks from the aged Sellotape which he would have cleaned off immediately in the spring but they could now remain for the next tenant.

Why?

'That's my saying not yours.'

Why take it down now?

'Because I have nothing to complain about anymore as it has all been self-inflicted pain. I can't simplify my life any further, unless there was absolutely no one else involved which is impossible and, quite frankly, I am not going to justify or engage with you about it, Nim.'

What's happening to you, Jack?

'Nothing is happening to me. That is exactly the issue. I need a new list starting with "BE ME" followed by "fuck the old crap", "fuck the people who say they are friends", "fuck my family" and "fuck everyone in general", as no one is fucking listening to me. Simple life is not achievable due to the intrusions of real life. Job done.' He used Manolo's expression to end the conversation and went to slump on the uncomfortable, old and musky-smelling sofa.

Looking at the digital clock on a shelf in the corner of the room he watched the red LED figures flicker, slowly counting away his life. At first he watched the seconds, then the minutes and finally the hours, synchronising his day and passing time but reinforcing his new perspective on life and what it really meant.

'It's just time passing, Nim. Fifty-three years down and forty-seven to go implies that I have to fill 17,000 days, 400,000 hours and 25 million minutes before I die. What the hell am I supposed to do with all that time?'

You have your simple life, so what else are you missing
to make you so introspective?

'Well there's the automatic toaster and kettle, instead of a manual grill and boiling water in a pan, plus a nice hot bath and … '

So nothing really?

'Fine, point taken, Nim, but I would like to get to a given date and have absolutely no practical plans after it, leaving a void to fill.'

To fill with what?

'The reality of my ideas. CITE. Writing. A Sun Sharer. That would mean I have achieved a simple life. I think that then I would have no emotional justification in any new relationship and that is also simple. I would have simplified life by communicating differently, stopping texting, not returning telephone messages and just never talking to people who are not true friends, by getting rid of my acquaintances.'

So nothing really. You have done all that.

'Fine again! But I have no money and no structure in my life. I have no family and all of this makes me feel so insecure, so "none".' Jack was quiet as he realised that he was scared of life now, whereas before he was only scared of death. His recurrent dream was with the shotgun being loaded and closed, but he would choose an easy suicide by overindulging in red wine and paracetamol; the fear of waking in the night and for a conscious minute realising his heart had stopped and he was dying. The red LED flashed away the seconds and he seriously contemplated the best methods of suicide to avoid his potential 25 million minutes of filling in time. He pondered whether he could make it seem accidental with his car skidding over the cliff by El Far and then the life insurance would pay off his debts to Melanie and Joseph. Pay off his guilt.

'I have no courage left, Nim.'

Why?

'Don't use my word.'

You can't buy time.

'Okay that one was mine too. No one is strong all the time, so stop taking the piss.'

It's up to you, Jack. Go ahead do it. Be dead.

'That's just Soul Shiner's reverse psychology. Go away.'

But it succeeded as he got off his settee and that was all that was important. He shook himself with his arms outstretched in a cross and pushed the negativity away by talking out loud as he left the house.

'Stay focussed, get the book completed and then reconsider the practicalities of living. You promised Mother you would never commit suicide again.'

The unique Ferrari rally car sped down the dirt track sliding around the corners to take negative Jack to see his best friend in Spain.

It was lunchtime on a Sunday and the small daily market in Palafrio had extended half a mile up the central road enticing extra people from the local vicinity, although none from more than five miles away. Inevitably, Jack had to park twenty minutes' walk away from the centre of town and slowly make his way in. As always, he never failed to marvel at the beautiful gardens and mansions secreted in the bland backstreets, harking back to earlier wealthy periods. As he closed on the plaza the shop windows declared "Sales" in large banners, in Catalan or Spanish, depending on the whim of the owner. The same tired façades always declared a final liquidation, because of moving to new premises or impending closure which never seemed to occur month on month. He couldn't understand how any of these small disparate shops survived. He surmised that the local shoppers didn't bother to travel or to shop in the same way as he was used to in England. It was only later he learned about the ingrained cultural support of the collective organisation created during the Civil War.

Maybe they have fewer cars in the family or prices are kept reasonable and close to the level of a big city as local costs are lower? Possibly it's the shoppers supporting their friends and families. But he never found the real answer and so, instead, he just enjoyed the convenience and excitement of the place he loved.

Manolo sauntered out of his office towards Bar Fun Fun and waved. Jack was saving him a stool from the marauding incomers who disrespected the boys' rights to their usual prime position. But it took another quarter of an hour for the Catalan to make the short journey as he chatted happily to passing friends and family on the way across. These chance meetings made the atmosphere joyful in the winter sun. Saunter and greet, wander and chat and that made Sunday special for everyone who flocked there 'to be' and not necessarily to buy. He clapped Jack on his shoulder.

'*Hombre, que tal?*'

'*Muy bien, amigo, muy bien.*' Manolo drank his beer greedily after a long morning of zero sales and rentals, and surveyed Jack with concerned eyes.

'Jack, my friend. My crazy English. I have some terrible news that I don't think you have heard in your splendid isolation.' Jack was mystified as he watched a dark beauty in sunglasses glide past.

'Good god, *amigo*, look at her.' Manolo watched the woman without comment.

'Jack I have serious news.' Jack turned his attention to his friend who carried on in a slow and sad tone. 'Dutch died in a car accident near Aguablara two nights ago. Nobody knows what happened but the police saw a bent and buckled section of Armco with silver paint grazes and so they investigated further.' There was no comment from Jack but he knew Dutch must have been driving the Duchess' Merc.

'They called in a boat with a diver from Palomost and that's how they found him. The convertible top was closed, but it wouldn't have mattered as he was smashed to pieces on impact with the sea, although he missed all of the rocks on the way down the 200 metre drop.' Manolo paused and shook his head. 'Jack, he was probably alive all the time until he hit the sea. Jack?' Manolo gently touched his friend's right arm as Jack gazed unseeing into the square. He prodded again but harder this time.

'*Hombre*, is the shock so bad, my friend? I feel so sorry for him.' Jack turned to Manolo with his lips pursed and a vein twitching in his left brow.

'Manolo, Dutch telephoned me last night.'

'That's impossible as he had already been dead for twenty-four hours.' Jack re-emphasised his words.

'Manolo, he rang me last night at about ten and warned me to be careful wherever and whatever I did, because he said *they* were out for revenge. He also told me half a dozen times to go to be blessed by the priest in Bagurr.' Manolo sank the rest of his beer and ordered two more. He had some more news to give and gulped nervously before he did so.

'There was also Rolly three nights ago.'

'Why?'

'Rolly drowned off the coast in Italy. His cousin telephoned me asking if I would go and inspect the house in Bagurr.' Jack said sarcastically.

'I suppose that was an accident as well?'

'He was swimming, Jack.'

'Sure, at night, in the cold sea, in November? I wonder if the coven helped him drown.' They sat silently, drinking the new beers and hearing nothing except their own breath as the hubbub carried on around them. Jack broke the silence with a grin and ordered the next round.

'*Mañana, hombre*. Life has its ups and downs and some of them are 200 metres. The lower the downs the higher the ups. *Abibajos* in Spanish I believe. Ups and downs.' He couldn't totally lighten the conversation as he had to ask. 'Do you believe in evil, Manolo?'

'Yes, Jack. My religion tells me it exists and my religion and belief protects me. If the expat women want me dead, well, *amigo*, they will want you dead more. Hoy!' They drained their glasses and ordered again. The alcohol made them relax and the fear dissipated with every swallow. Jack responded.

'Maybe your beliefs help, but maybe not. Remember they all went and saw the Priest in Bagurr.' There was a long pause, 'And that didn't work, did it? Anyway, *hombre* they will come for you first as I was far better at shagging them.' They burst into irreverent laughter before toasting the witches' coven. Nothing really mattered to the pair of them. Life was practical and real sitting there in the sun and it wouldn't be until the sun set that they would consider the real danger.

'How is Soul Shiner, Jack? Have you dumped her yet? You know you need to be cruel to be kind.' He explained her loving behaviour to the unemotional Manolo.

'She listens to me and hears my words but then she reads between the lines and even my phrases to give me a totally illogical answer to any question or issue concerning me and her. It's as if she bases everything on the in between things that are not heard and not based on the hard factual words.' Manolo tapped his nose before replying.

'Be yourself in a relationship.'

Jack, listen to your best friend.

'Fuck off, Nim.'

'Sorry?' Said Manolo.

'No don't be sorry, I was talking to Nim.'

'Jack, *hombre,* please let go of this thing with a spirit guide. Just forget he exists and move on, okay?'

'Okay, *amigo.*' But that meant not telling the truth to his friend as he still fervently believed in Nim, and he knew the spirit guide was protecting them both from the two remaining witches.

Jack quickly changed the subject back to a lighter note.

'You can't believe in anything, *amigo.* Spirit guides, TV and especially Internet sites. You see famous people portrayed in front of you as a sound bite or a flattering or unflattering photograph; a five-second clip cut from an hour-long speech, or a photo digitally enhanced to make them more beautiful or the worse for wear at an editor's behest. What is real?'

'*Hombre,* you are not going to rant and rave again, you crazy English. Relax let's have more beers instead of a serious conversation on this beautiful day. Tomorrow we could both be dead.' The truth of the words tailed off into the cold clear air. Jack continued without touching his beer and demanded to be serious.

'What sums it all up is when the good old BBC website has a video link called "One-minute world news". How impossible is that? One fucking minute, no fucking way. The *Daily Mail* had typical crap headlines all this week like THE GREAT LIGHT BULB REVOLT, when children in Gaza are dying, bombed by the Israelis as a *necessary* part of their actions. And how cynical is the Spanish Government donating five million euros to the visiting President of Gaza? Hey, Manolo? So the Spanish press can take a nice picture of your President and print it to keep the Algerians and Moroccans happy as the mainstay of your cheap labour.'

Manolo was shaking his head from side to side, disagreeing but not wanting to argue, although he did remember many parts of North Africa were once Spanish colonies. Jack was deeply upset by the latest world events.

'Keep the Moslems happy. Hoy! Leaving Prince Harry in *The Mail* to slag off the Pakis, and all in the same week! What a total coincidence or great fucking timing by someone and do you know what? Within a month it is all forgotten and everyone has moved on to something new and just as shallow.'

'Jack, you worry too much. Concentrate on light entertainment like me, and follow our beloved Spaniard Penelope Cruz, who has been on our TV constantly this month waiting to win award after award. She is the most beautiful woman in Barcelona and is the only one who will not take me as her lover.' They laughed so hard they fell off their stools.

'She lives in fucking Hollywood, *hombre,* and never comes home. Anyway let's face it, she's just a thin coat hanger, *amigo.* Every picture she has taken is in front of a brand name logo with someone's designer dress on. Fucking cynical, *hombre,* but at least she makes loads of money!' Manolo retreated to the toilets and so Jack started on Lluis the barman, who spoke poor English which suited negative Jack.

'Every company claims to be carbon-free on their literature and their websites, but do you know what that means, Lluis? It means nothing, as it's just marketing hype to keep the customers happy in their tiny little minds. Like a wind turbine that sits on top of a supermarket in full view of the mindless morons and barely powers five checkout tills. All fucking hype, Lluis.'

'No fucking, *Señor* Jack, please.' Lluis carried on tidying the emptying tables.

'What about the credit crisis, Lluis? What credit crisis, I say. I'm alright Jack, as I now own the Bradford and Bingley and Northern Rock banks. They are mine, as I am one of the people, and the people own things by paying more tax and financing the Government.

You know, Lluis. I've got nothing and so I can't lose anything. I have two banks now, but before all I had was an overdraft!' As the rest of his rich ex-acquaintances were running for safety into government bonds and multiple bank accounts, Jack sat as happy as Larry with zilch.

'People make money out of a crisis, Lluis.' Lluis walked inside but Jack continued to tell the passers-by. 'As oil prices plummet to a third of their levels, the futures marketeers are laughing all the way to the bank if they guessed right. The Arabs are making money by baling us out and the rich make more money buying properties at half their previous values and banking them away for a decade or two. The rich get richer in a crisis, trust me, I'm an estate agent.' Manolo returned having considered Jack's previous outburst.

'*Amigo*, maybe your ranting is due to your age; that is, fifty-three down and not a lot to go.'

'Thank you for your support, *hombre*, based on the exploits of the coven maybe we only have a couple of days left each!' Manolo chuckled nervously before Jack continued.

'You do know when you are getting old though. I know it hasn't happened to you yet, but a good example is when you get into a friend's car and you can't find where to secure your seatbelt buckle, just like your grandma used to do. Or when you permanently carry your reading glasses around in your pocket, for perusing menus or tins in supermarkets. You also need your glasses to see maps when you are travelling in your car, as it is impossible to drive and see your satnav at the same time.' Manolo was laughing at his friend and joined in.

'Old age is going to have a piss every half an hour in the middle of a sex romp, so in fact it is impossible to romp at all.'

'Who told you my secret, *amigo*? I bet it was Juicy Lucy, loud-mouthed whore. Anyway, it isn't strictly true. Pissing in the toilet without missing is the real issue, so I have to sit on the seat at night to make sure I don't pee on the floor.' Now they were both laughing in their drunkenness. 'As an old git, I now accept people for what they are. I don't judge them by my standards; I don't judge them by this society's standards or another country's standards, just by what they do to me and me only.'

'Bravo, Jack. That is enough for one day. *Adios, amigo*.' Manolo swayed towards his office for a long siesta as they remained closed every Sunday afternoon and Jack walked disconsolately in the opposite direction to sleep the booze off in his car before driving home.

The town had emptied by now and the market traders were clearing up and loading most of their goods back into their large white vans.

Crisis what crisis?

⋆　⋆　⋆

It took a fortnight for Soul Shiner to overcome her jealousy about Jack's unacknowledged affairs and then to telephone him to make up.

'Hello, poppet, I just need to say something, okay.'

'There's no need to say anything, Harry. Please don't say anything. It's just nice to hear your voice again.' She carried on regardless.

'I'm sorry for disrespecting you and I know I bent your words, but I have a feeling that you are not telling me the whole truth and never will.' Jack interrupted.

'Please don't say anymore.' But she wanted to finish her thoughts.

'I understand you are going through a difficult time and I accept that because I can't live without my best friend.' She started to cry. 'So please, Jack. Let's still be friends and anything else is a bonus.'

He answered truthfully.

'Soul Shiner it is inevitable that lovers have more emotions than best friends and more emotions mean more to hurt, with more jealousies, and this revolves in a vicious circle. So you want to be lovers and therefore you must accept that pain, if that is what you want. Do you want that?'

'Yes of course I do, poppet.' He told her straight.

'Being best friends without sex but still with genuine deep love gives more, as it helps all our inner needs, so truly less is more.' She replied.

'I understand that, Jack, but I can't help being in love, it just happened. I don't think about being in love, it just feels that way. I don't analyse it as there is nothing to analyse. I do know how I feel and that's what makes my day; feeling and not thinking. So as long as you can put up with me I want to be a lover and a best friend.'

'Of course I will put up with, you silly billy, but remember true love is not selfish and you may become selfish, as you will look after you and yours and *we* become old gossip in Cheshire. A Sun Sharer is never selfish; they always look after their partner with no balancing, no laying off one against another and never selfishness. They always think of the other person as they think of themselves in a oneness that is indestructible. I have always said you are not my Sun Sharer, Harry, and I have always been open and honest about us.'

'I know, poppet, and I thank you for your honesty. So let's just see where we end up, okay?' Jack was happy to leave it at that and invited her to bring him up to date on her life as he listened contentedly to his best friend in England.

She told him the details about Matt, the girls and the house in her divorce negotiations until Jack jealously pushed her away, prompted by her talking about two million pounds that was *her money*.

'I'm sorry I can't be with you more often, Harry, as you have everything and I have nothing. I can't even afford to fly home anymore. That's ironic I suppose as they say, "absence is a common cure for love".' He dismissed her after an hour of chatter. 'Speak to you soon, lovely, bye.'

'Night night, my knight,' she replied thoughtfully, but he had said the words and couldn't take them back. He received another telephone call from her in the early evening of the next day which was a Friday.

'Poppet?'

'Hi, Harry, how are you?'

'It's not a question of how am I but more one of where I am. Can you guess?' Jack didn't think too hard with his reply.

'You are in the Pheasant Inn having a friendly drink with my 'ex' wife Melanie?'

'Jack! No of course not. I am at Liverpool airport about to board a flight to Girona for the weekend, unless you say don't come. So tell me now, shall I get on this plane and be there in two hours, or shall I drive home a disappointed and rampant whore.'

'Oh god, it's that time of the month, is it? You want me so badly that you are flying over to shag me silly. Is that correct?' She replied excitedly.

'Yes, of course, unless you can't manage it ...'

Jack was sexually desperate to see her and also wanted the company of his best friend as he was incredibly lonely. He was smirking as he asked his next question.

'Before I decide, what is the fashion in underwear now?' She giggled.

'Big nicks are out, thongs are definitely out and my new highly fashionable knickers are more like a wide waistband with a hanging crotch; very pretty and very, very sexy. So do you want to take them off me with your teeth, or not?' There was no hesitation in his reply.

'Just get on that fucking plane and shut up.'

He hung up and checked the LED clock to see when he needed to leave to pick her up and then went to shave and shower. On the way to the airport he bought some fresh bread and different types of Spanish cheese and ham so they could eat simply and quickly on their return to his home, but the rampant sex was only fed by red wine as the first ten hours were spent fucking, bingeing and sleeping.

After a second bout of sex on the Saturday morning, when Jack failed to have an orgasm yet again, he suggested a walk up the hill at Torreolla Castle. The location had been chosen especially as it was well away from his friends and avoided any chance of potentially embarrassing meetings.

It was a beautiful clear day, nudging fifteen degrees, as they scrambled up the isolated peak surrounded by flood plain. The shape resembled a bishop lying on his back with his hands crossed, leaving the Bishopric ring as the castle on the top of a corpulent tummy. They passed altars and shepherd's huts built from the stones of the hillside, until they reached the large cross on the ridge. Here, they could marvel at the new monastery and the ruin alongside in the pretty and secluded valley behind the Bishop's belly and, in the far distance, they could see the Islas Medes islands.

Jack crossed himself in remembrance for Niiige who had died a few hundred yards away from where they paused. Turning 180 degrees and facing east they could also see the medieval city of Pals and its surrounding rice fields, resurrected after so many deaths had required their draining in 1835 due to the malaria epidemic. As they climbed higher, the worn but natural rocky steps took them on a white-grey path to the empty shell of the castle where they ascended a tower to sit in the chilly easterly breeze. She held his hand as they walked the ramparts and told him about her love.

'You can stop pushing me away now, poppet. You don't need to protect your independence, you know.' He gripped her hand tighter and leaned over the wall to stare into the dry moat before replying in a matter-of-fact voice.

'That comment goes to show how weak or how new is our relationship. You think that because I am pushing you away I don't care for you, but it's actually the opposite. I'm being defensive about me getting on with this new life. I don't intend making a mistake for a third time with someone I love.' She spun him round and stared into his eyes.

'Do you love me then?' He answered eventually.

'That's my biggest hang-up. Making a mistake in a relationship again. You see, Harry, I do love you, but I don't think I love you enough.'

'I know that. I also know that I'm not your Sun Sharer, but I will always be there for you.'

'And I know that too, Harry.' She smiled and hugged him as they looked at the Cadaques headland in the blue distance. She asked him.

'How do you know if someone is a Sun Sharer?'

'True love is never doubting someone. That's a way of knowing you have a Sun Sharer. In our minds we are always trying to mould people into a perfect person, a perfect image. Fat must be thinner. Dirty must be cleaner. Brunette to blonde. If you have no moulding to do then that person could be your Sun Sharer. There are hundreds of ways you could give marks to a person to reach a total, to judge a Sun Sharer, but none of them are applicable, as you would just know.' She hugged him tighter.

'Do you really believe you will ever find a Sun Sharer?'

'I suppose not. It could be a figment of my imagination to help the storyline in my book. Who knows? I don't even know if I would be happy with my Sun Sharer as that's not guaranteed. I do think there is a scale of unhappiness and even normal day-to-day life can be unhappy. The first kiss can be deliriously happy, looking at a sunset holding hands can be very happy, not seeing your son can be deeply unhappy. What do you think, lovely?'

'I think it is wonderful being here with you in your beautiful country that you keep calling *home*. That's all I need to think about.' They walked steadily back to the car, with Jack in the lead as the path was narrow and slippery and that effectively killed off any further serious conversation until later that night, after another three hours of love-making. They lay exhausted in the dark when she asked him a poignant question before they slept.

'Why can't you come, poppet? That's the third time we have made love and I feel so selfish as I have so many lovely orgasms and you have none. Why?'

'No one can use my copyrighted expressions like why? That is, unless you pay me royalties, of course.' She snuggled up to him and whispered sleepily.

'I want to make you happy, as I feel selfish. What can I do for you?' She had her hand on his still-hard prick but she was too tired to do anything with it. 'Tell me why, Jack. Why can't you come?' He knew she would be asleep in a few minutes and hedged his bets as she farted and then apologised.

'It's not you. It's not that you are not exciting or not beautiful enough. Maybe it's my age.' He let his answer hang. 'Yes that is probably the biggest thing, but at least I don't need to take drugs to get and keep an erection. Well, at least not yet.' She was quiet now so he whispered in her ear. 'We could have tantric sex if you like? You can just lie there not moving with me on top of you and then we mustn't speak for three hours and certainly not wriggle our parts about.' She was very sleepy now and farted again without an apology before her reply.

'But, poppet, how do I know you won't be asleep?' He poked his tongue in her ear and said.

'You don't need to know because I can guarantee that after ten minutes I will be.' She laughed and turned on her side with her back to him murmuring.

'Can you keep a hard on when you're asleep?'

'I'll give it a crack if you will.' But she was snoring gently before he could comment any further. Jack lay still and listened to her. He wasn't happy as she had started to resemble Melanie. The lack of respect as she farted and snored in bed were minor things. So was the extra stone of fat now that she was more content. The issue was trying to manipulate his life to be what she wanted and not asking or listening to what he wanted. He got out of bed talking to Nim in his mind.

'What the fuck am I doing here again?'

She doesn't understand you, Jack. It's all a sham, drawing you further into her world each day, but she is not the right one for you. You know that, despite the little things that you push to one side.

Fundamentally, you don't have the courage to end it all. It's not the grabbing the telephone whilst you were talking to Joseph, or telling you what you should be saying to him.

It's everything else, isn't it?

'I know, Nim. I know but ...' Jack went to fetch a drink of water to wash the wine through his liver and stood on the patio pondering the truth that his spirit guide didn't need to tell him.

Sunday was spent walking the coastal path between Tiramisu and Palomost and by the end of the afternoon they were both exhausted from the physical exercise, both in and out of the bedroom.

They sat on the *barraca* patio entranced by the view milking the last of the beauty before the sunset and the drive to the airport. It was Jack who, unusually, broke the silence, casting his mind back to his reading book a few days earlier.

'Don Quixote has a lovely poem in it called "The despairing Lover". It doesn't translate well but I want to read it to you. He went inside and fetched the worn book and finding the place where the page corner had been turned over he started to read.

'It was a poem by a shepherd who died because of his unrequited love for a beautiful woman called Marcella. This woman didn't welcome or invite any man's love and didn't want to be beautiful, but men fell in love with her constantly. So she never led the shepherd on or gave him any reason to want her, but men delude themselves, my best friend. We just delude ourselves and don't see things clearly as we aren't like women.'

'Read me the poem, Jack.' The red sunset burnt the tops of the pines as he read slowly and clearly.

'Relentless tyrant of my heart,
Attend, and hear thy slave impart
The matchless story of his pain.
In vain I labour to conceal
What my extorted groans reveal;
Who can be rack'd, and not complain?
But oh! who duly can express
Thy cruelty, and my distress?
No human art, no human tongue.
Then fiends assist, and rage infuse!
A raving fury be my muse,
And hell inspire the dismal song!'

Jack completed the story.

'It goes on after this and is all about being scorned, unloved and finally about pain and the shepherd's death.' Harriet leaned her head on his shoulder and whispered.

'How did the shepherd die, my knight?' Jack stroked her hair as he replied.

'From love, my darling, from love.'

Soul Shiner flew home happy. She had seen her knight and he had told her beautiful things. She had a wonderful lover and a best friend, but she wasn't listening.

★ ★ ★

The day after she had gone home, Jack woke up early with her visit still buzzing through his mind and that pushed his thoughts back to his old life in Cheshire which knocked onto his doubts about his new one in Catalonia.

The memories wouldn't go away and so after a quick coffee he strode the two miles down to Kaletta beach and, sat watching the sunrise from a rocky promontory next to the Hotel Sant Roque, with Nim sat invisible but tight by his side. You could tell the sun was now far to the south over Africa as its weakness left Jack yearning for the lost summer. He thought about his best friend in England and talked to Nim.

'People make things up as something to do and then they repeat those things, or complicate them to stay busy or to stay involved in their minds. Soul Shiner is like that. Then they don't need to think too deeply about life. They are happy to fill in time by thinking the same things, but slightly differently; staying within their comfort zone. You accumulate so much about life in your head, and physically in your house, that you spend all your time dealing with this accumulation, rather than developing something new and more important.'

Will there be no seven pleas today, Jack? Why won't
you join the Collective anymore?

'I'm not sure if a belief in anything really helps, never mind the Collective. Blessings and the Catholic religion weren't much use to Rolly, Dutch and Niiige, were they? All dead now, sought out by evil, and me next ...'

You will not die because of the coven, Jack. You only
met them because of Pippa, who you knew before.

'I have accepted your spiritual help and I also accept spiritual things, but I am puzzled by the plethora of beliefs and all without proof of existence.'

But it has taken centuries for you to reach this
conclusion and in all those years nothing has changed
in the beliefs. Only the people who pronounce on them
have changed through time and by continent.

'I thought Soul Shiner answered a spiritual need in me and that's why I called her by that nickname, but she is a sham, isn't she? Just as shallow as most others.'

Yes, Jack, she can never identify and live with your true
needs and there is only one person in the world who can.

'My Sun Sharer you mean?'

Yes of course. What about your pleas?

'I thought seven was a special number but it's not done me any good. I have seen and heard many beliefs, Nim, where different numbers are important. There are eight beats of a Buddhist drum to scare away eight devils, so I could buy a drum to keep the three witches at bay, and have double the protection. 111 is the sum total on numbered squares sold in the temples in Xi'an, China, where the terracotta army stands. The number brings good luck and as you manipulate the square all ways count to 111.

A typical Chinese mathematical conundrum and
not mystical.

'*Vale.* There are 108 sutras to read in Buddhism, with the words used to wash the body and mind. They dictate that improvement can only come from within you and not via others but, in England *we* blame everyone else for why *we* don't do something.'

The philosophy is sound and applies in all countries
but the number is unimportant. Think of it as running
out of ink and therefore unable to write some more.

Jack sighed and slowly stretched his arm to point towards the pretty holiday resort indented across the coves below.

'What a load of bollocks. See all this? It's not the real world, it is mundane and claustrophobic. We were made to do more than just exist.'

Exactly what I have been teaching you, but it applies to a limited number of people who are currently on this earth.

Jack remained thoughtful as the sun crawled slowly higher, as if afraid to meet the winter cold. He squinted into the brightening sunlight.

'Christians and Buddhists put light in front of their altars to dispel the dark as it's symbolic of ignorance, but we have all this light and are still ignorant. I think the Buddhists have a name like yours. *In ergin* is like Nim; life and rebirth expressed as something different in one of six ways. I can't remember exactly what though. Just like my mother forgets, I know I heard it long ago. They also have seven bowls of pure water on the altar. One is to drink, two is to wash ...' He was interrupted.

Jack. You can't take odd aspects of different beliefs and places of worship to give you an answer. You are confusing yourself.

'Okay! I agree. Forget the numbers from now on. I make a denial of seven. Now this minute I deny it is important. Is that good enough?'

The number isn't important but the pleas are. Nine was an important number for the Chinese. In Beijing you went to the ancient Temple of Heaven built on three tiers, representing the earth at the lowest point, with the mortal world in the middle and heaven as the top tier.

There were nine steps between tiers, nine slabs on each
tier, nine rings on the heavenly tier representing the
nine different layers of heaven.
It was a belief, the number didn't matter. But the fact
it was a temple of heavenly and spiritual purification
was all that mattered.
Do you understand now?

'Agreed, agreed, agreed.' Bored but emphatic, Jack was still confused. 'Take Taoism instead, as it explores the dynamism of nature and the operating force behind the universe. Numbers, temples or prayers don't count for anything. They said that achievement can even be by inaction, allowing things to develop and occur of their own accord.

Agreed, agreed, agreed.

'Very funny, Mister Spirit Guide. Listen to me. Buddhism seeks to cure suffering through the neutralisation of desire and following the noble eightfold path leads to Nirvana as a transcendent state of freedom.

And your point is?

Before he could shout at the invisible Nim and scare the women power walking along the beach, the church bells of Kaletta sounded eight times and calmed him down.

'My point is whether it is the pure sound of bells going direct to the heart of believers in Buddhist temples or Christian churches we were made to do more than exist, and a belief helps raise our performance to something we thought we would never achieve. Belief in something, not necessarily religious, just a belief.

Correct and now we can move forward. Did you
really expect a few words and the number seven
to make a difference? It's your attitude and your

> *example that will help others. It's your spirit and your*
> *vibrations as you interact in this and in other worlds*
> *through the Collective.*

'And that my friend is what I don't understand yet. Not the principle. The delivery.' He walked the extra two miles to the nudist beach and stripped before wading into the crashing and freezing surf in an attempt to purify his spirit, but he just got cold. He didn't know how to cleanse himself from the perceived debris of everyday life to get to his real life, and he had no Sun Sharer to help him. The cold, the thrill of his nakedness and being alone did not give him a purity of spirit, but it did make him happy in his heart. He trudged back towards Kaletta on the dirt track that wound through the pine trees and asked Nim a final question.

'I see a shotgun in my dreams every night and it is being loaded and then snapped shut. Can you see my end?'

> *No. I don't see an end yet, just a path to follow still. A*
> *shotgun is not effective in a battle of good versus evil.*
> *Only water quells the witches' souls.*

Jack stopped thinking as he was tired and hungry and used the thought of a *cortado* and croissant at one of the bars by the sea to keep himself moving.

Life closed in on Jack as people in England concentrated their November thoughts towards Christmas and so it became a time for brief emails instead of conversations. No one in England had time to talk as they were too busy in the mad commercial rush preparing for Jesus' birthday. It was a startling and direct contrast to his simple life. They were busy arranging family, friends, food and frivolous festivities, without a spiritual thought between them. Nobody rang except Harriet.

However, one day, Joseph left a tearful and garbled message about his guinea pig dying but never made a follow-up call. Jack rang him back immediately but found the line engaged as if the telephone was off the hook. After two days, he gave up, blaming Melanie and presuming it was deliberate. That was the saddest part of Jack's month. Not even Rodney or Edima telephoned him, but he thought of them all. In his imagination he watched them enjoy their bonfire parties and was envious of their happiness as he missed them desperately. The unreality of his life, that cut him off from everyone he loved, was eating into both his heart and his soul. He rang them but it all seemed so negative. His brother informed him politely that his mother was ailing and was now in a home specialising in dementia. Apparently she was completely devoid of reality and recognised no one from the family. JoJo gloated that Liverpool had lost to his all-conquering United team and had also been dumped out of the FA cup. What do you say to an eight year old?

'Never gloat if you win and always be gracious in defeat, Joseph.' Jack paused. 'Anyway my boys will stuff Man U next time we meet.'

Which left the ever-loving Soul Shiner to telephone him four times a day about nothing, added to the six emails and three texts. He resented the intrusion but enjoyed the unconditional love. It seemed like the wrong time to give up the pointless conversations at night or he would have been really lonely.

The ancient telephone struggled to ring its old bell.

'Hello, my knight, how's the book going?'

'It's hard, Harriet, as I am living every word. Hard as imagination causes pain. Hard as it is so unreal.' She thought about his use of the word hard before replying.

'Are you okay, Jack? Are you happy?'

'No, not at the moment, I don't think I have been happy for a long time and happiness seems to elude me.'

You are not here to be happy. You are here to achieve something with someone.

'Go away, Nim, it's a path too long.' Jack said this out loud.

'Are you still talking to your spirit guide?' Harriet asked in a disapproving tone.

'Yes sometimes. Why?'

'Because, Jack, a spirit guide who speaks to you is in your book, and doesn't exist, poppet. You need to stop thinking he's real.' Jack maintained his silence until she broke it for him. 'Get real, Jack, and find a real job with real money, and I will help support you through your personal crisis.' He stayed quiet again, affronted by the slur on his writing, his lack of strength and his beliefs. She carried on without listening to his silences. 'You've got too much time to think, Jack.'

'I know it, but that means I can think, and most people don't have the necessity of that time. They are too busy filling their lives with things; they are too busy to sit back and really question their lives, what they are doing, for whom, or why, and they never ask questions like how can I live better?' She ignored most of his comments but asked for one clarification.

'What do you mean *better?*'

'Better for other people, for my family, for my country even as we are rarely patriotic. Better for my world. It is a selfish greedy place we live in without thought for others, apart from our immediate family.' She was selfish in her thoughts and couldn't understand him.

'Is there anyone else in your life, Jack?' He thought of Karina and the women during the summer. Deliberately he asked in return.

'Why?'

'Jack, I am prepared to give you my heart and my soul, but I feel it's all one-sided and you make no commitment. I have so much to give and I want to give it to you. I love you dearly and want you in my life, but I don't want to be a part-time girlfriend anymore.' Jack thought carefully before replying.

'I didn't know that, Soul Shiner. We blokes are rubbish at emotional stuff, but I really didn't know that. The crux of the question is this. If you were here in my arms, looking into my eyes and said those things; if you told me face to face that you really love me as much as you say, then what would I do? That is the fundamental issue, isn't it, because if I said no it would destroy you.'

He paused and she didn't interrupt until he answered her question. 'To answer your question; no, there is no one else in my life, not even a spirit guide in your eyes.' She missed the sleight and he had answered truthfully depending on the meaning of the question. Are you shagging someone else or do you love another woman?

'But, Harry, if you keep asking me questions like that you are questioning my integrity and I will not stand for that, so why do you ask about it? I am not after your money for stability or for safety and I don't care about what you get from Matt. You are not convenient for me; you are not my safety net, okay? It's your life and how you sort it out with him is up to you not me, but I have been and will be there to help you work it out.'

'Thank you, poppet, I know that deep down, but I feel insecure sometimes and therefore I am no different from you.' He knew she was different before replying.

'I have always wondered if I had nothing and got rid of everything whether I would find the true me and find my real path.' He laughed quietly. 'But that's what I've done and now I'm scared about the future.' She tried to calm him down.

'I am always there for you, poppet. You know how much I love you.' The *love* word stabbed him in his heart because he didn't love her back. He asked her to remember something.

'Love is not on a scale of 0 to 151, like I thought it was last year. It's on a binary level 1 or 0. Yes or no, so be careful what you commit to, lovely.'

'Do you love me, Jack?'

'I love you most days.' She told him she was happy with that but under his breath he told himself it wasn't enough. 'Harry, also remember that circumstances change relationships and sometimes they are beyond our control, lovely.' She was crying, he could tell so he sat quietly to listen. Harriet told him what she wanted to do between sobs.

'I want to come to stay with you in Spain in December … permanently, poppet. It's too lonely here on my own and I want to be with you. The question is, do you want me there? I am arranging it so you have to stop me and say no don't come. It's up to you, Jack, and not me anymore.' She sobbed uncontrollably down the telephone for a full five minutes before he sighed a reply.

'That's okay. I am the one person you know who doesn't live in the past. I live in the future and I am always conscious of my Sun Sharer. But you understand that, don't you?'

'Yes,' she replied quietly missing the allusion to the presence of a Sun Sharer. He continued.

'I am not content with today, nor what I have done or achieved yesterday or last year. If you want to be here I see that as giving and taking on both our parts. I only give unconditionally and sometimes that makes me look weak.'

'You are not weak, poppet, you are very strong. Don't knock yourself.' He quickly added.

'People take continually and want to be on the upside of any balance but I give everything; body, soul and mind. That's me, okay?'

'Okay. Night night, my knight' and she replaced the receiver content with her man and her future.

Jack went outside and stared at the stars. The smell of the pines wafted over his face as he tilted his head back as far as it would go and he slowly pirouetted through 360 degrees. He thought of Niiige, Rolly and Dutch and where their spirits were now. He hoped they were looking at him as he said his goodbyes to them and nursed his regret that he hadn't understood and helped them. He stood enveloped in his guilt and selfishness. A cold northerly *Tramuntana* wind made him shiver as he remembered a card that Soul Shiner had sent to him earlier in the summer. "The road to a friend's house is never long." A Danish proverb.

But he felt nothing anymore just 'none'.

A 'none' mood absent from reality.

What are you, Jack?

He responded in a monotone.

'I am nothing. No one talks to me. No one sees me. No one cares about me. No one truly loves me. Therefore I am nothing. I don't belong anymore after two years. I have no children, no wife, no parents, no job, no home. Therefore I am nothing. In fact, the way I have lived my life this year means I don't even have any self-integrity, but I suppose that has been disappearing for a long time now.

'So I know what I am, Nim. I am nothing and therefore I am ready.'

9

The need for an ending

The weak sun was low in the sky in early December barely able to refract through the rain pouring off the clay roof. It dropped to the soil with such venom that it splashed earthy red water onto the lower front window of *la barraca*, but the weather was good company for Jack, comforting him with its gurgling down the tiles and splashing onto the earth, as he jabbed his treasured words into the computer. In his imagination he was naked and swimming away from Yapanc beach, parting the inhospitably dark waters and stroking his way to commit suicide.

The synthesised noise of a singular bell drew his attention to an incoming email. Stretching his arms towards the sodden clay tiles he stood and stared at his precious but damp view, rotating his body left then right to ease his back and hips. He shuddered at the thought of his suicide attempt the previous year and pushed away the emotion of the memory. Eternally grateful for his simple house and the countryside immediately around it, he lived his life immersed in his personal heaven on earth, Shangri La, but couldn't love it yet. He had reached his emotional nadir the previous month, and was now on a *crescendo* of goodwill and happiness, inspired by his vision for life in the New Year. He looked out of the window and saw that the sea was almost invisible, obscured by the rain, but he relished the idea of swimming in it once again.

Nonchalantly he clicked open the email expecting it to be routine; a bank statement or a solicitor's letter, but it was from his brother.

'Hi Bro, I have sad news. Mum passed away an hour ago in Leicester General hospital having been taken ill in the night. It looks like a stroke. Let me know when you can come over to settle the will as you are the executor not me.'

'Mother?' he said plaintively to the curtain of water as if she were still on the telephone with him. Immediately wandering outside for an explanation he looked to the heavens and let the rain bounce off his face and dilute his tears.

'My mother?' It was a painful cry to her spirit. 'Is that all you are worth in the end, lovey, just an email and a few thousand pounds?' He put his hands behind his head as he sank to his knees, as if ready for beheading, and then leaning forward he grasped the red mud with both hands, squeezing it hard to make sure he could be as close as possible to its physicality.

A red dye poured through his fingers like Bridget's blood and joined the rivulets heading down the slope towards the distant sea. There was no breath to draw and he gasped as his tight chest involuntarily relaxed so that he could take some air. He shuddered.

'I will remember everything, Mum, even though no one else will.' *Love* had been the title of her letter at age eighty. He recited it from memory as he sprawled forward and lay prostrate on his stomach feeling the cold eat into him like death itself.

'I love your dad, but I don't always agree with him.

I love to be alone, but not all the time.

I love beauty; it's always there if you look for it.

I love my family, but I found out I cannot live their lives for them.

I love life, because I don't want to die.

I have loved my work, but never believed I was indispensable. I find I can leave it now for somebody else to do a bit.

Love is difficult to define. It's like breathing, smelling and tasting; it's good and bad all at the same time.

I love each new day, as I know it will be different from yesterday.

If I'm not happy, or something isn't suiting me, I ask myself what am I going to do about it. If I can't do anything, then I put it to one side as tomorrow is another day.'

But there was no one to hear her loving advice and no one to share his grief, except Nim who kept quiet with Mother standing next to him under the pine trees, leaving Jack alone to say his goodbyes and reconcile her words with his own life.

The funeral was held a week later but Jack remained in Spain. He didn't want his family and they didn't want him anymore. He was a social outcast, 'a bit of a loner' and still considered to be crazy; in the midst of a mid-life crisis. The truth was he had nothing left to say to a body in a coffin since that spiritual farewell in the cold rain. He preferred the Spanish way of burying the body within twenty-four hours and driving around the town announcing the death from a loudspeaker on top of the car so that old acquaintances could share the burden of grief and the passing of a spirit. He also had nothing left to say to his family. On the day of the burial he went to pretty Besalu for a more personal memorial service, away from the closed negative energies of a church and a distant family.

Below the yellowed stone village and outside the old protective walls stood the old Roman Bridge, kinked to stop the evil spirits that moved in straight lines, or more likely to blunt the aggression of any attackers 1,000 years before. A bunch of lilies hung in a listless hand for a few minutes as he watched the fast flow of shining water twenty metres below.

Seven white lilies for seven pure memories which he mouthed quietly in the bitter northerly wind that cut across the Pyrenees behind him, and sped the words on towards the sea.

'For the hugs you gave me when I was a poorly little boy, that always made me feel well.

For those nights you let me come into your bed when I was scared by my dreams.

For working so hard to make our material lives better and always wanting us to have the best.

For being there on the telephone when I needed to share something as I grew into my own life.

For the vision of a different, more essential, world that inspired my thoughts.

For your love of my dad that gave me my life.

For being my mum and not somebody else's.

For these seven things I will always remember you, lovey.'

He crossed himself after staring down into the depths for a few more moments and walked away without watching the lilies toss on the torrent as they sped away. He passed the Mikva, or the ritual bath of the moneyed Jews before they were hounded out by racist jealousy, and was comforted by their belief in the ritual purity achieved from immersion in the flowing waters of the river. As he drove home to Palafrio he knew she and Dad were with him and he was comforted rather than scared. He was happy to know that they were together and pledged that he would see them again.

Late December and the view from the *barraca* patio was exceptional; a perfect blue sky and a mirror sea with no whispering winds disturbing the trees, or murmuring further messages to Jack. The place was essential to his equilibrium and the ever-changing days and nights gave him some substance in his new life, as he came to terms with himself, his path and his loneliness. It was exactly a year since the miracle rescue and the day that Manolo had embraced Jack's future on the harbour wall. For only the third time in four years, Jack stood motionless, staring at his reality and avoided his seven pleas for others in the world. The Collective dwelt on him that morning rather than his joining them, as there were too many questions in his mind. The first was easy.

'Why am I letting Harriet come and live with me this afternoon?'

Because you are emotionally weak and driven by sex.

'I know the answer, Nim, but where did the last year disappear to? I have no money left, just two real friends in Harry and Manolo, no stability and too much time for living.'

You didn't follow your path, Jack, and you exercised your free will, which was wrong.

'So what,' he retaliated childishly, 'you can't punish me, can you.' It was said in an angry and rhetorical tone.

No Jack, there isn't any punishment in the spirit world as you understand it. Just many pathways, and you have failed to follow yours, so now you are lost in the eternal void.

A more amenable Jack responded positively.

'I understand that now, but it's so hard, just too hard sometimes, Nim. In one way I have had the happiest year of my life. In another it was the unhappiest and they have balanced out leaving me none. I created my book, but have failed to get it published. I have lived life to the extreme, but have not seen my son. I have received love, but given nothing back.'

Jack just acknowledging the difficulty is a success and recognising you have a path is hard. Then you have to double your courage and carry on no matter what.

You know you can curb your greed for a good time; the sex and excitement was just like eating sugar. An incredible high that lasts but a moment. You buzzed like a bee but forgot the rest of the hive.

Jack laughed ironically.

'That's very apt, Nim; a man gorging on endless honey and unable to find his way home. Maybe I can follow my path now, just maybe through this experience and with your help, but I need some more time.' He saluted the sun to shield his eyes as he squinted at it. 'The sun today gives me that hope. I can feel it; there is something that is ready, something pending. I know what is needed, my friend, and I believe in my path, so with a little more time that can make me truly satisfied.'

Satisfied, Jack?

He replied with a new certainty.

'Yes because I'm not searching for an elusive happiness anymore. I need to avoid my self-need and give rather than take, to buck the trend of what is considered to be a normal life.'

I will help you, my friend, and that is why I am here.
However, your time is fixed by your path and cannot
be moved like the hands of a clock.

The perfect day held him captive and breathless as he widened his arms to encompass it. After a few moments he had to ask the obvious.

'Who sent you, Nim; you never told me?'

No one sent me, not a god. Spirit guides aren't sent by
someone or something. I exist for you and am part of
you as you called for me. I have mirrored your lives for
hundreds of years and when you achieve your Karma
you will become me. I am what you choose to see.

Jack reached across to the dusty radio which sat on the blackened barbecue and switched it on. Quarenta Principales was playing Take That for the thousandth time. 'Today this could be the greatest day of our lives'. He smiled as the catchy tune continued. 'Stay close to me, stay close to me'. As he walked inside he asked Nim to always do the same before turning to the mundane and habitual task of making a coffee with the tune still resonating in his mind. The sun rose higher to be shared with the characters in his completed book and started his perfect day.

Such a day demanded a telephone call to a perfect son.

'Hiya, JoJo, how are you?'

'Great, Dad. Did you hear we beat Chelsea and you went down at little old Stoke City?' Of course he had seen the weekend results on the Internet but played the game of distant father and son.

'Oh no, what a disaster! That means we are only nine points ahead of you in the league. Or is it ten?'

'Yes but Dad ...' came a firm reply, 'we have three games in hand, remember?'

'Have you? Have you really?' He questioned untruthfully.

'Yes, Dad,' was the emphatic response. 'You are hopeless at remembering.' Joseph sighed at his dippy daddy who remained competitive.

'Anyway, points in the bag are what count, mate, not promises in newspapers from big girls like Ronaldo.'

'Dad!' It was a sharp reply. 'He has a girlfriend, Dad, so he must be a boy and Dad ...' Joseph paused before delivering his pronouncement in a rising and incredulous tone, 'he was just voted the best player in the world and that was by all of the other players.'

'Ah, my big boy, I love you so much. Okay, okay he's a reasonable player on some days, but let's just see where we are at the end of the season, JoJo. I bet you a £100 we are at the top of the league.'

'No way, no bet, didn't shake. No betting as Mum says not to.'

'There you go then, scared already.'

'Dad ...' he strung the word out to chastise his beloved dad. Jack was smiling at the perfect day and sharing his sun with his lovely boy.

'You know, Joseph, the most important thing isn't the banter about a subject like footie, it's about not giving up even when things get tough. That is the most important lesson you can learn from me, JoJo.'

'I know, Dad, you always tell me that.'

'Well, that's because you need to practise it. Today I can feel the essence of not giving up swirling around invisibly in the Spanish air. If you can look at your life each day and see how you made people happy, you have given a lot. If you have tried your hardest each day at all that you do, you have given a lot. If you share the sun with your dad each day, then you have given everything.'

'I know that too, Dad, and I always think of you when I see the morning sun through my bedroom window.' There was a pause before his boy said, 'I miss you, Dad.'

Jack thought he had heard a sob but dismissed it not wanting to upset his son by asking. JoJo had never cried for the loss of him in the two years they had been apart.

'I miss you too, son.' A definitive sob in England filled the silence and Jack felt a lump in his throat. It was hard to keep his voice normal as he forced the words out. 'I love you wider than the sky and bigger than the sea, Joseph, and I always will, wherever I am.' The silence was broken.

'I love you more than that, Dad.'

'Bye, lovely. Be a good boy for your mum. We are Sun Sharers until the day we die. Love you. Bye.'

Jack replaced the receiver to cut short the conversation before they were both in tears.

Jack you need to be there for him. Go and see him and go soon.

'I can't go back at the moment, it's too hard. Maybe in January after Christmas and when the flights are cheaper.'

Go and see him now, Jack. He was crying. He needs you now, just do it.

Jack walked outside and stared at the sea searching for boats so as to ignore his conscience.

'Did you realise that, "win" is "Nim" written upside down? Nim … win. A win win situation. What a crap saying is that? We have a win win situation meaning exactly the opposite. I win, you lose, and you have no choice but to play along because of the circumstances. Pfur! How about it's time to wake up and smell the coffee. It means get real or you are in the shit, but what if you prefer tea hey?' He dumped the conversation with his son from his mind as it hurt too much to remember his boy.

Too much distance, too much sun-sharing and too much unconditional love to handle on this perfect day; so he jumped into his Korean prancing horse and went to find some company.

Palafrio village gossip is no different from Tarporley, everyone knows each other's cousins, wives, girlfriends, husbands and boyfriends, sons and daughters of cousins and even cousins of cousins and, of course, all of Jack's business, as part of the base fabric weaving their lives together.

Sunny stools outside Bar Fun Fun beckoned in the square and a *cortado* was ordered to relieve the chill that was still permeating the air.

'*Que tal,* Lluis?'

'*Muy bien* Jack, *muy bien.*' Lluis buzzed around the tables and was late as usual getting ready for breakfasts served between nine and ten.

'Did you see the TV coverage showing Gaza? All those dead children?' Lluis stopped and turned to Jack with lips pushed hard together in a disapproving grimace.

'I saw. I think dog eat dog is your expression. Did you know the Moslems held a peace gathering here in the square yesterday, to demonstrate against the Israeli incursion and the support of the Americans? I watched this Jack and it was very cynical. They placed the children at the front of the protest for the press photographs and denounced my government. "Allah Akbar", they cried but no good Catalans listened. They need to go home to Maroc if we are not good enough.'

'Lluis!' Jack expostulated, 'give them a break. Everyone has a right to protest.'

'But Jack, we gave them five million euros two months ago. We welcomed their President to see ours and also to see Prime Minister Zapatero, and then they stand in my square and say we aid Israel and America. These Moslems need to learn respect.'

'They are normal people, but you don't try and understand them at all, Lluis. Just Mussulmen from Maroc who run bazaars and the quality Halal butchers that you use! They are part of Palafrio too and you need to accept it because this area in the last two years has increased its immigration from four to twenty per cent. Fact!'

Lluis grunted and carried on cleaning quietly with a bowed head. Jack mused. 'I even bought a book about Islam and I used some of it in my book.' Lluis raised his head and shook it disapprovingly at Jack who continued his rhetoric.

'Tell me then! How many Catalans are afraid they are being invaded? Your views are like England thirty years ago when we were invaded by the blacks. Now we don't give a shit so long as they do the shit jobs at low pay. It's just market forces. Bring in the Poles instead. It doesn't matter you know. Or is it because they are a different colour never mind their culture? That's the way it is and that's the way it will stay. Soon your lot will be complaining about the Chinese and, finally, you will be really upset when the Arabs take over world finance behind the scenes.'

Jack crossed his arms in disgust. He couldn't be bothered to argue further. He knew many Catalans were racist and that they needed many more years to overcome this attitude. He changed to a non-controversial subject as there was no response.

'I have to go to Girona airport today to pick up a friend. What's the C31 like since the road works?' Lluis shrugged.

'Same problems, Jack. Too many cars too many people.'

Jack stared up at the bare tree branches and thought disappointedly, actually no different from the A51 in Cheshire then.

But his bad mood was worsening every minute of that perfect day because people make the day, not Nature or things. He grumped at the busy barman.

'So what about Russia cutting off the gas to Europe this weekend? Is that linked to Gaza or not? Is it politicking in the black oily waters of the Middle East? Hey, Lluis?' He tried to incite some biased comments rather than the *mañana* attitude. 'On a day when it was minus nine in most of Europe. How fucking cynical is that, Mister Catalonia?'

Lluis adjusted the chairs before replying. 'Dog eat dog. You said it. Who knows and who cares? I just need more customers and that's all because of some crisis!'

'Mark my words, Lluis, the Arabs and Chinese will do something similar and hold us all to ransom in our little service-orientated, material world. We have forgotten to keep it super simple and spend hours looking at the detail, rather than the big strategic picture; a small world with people looking at small world things.'

Lluis ignored him but inwardly thought that Jack was ranting.

'How cynical is power. Pay us more for our gas as we are in control. Real people in Bulgaria, real cold, real effects, real dog eat dog and, I suppose, *'Real Life'* hey!'

Lluis put his hand on Jack's shoulder as he walked inside.

'Jack you are having a bad day. *Mañana,* my friend, *mañana.'* The barman moved into the warmth of the interior leaving Jack huddled in his jacket regretting his own lack of gas in the empty and cold square.

'I'm not having a bad day; I'm having a perfect day.'

In the far corner he saw Nuria was walking towards the office and waved to her enthusiastically.

'Good morning, Mister Edmunson. How are you?' Time had at least made her polite since he had used her.

'Regular, normal, but I love the day. Tell me, Nuria, have *you* noticed the obscene rush to extract money from the Arabs to fund the credit crisis?' He emphasised the *you* to make it personal. 'Remember money and power are uniquely linked along with sex, of course, and the Western world will forget that adage of mine as they mortgage their countries' souls to the enemy. The old traditional Moslem enemies of Christendom.'

'My God you are so serious on a beautiful morning. No, I don't think about things like that, just my work in the *finques*.' She glanced around for reassurance that a Moslem face wasn't too close. 'Be quiet about religion, *señor*, or we will have a riot. Things are getting worse since Gaza.' The white Christians of Palafrio were running scared from the Moslem anger. The TV showed the demonstrations in Madrid and the locals were worried.

'Well, you should think about it, Nuria, because they are your friends now. At least to your face that is, but they can never respect any of us for the mess we in the West have created. They have the oil, the money, and control of our debts and soon many more Moslem countries will have nuclear weapons. Mark my words and remember in December 2008 it was me who told you so. Then they will start to flex their muscles and they are determined, having a belief built on a religion that is fundamental to their lives.'

'Really, *amigo*, so serious!' She laughed his comments away into the peaceful winter air and that made him angrier.

'And what is worse, Nuria, is they have no fear of dying as it is an honour to go to Allah early.' Breathing out an exasperated cloud she asked.

'What about sex then? Where does that fit into your crazy theory with money and power?' He swung off the stool and clutched the arm of her red woollen coat.

'Where does that come into it? That's easy in this case; they are screwing us, Nuria. They even have the natural resources, the new discovery of a type of rock that can be used to eliminate carbon dioxide and stop global warming. How unfortunate is that?' Nuria moved to walk away as quickly as possible.

'*Adios,* Mister Edmunson, I hope your day becomes happier.' As she took a step her mobile rang and she paused her life to answer it. The ring tone was 'I kissed a girl and I liked it' by Katie Berry. Jack shook his head in frustration and expressed a disgruntled 'pfur' as she took the call. He sat back on his stool and contemplated with dread what time he needed to be at the airport to meet Harry. Breathless now, the stress in his chest hurt as he thought of her living with him.

'Oh god, Nim. What have I done? I don't think this is a good idea.'

Jack, you did not follow the path I advised and so
you have to deal with it. This is not her problem, as
you created the whole situation by your weakness. She
taught you to say no and you forgot it.

He glanced at Nuria who was white-faced and standing stock still. As she turned towards him, he knew something was wrong.

'It's Manolo. He's in Salt Girona hospital and was rushed there earlier this morning after a heart attack at home.'

'Oh fuck.' Jack was suddenly colder in the winter sun. He pulled her to him and hugged her tight to stop the tears. After a minute he eased himself away from her.

'Are you able to cope?'

'I'm okay, Jack. It is such a shock.'

'Listen, Nuria, I'll go to the hospital immediately and ring you after I've seen him so you know exactly how he is, okay? Go and open the office and contact his friends and family as it's important to maintain that contact, and that's the most logical place for it, okay?' He held her eyes and he knew she had the message as she replied

'Okay, Jack.' He gave her one last hug.

'I'll get back to you as soon as possible. Okay?' He double checked.

'Okay, Jack. Kiss him from me.'

'I don't think so.' He grimaced as he said it and it made her laugh to ease the tension.

'Right come on let's go.' They marched swiftly away leaving Lluis perplexed as they hadn't paid him.

'Crazy English' he said under his breath.

Fifty minutes later the intensive care unit in Salt hospital was easy to find but a dose of ignorant English behaviour without admitting any understanding of Castellano was required to bluff his way in. There were six people lying in the darkened room that was full of silent machines, maintaining life as we know it; partly obscured by a light blue curtain was a sorry-looking estate agent. Jack walked up to him with a wide smile.

'What are you doing, my friend' he looked down at Manolo lying in a bed with an oxygen mask totally covering his usually happy face. He bent low to listen.

'Ah Jack, my friend, my best friend,' was muffled as he started to cry, shuddering with the enormity of it all under Jack's pacifying hand resting on his arm. As he recovered his composure he murmured.

'So, Jack, Job done? Did the coven win?'

'No, Manolo, my friend. Not job done. It's not over until the fat lady sings and my ex-wife isn't here.' The sorry patient smiled.

'You think so, Jack?' His friend looked at the patient with certainty.

'I know so, Manolo, I know so.' As a nurse started to usher the awkward Englishman out of the room, his best friend uttered quietly.

'Life is what you make of it. Isn't that what you say, you crazy English?' Jack touched his shoulder as a goodbye and squeezed gently.

'No, life is what it makes of you.' He followed the nurse out and walked quietly to his car, oblivious to the pain of all those visiting or leaving like him. Sometimes you had to be selfish to make things happen.

It was a short distance to the airport and the radio played Take That's 'Stay close to me' and it upset him. It took no more than fifteen minutes but there was only just enough time to meet the Ryanair flight from Liverpool. Soul Shiner skipped out of arrivals on a wave of happiness, her soulfulness influencing everyone around her. Jack smiled and saw the beautiful person inside her that he called his best friend in England. She had an inner glow and radiated love.

'My hero, Jack. My knight in shining armour. My little poppet writer.' She clung to him so tightly that he could hardly breathe, but as she let go his breathlessness continued. 'Why so serious a face, Jack?' She knew all of his emotions and knew something was wrong. He drew something from deep inside to answer.

'It's been a bad day, Harriet; please can we go to the bar and grab a drink?'

She gave a guarded, 'Of course,' and they walked hand in hand the short distance to departures, dragging her two suitcases and sat in the scruffy noisy bar.

'Talk to me, Jack. No secrets. Open and honest you say.' With his head bowed and hands held tightly together he leant forward on the table and told her about his belief in today being a perfect day and how he and Joseph had cried. He told her about his anger and frustration over nothing and everything as he sat in the square in Palafrio wanting to influence the world. Finally, he told her about his rock; his best *hombre*, Manolo.

'What are you building up to, Jack? You have been acting strangely for a few weeks now.' Her knight leaned across the dirty table to grasp both of her hands and then looked into her troubled eyes.

'Harriet, I have learned you can't own or possess anyone. You have to respect and trust them or you have nothing. You are trying to own and possess me, just like Melanie and now, at the point of no return, I know we can't be together.' Her mouth was apart and her lips quivered before she shut them tightly into a pinched line. He continued bravely without emotion.

'You have your children, you have money, a happy home and you are a good mum. In contrast, I am a bad dad; I rarely visit Joseph, who is becoming more distant and unhappy. I have no money, no home, no job and today it has all come together and I feel like the whole world has collapsed around me.' She made no reply but tried to move her hands away. He gripped them tighter, fighting her emotions.

'No, Harriet don't pull away, hold my hands and open your heart. You have to understand, my best friend, I have to say this.' He pulled her upper body closer so their heads were touching temple to temple and lowered his voice. 'We are so apart and yet so close, but we live in different circumstances and I know now that I just can't be with you. You are not my Sun Sharer, you are my *bestest* friend. It's not the end, Harriet; it's the start of something new.'

Her tears poured onto his grey denim jacket and she couldn't reply. He continued with his voice strong and determined, knowing his certainty for the first time. 'Promise me you won't let your emotions get in the way. Best friends like before, but not lovers and not living together. I know that is good and anything else would be bad. If not, we would just break what we uniquely have.' She looked into his dreamy green eyes and searched his face for clues. The anguish in her voice hurt him now.

'What is good or bad, Jack? Simple life or materialistic life? Normal or abnormal? You can't tell me what is normal, you can't judge as you are not God.' She pulled her hands away, mentally slapping his face, and sat back as if trying to be as far away as possible, shrinking from his touch, his words and his very thoughts.

Jack stood slowly, needing his arms to push up off the Formica table to allow him to move. Looking down at her red hair he placed a hand on its softness and said quietly.

'I know I'm selfish, but what I am doing is right and you will thank me for it one day.' She was crying silently.

'Go back to your children. Go and support Matt and be there for them so that you don't make my mistake.' Without a trace of emotion or a farewell kiss he turned and walked away, leaving her distraught with her head in her hands.

The sun set as he drove home and filled the sky with blood red clouds gathering from the west and Quarenta Principales transmitted 'Stay close to me' again, but the signal wasn't received.

Jack stopped at Grau, the wine warehouse on the outskirts of Palafrio, and walked purposefully to the most expensive section behind the reinforced glass. He couldn't be bothered to search and study, but walked down a single aisle looking at the prices. As soon as he saw a 100 euro bottle of Rioja he snatched it up and immediately went to the checkout.

'Ah, *señor, fantastic, muy bien vino, si?*' He wasn't listening.

'Yep' and bluntly handed over his credit card to the man, inviting him to stay quiet with a withering look. By the time he arrived home his body hurt so much with physical pain in his hips and back, plus his mental anguish from the horrific day, that he grabbed a packet of sixteen paracetamol to go with the wine. Remembering a corkscrew he took two analgesics and started the mile walk down to Yapanc beach.

It was dark now, but the day had turned warmer because of a Saharan wind and so he felt hot in his baseball hat and thick denim jacket. He took off the hat whilst slowing his pace to a Spanish wander and let the countryside talk to him. A giant owl flew low to his left and a fox barked at the potential incursion on its prey. Above them all, El Far beamed its welcoming light, in competition with the full moon, appearing above the headland and it helped him to breathe deeply and more evenly. The ancient dolmen stones called to him to his right but he couldn't stay and talk to dead people because his purposes were focussed on the living.

Jack, mind the …

As he tripped he swore.
'Fuck me, Nim, are you helping or hindering me.

Well, at least you have some life back in you now.

'Too fucking true, Nim, I will never give up on life. Never.'

So why the wine and Paracetamol, Jack?

'You need to trust me and not nanny me. I hurt so much and I have no way to share the pain except with two painkillers. Booze and drugs.'

You can talk to me, Jack.

'Therein lies a problem. You guide me, but you don't tell me what to do. Is it against union rules or something?'

Jack ... Nim said gently to admonish him.

Ten minutes later Jack was on the beach at Yapanc and the bottle was opened, with the first gulp poured down a willing throat.

He avoided sitting on the rocks where Joseph and he had shared the early mornings. He avoided Melanie's prime position for endless mindless days of sunbathing, but he felt happy sitting where his dinghy had stood and dreamed of the days he and Karina had sailed from the beautiful shore.

The sea was calm, reflecting Luna across the whole bay, and that helped him to calm down to match its eternal serenity. Four tablets more, half a bottle of wine but he still couldn't stop his thoughts.

'Two years on, Nim, and I am still the same person.'

You are different, Jack. The others in your life
have stayed the same and you have developed and
are now ready.

'Development, that's a new one. You develop breasts as a teenage girl. You develop a deep voice as a boy becoming a man, but my persona hasn't changed like that. That would be nice though. Going back with all my knowledge and experience and reliving my teens.' He used his right forefinger to draw sun symbols in the sand, enhanced by the moonlight casting deep shadows. He had seen the symbols in China. The original was a circle with a dot in the middle but he also drew the modern version resembling a squared off figure of eight.

'The sun is the moon, Nim. The sun reflects off the moon so that I have the sun for my whole day. There is no night when there is a full moon and the powers of darkness cannot exist in the power of the reflected sunlight.'

Keep saying and believing that, Jack, because the
power of the witches grows stronger.

He felt extremely drunk but still hurt and he took four more paracetamols with another pull of wine.

'100 euro wine and it tastes like shit, for fuck's sake.'

Go easy, my friend.

'So this true path thing … what the fuck am I supposed to do tomorrow, as I haven't got a fucking clue?'

Nothing, Jack. Let the day come and decide then, but you will have to choose soon.

The alcohol was too effective to allow any choosing.

'Very Taoist. Choose what? Come on. Make it easy for me.'

Between natural time now on earth or unnatural time to reach the Fifth World.

'No fucking chance.' As the reflected sun dropped behind the White Headland heading for Palomost, the Yapanc church clock struck three echoing chimes that fled across the sea, as belligerent Jack slumped onto his left side on the damp sands. He had stopped thinking at last and slept without dreaming, ignoring the Duchess's favourite but retreating moon and its symbolic connotations over history, on this fateful but perfect day.

At 8 am precisely a beautiful woman paused outside the *croisanteria* in Yapanc square with a bunch of keys in her hand, ready to open up. She glanced towards the harbour and saw a familiar figure slumped on the beach in a grey jacket and a pink Fat Face hat. There was no movement as she watched and so with a lump in her throat she started to walk towards him as quickly as possible, just in case there was something wrong. As she got closer she could see no movement in the awkward shape and started to run before collapsing on her knees to his side.

As Jack and Nim revolved between their conscious and unconsciousness state, Jack thought he could feel a hand on his shoulder roughly jerking his mind, but he couldn't see anything except the brightness of the rising sun through his closed and painful eyelids. Karina supported him, squatting on her now damp jeans and looked for a long time into his face. She realised she still loved him but could never admit it. As she stared closely she saw another face and imagined it spoke to her between the ebb and flow of the waves.

Karina, I am Jack's spirit guide, Nim, but you know me from centuries ago as Artemis. So accept me now, as I know Jack told you he talked to me.

I come to this world through people's own energy, generated by their thoughts and emotions.

You and Jack have always been part of me in every generation, and united by love over the centuries. You always knew in your heart that you and he must be together as one. You see the calm on his face?

She leant closer and her tears gently fell onto Jack's closed eyes and trickled down his cold cheek.

'But, Artemis, there's no breath.' She started to panic.

No and there cannot be unless you accept your shared path. Only then will he live. If not, you will lose another opportunity to be together.

She pulled Jack closer. 'I accept my path, but not now, Artemis. The time is wrong.'

The path dictates the time, so he will live.

Jack shuddered but failed to open his eyes. Karina knelt by him and he knew her from the Allure perfume she always wore, but he was blinded by the sun as he blinked slumped against her legs.

'You? Why you, my lovely?' He blinked again struggling to come round.

'That's a strange story, Jack, that I don't believe.' She sat by him and cuddled his head onto her shoulder as her tears finally overwhelmed her.

'My dearest Jack. What are you doing here?' He yawned.

'I just had a perfect day that's all and so I came to see the moon reflect the sun, and now I can see the sun again and so I'm happy because it's with you, lovely.' They sat still and listened to the world awake.

In a tired quiet voice he said, 'So you are here, but I am confused. What about you and I? Can we be together? Is that why you are here? To tell me that?' She shook him gently and smiled.

'Jack, please don't. That hurts me. You know I have Josep Maria and the children to think about. He relies on me so much more now. I don't know why, but he has been acting strangely lately. Maybe his brain is not quite right, Jack, but nothing has changed.' She shook him gently to check he was still with her.

'I saw you collapsed on the beach and came to help.' Jack closed his eyes and remembered the hospital ward nearly two years before. He decided not to remind her as she probably wouldn't remember. She was distraught at the time and must have blocked the episode out of her mind, hoping nothing would ever change, but he knew of course that it would.

'Karina, there is always so much that is unsaid between us.'

'I understand that, but everyone in England is looking for you. Don't you know that, my love?' He looked at her and knew without doubt that she was his Sun Sharer and that he must wait for her forever. He threw himself backwards onto the gritty sand and stared at the deep blue sky of another morning, before answering angrily.

'Why are they looking for me? Why does anyone care? No one bothers. Do they want more money? The shirt off my back, a piece of my soul?' he laughed awkwardly. 'Hoy, they've already had that, my friend.' He yawned widely, tired of what life had thrown at him.

'No, Jack my dearest love.' She paused and lay back beside him so they were admiring the sun above them.

'They just want to take a bit more of your life and your love.' Warily he turned onto his side and put his hands around her face in a gentle caress, his drunkenness gone. He watched her tears reflect the brightness as they fell and wondered how many tears were possible in a perfect day. The sea hissed across the sand and hushed the mourning sobs as they racked her body.

'What is it, Karina? What can be so bad? Nothing can be as bad as yesterday.' She struggled to say the words.

'It's Joseph, Jack. I'm sorry.' He thumped the sand hard with both hands in anger.

'No, that can't be right! No, Karina, no!' The tortured shout joined the breeze reaching to the four hills of Yapanc.

'It's true, Jack. I'm so sorry. He's dead.' He collapsed onto his face and buried it, painfully feeling every sharp grain.

'No, Nim, I didn't see it. I see these things. Why was that hidden? What have I done to deserve this?'

So the dream was a dream and now it was over, the shuddering return to reality. The search for the true path and death intervening in life with a certitude that should never be forgotten.

Practical, factual and uncaring. The inescapable realities of life.

> *'My darling, Joseph. My little boy. I wanted to share the sun forever. I hope you see it clearly now. Share it with me, my son. Please still share it with me.'*
> *'And, Karina, was it all a dream? It really does matter. Of course, more is less in this life, but now less is really less too.'*
>
> *Dear reader … remember and believe.*

Why

The first book in the trilogy was about how people treat each other. How they judge and justify and forget about *'Real Life'* as only their version of it exists. That truth hurt.

This sequel shows a way of escaping the daily *'mundanities'* and the issues that brings. It shows the insignificance of our lives as we strive to understand if there is more to existence than existing.

The third book 'Someone Something' is complete and gives the answers to why we should strive.

Jack George Edmunson
19th October 2010

Notes

PAGE   LYRICS, POETRY, ARTICLES AND BOOKS

23   If you have read Coelho's novel you must surely have
        questioned the meaning of life? No? Well hopefully mine is a
        little more practical for you.

        'Before a dream is realised, the Soul of the world tests
        everything that was learned along the way.'
        Coelho, Paulo. (1998). *The Alchemist.* UK, Collins. ISBN
        9780007233670

57   'I don't like Mondays'
        The Boomtown Rats. (1979). *The Fine Art of Surfacing.*
        UK, Ensign Records.

71   'Here we go again, my my how could I forget you'?
        Abba. (2004) *Gold.* UK, Polydor Ltd.

71   'How deep is your love, how deep is your love I really need to
        learn cause we are living in a world of fools breaking us down
        when they all should let us be.
        The Bee Gees. (2001) *How deep is your love.* UK, Polydor Ltd.

        Written by Barry, Robin and Maurice Gibb.
        Published by Gibbs Brothers Music, BMG Music Publishing
        International Ltd.

94   'It's time to move your body'
        Robbie Williams. (2010). *In and Out of Consciousness.*
        Greatest Hits UK, Virgin.

99   'I just want to feel real love
        Feel the home that I live in
        'Cause I got too much life
        Running through my veins going to waste.'
        Robbie Williams. (2010). *In and Out of Consciousness. Greatest
        Hits.* UK, Virgin.

104   'And through it all she offers me protection, a lot of love and affection. Whether I'm right or wrong.'
Robbie Williams. (2010). *In and Out of Consciousness. Greatest Hits*. UK, Virgin.

124   'It's only words and words are all I have to take your heart away'.
The Bee Gees. (2001). *Words*. UK, Polydor Ltd.
Written by Barry, Robin and Maurice Gibb.
Published by Gibbs Brothers Music, BMG Music Publishing International Ltd.

140   'When a wench perceiving he came no longer a-suitoring her, but rather tossed his nose at her, and shunned her, she began to love him and dote on him like anything.'
'That is the nature of women, not to love when we love them and to love when we love them not.'
Cervantes. (1992). *Don Quixote* UK, Wordsworth Editions Ltd.
ISBN 781853260360

148   'For we are going to be forever you and me. You will always keep us flying high in the sky. Love.'
Beautiful South. (2001). *Solid Bronze – Greatest Hits*. UK, Mercury Records Ltd.